THE HIGH DRUID'S BLADE

The DEFENDERS of SHANNARA
THE HIGH DRUID'S BLADE

TERRY BROOKS

DEL REY • NEW YORK

2015 Del Rey Mass Market Edition

Copyright © 2014 by Terry Brooks
Map copyright © 2012 by Russ Charpentier
Excerpt from *The Darkling Child* by Terry Brooks copyright © 2015 by Terry Brooks

Published in the United States by Del Rey, an imprint of Random House, a division of Penguin Random House LLC, New York.

DEL REY and the HOUSE colophon are registered trademarks of Penguin Random House LLC.

The map by Russ Charpentier was originally published in *Wards of Faerie* by Terry Brooks, published in the United States by Del Rey, an imprint of Random House, a division of Penguin Random House LLC, in 2012.

Originally published in hardcover in the United States by Del Rey, an imprint of Random House, a division of Penguin Random House LLC, in 2014.

This book contains an excerpt from *The Darkling Child* by Terry Brooks. This excerpt has been set for this edition only and may not reflect the final content of the forthcoming edition.

ISBN 978-0-345-54078-2
eBook ISBN 978-0-345-54071-3

Printed in the United States of America

www.delreybooks.com

9 8 7 6 5 4

Del Rey mass market edition: May 2015

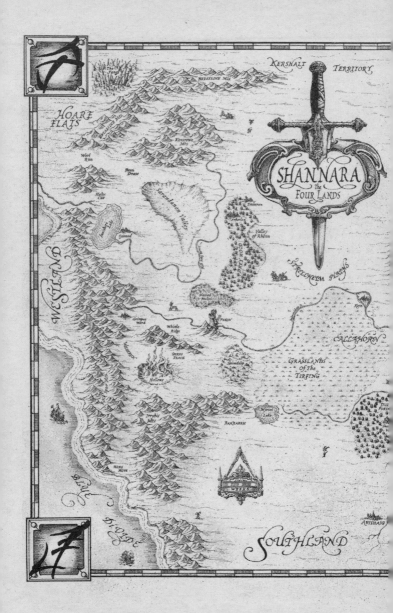

NORTHLAND
TIDERACE
KLU
TALVO ROUGH
The Lazareen
Razor Mts.
Skull Kingdom
Knife Edge Mts.
Rangling Story
Jannisson Pass
RABB PLAINS
PARANOR
Hall of Kings
VALLEY OF SHALE
DRAGON'S TEETH
Mountains of Rynne
Tyrsis
Rainbow Lake
UPPER ANAR
DARKLIN
Graymark
HIGH BENS
EASTLAND
ANAR FOREST
Culhaven
LOWLANDS of CLETE
PREKKENDORRAN HEIGHTS
PLATEAU
N
W
E
S

THE HIGH DRUID'S BLADE

I

PAXON LEAH PAUSED IN THE MIDST OF CHOPPING wood to gaze out across the misty Highlands surrounding the city of Leah. The Highlands were called Leah, too, and the confusion sometimes caused outlanders to wonder if the inhabitants were limited to a single name for everything. It was worse in his case, since his surname was Leah, as well, passed down through countless generations from the rulers of old, for whom the city and the Highlands had been named when the Leahs were their Kings and Queens.

But all that was long ago and far away, and it had little to do with him. He might be the descendant of those Kings and Queens, but that and a few coins would buy you a tankard of ale at the Two Roosters tavern. There hadn't been a monarchy in Leah for generations; the last members of the royal family had walked away from the responsibility not long after Menion Leah had helped dispatch the Warlock Lord by finding and employing the fabled Sword of Shannara. Vague history, long forgotten by many, it was a legacy he carried lightly and with little regard.

He chopped another dozen pieces of firewood for the winter stash before pausing again. The Leahs were commoners now, no different from anyone else. They hadn't even served on the Highlands Council, the current governing body, for many years. His parents had inherited the shipping business that had been in the family for half a dozen generations—a once-thriving but now marginal source of income and sustenance, operated by his mother and himself, but mostly by himself. He ran shipments on the average of twice a month, making just enough money to feed and clothe the family—the family consisting of himself, his mother, and his little sister, Chrysallin. His father had been gone since he was ten, killed in an airship accident while flying freight into the Eastland.

He finished cutting up the firewood, stacking it by the storage shed next to their cottage, still pausing now and then to take in the view and dream of better times to come. Not that things were bad. He had time to hunt and fish, and he didn't work all that hard—though he would have preferred the harder work if the business would improve. At twenty, he was tall and lean and broad-shouldered, his hair red in the tradition of his ancestors. There had been hundreds of redheaded Leahs over the years; he was just the latest. And he imagined there would be hundreds more before the line was played out.

With the wood neatly stacked, he carried his tools into the shed, cleaned and oiled the saws and ax heads, and went into the house to wash up. It was a small cottage with a kitchen, a central living space, and bedrooms for his mother, his sister, and himself. There was a fireplace, with windows to the west-facing front and to the south so there was always plenty of light—important in a climate where the days were frequently gray and hazy.

He glanced at the old sword his sister had hung over the mantel above the hearth, its metal blade, leather pommel, and strap-on sheath all as black as night. Chrys had found it in the attic and proclaimed it hers. The markings on the weapon indicated that the pommel leather and sheath had been replaced more than once, but the metal blade was the original. She said it had belonged to those Leahs of old who had gone on quests with the Ohmsfords and the Druids, all the way back to Menion Leah and forward to their great-grandmother Mirai. Paxon supposed it was so; he had been told the stories often enough as a boy by both his father and his mother. Even some of their friends knew the tales, which had taken on the trappings of legend over the years.

He washed his hands and face in the kitchen sink, pumping water from their well, dried himself, and walked back into the living area to stand before the fireplace. The tales about that black sword were cautionary, whispering of dark magic and great power. It was said the blade had been tempered in the waters of the Hadeshorn once, long ago, and thereby made strong enough that it could cut through magic. A handful of Leahs were said to have carried it into battle with the Druids. A handful were said to have evoked its power.

He had tried to join their ranks more than once when he was much smaller, intent on discovering if the stories were true. Apparently, they weren't. All of his efforts to make the magic appear—to make the sword do anything, for that matter—had failed. There might have been more to the process, but the blade didn't come with instructions, and so after numerous attempts he had given up. What need did he have of magic, in any case? It wasn't as if he were going on a quest with Druids and Ohmsfords.

If there even were any Ohmsfords these days.

There was some doubt about this. All of the Ohmsfords had left Patch Run—their traditional home for hundreds of years—when his great-grandmother had married Railing Ohmsford and brought him to the Highlands to live. His brother, Redden, had come with them, and for a time had shared their home. But eventually he had found a girl to fall in love with and had married her and moved out. Both Redden and Railing had stayed in the Highlands until they died, twins closer than brothers to the end. Redden's boys had moved away and no more had been heard of them. Railing's granddaughter, always closer to her grandmother's side of the family, had taken back the Leah name when she married and had eventually passed it down to her children.

Since then, there had been no Ohmsfords in the Highlands, only Leahs, and Paxon couldn't say if there were Ohmsfords to be found anywhere in the Four Lands these days. Certainly, he hadn't heard mention of any. Which was sad, considering that the families had been friends over many, many years, and the relationships had been close and personal, including most recently the marriage of his great-grandmother to Railing.

But everything comes to an end, even friendships, and families die out or move on, so you couldn't expect that nothing would ever change.

The Ohmsfords had possessed real magic, inherited over the years as a part of their makeup—a power born of Elven magic that had come to be known as the wishsong. Redden and Railing Ohmsford had both had use of it—though it had skipped other generations previously, and every generation since Railing's marriage to Mirai Leah. None of the offspring from that union and for the three generations following had possessed the wishsong magic, so for them—as for him—it was another slice of history that was interesting to talk about, but of little practical consequence.

Besides, he wasn't so certain that having use of such magic wouldn't be more of a burden than a gift. He had heard the stories of what using it had done to the twins, particularly Redden, who had been rendered catatonic after employing it in the terrible struggle against the creatures of the Forbidding. He had recovered, but his brother and Mirai had feared he wouldn't. All magic was dangerous, and any use involved a certain amount of risk. It didn't matter if it was something you were born with or not—it still posed a threat.

Which was in large part why magic was outlawed all through the Southland—everywhere the Federation was in control, which these days included everything south of the Rainbow Lake, including Leah. The northern territories didn't feel the Federation presence as heavily as did the major Southland cities, and in truth Leah and the villages of the Duln were still disputed territories, with the Borderlands laying claim to them as well. But no one wanted to risk bringing the Federation authorities down on their heads by testing out their tolerance for those using magic in deliberate defiance of the edict—especially when the prevailing view in the Highlands was that magic was a source of power best left to the Druids, or left alone entirely.

Paxon studied the sword and scabbard a moment longer, then turned away. A relic, an artifact, or his sister's momentary infatuation—what difference did it make? It was nothing to him.

He went back outside and glanced at the sky. A few clouds were moving in, but nothing threatening. Still time to work on those radian draws he had been mending for the transport. He had a run to make the following week, and he wanted the airship to be fully operational well before then. He was thinking Chrys should go with him. It was time she began taking an active interest in the business. Still only fifteen, she was wild and impetuous, just beginning to recognize her lack of interest in authority and fully engaged in finding out how much trouble she could get into. At least, that was what he perceived. His mother was more tolerant, seeing Chrys as a young girl growing up and still finding herself, while Paxon saw her as trouble on the prowl.

Like the time she found a way to haul the Radanians' tractor onto their barn roof. Or the time she put twenty live pigs in the butcher's bedroom. Or the time she and three others went down to a council meeting to protest involvement with an irrigation plan that potentially would have dammed up the Borgine River and killed thousands of fish, dumping vats full of dead fish on the chamber floor to emphasize their point.

Or all the times she stayed out all night with boys. Or the times she came home from the Two Roosters walking sideways and singing bawdy Highland drinking songs.

His sister needed something to focus on besides finding new and creative ways to entertain herself, and it was time she began contributing more than housecleaning and dishwashing to the family effort. She already knew a sufficient amount about flying airships to help him on his runs, and eventually she would be old enough and might become sufficiently dependable to make runs on her own. In the meantime, she could learn to fly the transport and lend a hand with crewing.

Maybe that would help keep her out of the Two Roosters and similar drinking holes, where she already spent far too much time.

He walked back into the kitchen and began looking through the cold box and pantry. His mother had gone to her sister's house for a few days, helping with the new baby. So it would be up to him to make dinner for himself and Chrys—assuming his sister put in an appearance. These days, it was no sure thing. He worried for her, and it frustrated him that she paid him so little attention.

You aren't my parent, she would say. *You can't tell me what to do.* Aggravating.

Sometimes, he wished their father were still there. Chrys had grown up too fast and too independent without him there to help rein her in. Maybe he could have exercised better control over her than Paxon.

He shook his head doubtfully. As if *anyone* could control Chrysallin.

He left the kitchen with a glass of ale and went out to sit on the porch rocker. Maybe he would have to go looking for her, bring her back to share dinner. He didn't like eating alone. He didn't like eating while worrying about her. It was bad enough that he had to do everything when their mother was away. Chrys didn't seem to think she had any responsibilities at all. She acted like she could do what she wanted and that ought to be the way of things.

She acted like a child, he thought, fuming. She acted like no one mattered but her.

But she was a child, of course. She was fifteen—and when you were a fifteen-year-old girl, no one else mattered but yourself.

She had a good heart; he would concede that. She was kind to others, especially to those in need of kindness and less fortunate than she was. She was quick to lend out or even give away what she had to those who didn't. She could be your friend in a heartbeat, if she saw you wished it. She stood up for what she believed in. She would not back down or be intimidated. His memories of her growing up softened his momentary frustration. She would get back to who she had been; he was sure of it. She would be all right in the end.

He finished off the ale and took the empty tankard back into the kitchen. He should go down to the airfield and work on mending those radian draws, he thought for the second time in the last few minutes. He should forget about Chrys and dinner until the day was a little farther along. Worrying about the future seldom did anything to help improve it. If you wanted to do something about the future, you had to put some effort into it. That usually involved working on something that would make the future you sought more attainable.

As he was going out the door, he glanced once more at the ancient sword above the fireplace. It'd be nice if you could make things better just by using magic. If you could skip the work part. Even if you could only do it once.

Staring at the sword, he wondered suddenly if his life was going in the right direction. He was flying freight on airships because his father had. He was running the family business because he was the oldest, and if he didn't do it no one would and his mother would have to sell. But was this what he really wanted to do? Or was he just marking time, doing what was easiest, taking on the familiar and not risking anything?

The front door flew open.

"Paxon!"

He turned around to find Jayet, one of the serving girls at the Two Roosters, standing in the entryway, looking distraught. "What's wrong?" he asked quickly.

"Your sister!" she snapped. "That's what's wrong. You'd better come right away!"

Chrys. Of course it would be Chrys.

He didn't argue with Jayet. He just did what she asked and went out the door behind her, working hard at keeping up because she was striding ahead so quickly.

"What's she done now?"

"Gotten herself in trouble. What do you think?"

Jayet was small and tough, physically compact, emotionally cool, and a bulldog at everything she did, which made her perfect for working at the tavern. She was Chrys's friend—or as much of a friend as anyone could be to his sister—always there when it mattered, ready to keep Chrys from getting in too deep with whatever mad scheme or stunt she had taken it into her head to try out.

Her mop of spiky white-blond hair bounced as she glanced over her shoulder at Paxon. "She got into a dice game. There were five of them, all locals except for this one man, who claims to have flown in on business from the Southland cities. Doesn't look like a businessman, but who knows? Anyway, I'm not paying much attention to them. No one's causing any trouble—Chrys included—when all of a sudden she leaps up and starts screaming at him. Just screaming like she can't stand to be in the same room with him."

"He did something to her?"

"He cleaned her out. He threw five sevens, a sweep, took the pot and everything that was bet. Including what she wagered and didn't have on her. Apparently, she was so confident about winning, she told him that if she couldn't pay him one way she would pay him another. He took her at her word, but I don't think she saw it the way he did. Chrys would never agree to anything like that."

He assumed not, but his sister was growing up fast and the boundaries of what she would allow might be expanding.

"Anyway, she claimed he cheated. The other players backed right off, refusing to get involved. If Chrys hadn't been so furious, she might have thought twice, too. This man didn't look like the type you wanted to go up against. He told her she lost, so if she couldn't pay, she belonged to him. That was the bargain. She told him what he could do with his bargain, and when I left they were standing toe-to-toe with everyone else standing back."

They were past the yard and down on the road now, heading into the city. He could see the sprawl of buildings below, the businesses surrounded by residences,

the airfield situated south, and the barracks and training field for the home guard and airmen set west.

"No one got between them? Not even Raffe?"

She shook her head. "Especially not Raffe. He knows
this man, I think. They might even have done business
together in the past. You know Raffe, always on the
prowl for an easy score, always walking on the edge. I
think there's some of that in play. Raffe just stood back
and watched it happen."

"What about City Watch? Did you think to call them
in?"

She wheeled back on him. "Look, I risked a lot just by
coming to tell *you*! Raffe told me not to do even that
much, warned me to mind my own business. But I came
anyway, and I might lose my job because of it! So don't
be asking me about City Watch."

He shut up then, deciding she was right, this wasn't
her problem in the first place, and he should just be glad
she'd bothered to come tell him what was going on
while there might still be time for him to do something
about it.

She started off again, walking more quickly than before, and he hurried after. "Sorry about the City Watch
comment. Thank you for coming to get me. I owe you."

"You bet you do," she threw over her shoulder.
"Come on! Walk faster! Chrys is in trouble!"

Picking up the pace, he did his best to comply.

2

IT WAS NOT AN OVERLY LONG WALK TO THE TWO Roosters, which was situated at the northern edge of the city, just a quarter of a mile downhill from where Paxon's parents had built their home. It was a small, intimate tavern, the sort Chrys would choose because she liked to claim places as her own. She had been Jayet's friend all her life, and that had probably contributed to her choice of taverns after her friend went to work there. Jayet was older, but not necessarily more levelheaded. Chrys was clearly the wilder of the two, the one who needed an older sister to help guide her. Unfortunately, Jayet wasn't up to the job.

Still, she was better than nothing. At least she thought to voice an objection now and then, and occasionally to provide a different point of view before things got too far out of hand.

Paxon was thinking about this as they reached the Two Roosters and pushed through the doors into the main room.

Everything was quiet, as if nothing of what Jayet described had occurred. Paxon glanced around the room. There was no sign of Chrys.

Raffe was behind the bar trying hard to look like he was busy but not succeeding, his eyes shifting to find Paxon then moving quickly away again.

"Do you see the man she was with?" Paxon asked Jayet.

She shook her head. "He's gone. So is she."

Paxon could see that for himself. He strode over to the bar and Raffe. "Where is my sister?"

Raffe glanced up and shrugged. "She left with some man. Not too long ago. Why?"

"Where did they go?"

"How should I know?"

"Think about it."

"Look, Paxon, it isn't my job to look after girls who make foolish bets and then find out the hard way when they have to pay the price. Especially ones who just seem to be asking for—"

He never finished whatever it was he was going to say. By then, Paxon had seized him by his tunic front and dragged him halfway across the bar. "I'm only going to ask you once more before I break your arm. Where is my sister?"

"Let go of me, or you'll . . ."

His hand was groping for the club he kept under the counter, so Paxon dragged him the rest of the way across the bar and threw him on the floor, stomping hard on his wrist for good measure. Raffe screamed as the bones crunched.

Paxon knelt with his knee on the tavern owner's stomach and his hand around his throat. "You should answer me, Raffe. Right now."

"Airfield!" the other gasped, grimacing in pain. "He has a ship there!"

"What's his name?"

Raffe shook his head.

"Answer me or I'll break your other arm."

Raffe spit at him. "Go ahead! He'll hurt me worse than you can even imagine if I tell you who he is!"

"Paxon!" Jayet was beside him, pulling him back.

"Forget this! Go after Chrys. That's what matters. You know where she is. Maybe you can still reach her before they leave!"

He was so enraged he almost didn't hear her. But she yanked him backward again and he finally rose, taking a moment to look down at the man at his feet. "If I find out you've lied to me, Raffe, I will be back for you. If I find out you lied, I'll kill you. She's fifteen years old!" He stepped away. "Let me know if he does anything to you because of this, Jayet." Then he was out the door.

Maybe he should have taken time to find out more, he thought as he raced toward the airfield. Maybe he should have beaten it out of Raffe. But there wasn't time. There was every chance he was already too late to catch them. If the stranger, whoever he was, had an airship waiting, he was likely already on his way back to wherever he had come from.

But why he was bothering to haul along a fifteen-year-old girl, lost wager or no, was troubling. Most men wouldn't have made the effort. Most wouldn't have gotten into a dice game with her in the first place. But Chrys was tall and mature looking for her age, so he may have thought her much older than she really was. What really distressed him was the thought that it wasn't the money that mattered, that it was Chrys he had been after all along. Young girls were taken by force all the time to work in the pleasure houses of the large Southland cities. Chrys wouldn't be the first to end up that way.

Except that she wouldn't end up that way, he reminded himself. He would find her and bring her home long before she got anywhere near that life. That was a promise.

He ran through the city, charting as direct a path as he could to the airfield, avoiding major avenues and crowds, trying not to exhaust himself before he reached his destination. If Chrys had been taken to the airfield on foot, he might still be able to catch up to her. There was no mention of horses or carriages or other travel. He had to hope. Using alleyways and cut-throughs, he shaved a few more minutes off his time. And the airship would not necessarily be prepped and ready to lift off. It would take time to attach the radian draws and power her up.

He ran faster, close now, the buildings beginning to thin out and become smaller as the edge of the city neared. He was running full-out, eating up the yards, setting a blistering pace. He would reach her, he told himself. He would find her.

And suddenly it occurred to him that he had no weapons.

After all, talk might not be enough to persuade the stranger to let his sister go. Just the fact that he had taken her in the first place—an act that amounted to the kidnapping of a fifteen-year-old girl—showed a certain disdain for authority or any interest in the moral high ground. By deliberately taking Chrys, this man had revealed his character and likely his intentions.

Paxon slowed, trying to think what to do. He should have brought that old sword. Weapons weren't something they kept in large numbers in his home, although there were hunting knives and a solitary long knife. But the black-bladed sword was a real weapon, and he should have thought to bring it.

Too late for that now. He began to run faster again, catching his first glimpse of the airfield through gaps in the buildings at the end of the street. He would try to find a weapon on the way. Anything would do.

Then he was past the last of the buildings and out on the open field amid the airships. Leah was small compared with the big Southland cities, but even so there were dozens of vessels moored over acres of ground. He slackened his pace, casting about anxiously. He searched through the ranks of airships, advancing slowly as he did so, trying to find something that would show him the way. There were men and women everywhere, servicing the airships. A few pilots stood by watching or walked the decks of the vessels or stood in the pilot boxes. He scanned the insignia emblazoned on the pennants that identified the ports of registration of the airships.

He did not see Chrys anywhere.

And then he did.

She was being led up a mobile boarding ramp to a sleek vessel of a sort he had never seen before. The ship had caught his eye because it was so different, and there was his sister. He charged forward, breaking into a run once more, darting through the forest of hulls and masts as he did so. He kept searching for a weapon as he ran, but none appeared. The workers on the field were not wearing weapons, and there were none lying about.

Finally, in desperation, he snatched up an iron bar. It wasn't much, but it would have to do.

When he was still fifty yards or so away, he slowed to a walk. He could tell the ship wasn't leaving quite yet. The crew was still rigging her; the diapson crystals hadn't been powered up. He had time. He wondered suddenly why Chrys wasn't fighting. She seemed to be boarding willingly, offering no resistance. That didn't seem like her, especially given the story behind her abduction. The confrontation at the Two Roosters did not suggest that she had suddenly changed her mind about accompanying the stranger to whatever fate he had in store for her. No, something about what he was seeing wasn't right.

Chrys was no longer in sight. The stranger who had

led her aboard reappeared at the railing of his vessel, caught sight of Paxon, and moved to the boarding ramp. Paxon continued to approach, but more cautiously than before. He watched the stranger descend and walk out to meet him.

"You would be the brother, I expect."

Paxon stopped six feet away. "I want my sister back."

"She hasn't stopped threatening me with you since I brought her to my vessel." He smiled. "She keeps telling me what you will do to me once you get here. I must admit to a certain curiosity, given all the terrible injuries she has assured me you intend to inflict. Is she always like this?"

Paxon was a little taken aback by this friendly chatter, but he was in no way deterred from his purpose. "You've kidnapped a fifteen-year-old girl," he snapped. "That's an offense everywhere. It doesn't matter what she did, you have to let her go. But I will make good on her debt, if that's what it takes."

The man shrugged, but the smile did not fade. He wasn't a big man, wasn't even striking in any particular way. Yet there was an unmistakable confidence about him, and no visible sense of concern over Paxon's appearance. "I'm afraid her debt is much more than you can afford, young man."

"I'll work it off."

The smile widened. "In a couple of months, if you work hard, you probably can. But she can work it off more quickly by coming with me."

Paxon was both enraged and frightened on hearing this. He was beginning to feel that talk alone was not going to be enough to get Chrys back. He was going to have to be more aggressive, and he wasn't sure he was up to it. "The City Watch is on its way," he warned.

The stranger shook his head. "I doubt it. But even if it is, they won't be able to do anything about your sister. I have immunity from interference from the local authorities. I can pretty much do what I want. Which, in this case, means taking your sister with me to pay her debt." He paused. "She might be willing to go with me by now, you know. She might have reconsidered; she knows she is in the wrong, and she might be ready to pay the price for her foolish behavior. You should be proud of her."

Paxon shook his head in denial. "I don't know what you are talking about. She would never go anywhere with you willingly, whatever you say. Let me ask her face-to-face. Let me talk to her."

"Oh, I don't think so. It would be better if you just turned around and went home again. She'll be back in a few weeks. There won't be any permanent damage. And she will have learned a valuable lesson."

Paxon hefted the iron bar. "If you don't release my sister right now, I will board your ship and take her back myself!"

The stranger nodded. He raised his arm, making a small gesture with his hand. A signal "I was afraid it might come down to this. You have no idea who I am, do you? If you did, you might think twice about threatening me."

"I doubt it. Are you going to set my sister free or not?"

"What I am going to do is to give you one last chance to walk away. You should take it."

All at once there were three men standing behind him, crewmen from his vessel from the look of them—big and strong, hard men much older and undoubtedly more experienced at fighting than Paxon. They carried no weapons, but gnarled hands and muscular arms suggested they did not need them.

The stranger had quit smiling. "Drop your iron bar,

Paxon," he said. "Let's make this fight more even. Fists only."

To Paxon's surprise, he did as he was ordered. He couldn't have explained why; it just seemed that it was something he had to do, and so he did it. He stared down at his discarded weapon, horrified.

"Much better." The stranger stepped back and his men stepped forward. "Don't hurt him too much," he told them. "Don't break anything. Just show him the error of his ways."

They came at Paxon in a rush, slamming into him with such force that they knocked him off his feet. They were on top of him instantly, fists pummeling him as he tried to fight back. He might have landed a few good blows in the struggle, but in the end there were still three of them and only one of him, and he was overwhelmed.

Eventually, the pain and the shock caused him to lose consciousness. When he came awake again, a hand was slapping his face in a rhythmic fashion while another was holding up his head by his hair.

The stranger was kneeling before him. "My name is Arcannen. If you wish to pursue this, you can find me at Dark House in the city of Wayford. You should stay away, but if you can't help yourself you had better bring a real weapon, not an iron bar. Because if I see you again, I will kill you."

He rose and stood looking down. "Let him go."

The fingers tangled in his hair released their grip and his face slammed into the earth. Pain exploded in his head, and bright flashes appeared behind his eyelids. He lay helplessly, fighting to stay conscious. But it was long minutes later before he could bring himself to open his eyes and turn himself over to discover that the stranger's airship had begun to lift off, light sheaths gathering in sunlight for the radian draws to channel to the parse tubes, thrusters powering up. As battered as he was, as defeated as he felt, he found himself admiring the sleek lines of the vessel, wondering again why he had never seen this sort of airship before. He made himself memorize her look, the emblems on her pennants, the insignia on her bow.

A black raven, wings spread, beak open wide. Attacking.

Then the vessel wheeled south and sped away. By the time Paxon was back on his feet, she was little more than a dot in the distant sky.

He stood looking at nothing for a few moments, waiting to recover from his beating, then turned about and stalked from the airfield. He had really never had a chance at getting Chrys back from the stranger. Arcannen—that was a name he wouldn't forget. He had provided it willingly—something Raffe had refused to do—so he was confident that it wouldn't help Paxon to know it. He was a man possessed of a new style of airship and a crew that likely would do anything he asked them to. Somehow, he had been able to persuade Paxon to put down the iron bar when that might have made the difference in the fight.

And he had Chrys in his possession. He was flying her back to Wayford to something called Dark House. Paxon could only imagine what that might turn out to be.

Come find out, Arcannen had challenged. Believing Paxon would never dare to do so, that he had found out the hard way what would happen if he did. The beating was a warning. *Stay away. Don't come after me. Let your sister go. She belongs to me, and I can do with her what I like. You can't prevent it, and you shouldn't try. You are a Highlander of no importance living in a place of low regard, and you can never hope to be the equal of me. Stay where you are and stay healthy.*

He left the airfield and trudged through the city toward home, picturing Arcannen's face and hearing his smooth voice in his mind.

So certain that Paxon had been put in his place.

Well, he was in for a surprise.

3

BY THE TIME HE REACHED HIS HOME AND WALKED into the kitchen to wash off the dirt and blood and put cold compresses on the worst of the bruises, Paxon had made up his mind. He was going after his sister, no matter what Arcannen threatened or what sort of obstacles he might encounter. Any further consideration of the matter was beyond discussion. But he would not be so reckless as he was before. He would not let himself be caught in a situation where he clearly had no hope of accomplishing anything. The outcome would be different this time around.

After he finished washing and applying cold cloths to his battered face, he retired to the front porch to sit and think for a few minutes. Chrys was already at risk, and he didn't believe for a minute that her captor would sit around deciding what to do with her. If he was to get to his sister before she was subjected to a whole raft of unpleasantness that could easily result in both physical and emotional damage, he needed to do so sooner rather than later. It was helpful knowing who it was he was looking for and where to find him. Arcannen had told him pointedly enough that he would be at Dark House in the city of Wayford, so all Paxon needed to do was to power up the Sprint he had built for himself some years back and fly down there. Someone would be able to give him directions once he arrived, and then he could start looking for Chrys in earnest.

Simple enough, if you didn't dwell too long on the lack of details—like how he was supposed to get her out of Arcannen's establishment and safely out of the city without anyone stopping him.

He imagined there would be guards—and probably large numbers of them. On further consideration, it seemed to him that if Arcannen could make him put down that iron bar simply by asking him to do so, he probably possessed magic. Even though it was outlawed in the Southland and any use of it would be dealt with swiftly no matter what sort of immunity he enjoyed, Arcannen did not seem the type to worry much about authority and acts of law. If he had a way to do so, he would have magic in place to defend his home and business, whether they were separate or not—something he needed to consider when he went in search of Chrys.

And he would need one thing more.

He would need a weapon.

Arcannen had told him so, and even if it was simply an embellishment to the dare he had thrown up, it was good advice. After what had happened today, Paxon certainly didn't intend to face the man again without protection.

He thought about taking someone with him, but that meant calling on friends for a favor they didn't owe and shouldn't be asked to give, considering the danger. Better he go alone than risk somebody else's life as well as his own. A large armed party would attract more attention, anyway. One man, keeping to the shadows, would have a better chance.

Sure he would.

He grimaced at his own facile analysis of the situation. But it was best to stay positive. Pushing aside his doubts, he walked back into the house, dumped the bloodied cloths and cold packs, and changed his clothes. He was in the midst of packing a bag with a few essentials when Jayet appeared in the doorway, calling out to him.

He walked out to face her.

"You look like you got the worst of whatever happened," she said quietly. "You didn't get her back, did you?"

"No," he admitted, "but the matter isn't finished. I know who he is now and where I can find him. I'm going after him."

She nodded. "I thought you would. Have you anyone to help you?"

"I think it's better if I do this alone. Other people might get underfoot. I would have to worry about protecting them as well as myself. If something happened to them, I'd be responsible."

"There are those who would come with you if you asked," she said. "You might need someone to watch your back."

He smiled. "Perhaps you could come," he joked.

She cocked her head, squaring up to him. "Funny you should say that. I'm exactly who I had in mind."

He stared at her, then quickly shook his head. "Oh, no. Out of the question, Jayet. You don't know what this man is like! Arcannen, he calls himself. He's very dangerous. Ruthless. I'm not letting you risk yourself for me."

"I wouldn't be risking myself for you. I'd be risking myself for Chrys. I should have stopped her the moment I saw her getting into that game, begging for a chair, making wild promises and talking like she was something special. I saw all the signs, and I didn't do a thing to stop it from happening. I just went about my business."

She ran a hand through her mop of white-blond hair.

"Besides, I don't have anything else to do. I'm out of a job."

"Raffe let you go?"

"I quit. I've had enough of working for Raffe and putting up with his constant badgering and groping and talking about how great he is. Believe me, Paxon, I've given this some thought. Anyway, that has nothing to do with why I'm here. You were seen coming back through the city and up the road past the Two Roosters. I knew then you hadn't gotten Chrys back. And I knew you wouldn't give up on her. So I thought maybe I could find a way to help."

"Jayet . . ."

"Please don't say that if you needed help, you would ask a man. If you did that, I would have to hurt you. Just listen a moment. For one thing, I can get into places where a man can't. For another, I can fly an airship. You might need me to do that if you get hurt. You might need another pair of hands to back you up. I can provide all that. I'm tough enough; you know that. Let me help."

He thought about it a moment. There were enough reasons against agreeing to her suggestion to fill a good-size shed. But there were reasons in favor of it, too.

Her blunt features tightened. She was waiting for him to say no. "All right," he said, less certain about it than he wished. "But you have to promise to do what I say, no matter what."

Her nod of agreement was brisk, sharp. "Whatever you say."

Not entirely to his surprise, she had already packed a bag. It was sitting on the front porch where she had left it, and she shouldered it as they went out the door together. He had written a note to his mother just in case she came back early, telling her that Chrys had gone with him on a transfer—a short run over to the east end of the Rainbow Lake—and he would be back in a couple of days. She was supposed to be gone for a week, and for once he hoped she would not hurry back.

He was on his way out the door when he caught sight of the sword hanging over the fireplace and stopped. He needed a weapon, and he didn't have anything better. The sword was a relic from the past, but he released it from its fastenings and took it down. He studied it for a moment, taking note of the emblem stamped on its leather sheath—a seal he assumed once identified the royal house of the Leahs. He pulled the blade free and balanced it in his hand. He ran his finger carefully along its edge. It was still razor-sharp, and unblemished.

The Sword of Leah.

He sheathed the blade anew and strapped it across his back. It was better than nothing. Maybe it would finally provide him with a little magic of his own.

With Jayet in tow, he walked back down to the north end of the airfield where he kept his vessels moored. He had several—or, he amended quickly, the family had several. The transport—a big, looming carrier with four masts and multiple light sheaths that required a crew of four, the balance of which he usually found from a pool of airship fliers who worked as independent contractors—an elderly skiff that wasn't good for much, and his Sprint. He would take the Sprint, of course; it was small, fast, maneuverable, and very dependable.

He walked over to where it was docked inside its locked hangar—a building that was more shed than hangar, constructed specifically to shelter the vessel from weather and tampering. He checked the lock, then released it and opened the door. With Jayet's help, he pulled the Sprint clear, put up its raked single mast, and fastened down the radian draws. Then he closed the door to the shed and locked it anew.

"Ready?" he asked her.

She nodded. "Let's fly."

Moments later they were airborne, winging their way south. Paxon had traveled to Wayford on cargo hauls a few times, and he could find his way without maps or compass. But he didn't know anything much about the city proper, having flown in and out again without leaving the airfield. Once they got to Wayford, he would need help.

He wasn't taking anything about this mission for granted. He knew he was going to need all kinds of help from one source or another. Maybe Jayet would provide some of it. Maybe strangers would provide the rest. But he would need luck, too. Probably a lot of it.

Even so, his conviction that he could find his sister and bring her home again remained undiminished. Nothing would prevent that from happening.

They flew south through the rest of the day and into the night. By the time the lights of the city came in sight, it was well after midnight. Jayet was sleeping, curled up in her seat behind him, her spiky hair flattened against the cushions, her face relaxed and bathed in starlight. He found her suddenly pretty—an attribute he'd somehow overlooked before. He smiled in spite of himself. She didn't look so tough now.

Wayford's airfield was three times the size of Leah's, and the sea of ships that filled her acres of open grassland and landing pads seemed to stretch away for thousands of yards. He maneuvered the Sprint onto a pad that was vacant, close to the field manager's office, and shut her down. Jayet was awake, looking around sleepily.

Paxon climbed out of the pilot box and stretched. "Wait here."

He reached inside the pilot box, pulled out the Sword of Leah—which he had taken off while they were flying—and strapped it across his back once more. Then he walked over to the field manager's office and stepped through the door. The boy sitting at the field manager's desk might have been thirteen or fourteen, but no older. "Kind of young to be an airfield manager, aren't you?" Paxon asked him.

The boy shrugged. "I'm old enough." He was looking at Paxon's sword, its black length poking up over the latter's shoulder.

"Can you give me that pad for one night? Maybe for two?"

"Yours as long as you want it. Just sign the register."

He shoved a book across the desk, and Paxon filled in the requisite space. "How much?"

"Pay when you leave." He gestured. "Nice-looking blade. Old, but it has clean lines. Bet you know how to use it, too."

"Want to take a look?"

The boy rocked forward and stood up. Paxon un-sheathed his sword and offered it to him. The boy examined it carefully, handed it back, and once it was sheathed again extended his hand. "I'm Grehling Cara. My dad's the airfield manager. He's off for the night, but I fill in for him. He's teaching me the business."

"Paxon Leah. Your father must have some confidence in you."

The boy pointed out the window at the Sprint. "I like your ship, too. Did you build her yourself?"

Paxon nodded. "From the ground up. Can I ask you something? Do you know a man called Arcannen?"

The boy gave him a look. "Why do you want to know?"

"I need to find him. I need directions."

"Are you friends with him?"

Paxon shook his head. "Why do you ask?"

Grehling sat down again. "Oh, just because. He flew in earlier today and told me he had a friend coming in

from the Highlands who might ask how to find him."
His eyes fixed on Paxon. "I thought you might be that
friend."

So Arcannen had expected him to follow, after all.
Paxon felt a surge of anger at the other's arrogance, but
quickly tamped it down. "Well, you should know he is
not my friend."

Grehling nodded. "I thought that might be. Arcannen
doesn't have many friends, just lots of people who do
business with him. He owns Dark House, a place where
they do things my father won't talk about. But I know
anyway. He's a magic wielder, a sorcerer. He's very
powerful and very dangerous. People disappear around
him all the time. Maybe you should think twice about
trying to find him."

"I should, but I can't. He's taken something that isn't
his, and I intend to get it back."

"A girl?"

"My sister, Chrysallin. You saw her?"

He nodded. "Coming off his airship earlier. I keep my
eyes open. Look, I can give you directions if you want,
but they might be a little different from the ones Arcannen would give you. Mine might help keep you safe. I
don't like Arcannen, and I don't like doing anything
that helps him. So maybe I'll help you, instead. But if I
do, I'll need some extra coins for making sure your
Sprint is kept safe and ready to lift off the minute you've
finished your business."

Paxon sat on the edge of the desk. "You seem awfully
eager to help someone you barely know, Grehling. Why
is that?"

He shrugged. "I knew someone Arcannen took to
Dark House, someone like your sister. Someone I liked."
His lips tightened. "She never came out again. Do you
want my help or not?"

"I'm listening."

When the boy was done explaining, Paxon thanked him for his help and paid him the coins he wanted. "You'll find your sister on the top floor," Grehling said in parting. "That's where he keeps all the new ones, at first."

He offered his hand, and Paxon shook it. "Better keep that sword of yours handy."

Paxon went back out to the Sprint and Jayet. She was still in the pilot box, eyes half closed. "Time to go," he said.

"Was that a boy you were talking to in there?" she asked. She rumpled her hair and yawned.

"A boy who is a lot older than he has a right to be," he answered. "Watch out for that one."

Jayet nodded sleepily. "I watch out for all of them. Can we please eat something? I'm starved."

They walked from the airfield into the city, following the directions Grehling had provided, and quickly found a tavern that was open all night. They took a seat at a table at the back of the room, ordered ale and soup and bread, finished it off, and quickly left. No one paid any attention to them.

Back on the streets of Wayford, Paxon explained what Grehling had suggested they do.

"Arcannen lives at Dark House, which is what I thought it was—a pleasure house specializing in exotic and forbidden acts. Very exclusive. Chrys will be there, probably locked up in a room somewhere on the upper floor, according to Grehling. He says other girls who work for Arcannen are kept there, too, at first. He told me how we can get inside, but then we still have to find out which room she is in."

"That might be difficult if there are guards."

"There are, but not so many at this time of night because everything shuts down after two until late morning. There will only be a few, and all but one of them will be watching the doors. The other one roams the halls. He'll be the most dangerous, the way we're going in. We'll have to get rid of him right away once we're inside."

"You're going in tonight? Without sleep?"

"Do you think I should wait until morning, Jayet? This is my sister we're talking about."

She shook her head. "I suppose not. But maybe a few hours wouldn't hurt. You haven't slept at all. What difference would it make if you waited for first light?"

"I don't know, and I don't want to find out. I'm going in now."

They walked on in silence. The streets were still busy, the taverns and pleasure houses still open, but the night was winding down and many of the patrons were hauling their drunken, sated selves home again. One made the mistake of groping for Jayet as she passed, and she hit him so hard with her fist that she knocked him unconscious.

"Hands to yourself!" she hissed at him as they moved past.

Following Grehling's instructions, they found Dark House in a little under an hour. It was a big, brooding structure situated at the end of a block on one corner, surrounded by stone walls with iron spikes embedded at the top, its windows curtained and shuttered, its lights dimmed to almost nothing. It was black and unfriendly. Paxon and Jayet stood across the street from it and stared.

"I don't want to find out what goes on in there," the girl said softly.

"You won't have to," Paxon said. "You're staying out here."

She kept looking at the building across the road for several seconds. Then she said, "I think you should take me with you. You might need me to distract that guard. You might need me to get in somewhere you can't. I can't help you out here."

"Out here, you're safe."

"Out here, I'm useless."

He gave her a look. "What did I tell you before we set out, when I agreed to let you come along?"

"That I would do what you told me to. And I will. But that doesn't mean I can't argue about it. Leaving me behind is a mistake. Think about it. Chrys means something to me, too."

He remembered the way she had flattened that drunk on their way here, and then imagined a few scenarios where being a woman might prove useful. Keeping Jayet safe was important, but getting Chrys out of Dark House was even more so.

"All right," he said finally. "But stick close to me and do what I ask you to do."

She flashed him a smile, her face brightening beneath the mop of white-blond hair. "I promise."

He wasn't sure it was a promise she could keep, but she was right about her value to his effort to free Chrys, so he could ill afford to be pessimistic about her conduct. Jayet was smart; she would know what to do once they were inside.

They waited a few minutes longer, watching as a final few customers straggled out the front door of Dark House, then they crossed the road with Jayet hanging on one arm, the two a couple out on the town, but heading home. Once across, he steered her to a wall separating Dark House from a shuttered and empty-looking building situated on the adjoining lot. Off the street now and out of sight, they followed the wall almost to its end before discovering a small wooden door set within the stone. Searching the door, Paxon found the button that released the lock, just as Grehling had told him. The door swung open, and he led Jayet inside.

Now they were standing in a cluster of sad-looking flower gardens that filled the space between the wall and Dark House. Moving straight across the gardens to the building in a crouch, they turned left to find a small window set between two larger banks. Paxon twisted the latch, and the window opened easily. Indicating that Jayet should go first, he boosted her through the opening, then pulled himself up behind her.

They were in a cluttered storage room that appeared to serve as a pantry. At least, that was what they could see by the dim glow cast from the streetlights outside the wall. Paxon moved to the doorway, stood listening for a few moments, cracked the door, and peered out. Then, beckoning for Jayet to follow him, he stepped through into the room beyond.

They were in a kitchen now, but it was empty and dark. They moved through it cautiously, not wanting to bump up against anything. After agonizing seconds of maneuvering in the near dark, they reached a door that opened into a servants' eating area and from there into a hallway beyond.

Paxon was sweating now, adrenaline rushing through him, his fear and excitement held in precarious balance. He could feel the weight of the Sword of Leah across his back, pressing against him uncomfortably, but it gave him reassurance that, if caught out, he would have a chance to fight his way free. Because Arcannen had been so open about telling Grehling to offer directions, Paxon knew the sorcerer would be ready for him. Somehow, somewhere, he would be waiting. Maybe personally, maybe using magic—but there was little chance Arcannen would be caught off guard.

The best he could hope for was that he could avoid any traps, find his sister, set her free, and maybe get all of them out of there before Arcannen knew what was happening.

It was not a particularly reasonable expectation, but nothing about any of this was reasonable at this point.

He was so deep in thought he almost missed hearing the approach of the roving guard, and only barely managed to flatten himself within the narrow recessed space of a closed doorway before the man appeared. Jayet kept walking, pretending nothing was wrong, that she belonged and was on her way to somewhere specific.

"No walking around after hours," the guard snapped at her as she reached him. "You know the rules."

She slowed, moving just past him, causing him to turn so that he was looking away from Paxon. "I must have lost track of time. I was thirsty."

"There is water in your room. Are you new here?"

She nodded. "Just got in. You're kind of cute."

Then Paxon clubbed him from behind, and he dropped like a stone. Jayet slowed the man's fall enough to muffle any noise, and after trying a few doors found a closet and helped drag him inside. Using cleaning rags, Paxon bound and gagged him and lashed him in place to some iron shelves. Not a perfect solution, but it would have to do.

Leaving the closet, they continued down the hall until they found a set of stairs. They climbed to the next floor and stopped when they heard signs of activity behind the doors of the rooms down the hall. When it was quiet again, they continued up to the top floor. It was an attic space, and there were only three doors: two to either side and one at the end. The last was padlocked and chained.

Paxon moved over to it quickly, put his ear against the door, and listened. No sound came from within.

He exchanged a quick glance with Jayet and shook his head. But it was the only door locked, so there was reason to think it was the right one, and he had to take a look. Which meant he had to smash the lock and break it down. But first he decided to peek inside the other two, just to be sure. He moved over to each as quietly as he could, cracking the doors and peering inside. Bedrooms, both of them, sparsely furnished, walls bare, windows shuttered.

The one on the right was empty.

Chrysallin was in the one on the left.

So was Arcannen.

4

PAXON FROZE, AND FOR AN INSTANT HE WAS UNDE-cided about what he should do. It had never occurred to him that Arcannen might be with his sister when he found her. She was tied to the bed, spread-eagled and lashed in place, her mouth gagged. Her gaze found his, eyes wide and staring and frightened. She was dressed in the clothes she had been wearing when taken and did not appear to have been harmed.

But appearances could be deceptive, he reminded himself.

Jayet was still outside the room, so he moved to block the entry to hide her from Arcannen. He was trying to think of something to say to warn her when the sorcerer saved him the trouble.

"Don't look so surprised, Paxon. We've been waiting for you since nightfall. She said you would come, and I believed her. Too bad for you, isn't it?"

Paxon closed the door behind him. Smokeless lamps on the nightstand and on the wall bracketing a large mirror across from the bed lent sufficient light for him to see clearly. Arcannen was sitting on the bed next to his sister, his black robes wrapped about him. His small, pinched features were crinkled with amusement, his black eyes bright and eager.

"You should have taken my advice and stayed home, boy. This probably won't end well for you."

Paxon held his gaze. "Maybe you are the one it won't end well for."

"That seems unlikely. Have you discovered who I am? Did the boy at the airfield catch you? He was supposed to give you directions."

Paxon ignored the questions. "What do you want with my sister, anyway? Isn't this going to an awful lot of trouble for one girl?"

Arcannen smiled. "Depends on how you value things. I value young women. I insist they keep their word when they make bets with me. This one made a bet and couldn't pay when she lost. Bringing her here isn't all that much trouble. Putting her to work is easy enough. Maybe she will like it well enough that she will want to stay on."

He shrugged. "You, on the other hand, are a bit of a problem. I have no work for you. I would have preferred it if you had stayed in the Highlands, but since you have failed to do even that much I have to deal with you more harshly than I wanted to. I hoped the beating would be enough to keep you from coming here. But your sister was right. You are beyond stubborn."

Paxon noticed the deep bruise across the far side of his sister's face for the first time. She had been struck and struck hard. He felt his anger resurfacing, crowding out his fear. He had to get Chrys out of here, no matter what it cost him.

Arcannen seemed completely at ease. He didn't appear to have any weapons, and none of his men seemed to be about. His confidence was troubling. It suggested that whatever magic he had was more than enough to disable or kill Paxon.

"Did you bring any money?" Arcannen asked suddenly.

Paxon shook his head. "I don't have any money."

"So you decided you would steal her back? That's not

very honorable of you. Didn't your parents teach you better?"

"I don't think you should be talking to me about honor. Why don't you just let me have my sister back?"

Arcannen shook his head. "We are covering familiar ground. I think I've made my position clear on the matter. There's no reason to talk about it any further."

He got to his feet, still smiling. Then he stopped suddenly, as if something had just occurred to him. "I have a thought. Perhaps you would be willing to trade me something for your sister, something you don't value as much as you value her. For instance, that sword."

Paxon automatically glanced over his shoulder at the handle of the black blade. The Sword of Leah. "Why would you want that?"

Arcannen shrugged. "I collect old weapons, especially blades. That one seems very old and might have some real value. I could be wrong, but if I'm right I will make back what I would lose by letting you have your sister. You, on the other hand . . ."

He let the rest of what he was going to say hang. But it didn't need saying. Which was more valuable to Paxon—his sister or the sword?

But he hesitated anyway. Something about this felt wrong. Instinctively, he sensed that Arcannen recognized the weapon and knew something about it he didn't. He was awfully quick to give up on Chrys after refusing even to consider releasing her before.

"The offer is only good for the next ten seconds," Arcannen threw in, looking suddenly bored. "I am already beginning to lose interest. After all, I can do so many more interesting things with your sister than I can with an old sword."

Paxon was certain something wasn't right now. Arcannen was pressing too hard. "All right, but only if you release my sister first."

The sorcerer gave him a sharp look. "Why would I agree to that?"

"If I give you the sword, you will have both the sword and my sister—here, in your own building. I'd be a fool."

Arcannen studied him further, then shrugged. Pulling out a knife, he severed Chrysallin's bonds and removed the gag. She scooted off the bed and stood uncertainly, as if perhaps she hadn't gotten her balance back. Then she moved over to stand beside her brother, ignoring Arcannen.

"Are you all right?" Paxon asked. "Are you hurt?"

His sister shook her head. She was almost as tall as he was, though still gangly and awkward in the way of very young fillies, but there was such determination in her eyes that it gave him pause.

"Now give me the sword," Arcannen ordered, still standing next to the bed.

Paxon leaned over and kissed his sister's cheek. "Get behind me," he whispered, keeping his face hidden with hers. "Jayet is outside the door."

She moved behind him obediently. "Open the door, Chrys," he told her, facing Arcannen again. "See what's out there."

She did as he asked, then rushed out into Jayet's arms.

"The sword?" Arcannen pressed. "You won't get out of here alive otherwise."

"Go downstairs," Paxon called over his shoulder to the girls. "Get out of here. I'll catch up to you in a minute."

"You try my patience!" Arcannen snapped, starting toward him.

But Paxon quickly reached over his shoulder and unsheathed the sword. "Don't you want to examine it first and make certain of what you are getting?" he asked, holding the blade in front of him. The black metal glittered in the dim light. "Come, have a look."

The sorcerer smiled. "You never intended to give it up, did you? You intended to keep it all along."

"Remember what you said about me a moment ago, about not being very honorable? It seems that, where you are concerned, it's true." He backed toward the doorway, eyes fixed on the sorcerer.

"Put it down!" Arcannen ordered, his face flushed, throwing back his robes. "Do it while you still have the chance, boy!"

"Stop calling me 'boy,' and I will consider your suggestion."

"You have no idea what I will do to you if you refuse! Don't be a fool. I'll finish you and go after your sister, and you will both be dead!"

Paxon was within the open doorway now and almost clear of the room, still watching the other closely. Arcannen was going to do something; he just didn't know what the other's magic allowed. He backed up another step. He had no idea how he was going to get out of this; he only knew he wasn't giving up the sword willingly because he knew now how badly Arcannen wanted it.

He risked a quick look out of the corner of his eye. The hallway was deserted. Chrys and Jayet were gone, and there wasn't any sign of Arcannen's men. Time to make a run for it.

But Arcannen was already moving. He seemed to gather himself all at once, everything folding into his body—almost as if he were collapsing. His arms thrust outward violently and wicked black light exploded from his fingertips, shooting across the open space that separated him from Paxon.

Paxon, acting without thinking, brought the blade of his sword up sharply to deflect the attack.

Then something strange happened. A surge of heat

burst inside him and the black blade of the Sword of Leah flared to life, its length gone bright and reflective, its metal infused with greenish snakes that wove their way through its length. It happened all at once—so quickly that Paxon had only a split second for it to register before the sorcerer's magic struck, throwing him backward through the doorway and across the hall to slam into the wall beyond.

But the magic expended by Arcannen did not touch his body or harm him in any way. Instead, it dovetailed into the blade of his sword and was absorbed as if by a sponge, sinking into the metal and disappearing.

In seconds it was gone.

Paxon heard Arcannen scream in fury as he saw what had happened. He pushed himself back to his feet quickly, the sword still held out protectively in front of him, the black metal alive with the green snakes, its surface a bright and shining mirror.

Arcannen struck at him again, advancing on him. But Paxon was ready this time, braced as he had not been before, and when the magic struck him it did not throw him back but instead exploded into shards that deflected in every direction as the attack collapsed.

Then Paxon was running down the hallway, amazed to find that he was all right, even more amazed to find that the Sword of Leah was magic-infused after all and that the attack by Arcannen had apparently brought that magic to life. He reached the stairway and started down, not looking back to see if he was being followed, but knowing he was.

The next attack caught him midway down, and because he was too slow in blocking it, he was thrown the rest of the way to the floor below. He struggled up and kept going, vaulting down the stairs three and four at a time, flinging himself over the landings. Behind him, he could hear multiple explosions as stairs and railings burst apart only inches away, splinters of wood slashing at his hands and face.

His thoughts raced, his fear propelling him on.

Can't stop!

Run faster!

He broke for the front entry when he reached the ground level, charging right at the guard who stood ready to stop him. A section of the wall exploded, just missing his head as more splinters and a few larger pieces of wood flew past. He kept going. The guard blocking the way stood his ground for about two more seconds and then flung himself clear, letting the Highlander pass without challenge. Paxon brought up his sword, intending to shatter the lock and break clear of Dark House, but just thinking of what he wanted seemed enough. The blade turned to fire, bright and terrible, exploding onto the door and incinerating it in seconds.

Paxon reached the smoldering ruins and kept going, racing from Dark House into the street beyond. He risked a quick look behind him. Nothing. The entry was empty, no sign of Arcannen anywhere.

And then there he was—higher up on a second-story balcony, hands weaving, strange sounds breaking from his lips. The stone of the roadway began to buckle and heave beneath Paxon's feet. He was caught by surprise and stumbled, sprawling to the cracking earth.

As he did so, he dropped the sword and watched it skitter away.

Now Arcannen came after him with everything he could muster—bolts of fire to scorch his skin, flaming daggers to pierce his body, and thunderous explosions to render him unconscious. Somehow, through a combination of desperation and luck, the Highlander managed to avoid all of it, throwing himself aside, rolling away, and finally retrieving his lost sword.

He was up at once, running once more, dodging left and right, reacting instinctively, trying to escape. He kept hoping he would see Jayet or Chrys, but neither appeared. If they hadn't fled to the airfield, he would have to come back and find them, and he had no idea at all how he would accomplish that.

In his hand, the Sword of Leah blazed with magic that wove through the metal and into his body, filling him with confidence and strength. Addictive, euphoric, it swept through him in wave after wave.

"Leah, Leah!" he shouted to the empty, darkened streets, giving out the battle cry of his ancestors.

He carried their sword; he was entitled to their battle cry. He almost laughed, he felt so gleeful.

Behind him, a pack of wolves appeared, yellow eyes gleaming. Their snarls warned him of their coming, and the sound of their claws digging into the roadway sent chills up his spine. He was beginning to wonder if there was anything Arcannen couldn't do. This sort of magic hadn't revealed itself in the Southland since the time of Edinja Orle, and she had been dead for more than a century. No magic of this magnitude was even suspected to exist anywhere within Federation rule. Magic much smaller and less dangerous would have been swept up and locked away in a heartbeat. How Arcannen had avoided that was troubling.

But there was no time to think about it now. The wolves were advancing on him. Big, shaggy beasts, they were more than twice the size of normal wolves, slavering and growling, long tongues lolling from mouths filled with razor-sharp fangs, and hunger in their eyes. Paxon ran from them. Sword or no sword, he didn't care to stand and fight so many. If even one broke through his defenses, it would rip him apart.

He searched for a way to escape them, for any refuge at all that would put him beyond their reach. But it was well past midnight, with dawn still hours away, and no one was on the streets and no lights shone in the windows of the houses. He thought momentarily to climb a tree, a few of which were in evidence, but doing that would put him at the mercy of the sorcerer if he were tracking him, and Paxon felt pretty certain he was.

Finally, he turned, his back against a stone building wall, and used the magic of the sword once more. Sheets of fire cut him off from the wolves, which slowed and backed away, snapping and tearing at the flames with their huge fangs, searching for a way to break through his defenses. Using magic was new to Paxon, and he was uncertain of its limits. He could feel his grip on it slipping away, suggesting it was neither unlimited nor certain. If he didn't break free of the wolves quickly, he would have to start running again.

But this time, they would be right on his heels.

How, he kept wondering, could a sorcerer conjure something of substance out of thin air? That shouldn't be possible.

So maybe it wasn't.

He dropped his broad defense against the pack and turned the sword on the closest wolf. Fire sheeted into the beast, and it vaporized instantly. Nothing but an image, he realized. He went after the others, disintegrating them one by one, until they were all gone.

Then he began to run again.

Behind him, the streets were quiet. No pursuit showed itself; Arcannen remained a threat that did not materialize.

He ran for what seemed like hours before he reached the airfield. To his relief, both Jayet and Chrys were already there, waiting by the Sprint. Grehling, as good as his word, had the vessel powered up and ready for liftoff.

"I owe you for your help," Paxon told the boy.

Grehling shrugged. "You already paid me. Remember? And if anyone asks—Arcannen, especially—I never saw you."

Paxon and the girls climbed aboard and buckled on their safety harnesses. In seconds they were airborne and flying north toward the Highlands and home.

5

ONCE THEY WERE BACK IN THE HIGHLANDS AGAIN, Paxon Leah did his best to put the entire incident behind him. From his point of view, the less said about it, the better. He was no hero, and he didn't want anyone in Leah or anywhere else trying to make him one.

Mostly, he didn't want any word getting out about the Sword of Leah and its magic. Even though neither Jayet nor his sister had been present to witness the events surrounding his use of the blade, he had warned them not to talk to anyone about anything that had happened. He could assume that neither girl knew anything that might give away the sword's secret, but there was no point in taking chances. As an added precaution, he started carrying the weapon with him, keeping it close at all times. Hanging it back over the fireplace was out of the question.

The girls, of course, were already proclaiming him a hero and were quick to insist that even if they couldn't talk about it to anyone but each other, their opinion of him was not about to change. He could live with this, even though he insisted he hadn't done that much; he never said a word to them about what he had discovered the sword could do or what he had witnessed in his battle with Arcannen. He simply told them that it was a difficult struggle and they were all lucky to escape.

Neither girl argued with what he was telling them—

both grateful just to be home again and away from Arcannen and Dark House—but he knew Chrysallin suspected he wasn't telling them everything. She was particularly suspicious about the sword, even after he tried to explain it away by telling her that the sword served as protection against any further attacks. The way she looked at him as he offered this explanation let him know she thought there was something more to it.

But Paxon refused to talk about it, repeating at every opportunity that she should do as he had instructed and keep this whole business to herself. Especially from their mother, who fortunately hadn't returned in time to discover any of what had happened. She might hear of the confrontation at the Two Roosters, but she was not to hear of the kidnapping or the events that took place in Wayford.

For the time being, they all needed to be very careful of where they went and what they did. Given Arcannen's reputation, this might not be finished. Even though Paxon could not believe the sorcerer would risk a return visit to Leah and the Highlands anytime soon, it would be a mistake to take that for granted. So they all needed to keep alert, and if they went anywhere they were not to go alone. Chrys, particularly, had to do better about watching out for herself. She had to stop putting herself at risk.

His sister was quick to shrug off his warning, but he had seen the look in her eyes when she was in Arcannen's hands. She was lucky she hadn't been hurt or molested in any way, and she knew it. Staying close to home and out of trouble would appeal to her for a while at least, and Paxon hoped that would be long enough.

Meanwhile, he asked about in the city, speaking of a rumor he had heard—that there was a sorcerer in Wayford named Arcannen who owned a business called Dark House and not only commanded magic but was using it in defiance of Federation law. He communicated with those he knew who served on the Highlands Council, the official governing body of the country, and again with a select group of men and women who had family and friends living in Wayford, but his inquiries always ended in cautions. If anyone knew of this man and this place, it might be a good idea to speak with someone in the Federation government about what might be happening and see if something couldn't be done about it.

And he asked everyone to be sure to let him know if they found out anything useful.

But no one had heard or knew anything about Arcannen and Dark House. After a day or two of asking, he quit. He could only do so much without engaging in a full-on confrontation with the sorcerer.

Even so, he asked the airfield manager and his mechanics to keep watch for any vessel bearing an attacking raven as its emblem or flying a pennant designating it as a ship registered out of Wayford.

Life went back to the way it had been. He continued making shipping runs into other regions of the Four Lands, but he took Chrys with him when he did, teaching her what he knew about airships and flying, doing what he could to distract her from what had happened and from thoughts of Arcannen's possible return. Jayet had found another job with another tavern, working once again as a serving girl, but with better people around her. She had grown much closer to Chrys since the Two Roosters incident, and they had started to talk about forming a business making jewelry and baskets. It gave Paxon considerable peace of mind to know that his sister was spending most of her time with someone who would have at least a reasonable chance of keeping her out of trouble.

He couldn't have said why Chrys was the way she

was. They had grown up in the same household with the same mother, and they had both suffered to some extent from the death of their father. But nothing dramatic or life changing had happened to his sister to turn her into such a wild creature. Nothing had happened to her that hadn't happened to him—nothing that would explain why she was so reckless and unsettled.

He watched her while they made their airship runs, working the lines of the trader, tying off radian draws onto the parse tube connectors and hoisting light sheaths and spars. Tall, rangy, already beginning to grow out of her midteen awkwardness, she had all the makings of a first-class airman. She learned quickly, she worked hard, and she listened.

But in spite of her skills and her potential, she spent her free time down in the taverns anyway—usually with Jayet—drinking with the men, throwing dice, being rowdy and wild. She didn't get in fights anymore, but she remained confrontational and fiercely independent, and there was nothing he could think to do to change that. Even though his mother asked him now and then if there wasn't something he could say to her, or a means of persuasion he could employ to help change her, he knew it was a waste of time.

Chrysallin Leah was who she was, and she was the only one who could ever change that.

Paxon was aware that he wasn't all that settled, either. Hero status notwithstanding, he was always looking for something better to do with his life. Much of the time he felt he was drifting, following through with his mother's expectations and the family's needs and ignoring his own. Money for food and clothing was a life requirement, and it had to come from somewhere. In this case, it had to come from running the family business. The trouble was that, as a prospect for his life's work, it was far from satisfying. But he had never found anything else—or at least anything that excited him sufficiently to justify moving away from cargo hauling and into what might turn out to be a reasonable alternative.

Yet he found himself wondering in the days following his encounter with Arcannen and uncovering of the Sword of Leah's strange power if perhaps he wasn't on the verge of doing so. His discovery was exciting and seemed indicative of better things to come. That he had managed to unlock the sword's power and wield it, that he could use it as a weapon against even the darkest sorcery, was both awe inspiring and thrilling. It was an important responsibility, laden with possibilities, and he wanted to take advantage of them.

It made him remember some of his ancestors, the ones who had carried the sword on remarkable quests and accomplished great feats—Rone, Morgan, and Quentin—Leahs one and all.

It also made him think more carefully on Arcannen's involvement with the sword. The sorcerer, he now believed, had known what the weapon could do when he first saw it. That he would try to come after it at some point seemed almost certain. But how would the sorcerer go about it? And what could Paxon do to prevent it from happening? Certainly, he had managed to escape once. But he had to admit that Arcannen was far more skilled and experienced with using magic than he was, and a second encounter might not turn out as well for him as the first one had.

Yet his options were limited by his circumstances. He was locked into fulfilling his family's needs, making cargo hauls, and staying in Leah, and into living with one eye open while sleeping and looking over his shoulder at every sound and shadow while awake.

He thought about moving away. Maybe it was time. Another man, someone with flying and business skills, could be brought in to run their airfreight service. He could find another city with another kind of work that would better suit him and help keep his family safe by removing himself and the sword from the picture. Maybe Arcannen would lose interest in the talisman if it wasn't around, and the danger would fade after a year or so and he could come home again.

He spent much of his time mulling this over, considering the risks and benefits and looking for a sign that would indicate which way he should turn.

On the first day of the third week following his return from Wayford, that sign appeared.

He was working down on the airfield, mending the frayed ends of lengths of radian draws that served as replacements for ones that had broken midflight, when a man approached, coming down from the airfield manager's office at a slow, steady pace. Paxon had never seen him before, but he knew what he was the moment he caught sight of him. Black robes that reached to the ground and covered him from head to foot, a deep-set hood pulled back in the midday sun, and a silver medallion with a hand clasped about a burning torch marked him instantly as a Druid.

Paxon put down his tools and stood, a dark premonition forming in his chest, quickening his heart.

The stranger walked up to him, his blue eyes bright and cheerful. "Well met, Paxon Leah. My name is Sebec. I serve in the Fourth Druid Order."

He held out his hand and Paxon shook it. Sebec was not particularly tall or imposing looking. If anything, he was slight of build and rather bookish in appearance. And he seemed very young. But there was an intensity to his gaze and a confidence in his manner that let Paxon know not to misjudge him.

"Your robes and medallion give you away," the Highlander observed, releasing the other's hand. "Can I help you?"

"It might be the other way around." Sebec gave him a brief smile. "Is there somewhere we can go to talk?"

Paxon knew what he was suggesting. That it would be better not to talk out in the open where they could be seen, that whatever the Druid wanted to say would be better said in private. Paxon glanced around, trying to think where the best place might be.

"Perhaps we could go up to your home and sit outside in the yard while we talk," Sebec suggested suddenly, revealing he knew more than a little about Paxon already.

Paxon didn't argue. Together, they walked up from the airfield, skirting the edge of the city to reach the roadway leading to his home. Paxon watched the Druid out of the corner of his eye, still taking his measure, trying to decide what this was all about—even though he was afraid he already knew. It had to be about his confrontation with Arcannen. It was the only thing he could imagine the Druids would be interested in, although he wasn't sure how the order had learned of it. He worried it might be because he had summoned the magic of the Sword of Leah, and they had a way of tracking such magic.

He worried they intended to take his sword away from him.

Once they had climbed the hill—a task Sebec accomplished without breaking a sweat—they sat down together on the porch steps. His mother called out from inside, then appeared in the doorway, brushing flour from an apron and smiling.

The smile dropped away when she saw Sebec. "Well met," she greeted the Druid, quickly putting the smile back in place. "I'm Zeatha Leah."

The young Druid stood. "Sebec, of the Fourth Druid Order."

Something in his manner made her smile widen in spite of what Paxon recognized as her obvious discomfort. "Welcome to our home, Sebec. I've just baked cookies. Would you like some?"

So Paxon and Sebec sat together on the porch eating cookies and drinking cups of ale while looking out over the city. For a while, neither said anything, concentrating on their eating and drinking, lost in their separate thoughts.

"You have a beautiful view of the Highlands," Sebec said finally.

"The land belonged to my family for centuries," Paxon replied, nodding in agreement. "Once, we owned for as far as the eye can see. But now we make do with fifteen acres and this view."

Sebec loosened the ties on his black robes to open them at the neck and let the breeze cool him. "This would be enough for me, if I lived here."

Paxon didn't respond, thinking it was enough for him, too, but he would have liked to experience the time when it all belonged to the Leah family and they were Kings and Queens of the Highlands. Just to see what it would have felt like.

"I've come to ask a favor of you," Sebec said, putting down his empty cookie plate and cup. "I want you to come with me to Paranor to speak with the Ard Rhys. You won't be gone long, maybe one night, maybe two. No more, and then I would bring you back again."

"She's going to take away my sword, isn't she?" Paxon declared, unable to help himself. The words just tumbled out of him, and he felt a deep emptiness at the truth he knew they carried.

Sebec stared at him. "Do you mean the one you wear strapped across your back? That one? No, I don't think that's what she has in mind. She wants to talk to you about something else. But it isn't my place to speak for her. She wants to do this in person."

"But she did not choose to come herself, did she?"

"She doesn't go much of anywhere these days, Paxon. She is very old and frail, and it is an effort for her just to get through the day while staying at home. You would be doing her a service by going, and I think maybe doing a service for yourself before matters are concluded." He paused. "You know of her, don't you? You are familiar with her name and history?"

Paxon nodded. "Aphenglow Elessedil."

He knew very well who she was. Almost everyone did. And almost everyone knew her history—or as much of it as she allowed them to know. She had been alive for more than a century and a half, kept so by the Druid Sleep. Once within the protective confines of the sleep, Druids stopped aging until they woke again. An Ard Rhys was entitled to use it as often as he or she thought advisable, maintaining consistency in the rule of the Druid Order through longevity.

But Aphenglow Elessedil was famous from long before her time as the Ard Rhys in the Fourth Druid Order. She was a member of the Elven royal family, and in her youth she had helped her sister Arling, a Chosen of the Ellcrys, pass safely through the ordeal required for her to become the successor to the Ellcrys when the old tree died. She had stood with the Ohmsford twins, Redden and Railing, against the demon hordes when they had broken free of the Forbidding. She had spearheaded the quest undertaken by the Druid order under Khyber when it had gone in search of the missing Elfstones of Faerie, and because of her efforts one set of the precious Stones, at least, had been recovered.

There were rumors that all of them had been found and returned to the Four Lands but that the others had been lost again. The ones that remained were said to be scarlet in color, but few had ever seen them. They were kept at Paranor in the possession of the Druids as a part of the edict regarding recovered magic and its care and usage. The Elves, he knew, had laid claim to those Elf-stones, demanding their return. After all, the Elves already had the blue Stones in their care. Why shouldn't they be given possession of the scarlet Stones, as well?

But Aphenglow had denied their demands repeatedly, insisting that the Druid edict on the collection and preservation of magic superseded any nationalistic claims. She was content to let the Elves keep the seeking-Stones, which had been in their possession for thousands of years, but not those scarlet talismans now referred to as the draining-Stones.

So the antagonism and suspicion that had plagued her throughout her life continued, and Aphenglow Elessedil was never accepted back into the Elven nation as one of their own. She had made her choice, and she would have to live with it. She had chosen the Druid way, embraced its creed and enforced its laws, and it was clear that this is how it would always be. She was a Druid first and an Elf second.

All of this was common knowledge. Or common to the Leahs and the Ohmsfords who had grown up with it or heard about it later from their parents and grandparents. So Paxon knew something of Aphenglow, but none of it lessened the wariness he felt for Druids in general.

"I'm not sure how I feel about all this," he admitted, locking eyes with Sebec. "Even the thought of going to Paranor makes me uneasy."

Sebec nodded. "I understand. But I can assure you that you will be in no danger if you come and will be brought back whenever you are ready. The Ard Rhys only desires a chance to talk with you, nothing more."

Paxon thought about leaving Chrys behind, about the risk that might be involved if he did. Arcannen might discover he was gone and take advantage of it. But he didn't want to say anything to Sebec about that particular concern because the Druids might not know about those events after all. Sebec didn't even seem to know the truth about his sword.

He looked away. He could simply refuse to go. He probably should. But what if what Aphenglow Elessedil wanted to talk to him about was important? What if it concerned Arcannen and might give him a way to help protect Chrys? What if it did have something to do with the Sword of Leah, and he would anger her by refusing even to discuss it?

What if he were simply being foolish and cowardly by imagining all sorts of things that weren't real? Wasn't he better off just going and getting it over with?

"All right, I will come," he said. "But I'll need time to say good-bye to my mother and sister. I need to make sure they will be all right without me."

The young Druid smiled. "Why not let me speak with them? I can reassure them that they won't have to worry about you." He climbed to his feet. "I shall start immediately with your mother."

And before Paxon could collect his wits sufficiently to question the suggestion, Sebec was walking into the house, calling his mother's name.

6

PAXON WAS ASTONISHED AT HOW AMENABLE BOTH his mother and sister were to the prospect of his traveling to Paranor. This felt entirely wrong, but the matter was settled almost immediately. Once Sebec had made the suggestion and explained how important it was to the Ard Rhys, neither said a word in opposition. Perhaps it was the young Druid's earnest demeanor that convinced them. Perhaps he used magic. Whatever the case, his persuasive skills exceeded anything Paxon had ever seen this side of Arcannen. His mother, so reticent about the Druids beforehand, was suddenly excited at the prospects she envisioned would be generated by her son's newfound importance. His sister, in typical fashion, seemed more interested in Sebec himself than in his news, and dismissed Paxon's departure with a casual wave and a cryptic remark about staying out of trouble.

As if he were the one who needed to worry about that particular problem.

At least he got his mother and sister to agree to take a few days to visit his mother's sister in the town of Agave, at the eastern edge of the Highlands. It would take them away from the capital city while he was gone, hopefully removing them from any immediate danger of another visit from Arcannen.

"Are you sure about this, Mother?" he asked her when Sebec had finished speaking with her and had gone back out onto the porch with the fresh glass of ale she had pressed on him. "You don't mind my going? You won't worry about me?"

"I will always worry about you, Paxon," she said, "but I don't think there is any risk to you here. I don't sense any duplicity in this young man. On the contrary, I think him honorable. He intends you no harm. You will be fine, and so will we."

So he went, walking down to the airfield with his sword strapped across his back and his travel pack slung over one shoulder, less certain of what he was doing than either his sister or his mother, but doing his best not to show it. Sebec's vessel was a Rover-crafted double-mast with good lines and black-dyed light sheaths bearing the emblem of the Fourth Druid Order emblazoned in gold. A crew of three awaited them—Trolls serving in the Druid Guard, chosen by the Ard Rhys herself from among volunteers who all came from the same village in the Northland and whose ancestors had served in the guard before them. Big, hulking men, they spoke not a word to either Sebec or Paxon, but simply went about their business, hoisting sails, tying off lines, powering up the diapson crystals in their parse tubes, and setting out.

They flew through the remainder of the day, crossing the broad expanse of the Rainbow Lake, navigating the blunt peaks of the Runne Mountains, sliding down the jagged length of the Dragon's Teeth to the Kennon Pass, and completing their journey to Paranor by midnight.

By then, Sebec had recounted to Paxon a great deal about the work of the current Druid order, which far exceeded anything Paxon might have imagined. Most of what he knew had to do with the order's ongoing efforts to find and retrieve errant and lost magic throughout the Four Lands. Sebec mentioned this in passing and quickly moved on. Those who joined the order did so to learn magic and to assist with its care and protection, but they were required to complete many other duties, as well. Upkeep of Paranor was a major effort, much of it undertaken by the Trolls of the Druid Guard, but some tasks required the more skilled and talented hands of the members of the order themselves, particularly in the rooms where the records and books were stored and in such chambers as the cold room and the Tower Watch. The older members of the order offered daily instruction, and the younger were required to attend and practice what they learned. Reading the Druid Histories was a part of training, mandating a familiarity with the events that had led the order to its present state, from the inception of the First Druid Order to the present.

"Before anyone can begin to master the use of magic—even in the smallest of ways—they first have to understand the nature of its usage," Sebec explained. "How was it created in the first place? What was its intended use? Does it always function as it should? Is it reliable? Are there ways to keep it in check that will protect not only the user but also those nearby?" He smiled. "It's complicated, but fascinating."

It didn't work that way for me with the sword, Paxon thought.

There were visits to the cities of the Four Lands to learn of their histories and cultures, including meetings with their leaders and governing councils. Avenues of communication were opened and maintained, with an emphasis on a sharing of information and ideas. The secrecy that had once shrouded the Druid order was slowly but steadily being removed as an obstacle to better relations with all of the Races, and cooperation was being fostered on all fronts.

"We don't hide behind our walls anymore," Sebec

continued. "We work side by side with people and governments in all of the Four Lands. Even the Federation."

But Paxon had heard that relations with the Federation and most of the lower Southland were still tense. There was a willingness to communicate, but mostly he sensed that both Druids and Federation officials wanted to keep an eye on each other. It didn't help that the Federation had outlawed all use or possession of magic in the Southland or that its avowed goal was to do away with magic entirely and turn back the clock to the days when science was the dominant tool for stimulating progress in the world.

That view wasn't universally shared, as the other lands remained reticent about both, but there were indications that opinion was swinging in that direction.

The hours passed and the young Druid talked on about the work of the order while Paxon listened and considered. After it started to get dark, they ate a dinner of meat and vegetables heated over a small brazier along with bread and ale, all of it shared with the Trolls. Paxon had seen enough of Trolls in his lifetime not to be taken aback by being in their midst, but he was intimidated nevertheless, by both their size and their rough look. They wore tunics with the Druid insignia woven into the fabric on the left panel with scarlet thread, and all of them carried weapons.

Sebec made no mention of Paxon's sword. Not once. He rarely even glanced at it, seemingly caught up in discussing the work of the Druids. But Paxon still worried about what he would do if the order tried to take the sword away from him. How would he respond? He could not let them do it, but how far was he willing to go to prevent it from happening?

By midnight, when the lights of Paranor began to appear, Paxon was nodding off, his eyes heavy and his body lethargic. But his first sight of the Druid's Keep brought him awake again in a hurry. The very size of it took his breath away. Massive walls, great towers soaring skyward, clusters of buildings sprawling over acres of ground, the whole of it made dark and shadowed by the ancient trees of the surrounding forest—the Keep was overwhelming. Sebec was at his side to point out which rooms each building housed, eager either to display his knowledge or to further intimidate a first-time visitor, Paxon wasn't sure which. Perhaps both. Whatever the case, the Highlander couldn't take his eyes off the complex, scanning everywhere, searching out shapes and forms through the shadows, imagining what was there that he couldn't see, hoping he would be given a chance to find out before he was sent away again.

The sloop set down on an elevated landing platform, and Sebec led him off the vessel and down a ramp to a doorway opening into a tower connected to the main building. From there, he led him downstairs to where the guest quarters were located, choosing a door midway along a corridor of matching doors and guiding him inside. The room had a bed, a table next to it, a dresser with a washbasin and towels, and a single window that looked out on a courtyard one story below.

"This is your room," Sebec said. "Sleep here tonight. Tomorrow you will see the Ard Rhys and visit with her. I will come for you when it is time. Sleep well."

Then he went out the door, closing it behind him.

Paxon looked around the room, dropped his bag, pulled the drapes, stripped off his travel clothes, washed, and climbed into the bed.

He was asleep in seconds.

When he woke the following morning, the sun was just coming up over the eastern wall of the Keep, a brilliant gold light in a clear blue sky. He lay where he was for a few minutes, languishing in the bedding, enjoying the feeling of comfort and ease, then rose and walked to the window to peek through the curtains. Sunlight filled the courtyard below, and several black-robed figures were at work in the gardens. He stared down at them for a moment, but when he heard voices in the hallway he turned away to wash and dress.

He was just preparing to depart for a look around when a knock at the door and a greeting announced the arrival of Sebec. "One minute," he answered.

Glancing over to where the Sword of Leah lay across the bed, he made a quick decision. He would take it with him. Leaving it behind was just asking for trouble. If he was going to lose it, they would have to take it from him by force and not through subterfuge or carelessness.

Strapping it across his back, he went out the door to join Sebec.

Together, they walked down to a dining room in which a handful of Druids and Trolls were eating breakfast. Sebec had them sit apart from everyone else, perhaps because he felt Paxon would be more comfortable that way. But it also gave them a chance to talk freely, and Paxon had more questions by now about the Druids. Sebec answered all but one—he declined to say anything further about what the Ard Rhys intended to talk to him about. Mostly, he claimed not to know. The Ard Rhys would speak for herself, and it was not his place to speculate about what she would say.

Paxon, though impatient with the secrecy, did not press him. Instead, he accepted the answers he was given, enjoyed his breakfast, and tried as best he could to prepare himself for what was coming.

When the meal was finished, Sebec took him from the dining room deep into the interior of the building, across a narrow bridge to a second building, and onto a rooftop garden. It was small and very private, but incredibly beautiful, the bedding plants a rainbow of colors set amid stone walkways and benches, all of it screened away from the rest of Paranor by a high hedge wall.

"Find a comfortable seat, Paxon," Sebec directed. "The Ard Rhys will be with you shortly."

He moved off, returning the way he had come, leaving Paxon on his own. The Highlander glanced around, found a bench in the sunshine, and took a seat. As he waited, staring off into the distance where the tips of the trees in the forest surrounding the Druid's Keep shimmered with a light breeze and birds circled in the skies overhead, he kept thinking of the sword strapped across his back. Of what use was it to him now? As protection against Arcannen and for Chrys certainly, but beyond that, what was he supposed to do with it? It was a powerful magic, one that had served various Leahs over the centuries in their support of the Druids and their numerous quests. Was there a quest in his future, one not yet made clear to him? Or was he clinging to the weapon because it was the only thing he had that made it seem as if there might be something more for him than continuing to run an airfreight service?

He could smell the scents of the flowers that surrounded him, pungent and fragrant as they wafted in the breeze. He closed his eyes and breathed in those scents, and the memories they generated of the Highlands and home and family were so strong and poignant they almost brought tears.

"Paxon?" a soft, lyrical voice asked.

He opened his eyes quickly. Aphenglow Elessedil stood before him, wrapped in her Druid robes, the Eilt Druin laced around her neck, its silver emblem flashing in the sunlight. He had never seen her before, but he knew who she was instantly. She was tall and sparely built, her gaze steady, a smile on her face. She must have been very beautiful once, when she was young. She was still beautiful in the way some older women are, made so more because of her regal carriage and the proud, calm certainty she radiated than simply because of her physical features.

He rose to greet her, flustered by the direct look she gave him and by the knowledge of what she represented. "Lady," he responded and managed a short bow.

She extended her hand and held his briefly. "Are you well rested?" she asked him.

"Very well." He glanced around appreciatively. "This is a beautiful place. The gardens, of course, but all of Paranor, as well."

"You have never been here, but you must have heard stories from your family."

"I have heard many. From my grandparents and my mother—of Mirai Leah and Railing and Redden Ohmsford. And of you."

"May I sit with you?" she asked.

He moved over to allow her to do so. "I am surprised to be here," he admitted. "Why did you ask me to come?"

"You never knew Mirai, did you?" she asked instead of answering him. "She was a brave and resourceful young woman. You would have liked her. I think she had as much to do as anyone with the outcome at the Valley of Rhenn when my sister became the Ellcrys and the demon hordes were sent back into the Forbidding. You carry her blood in your veins; you carry Ohmsford blood within you, as well. A very potent mix that allows for special abilities. Even, perhaps, the presence of the wishsong."

He had thought of that possibility more than once over the years, ever since learning of the complexity of his family's history, of Leahs linked to Ohmsfords. But there had never been even a hint of such magic in his blood—not even the smallest suggestion that it might be present.

"I don't think I have any use of magic," he said. "I don't think anyone in the family has since the Ohmsford twins."

"But you have something else of value, don't you?" She gestured to his sword. "You have the blade that is your family's legacy from centuries ago, the blade Allanon dipped into the black waters of the Hadeshorn and infused with his own magic. The blade he then returned to Rone Leah, naming him protector of Brin Ohmsford when she went in search of the Ildatch in order to destroy it."

So she knew about his sword. Paxon nodded but did not reply. He feared the worst now, could almost feel it happening. She had brought him here to claim the sword for the Druid order, and she would take it away in spite of his protests. He would want to do something to prevent her, but in the end common sense would prevail. Her magic was too powerful for him to resist. And he would never even think to try to use the sword against her. It would be pointless.

"Do you have to take it from me?" he asked finally.

"I don't have to," she answered, "but I should. Magic is not allowed in the hands of those who are not trained to use it, even if they have come by it in a legitimate way. It is a matter of public safety that such magic should be collected and held by the Druids."

"The Druid Edict," he said. "I know."

"Still, that is not why I brought you to Paranor." She looked off into the gardens, as if measuring something with her gaze. "You discovered the magic quite by accident. But you used it to good purpose—to save your sister. And you exercised reasonable judgment in doing so. What do you intend to do with it if you keep it?"

He thought a moment, and then shook his head help-lessly. "I don't really know."

"Who else knows of the sword's power besides you? Your sister? Does your mother know?"

He shook his head no. "Just Arcannen, as you might have already guessed if you know how I rescued my sister."

"Tell me what happened, Paxon. Don't leave anything out. I may be able to tell you more than you know about this business by the time you've finished."

So Paxon, curious now as to what she meant, told her everything, from when Jayet came running up to get him at the cottage to when he returned home safely from Wayford with Chrys in tow. Aphenglow listened without interrupting, attentive to his every word.

When he finished, she gave a deep sigh. "The Druid order knows of Arcannen. This is not the first time he has been involved in something that works counter to our purposes. He will have to be dealt with eventually. He is a skilled sorcerer, but he is also venal and treacherous. You are right to be worried about him. He will come after you sooner or later. He will still want your sword, and he will not give up on trying to get it until he has it."

"I thought as much."

"You don't know the half of it yet. Let me tell you what I suspect is the root. Ostensibly, your sister got involved with throwing dice at a tavern with a stranger, who later turned out to be Arcannen. She bet more than she had, lost, and couldn't pay. So he took her out of the tavern and back to Wayford where she could work off her debt at his pleasure house. You tried to stop it from happening, failed at the airfield, but picked yourself up and went after them. While you were attempting a rescue at Dark House, you drew out your sword and discovered it contained magic that responded to you. The magic saved your life. You fought your way free and rescued your sister. All well and good."

She paused. "But ask yourself this. Isn't it odd that he made a point of goading you into coming after him to save your sister and while doing so pointedly suggested you bring a weapon? So you did; you brought the Sword of Leah. But what if that was what he wanted you to do, what he expected of you all along? You've said you believe he recognized the power of the sword when he saw it—that you could tell as much when he tried to prevent you from drawing it out of its sheath. What if I told you he knew about the power of the sword all along? That he lured you to Dark House by kidnapping your sister so you would bring him the sword?"

Paxon frowned, considering. Arcannen *had* seemed suspiciously interested in the sword. "But if he wanted it so badly, why wouldn't he just steal it from the cottage in the first place? It was hanging in plain sight over the fireplace. If he knew of it beforehand, wouldn't it have been easier to get possession of it that way?"

"What if he wasn't interested only in the Sword of Leah, Paxon, but in you, as well? What if the sword was of no use to him without someone who could wield it—someone who was a member of the Leah family, a descendant of all those Leahs who actually used the sword in times now past?"

"How would he know that?"

"Let's assume for the moment that he did."

"All right. Then how could he make me use it the way he wanted?"

"Perhaps in the same way he used his own magic to make your sister play a game of dice she could not possibly win."

So Chrys hadn't really been careless; she had been tricked. Paxon thought back on what had happened at the airfield when he had faced Arcannen and again when the sorcerer had been waiting for him at Dark House. What the Ard Rhys was telling him seemed to fit.

"So he knew of the sword and wanted it, but needed me to release its power, and that is why he kidnapped Chrysallin?"

"Except his plan fell apart when you drew out the sword and decided to stand up to him. The magic responds to attacks faster than you can think to ask it to. That has always been the hallmark of Faerie magic. What Allanon did to the Sword of Leah all those years ago at the Hadeshorn was to infuse your blade with that same kind of magic. So it acted to protect you and defeat Arcannen. But that's not going to be the end of this, is it?"

"No, it doesn't seem likely," he agreed. He felt a sinking in his stomach. He was in a lot more danger than he had imagined. "If he went to all that trouble, he won't give up until he has the sword in hand. He'll keep coming after me until he gets what he wants. What should I do?"

Her smile returned. "This is what I brought you here to talk about. I want to make you an offer. Come to Paranor and live with us. Learn to use the magic of the sword fully and responsibly. We can help you do that. When your training is complete, remain here with us for three years as our paladin. It would constitute repayment in full for our services and provide you with practical experience using your sword. You would be given tasks to complete, helping us to secure various items of magic and to deal with those who refuse to cooperate in our efforts to protect against misuse of that magic. At the end of three years, if you so choose, you would be free to go."

She paused. "And you would be allowed to take your sword with you when you leave."

Paxon stared at her in disbelief. "Are you asking me to join the Druid order? To become a Druid?"

She shook her head. "I am asking you to serve with the order, not to join it. But there is work and responsibility enough just in that, Paxon. I wish you to be what was once called a Knight-errant. Our order comprises students and teachers, but few are trained as warrior Druids, as some once were. Few have fighting skills and weapons knowledge. And no one has a weapon like you do. You could accompany our Druids while they do their work searching out and recovering lost magic and confronting the threats such magic poses. You could help keep them safe. You could act as their protector. Will you consider doing so?"

He knew right away it was what he wanted, what he had been searching for—a chance to do something besides haul freight and pass the time between runs. He also understood the importance of what it would mean to be associated with the Druids. He was not afraid of what that might involve or of the Druids themselves; he was confident in his ability to make good choices when the need arose. Still, an acceptance of the offer could not be given lightly, and the offer itself should not be accepted out of hand. There were still uncertainties to be resolved.

"By doing this, you would remove me from Leah and from any danger of Arcannen catching me unawares? Or coming after my sister again?"

"That is my thinking." She arched one eyebrow. "Though we might need to do a little more early on."

"But my mother and sister depend on me to work the airfreight business," he said. "There is no money for them if I leave."

"We will give them money to replace what your departure will cost them, enough so that they can live comfortably. You can either sell the business or ask someone to run it for you in your absence. I will repeat what I said before. You needn't worry for your family's welfare. If I deem it necessary, I can provide them with someone to help look after things."

She was promising an awful lot, and it suggested that she badly wanted him to accept her offer, which was both reassuring and a bit intimidating. What would she ask of him as an agent of the order? How much would he be expected to do in her service?

"What if, after you've trained me, you ask me to do something I don't feel right about, something I can't make myself do?"

She regarded him steadily. "I won't ask you to do anything like that. We aren't what some people say we are, Paxon. We don't act in ways that bring harm to those who don't invite it. And should you feel we are crossing a line you yourself would not cross, we will let you step aside."

"But I will be expected to fight?"

"Mostly, you will need to be *prepared* to fight. Your presence alone should help deflect most of the violence."

Paxon wasn't sure that was true, but he saw no point in arguing about it. What really mattered was whether or not this was something he wanted to do badly enough to take whatever risks the work offered. "I don't know if I'm up to this," he admitted. "I don't know if I'm good enough to do what you expect. What if I'm not?"

The smile returned. "Paxon, I've lived a long time, and I've come to be a pretty good judge of character. I've been wrong about people, but not very often. So when I tell you I believe you are what we need and will be able to do what's expected, you can feel confident that I am right. I think you should consider giving it a chance. If we are both wrong, you can walk away."

She held up one cautionary finger. "You've been look-ing to do something more with your life; I could see it in your eyes when I told you what I wanted you to do. You want a chance to do something important, something that matters. You want your life to have real purpose. Why not see if the opportunity I am offering you isn't what you've been looking for? Why not discover if it isn't the chance you are seeking?"

"You make a persuasive argument," he admitted, smiling back at her. "How long do I have to decide?"

"Do you really need time to make this decision?" she asked gently. "Don't you already know the answer? Isn't the answer in your heart?"

He stared at her in surprise. He hadn't expected this. He had believed she would tell him to take the remainder of the day to think it over, maybe more. He waited for her to say something more, but she remained silent, watching him.

He looked down momentarily, considering her words, and then met her steady gaze once more. "All right," he said. "I'll do it."

She rose and extended her hand to him. "Welcome to your new home, Paxon Leah," she said.

And immediately he knew he had made the right choice.

7

SO PAXON WENT BACK TO THE HIGHLANDS OF Leah, departing Paranor with the young Druid Sebec at the helm of the same two-masted clipper that had brought him there. The Ard Rhys had given him two days in which to make his arrangements at home before returning to the Druid's Keep and his new life, and he was aware of how little time that allowed him to do what was needed. To begin with, he had to figure out how to tell his mother and his sister what he had committed to, and he had to do so as soon as they returned.

Which meant, in turn, that he had to figure out how much he was going to tell either one of them about why Aphenglow Elessedil had asked him to come to Paranor at all.

After all, neither one knew anything about the magic contained in the Sword of Leah. He had kept that secret from both. His mother didn't even know what had happened to Chrys in her absence—his sister's kidnapping and rescue. Everything surrounding that episode was still just between himself and Jayet.

But he had to offer some sort of explanation about why the Ard Rhys of the Fourth Druid Order had suddenly decided that Paxon was a candidate for training with weapons and magic until he could serve as a protector and paladin on quests to seek out errant and stolen magic for collection and storage at Paranor. Or, even if he left out the part about training with magic, why she would even have known about him in the first place. It wasn't as if the Leahs had maintained a close personal relationship with the Druids over the years.

He thought about it all the way home, and he was still mulling it over when they landed at the airfield and Sebec sent him on his way.

"I will be here again in two days at midday, waiting for you," the other told him, and then added cheerfully, "Don't be late."

Then he was off, the clipper lifting away and disappearing north. Paxon watched it go and set off for the cottage. He would talk to his sister first. Whatever he ended up telling his mother, he wanted to be sure Chrys would not contradict him.

Neither she nor his mother was home when he arrived, so he dumped his backpack on his bed and went off to Brew Tide, the tavern where Jayet now worked and where he imagined he might find his sister. He went down into the valley and the city, angling east, away from the airfield and toward the army barracks. Upon reaching the tavern and stepping through the doors, he found the girls engaged in conversation at the far end of the bar.

They rushed over to welcome him back, hugging and kissing him, though it seemed to him that Jayet did so with a little more enthusiasm. After exchanging a few words with both, he separated his sister from Jayet and sat her down at an empty table. The tavern was quiet in the midafternoon hours, so they were able to talk uninterrupted and in private.

"Does Mother know anything yet about what happened to you?" he asked.

"Not from me," she announced flatly. "I wouldn't tell her."

"Then we won't start now," he said. "But I do have to tell her something because I've been asked to come train at Paranor by Aphenglow Elessedil."

Chrys gave a surprised gasp. "Paranor?" she whispered, leaning close. "How did that happen?"

What he told her was that word had gotten back to the Ard Rhys about what had happened at Dark House. Because she knew of Arcannen and considered him an enemy of the Druids and opposed to their efforts to find and reclaim magic throughout the Four Lands, she had paid close attention to the news and made an effort to find out more about Paxon. Having done so, she decided she wanted him to come to Paranor to train in the use of weapons—and perhaps, one day, with magic, as well. After his training was complete, he was to take a position for a period of three years in the service of the order, aiding Druids in their efforts to track down rumors of magic, acting as protector and companion to them while they were away from the Keep.

"You've decided then?" she asked. "Are you certain about this?"

"She made me the offer and said I had to make up my mind right away. Otherwise, I would have come back and discussed it with you and Mother first. But the truth is, I knew this was what I wanted. I've felt trapped in the airship freight business. It was a living for us, but I never wanted to do it forever, and now I don't have to. You and Mother will be given money to live on. I'll find someone to run the freight business in my absence. If you want, you can help with this. And you don't have to worry about Arcannen. For a few months, there will be someone from the Druid order living in Leah to keep an eye on you, just in case Arcannen decides to pay a return visit. You won't know who is looking after you, but you will be safe while I'm gone."

"I'm not worried anyway," his sister declared, looking irritated. "I won't be caught off guard like that again."

Paxon almost said, *Magic can always catch you off guard, and that's what happened the last time,* but he decided to keep his mouth shut.

"Will you be all right if I do this?"

She grinned. "I want you to do this. I want you to be happy. If this is what you've been looking for, then you should go. Mother and I will be fine." She paused, turning suddenly serious. "But you'll come back to visit us, won't you?"

"You know I will. And if you have need of me, for any reason, you will be able to contact me at Paranor." His smile, when he unleashed it, made him feel suddenly giddy. "I can't tell you how excited I am to be doing this!"

She snorted. "I can't believe they want you, of all people. And all because of me. I guess you owe me for that, big brother."

"Just promise me you won't ever do anything like that again, and I'll be even deeper in your debt. We have to go now. I need to sit Mother down and tell her what I'm going to do, but I wanted to tell you first. I want to be sure you will back me up. I don't want to tell her about Dark House and Arcannen. That will only cause her to worry. So even though that is the real reason the Ard Rhys found out about me, I'm going to tell Mother it was because she knew of the Leahs and their long history with the Druids and thought I might be a good choice because of that."

His sister's brow crinkled with doubt. "You think she will believe that?"

He shrugged. "Let's go find out."

It turned out their mother never questioned it. She was so happy that her son was finally receiving the recognition and opportunity she felt he deserved that she skipped right past the part about why he was being asked and simply accepted it as his due. He did have to reassure her that he would be all right, that none of this was particularly dangerous, even though he knew in his heart it could be. He shaded all his dissembling just so, both with his mother and his sister, and the matter of the Sword of Leah never came up.

When he went to bed that night, he had mixed feelings about what he had done. He felt it was for the best that he kept certain things back, offering just enough details for reassurance but not so much that it would cause them to worry. Still, lying to them felt wrong. At some point, he would have to tell them about the sword. He wasn't sure why he was keeping it from them now except he was afraid that knowing he would be involved with magic would cause them to feel less excited about his choice and to view his departure with more trepidation than pleasure. The less they knew—or could talk about—the safer they would be.

Whatever the case, it took a long time before he fell asleep.

Two days later, as scheduled, he flew out of Leah for Paranor and the Druid's Keep. Sebec was waiting for him at the airfield, as promised, and welcomed Paxon warmly. Stowing the Highlander's bags in a rear storage compartment, he took the clipper up for a final slow circling of the city that allowed Paxon to enjoy a prolonged last view of its buildings and hills, and then headed north.

In the interim since his return from speaking with Aphenglow Elessedil and pursuant to her suggestion that he set his business affairs in order, Paxon had approached several friends to see if they might be willing to take over the running of his airfreight business. But none of them had either the time or the inclination to take on the extra work, so he had been forced to talk to his larger competitors. None of them was interested, either, but three made offers to buy the business outright. Two of the offers were so ridiculously low that Paxon walked out on them. The third was reasonable, and he liked the man he was dealing with. So on impulse, and with time slipping away, he agreed to the sale. He realized he was cutting ties with the city and his life that he hadn't planned on, but sometimes when you took a chance it was better to hold nothing back and to go all-in.

He was paid that very day and signed papers for the transfer of all airships, spare parts, and the storage shed. He kept his Sprint and arranged for the manager of the airfield to store and care for it in his absence. He told his mother and his sister what he had done, but neither complained or voiced concern. It was the right thing to do, his mother insisted. Just so long as we have money to buy food, said his sister.

Though hesitant about doing so, he went to Jayet at the Brew Tide to tell her good-bye. She was cheerful and calm until the very end, when she broke down in tears and kissed him and told him she would think of him every day and pretty much clung to him until he pried her loose. It was a little disconcerting, but he supposed she felt a little more possessive of him because of her involvement in getting Chrys back from Arcannen. Whatever the case, he promised he would take care of himself and not indulge in reckless behavior and be back to see her no matter what when he returned to visit his family.

So with farewells exchanged and the airfreight business disposed of, he departed with a sense of finality, prepared to begin anew, his future a bright uncertainty that beckoned with all the flash and elusiveness of a colorful songbird. Nothing was promised him, and what he might gain from this experience was yet to be determined, but the possibilities were out there in recognizable and tempting forms that drew him on.

He made the journey in relative silence, wrapped in thoughts of what lay ahead. Sebec let him be, perhaps sensing what he was going through. It took them all day to reach Paranor, the sun just setting as they skimmed the forests surrounding the Keep before setting down on the airship landing pad. Sebec took Paxon to his new quarters, a room higher up in the building this time, and got him settled in. Then he accompanied Paxon to dinner and introduced him to a few of his friends— Avelene, with her lavender eyes and bladed features; Zabb Ruh, come from a farming village in the deep Southland called Terran, where he had been viewed as a warlock and worse because of his talent with magic; and Oost Mondara, who would be Paxon's instructor in the use of weapons.

This last introduction was a bit unsettling for a couple of reasons. First, Oost was a Gnome, which meant he was small and wiry and not very impressive physically. How he could instruct anyone as big as Paxon on how to use blades, where close combat was almost always necessary, was difficult to imagine. Second, Oost barely gave him a glance, providing a perfunctory greeting and going right back to eating his meal. Already, Paxon didn't like him.

But when they were alone again, Sebec told him not to prejudge the Gnome. "The Ard Rhys could have chosen a different instructor," he said to the Highlander, "but she very deliberately chose Oost because he is the most talented and skilled of those who serve the order." He paused. "Also, you might want to know that Oost was less than thrilled about the assignment. He thinks you won't last because people like you always believe magic can get them out of any sort of trouble and fail to concentrate on the skills a real swordsman needs to survive."

"Then he knows about the Sword of Leah? The Ard Rhys told him?"

"She did. She knew he would want to know, even though he wouldn't like it. But Oost will do what he's told, and he will do his best. It's up to you to prove him wrong. And don't underestimate him. You do that at your peril."

Paxon had no intention of prejudging or underestimating anyone while he was at Paranor, and all he asked was that he be extended the same courtesy. From what he had seen and heard so far, he wasn't sure this would happen with Oost Mondara.

His final introduction that evening was to a tall, lean Elf named Isaturin, who was second in status only to the Ard Rhys and widely considered to be the favorite as her successor. He greeted Paxon warmly and told him he was most welcome, and they were all looking forward to his contributions as a paladin for the order. He knew Leah and talked about the Highlands in such familiar terms that Paxon was immediately put at ease in his presence.

When he had moved away, Sebec said, "He is our designated ambassador to most of the governments and monarchies of the Four Lands. When the Ard Rhys doesn't travel, which is most of the time now, Isaturin goes in her place. He is a skilled orator and negotiator, as you might have guessed. He is very well liked everywhere, and he has done more to bring about a change in our relationships with the Races than anyone." He paused. "He must have taken a liking to you. He isn't usually so enthusiastic about newcomers. I know he's spent time in Leah, so maybe that's it. For an Elf, he's very open about his admiration for the Southland and its people."

"I don't remember ever seeing him in Leah, but he certainly knows his way around. He even knew the tavern where my sister's friend Jayet works."

Sebec shrugged. "He knows a lot of things others don't. And he is a skilled magic user, perhaps the best at Paranor. He can do things I've never seen anyone else do—not even the Ard Rhys. He can disappear while you're looking at him. He can move short distances through space, disassembling and reassembling himself in the process." He shook his head. "I don't know how he does even half of it."

He returned Paxon to his room then and told him he would come back for him after sunrise. "We'll use the morning to give you a tour of the buildings and grounds. In the afternoon, you will begin your weapons training with Oost. Better get some rest. You're going to need it."

Paxon took him at his word and said good night. Inside his room, he stood looking out the window, taking in the torchlit stone walls and ironbound gates, the lighted windows in the buildings all around him, the parapets and battlements, the soaring towers, and the layers of shadows draped everywhere. It looked and felt so different from home that for a moment he felt a keen disappointment and a sudden homesickness for the familiar Highlands.

But the moment passed, and he went back to thinking about what would happen tomorrow. Would he be allowed to use his own sword? Or would Oost feel its inherent magic a distraction that should not be allowed? When would he be permitted to start training with magic? Were there other students like himself, others with the use of magic brought in to fill the same position? Was he in competition with anyone?

The questions swirled around him like moths drawn to a flame, and even after he had shed his clothes and climbed into bed they were still flitting about, erratic little gadflies inside his head, pressing for attention.

It was a long time before he closed his eyes, brushed the questions away, and fell asleep.

He woke at sunrise and was dressed and waiting when Sebec came for him. The young Druid looked fresh and rested in a way Paxon did not feel, and as always he was cheerful as he took the Highlander down to breakfast and then began their tour of the Keep.

As they moved from building to building and room to room, Sebec kept up a running commentary on recent Druid history.

"Everything changed after the collapse of the Forbidding and the escape of the demons into the Four Lands," he told Paxon. "The Fourth Druid Order was almost decimated, all of them killed save Aphenglow Elessedil and a Dwarf named Seersha. When the Forbidding was restored and the escaped creatures were locked away again, those two were all that was left. The order almost collapsed. But Aphenglow chose to go back to become the Ard Rhys, even though she had doubts about doing so. Her Elven heritage made the choice difficult. At that point, the Elves neither trusted nor supported the Druids. Anyone from the Westland who joined the order became something of an outcast. That was the case with Aphenglow, even before she became the Ard Rhys and undertook the job of rebuilding the order.

"But she felt strongly about it. Her younger sister, Arlingfant, had become the new Ellcrys, and she believed her own sacrifice should be at least as meaningful. So with Seersha and a shape-shifter named Oriantha, she rebuilt the remains of the Fourth Druid Order. Afterward, she immediately began to search out new members, traveling the length and breadth of the Four Lands to find suitable candidates for training. Surprisingly, there were dozens. But she kept the number small at first, choosing only those who had a natural affinity for or actual possession of magic. She rebuilt the order slowly and with care. Then she reached out to all the governments and rulers of the Four Lands to ask for their support. Some gave it freely; others did not. Interestingly enough, it was the Dwarves and Trolls who were most supportive at first. The Elves remained reticent, even with Aphenglow as the Ard Rhys and her uncle as King of the Elven people."

"But she must have found a way to break down that barrier," Paxon interjected.

"Time and patience." Sebec stopped them at an overlook and leaned on the half-wall contemplatively. "When her uncle died, a member of the Ostrian family ascended to the throne. She was less inclined than others to vilify the Druids. She was a more pragmatic and farseeing ruler, and she understood that the Elves and the Druids were natural allies. They had always shared a belief in the importance of and need for magic in the world. The Southland had already banned the use of all magic within its borders, and their position on the matter was intractable, not open to discussion. Although Arishaig had been rebuilt as the capital city, and a new Coalition Council with a new Prime Minister had been installed, the same old prejudices were embraced. Science was the path to prosperity and a better world; magic was outdated and dangerous and elitist."

He paused. "Seersha was dead by then. She died in her sleep, the Histories say. Oriantha was acting Ard Rhys during a long period of time following Seersha's death when Aphenglow went into the Druid Sleep. While she held that position, she did something Aphenglow had never been able to do: She managed to open lines of communication with the Federation and arrange for an exchange of ambassadors. Perhaps it was because she put a new face on the order or perhaps the Federation grew tired of its isolation. In any event, even with their differences about the need for magic still a barrier between them, they began talking to each other on a regular basis. It was the beginning of a more open relationship between the Druids and the Southland. The other lands quickly took advantage of this and joined in. Delegations visited and information was exchanged. Even the Gnome tribes participated, insofar as they could manage any kind of agreement regarding who was to represent them. It was the first time in history that this had ever happened.

"By the time the Ard Rhys awoke from her Druid Sleep, Oriantha was old and worn out, and she left the order shortly after. She was never seen again. The entire order was new, and Aphenglow found much that was different from when she had gone into the Druid Sleep. This was eight years ago. I came to her in her first year after waking, sent by a friend of one of the other Druids. She interviewed me, and I was accepted into the order. I already knew a little magic, so that helped. Two weeks later, she made me her personal assistant. She says she likes the way I think. She says I am more organized than she is, and I am younger and have greater energy. That helps to prevent her from wearing herself too far down."

He smiled ruefully, running his fingers through the dark curls of his hair and shrugging. "She's coming to the end of her life. I can't imagine the world without her. I have been her assistant for seven years now, and I would gladly serve her for fifty. It has been my great privilege. She is the kindest person I have ever known."

He was lost in reverie for a few seconds, and then he straightened abruptly and started ahead once more. "We'll have a quick look at the study rooms and lecture halls and then go down to lunch. Afterward, you can start your training with Oost."

8

As he had promised, following lunch Sebec delivered Paxon to Oost Mondara, who was waiting for him in the courtyard of the Keep reserved specifically for weapons practice and training. The yard was dusty and sunlit, and there were no other Druids or trainees about. Oost was standing by a rack of weapons, arranging them in a manner that suggested the paternal love of a father for his children.

"From now on," the Gnome said without turning around, "I will expect you to be here promptly at noon. This area is reserved for your training each day for three hours exactly, and I know you don't want to waste a minute of it."

"Good luck," Sebec whispered to Paxon, and hurried away.

Paxon, determined to do whatever it took to prove he belonged, stepped forward and bowed. "I apologize."

The Gnome turned slowly to face him. In the daylight, he was even more gnarled and bent. "Apologies are not necessary between a teacher and a student. Nor is bowing required. Now, let's have a look at you."

He made a slow circle of Paxon, saying nothing until he had completed his study of the Highlander and was facing him anew. "You have a solid build and good posture. You might not think that's important, but how you carry yourself defines how you will perform with a blade. Is that your sword you have strapped to your back?"

"It is," Paxon said. "I thought—"

"Take it off." The command was brusque, perfunctory, as if perhaps it shouldn't have even been necessary. "You won't be needing it today. Or for quite a while yet. Tell me of your training. Formal or informal?"

"Informal," Paxon admitted. "But I drilled with members of the Border Legion and the Red Guard while they were on leave and visiting Leah. A few were stationed in the Highlands and offered to teach me."

The Gnome's face crinkled in distaste. "How wonderful for you. But your education here will take a slightly different direction. I am sure you know how to use your sword in at least a rudimentary way. I am sure you could defend yourself, if need be. I am equally sure that once you discovered your sword possessed magic, you began thinking you might never again need to worry about fighting an average sort of battle. You could just use magic if things got too rough."

Paxon almost said no, just to be perverse. But instead, he nodded. "It crossed my mind. But obviously you don't approve."

"Obviously I don't. That sort of thinking can get you killed. Magic is a wonderful thing, but it is unpredictable and treacherous. It cannot be relied upon one hundred percent of the time. And it only needs to fail you once to put an end to your life. An ordinary blade, on the other hand, is always constant. Learn to use it, and you have only the limitations of your education and skills to hold you back. My job is to provide instruction that will allow you to know going into any battle what you can expect from your weapon and yourself. If you are forced to fight, you want no hesitation. Am I making myself clear?"

"Very." He reached back, released the buckle that held his sword and sheath in place, and removed them.

"Give them to me, please," Oost Mondara ordered, and held out his hand.

Again, Paxon almost declined. But what he hoped was good judgment and common sense overruled his reluctance, and he gave up the weapon to the Gnome. Oost took it from him, balanced it in his hand, drew out the blade and examined it from every angle, struck a combat stance against an imaginary foe, and sheathed the blade once again.

He carried the sword over to a rack, hung it from a peg, and walked back again. "That is a very fine weapon, young Paxon. Perhaps too good a weapon for you; that remains to be seen. At the very least, you owe it to yourself to become a swordsman worthy of such a blade. You owe it to those who carried it before you to be their equal. Let that be your goal in the time we are together."

He paused. "Now walk over to that barrel, pull out one of those wooden swords, and follow me."

With a final reluctant look at his own weapon, Paxon did as he was told. The swords in the barrel were battered and unwieldy and appeared to have been used by thousands of hands before his. Feeling less than enthusiastic, he chose the best of the bunch and rejoined Oost, who was standing by an odd contraption a few yards away. It was a six-foot-long log embedded upright in a circular platform that rested on wheels. It was shaped to resemble a human, with poles for arms attached to the makeshift body by heavy springs and a head consisting of a helmet set upon the upright end of the pole. A wooden sword similar to the one Paxon held was tightly attached to one of the pole arms.

"Meet Big Oost," the Gnome announced, gesturing toward the creature. "He will be your sparring partner until you can knock his helmet off with your wooden sword. He will be my surrogate in this early part of your training." He caught the look that passed across Paxon's face and laughed. "What, you thought you would train with me, personally? But look how small I am! What chance would I have against someone as big and strong as you? You try your luck with Big Oost first. Who knows? Maybe you will get a chance at me quicker than you think."

Paxon didn't know what to say. He started at the Gnome and then at the contraption. "Just hit it?"

"Wherever you can."

Paxon eyed Big Oost warily. "This isn't what it seems, is it?"

"Nothing much is when it comes to fighting an enemy. You are right to be wary." The Gnome smiled crookedly. "But do something anyway. This is just a lesson."

Paxon took a guarded stance, and Big Oost immediately mimicked him, bringing its wooden sword about in guarded fashion. Paxon hesitated and then swung a mighty blow at the other's helmet. But Big Oost's sword blocked it so quickly that Paxon's sword arm shuddered from the force of the blow. The Highlander tried again, this time with a feint and a follow-up thrust. Again, he was blocked. He went into a crouch, angry now, circling the contraption, watching it follow his efforts smoothly, rolling on its wheeled base, always keeping Paxon in front of him. Three more times the Highlander tried to get past the machine's guard and three more times he failed.

He stepped back, winded and frustrated, his arm aching. "How does it do that?"

"Magic," Oost Mondara replied. "How does it feel to be on the receiving end? But you have to expect the worst and be ready for it every time. Take nothing for granted. Expect the unexpected. Take me, for instance.

I am a weapons expert who trains others, but I also have the use of magic. I animated this pile of wood and metal and infused it with a generous portion of my own combat skills. I have no desire to wear myself out on those who can't defeat an inanimate hunk of spare parts. You will spend the rest of the day looking for a way to break through its guard. If you fail—which I fully expect you will—tomorrow will be another day of the same. I will offer helpful hints when I can. I will suggest ways in which you can improve. But mostly, you will learn on your own. There is no better teacher than experience. Now have at it."

So Paxon did, renewing his attack on Big Oost, slowly accepting that the machine was better at protecting itself than he was at attacking it. He tried everything he knew to break past its defenses, and nothing seemed to work. All the while, Oost Mondara stood by, watching. Now and then, he would offer suggestions on Paxon's form and choice of stance and approach. But mostly he said nothing. Every fifteen minutes or so, he would call a halt and let Paxon have a short rest and as much water to drink as he wanted.

The three hours went by more quickly than the Highlander would have expected, and he was surprised when Oost called a halt to the day's training. On the other hand, he was so sore and winded from his efforts he could barely stand.

"A hot bath with plenty of soaking, a good dinner with ale to wash it down, and a solid night's sleep will help." The Gnome retrieved the Sword of Leah and handed it to him. "You can leave that in your room tomorrow. As I said, you won't need it for a while. What you need first is a better understanding of your shortcomings." He gave a perfunctory wave as he walked off. "Remember. Noon sharp."

Paxon soon discovered that three hours of attacking

Big Oost had left every part of his body aching. His sword arm, in particular, hurt so badly that even lifting it was a problem. He took the bath as suggested, lying about in the water until it was cold, and then dressed and wandered down to the dinner table. He found Sebec sitting with Avelene at one end of a long table, both of them grinning.

"How's the sword arm?" Sebec wanted to know.

"Need me to help feed you?" Avelene asked.

He laughed along with them, but even laughing hurt. "Did you have to go through this?" he asked them. "Does everyone have to train with Oost?"

"Druids don't train with weapons unless they are warrior Druids, and we have very few of those," Avelene said. Her lean face bent close to her food, as if she was afraid it might get away from her. "There hasn't been a single one since I came to the order five years ago. Training is reserved mostly for those in the Druid Guard and when Oost decides it is needed for men and women like yourself who are asked to serve as protectors and paladins for the order."

"Well, how many of those are there?" Paxon demanded.

Sebec cocked an eyebrow. "None, right now. The last was several years ago. He didn't complete the training. It's rigorous, I hear."

Then he and Avelene began laughing anew, trying to muffle it but failing miserably. "Look on the bright side, Paxon," Avelene declared. "You've got no competition! You've got the field to yourself."

Paxon nodded along agreeably and finished his meal quickly so he could go off to bed and suffer alone.

The following morning, Sebec took him up to the cold room and let him have a look at the scrye. Paxon was still sore, but feeling better after his night's sleep, ready enough for the afternoon weapons practice and confident that he wouldn't have to limp through it.

They climbed to one of the highest floors in the main building and down a long hallway past many closed doors to one that looked the same as the others, but wasn't. Inside, a huge stone basin resting on a circular riser housed the scrye's magic-infused waters. A single Druid sat next to the basin, keeping close watch, monitoring its responses. Or in this instance, its lack thereof, because nothing was happening.

Nodding a greeting to the other Druid, Sebec offered a brief explanation of how it all worked. The basin bottom was inscribed with an intricately drawn map of the Four Lands and surrounding bodies of water and scattered islands. If magic was used anywhere within the Four Lands, it would register within the waters— sometimes as ripples on their surface and sometimes as a boiling deeper down. Now and then, there would even be changes of color.

"This is how we first learned about your sword," Sebec said. "When you ignited its magic in your confrontation with Arcannen, it revealed its presence in the scrye waters. We followed up from there."

"So the response of the waters varies according to the strength of the magic expended?" Paxon asked. "The amount of turbulence is directly proportional to the nature of the magic used? And you can read the nuances?"

"Pretty much. A weak usage might not even register, but we aren't really looking at those incidents, in any case. We are mostly interested in the stronger ones because they indicate a more powerful form of magic and the possibility of greater danger to anyone close."

"The reaction to my fight with Arcannen must have been fairly dramatic."

Sebec cocked an eyebrow. "Enough so that the Ard Rhys was summoned immediately. The search to uncover the source of the magic was begun that very night. We found Arcannen quickly enough. It took a little longer to find you."

"How *did* you find me?" Paxon pressed. "How did you even know I had been to Dark House?"

"Oh, that wasn't so hard. At the direction of the Ard Rhys, I flew to Wayford and asked around. We have people living there—friends of the Druids—who keep us informed. Once we knew of Arcannen's involvement, one of those friends advised me that the sorcerer had just that day flown in from Leah with a new girl for one of his pleasure houses. When I spoke with the airfield manager, he pointed me toward the boy Grehling. He told me about you."

Paxon pursed his lips doubtfully. "He didn't seem the type to tell much of anything to anyone."

Sebec shrugged. "He isn't. But I can make almost anyone tell what they know, if I wish it. That's part of what I can do with my magic."

Paxon wasn't all that happy to hear that magic had been used against Grehling, but he supposed it was in a good cause if the end result had led the Druids to him and in turn brought him to Paranor. He didn't think Sebec would do anything to hurt the boy. Still . . .

"Sebec!" the other Druid called out, pointing at the basin waters, which were shimmering and giving off tiny ripples just above the outline of the rebuilt Southland city of Arishaig.

Sebec and Paxon moved over for a look. "A medium disturbance, nothing too overt, but heavily concentrated on one area. Or person." He caught the Highlander's quizzical look and smiled. "Once you learn to read the waters—something all Druids have to learn how to do—you can pretty much tell what is happening when magic is used." He nodded to the other Druid. "I will let the Ard Rhys know of this."

He left the room at once with Paxon in tow, and it seemed to Paxon they were departing with more alacrity than he would have thought necessary, given Sebec's disclaimer about the disturbance. Then he remembered how Sebec had told him that his own use of magic had warranted summoning the Ard Rhys, and wondered if this instance wasn't more serious than the young Druid was letting on.

They went up to the top level and the quarters of the Ard Rhys. Sebec knocked, waited for permission to enter, and left Paxon outside to wait. The Highlander moved over to a bench on the other side of the hall and sat down, thinking it over. He supposed it wasn't strange that Sebec would shade the truth about the seriousness of any particular magic's use. Why should Paxon be allowed to know the truth of such things? He was only in training, and there was no guarantee he would still be around in a month or two. Even though he believed he would be, no one could be sure.

He remained where he was until Sebec emerged and then rose. Sebec came straight over. "She seems to know what it means, but it doesn't hurt to make certain. Are you hungry yet? Would you like to go to lunch?"

That afternoon proceeded in very much the same way as the one before it. Oost started off with a short lecture about positioning and stance, then set him against the machine once more. This time Paxon felt he made Big Oost work a little harder, but the end result was pretty much the same. Though he strove mightily to break through the other's defenses, he was blocked every time. The closest he got was when by accident, on a misstep, he struck back almost out of reflex and seemed to catch his sparring partner off guard, nearly getting past its belated block.

It started Paxon thinking, and when the session was

over he found himself wondering if he couldn't take advantage of what he had learned that afternoon. Shouldn't there be a way to catch Big Oost by surprise? A way that would allow him to break past the machine's automatic defenses and strike off his protective helmet?

Then late that night, when he was lying in bed still thinking about what might work, something occurred to him. He was looking at things the wrong way around. Oost himself had given him the clue he needed, and he hadn't paid close enough attention to it at the time.

But he was paying attention now.

On the third day, he had the morning to himself. Sebec was otherwise occupied, and Paxon took advantage of the free time to explore the outside world from atop the walls of the Keep, viewing the surrounding forestlands and the distant mountains, orienting himself with his surroundings by direction and points of reference.

Skipping lunch, he went straight to the practice yard. He sat through another short lecture from Oost Mondara and then picked up his sword. Standing toe-to-toe with Big Oost, he started his regular feints and cuts and slashes, and then stopped thinking about what he was going to do and just reacted. He wheeled about so that his back was to the machine, then finished the movement by coming full circle. As he came around, he thrust swiftly and without thought at the helmet atop the pole, broke cleanly past the defensive block Big Oost tried to employ, and sent the helmet spinning away in a bright flash of metal to slam against the stone wall twenty feet away.

Oost Mondara climbed off his perch, grinning wickedly. "So, young Paxon, you figured it out, did you?"

"You said early on that nothing is what it seems when you face an enemy in combat, and that you should be ready for anything. Then I started mulling over what you said about infusing a piece of wood and metal with magic. But wood and metal aren't sentient, so how could you do that? It seemed more likely that you were operating Big Oost yourself, controlling its movements by thought. You could see what was coming; you could anticipate what I was going to do. So Big Oost was responding to your own instincts. I was fighting you, after all."

"Exactly. You were trying to break past my defenses, and I was trying to stop you. So it's time we move on. Until now you hadn't gotten to the place where you were ready to test yourself against an attack I might mount. That's what we will work on next. Sit and have a drink of water, and we'll start anew."

Starting anew, as it turned out, quickly washed away any lingering sense of accomplishment and thrust the Highlander directly into a fresh kind of suffering. Now Big Oost was free to attack him, and he was forced to defend himself. He was allowed to counter, but not to directly attack his adversary. This was the next phase of his training, Oost Mondara advised. Now he would be required to concentrate solely on defensive work and holding strategies until he mastered those sufficiently. His reward for this promotion was a body that ached all over from blows struck by his attacker that he failed to adequately block and that left him bruised and battered.

When that day's session had ended and he went back to his room and peeled off his clothes to bathe, he found his body was a rainbow of dark colors that formed intricate patterns over torso and limbs with barely a patch of skin untouched. Everything hurt from head to foot, and while nothing appeared to be broken, his muscles and joints were raw with pain. He bathed in salt water in an effort to ease his discomfort, then slept until dinner and went down to the dining hall.

Neither Sebec nor Avelene, sitting across from him, said a word to him while he ate. When the meal was finished, he rose, nodded to them, and went directly back to bed.

The days and weeks that followed were marked by further battering and bruising, but after a time it lessened as he slowly improved his responses to the attacks and his anticipation grew sharper and more effective. After two months, he was skilled enough to be able to block almost every blow Big Oost gave him and to keep the other not only at bay but also off balance with counterstrikes. His body toughened, and his confidence grew by leaps and bounds.

Even his taciturn, acerbic trainer began nodding and voicing approval, and Paxon was starting to feel he might really belong at Paranor with the Druids.

By then, he was studying magic with Sebec in the mornings—classes that were informal and mostly a sharing of the young Druid's information on how magic worked rather than actual practice.

"Before you can learn magic, you have to understand it," he told Paxon. "Not just in the raw, instinctual way that you came to discover the magic in your sword, but in an intellectual fashion. You have to appreciate the ways in which it can both help and hurt you. Because it can, sometimes without your meaning it to do so, sometimes without warning or reason, and mostly because you are too reckless and unthinking in your use of it."

"I didn't feel any of that when I fought against Arcannen," Paxon pointed out. They were sitting in one of the classrooms, just the two of them. "If anything, it felt exhilarating."

"Yes, and there's danger in that, too. Magic can become addictive. Magic *is* addictive. You need to be aware of that and not let it become so much a part of your life that it comes to dominate it. All Druids run this risk. Every time they use magic, they chance crossing a line that they can't cross back over. Brona, in the time of Allanon, was one such Druid—a man who delved too deeply into the arts and was consumed as a result. I'm not saying this would happen to you. But you need to know that magic is never safe and never predictable. It responds to you—to who and what you are inside. It adapts, and sometimes it wants to change you."

"How am I supposed to protect myself against that?" Paxon wanted to know. "How do I measure the amount of magic expended so that it doesn't do me some sort of damage?"

"Practice, mostly. But understanding the danger and being aware of it beforehand helps, too. You are less at risk than the Druids who use magic all the time and in varying forms. Your sword is a limited, recognizable sort of magic. There aren't that many parameters to its use. Eventually, you will come to know them all. Unless you over-engage in use of that magic, your exposure and the resultant danger isn't so great."

So it went. They discussed how a nuanced use of magic could be mastered, how emotional control could help create the necessary balance between what was intended and unexpected consequences. Sebec explained how, over time, Paxon would come to understand uses of his sword's magic that he could not even imagine now. The magic's well was deep and cold, but its taste was sweet and life giving. Paxon's choice to embrace it would give him strength and purpose; he need only be aware of its limitations and vicissitudes.

Mostly, Paxon agreed with Sebec in his analysis and explanation of magic's workings, though he longed to experiment and discover its limits. But the young Druid was adamant: He must be patient and he must wait. His concentration now must be on his weapons training. Oost Mondara would not stand for distractions that using magic at this point—even if it was only testing the limits of his sword—would cause.

So more time passed, and more lessons were learned, and better results were achieved on the practice field, but Paxon's patience was slowly, steadily eroding.

Then, just over two months into his time at Paranor, he was summoned to the chambers of the Ard Rhys.

9

It was Sebec who brought Paxon the message and who delivered him to the door of the room where Aphenglow Elessedil waited. But then the young Druid told him he was to enter alone and left him there. Paxon watched the other's back recede down the hallway, not quite believing he was being left alone for this meeting. But then he took a deep breath and knocked.

"Come in, Paxon," the Ard Rhys called out from inside.

He entered and found her waiting in the company of another Druid, a man of ordinary size and appearance, a Southlander by the look of him, one possessed of eyes that were of two different colors—one deep blue and the other lavender. The Druid nodded to him but said nothing.

"Close the door, please," the Ard Rhys ordered.

He did so and stepped up to where she sat at her writing desk, its small surface cluttered with papers of all sizes, shapes, and colors. "This is Starks," she said. "I've asked him to travel to the Westland to Grimpen Ward where there is evidence of a magic in use. I want you to go with him."

Paxon didn't know what to say. "As his protector?"

"That, but mostly as a student assigned to learn from a more seasoned member of the Order. I have spoken to Oost and he tells me you are well along in your training with weapons. He thinks you are ready for some practical experience. This particular journey should suffice. The magic the scrye has discovered is not large and is being applied in a haphazard manner. Whoever has it likely found it by accident and has no real idea how to use it. Or, perhaps, even of the danger it poses. To the finder, this is mostly an interesting toy. Starks will show you how to find such magic and how to retrieve it without calling attention to yourselves or causing harm to anyone else."

"Will I be allowed to take my sword with me?" he asked.

She nodded. "But you are not to use it unless Starks tells you to or either of you is threatened in a way that absolutely requires it. *Absolutely,* Paxon. Do you understand why?"

"Because I am still learning about magic? Because I don't have enough practice with it?"

"Because every time you use magic, you risk someone finding out about it. The Druids are not the only ones who scour the Four Lands in search of magic. Others, many not friendly to the order and not respectful of its goals, hunt it, too. We don't always know who these people are or where they can be found, so we use caution in employing magic and avoid invoking it whenever we can."

"I'll be careful," he promised.

"I'm counting on it." She gave him a brief smile. "Now go along with Starks and let him explain more about the details. You'll leave tomorrow."

She went back to sorting through her papers, and Paxon went out the door with the other Druid. As they walked side by side down the hallway, Starks asked, "How long have you been here, Paxon? It's been awhile, hasn't it?"

"A little more than two months."

"Working with Oost the entire time?"

"Mostly. In the afternoons. Sebec teaches me about magic in the mornings—about how it works and what to look out for when using it. How long have you been here?"

The other shrugged. "Maybe six years. I'm impressed by the fact that you had a run-in with Arcannen and lived to tell about it."

Paxon suppressed a grin. "I was lucky. The sword's magic saved me. How do you know about this?"

Starks gave him a look, his bland expression shifting into something resembling amusement. "Everyone knows, Paxon. Everyone knew even before you arrived. The Druids keep few secrets from one another."

The Highlander frowned, looking off in the distance. "Apparently."

Starks laughed. "You didn't think there wouldn't be talk of you before you arrived, did you? Not when you are the first paladin selected by the Ard Rhys in five years. You did know that, didn't you?"

Paxon managed a sheepish smile. "I think Sebec said something about it. I guess the one before me didn't last."

"Didn't and shouldn't have. You, at least, seem better settled and certainly more seasoned. Oost talks, too, you know—even if you don't see him doing so. He likes you."

"He does?" Paxon was genuinely surprised. "I always believed he was pretty much just putting up with me."

Starks came to a halt. "If he didn't like you or think you were adequately prepared for it, you wouldn't be going with me. You can be certain of that."

He started away, and then he turned back. "You should also know that I asked for you to come with me. That ought to tell you something."

A moment later, he was gone.

* * *

They set out at dawn, flying the familiar two-masted clipper crewed by a pair of Troll guards. One of them took the helm and the other managed the lines and light sheaths. Starks showed no interest in helping out; indeed, he placed himself squarely in front of the pilot box upon a folded blanket, his black robes wrapped about him, and disappeared into a book he had carried aboard. After stowing his bag, Paxon stood around for a bit, trying to decide what to do. He didn't want to interrupt Starks, and the Trolls seemed fine without him.

Finally, he moved to the bow of the clipper and started working through the list of exercises that Oost Mondara had given him to loosen up every afternoon before weapons practice. But he was free to use his own sword now, and he did. The blade felt so much lighter and more balanced in his hands than the wooden model he used in field practice that he practically flew through his exercises. When he finished the first run, he drank some water from the deck barrel and began again.

Two hours later, he felt hot and vaguely light-headed, perhaps from doing so much at a higher altitude. In any case, Starks told him to break it off and have some lunch.

They sat together with tins of hot vegetable stew and bread and washed it down with ale. Surreptitiously, Paxon watched the other man, trying to make sense of him. He seemed so removed from everything, as if he was always somewhere else in his mind. He showed no obvious concern for the mission on which they had been sent, having not once bothered to discuss it with his companion.

Finally, Paxon said, "Do you think we'll have any trouble with getting this magic away from whoever has it?"

Starks smiled. "You want to know why I don't seem worried about it. Maybe why I don't even seem interested. It's just the way I am. I don't like to think too far ahead about what's waiting around the corner. I like to be prepared, but not troubled. We've got two days before we reach Grimpen Ward. There is no point in fussing about it until then."

Paxon frowned. "I don't know if I could do that."

"Most can't. Other Druids wonder about me. I hear them talking sometimes when they think I don't hear. But I've always been different from most of them anyway."

"What do you mean?" Paxon said.

"I'm from the deep Southland. From Sterne. Not too many raised that far inside the Federation find their way to Paranor."

"But you did?"

"I wasn't satisfied with what the Federation had to offer. I didn't accept that I wasn't supposed to use magic if I could manage to do so. That sort of rule feels artificial. So I went north and asked the Druids if they would take me. Some of them wouldn't have, I suspect. But the Ard Rhys did. She never questioned me, never asked for a reason, and never suggested I wasn't to be trusted because of where I came from. She worked with me personally for a time, and then gave me over to Isaturin. That was daunting. He was very precise, very demanding. A tough teacher. But I came through, and now I am a full-fledged member of the order."

He gave Paxon a look. "You know, you should give some thought to joining the order, too. It might be possible, once you've proved your value as a paladin."

"I didn't come to Paranor to join the order," Paxon said quickly. "I don't think it's for me."

Starks rose and stretched. "Give it time. You might

not know what's for you this soon. And don't underrate yourself. You can do and be anything you want."

He went off for a nap, leaving Paxon to clean up the lunch, which the Highlander set about doing. At least he was performing a useful task.

They set down for the night halfway across the Tirfing in a copse of conifers that offered some protection from winds that had picked up late in the day and suggested a change in the weather. As the pair ate dinner with the Trolls, they could feel a sudden rise in the temperature.

"We're going to get some rain," Starks declared, the firelight reflecting from his different-colored eyes. "A lot of rain."

They went belowdecks to sleep that night, heeding the Druid's warning, and by midnight the rain was hammering against the sloop's hull and the vessel was rocking and straining against her anchor ropes, buffeted by the heavy winds. The motion was familiar to Paxon, who had been aboard airships all his life, so he slept undisturbed until one of the anchor ropes broke and the clipper began slamming against the trunks of the trees in which she had been moored.

So throwing off his blanket, he went topside with the Trolls and down the rope ladder to fasten fresh ropes in place to resecure the ship. By the time that was done, he was drenched, and because it was near morning he chose not to try to go back to sleep. Instead, he sat up until dawn, listening to the howl of the wind and thinking about other times. He wished that Starks would be more open with him about what to expect, but he accepted that this might not happen. Starks was closemouthed and reticent, and Paxon believed the man pretty much preferred his own company. That he had taken as much time with the Highlander as he had at their initial meeting seemed surprising in retrospect.

He found himself thinking of his family and home. He had been back only once since coming to Paranor, in spite of his promises to his sister and mother—a fact he found troubling. He could argue that he had been too busy with his training, which was admittedly demanding, but the truth was that he had chosen to stay away. Going back before he had accomplished something worth talking about didn't feel right. And to date, that hadn't happened. Perhaps after this journey was over and he had helped retrieve the magic they sought, he would make another visit.

Perhaps.

When dawn arrived, the storm departed, moving eastward. The winds died and the temperatures dropped enough that the humidity faded. Starks, Paxon, and the Trolls ate their breakfast, released the mooring lines, and set out anew. They flew through the better part of the day, crossing the Tirfing to the Rock Spur Mountains, and finally descended into the Wilderun and the frontier town of Grimpen Ward.

They landed some distance away from their destination, choosing a spot within the forest where the ship wouldn't be likely to be found. Starks shed his black robes in favor of woodsman's garb similar to what Paxon was wearing, and then the two set out on foot. Twilight was approaching, and the shadows cast by the trees were lengthening, absorbing the fading splashes of sunlight. The woods felt empty and watchful, its eyes those of creatures that made their homes there. They found a footpath that took them a short distance to a road. From there, they could just make out the outlying cabins and sheds of Grimpen Ward's residents—ramshackle affairs with no sign of life. The road they followed was empty until they neared the main part of the town, where the first of the taverns spilled its patrons out one door and on to the next while new patrons pushed their way inside and women from the pleasure houses called out to them from the doorways and windows of their workplaces.

A few dogs roamed the streets and alleyways as they made their way through the town, and carts and horses passed them by in a rumble of wheels and a clopping of hooves. Beggars came at them from everywhere, and pitchmen from the more exotic shows called out their promises, wild and tempting. *Come see, come experience!* Paxon glanced everywhere at once while Starks looked at nothing but the road ahead.

When they reached the crossroads marking the town center, Starks brought them to a halt, then moved out of the road to an opening between two buildings and stood with his back to the wall. "Keep your eyes open," he said to Paxon.

Then he closed his own, and for long minutes was very still. When he opened them again, there was a hint of confusion on his face. "I'm picking up on more than one form of magic. That shouldn't be."

"You can tell where it's coming from?" Paxon wanted to know.

"In general. I can sense the residue. The two are close to each other. Maybe they are even the same, reflecting different uses. In any case, we are not near them. They are all the way on the other end of the town." He glanced about, looking up at the sky. "We should go before it gets any darker."

They set out anew, maneuvering their way through the growing crowds, keeping to themselves, trying to avoid unwanted encounters. It was difficult to make headway, the streets filling quickly with the approach of nightfall and the air pungent with the promise of nighttime pleasures. Several times they were accosted, but Starks gently moved those who stopped them away with a touch of his fingers to his lips and a small twisting gesture.

Eventually they reached the far end of the town, the buildings just beginning to give way once more to the forest, lights in windows and streetlamps brightening with the coming of darkness. Starks slowed as they reached a tavern whose sign announced it as the Mudland Rose.

"This is where we want to be," he said to Paxon. "The magic is close by, but we will have to sniff it out. I will ask the questions, and you will watch my back. If anything looks awry—anything at all—tap me on the shoulder. Don't hesitate. If there is another magic hunter inside, we don't want to be caught off guard."

Paxon nodded. With Starks leading the way, they pushed through the double doors and entered the tavern.

Inside, it was a madhouse. Men and women were crowded up against one another shoulder-to-shoulder, with barely space to move about. The room was cavernous and so dark and smoky that Paxon could not see into the murky corners and higher spaces at all. Patrons stood three-deep at the serving bar, and all the tables were filled. The laughter and shouting were deafening.

Starks took a quick look around, then began maneuvering his way toward the end of the counter where the serving girls were gathering tankards of ale on trays to carry to the tables. Paxon followed, trying to stay close. It required considerable effort, but they eventually reached their destination. Starks immediately bent to the closest server and whispered in her ear. She went white, nodded slowly, and did not turn to look at him. Instead, she mouthed something Paxon couldn't hear, picked up her tray, and swiftly went about her business. Starks moved deeper into the room, Paxon following in his wake, using him as a buffer against the crowds. Although he was repeatedly jostled, he kept his feet and stayed close, scanning the crowds, taking in everything, thinking he might see something that mattered.

And then he did. At the very back of the room, a tall figure, cloaked and hooded, rose from a table and went out through the back door. Two others sitting with him, thicker of build and heavily muscled, moved in front of the door and stood blocking it.

"Starks!" Paxon hissed, tapping him hurriedly on the shoulder.

The Druid glanced back at him, followed his gaze, and nodded. "How many others?"

"Only one that I saw. He went out through the door just ahead of those two. I can't be certain, but it looked like . . ."

• He let the rest hang, so uncertain his eyes had not deceived him he didn't want to finish the thought. Starks was already moving anyway, making for the door and the men guarding it, no longer evidencing even a trace of the careless disinterest that had marked his earlier behavior aboard ship. Paxon started to reach for his sword, but the patrons of the tavern were packed together so tightly that he couldn't find space to maneuver.

Starks wasn't waiting anyway. He came up to the men without slowing, felled one with a fist that shimmered with blue fire as it connected, and stunned the second with a bolt of that same fire flung from his hand in a brilliant flash. Both men went down, and Starks was past them and out the door to the yard behind the tavern, Paxon at his heels.

In the next instant a shock wave of black light exploded into them, throwing them back against the rear wall of the tavern. Starks was leading, so he took the brunt of the strike and lay motionless on the ground. But Paxon was only momentarily stunned, and he came back to his feet swiftly, drawing the Sword of Leah as he did. Another flash of fire exploded toward him, but this time Paxon caught it on the edge of his black blade and shattered it into harmless fragments. In the dying light, he saw that the attack had come from a stable set out behind the tavern at the end of the lot—a smallish structure with a handful of stalls and a maintenance shed. He also caught a glimpse of two figures crouched within the shed's entrance.

Then everything went dark again, and Paxon was forced to wait until his vision adjusted. Crouched in the night's gloom, aware of Starks unmoving behind him and the figures ahead waiting, he held his ground, ready for a fresh attack.

When he could see again, the entrance to the stable was empty, and the figures were gone. He advanced warily, thinking it might be a trap. But when he reached the building, he could tell it was deserted. There weren't even any horses in the stalls.

He was about to go back to see to Starks when he noticed the dark bundle in a corner at the rear of the structure. Casting a quick look around, he went over for a closer look and found a boy of perhaps eighteen, his hands and feet bound and his body badly mutilated. It looked as if he had been cut and burned repeatedly. His eyes were wide and staring, and his mouth was stretched as if trying to scream. He must have died in the midst of whatever torture he was enduring. Paxon found and lit a lamp and bent close to the boy. Blood stained the ground surrounding the body, and he could make out the markings of strange boot prints.

"Federation issue," Starks said, bending close. He was back on his feet, but one side of his face and body were heavily singed. "But these were people who knew magic, not common soldiers. That boy was subjected to a lot of pain, both internal and external. They wanted something from him, and I would be surprised if they didn't get it."

"The magic we were hunting?"

"That, for certain. But I think they wanted something else—something that wasn't so tangible. Perhaps an explanation for how he found the magic. Or how he learned to use it. Or where he heard of it." He looked at Paxon. "How many of them did you see?"

"Two. The one who left the tavern ahead of us and a second who must have already been out here waiting. What's going on? Did both forms of the magic you sensed earlier belong to these two men? Or did one belong to whatever talisman the boy was hiding?"

"I'm not certain. At least one form of magic was what killed this boy, so we know that much. To know anything more, we would have to find the men who did this. If they were men."

Paxon stared at him. *If they were men?* What else would they be? Were they dealing with some other form of creature?

"Let's go after them," he said abruptly. "Maybe we can still catch them."

Starks gave him a look. "Maybe they would like that." Then he shrugged. "Let's do it anyway."

They set out at once. Starks seemed to know where he was going, his head lifted, his eyes peering through the darkness as if he could see beyond it. They went at a fast trot, heading farther outside the town in the opposite direction from which they had come, following a narrow pathway into the trees. The shouts and laughter of Grimpen Ward slowly faded away, and the night's stillness grew deep and pervasive. The only sounds now were of their own breathing and footfalls as they ran. Paxon had his sword out, ready for use, fully expecting that he would need it. Starks didn't object. Once or twice, as they were running, Paxon caught sight of familiar boot prints in the soft earth ahead, and he knew they were on the right track.

Ahead, the woods opened onto a broad treeless stretch of pasture, and an airship sat bathed in moonlight on its far side. Two figures were running toward it and had nearly reached it.

"Leah! Leah!" roared Paxon, caught up in the moment, and with a sudden burst of speed he raced right past Starks in an effort to catch the fleeing men.

He should have used better judgment. Ordinary men would have offered no threat to him from this distance. But magic users were another story. They turned, and the entire pasture lit up with explosions of green fire. It had the look and feel of an attack by flash rips and fire launchers, and Paxon was suddenly dodging this way and that to avoid being struck. He heard Starks calling out to him from behind, but he was too busy trying to stay alive to respond.

One of the men abandoned the attack and scrambled aboard their two-man, powering up the diapson crystals and preparing to lift off. Paxon ran harder, close enough now that he thought he could launch his own attack.

But in the next instant he was struck a powerful blow that lifted him off his feet and threw him backward, his clothing on fire and his ears ringing. He collapsed, still clinging to his sword, fighting to stay conscious. An instant later Starks was bending over him, smothering the fire with a sort of dry mist that spilled from his fingers. Paxon gasped for breath and tried to sit up, hearing the sound of the airship ascending into the night sky.

"Stay where you are," Starks ordered, pushing him down again. "It's too late now. They've gone. What were you thinking, anyway?"

"I just thought . . . they might panic . . . and then I could catch them," he gasped. "Stupid, I know."

The Druid felt carefully along his arms and legs and torso. "No harm done, apparently. But don't ever do that again or it will be your last outing with the Druids. Am I understood?"

Paxon nodded. "Can I get up now?"

Starks pulled him to his feet. "At least we know a few things we didn't know before."

"We do?"

The Druid grinned. "Well, for one, we know you can't readily disengage your brain from your impulses. You'll have to work on that. I'll tell you the rest on our flight back to Paranor. Come along. And put that sword away, please."

Feeling both exhilarated and sheepish, Paxon Leah did as he was told.

10

On their return from Grimpen Ward, Starks and Paxon went immediately to the Ard Rhys to give their report. It was not a comfortable situation. Nothing they had set out to do had been accomplished. They had failed to find and claim the source of the magic the scrye waters had detected. The user—a boy not yet fully grown—was dead, likely at the hands of the men who had stolen the magic and escaped the Druids. A thorough investigation of the matter failed to turn up any explanation of what the magic was or how the boy had found it in the first place. No one had seen him use it; no one knew anything about how he had found it. No one even knew much about the boy himself. He was an orphan who had come looking for work several years ago and been hired to care for the horses of the inn guests. He lived in the maintenance shed and had no friends.

But, as he had indicated to Paxon, Starks had a couple of pieces of information he felt the Ard Rhys would find useful. First, it was clear that at least one of the men they had fought was a powerful magic wielder with skills the equal of his own. Second, the Druid had noted that the vessel their attackers had been flying had Federation markings, and it was likely the men aboard were in some way connected to the Southland.

"But this is the most important piece of information,

Mistress," he finished. "The men who stole the magic were expecting us. Clearly, they were magic hunters, and they would have taken precautions in any case. But they had set up a watch inside the tavern, and they knew us for who we were even though I wasn't wearing the Druid robes that would identify us. They had it in their minds to kill us, and they very nearly did. But how did they know to look for us? How did they know we were coming?"

Aphenglow regarded him steadily. "You don't think it was simply luck, I gather?"

"I don't. I wish I did. But I think someone knew we were coming and told them so."

"A spy."

"Within the order. Yes. It is the best explanation, though not the easiest to accept."

"No, hardly that." She looked out her window for a long time, saying nothing. "Why would anyone go to so much trouble to claim a magic that seemed to have so little value? It was a minor magic when it revealed itself to the scrye. Is it possible it was much stronger than we believed? Or that it somehow evolved?"

"That would be unusual," Starks offered quietly.

The Ard Rhys glanced at Paxon, who was doing his best not to be noticed. "What do you have to add to all this?" she asked suddenly. "You were there. What did you see that Starks didn't?"

Paxon hadn't planned on saying anything, so for a moment he was left speechless. "I only saw what he saw. Except . . ."

He paused, remembering suddenly. "Except that the man sitting at the table who went out the door ahead of us looked familiar. I didn't see his face. It was the way he moved, how he held himself." He shook his head. "But I'm not sure."

"He reminded you of Arcannen, didn't he?" she pressed him.

He nodded. "He did. But I just don't know."

"Well, he would be one who would be magic hunting. And he is a powerful magic user." Starks smoothed back his dark hair and shrugged. "We should put an end to him, Mistress. Whether he was there or not, we've had enough of him."

The Ard Rhys made no response, but instead got to her feet. "Is there anything more to report?"

To Paxon's relief, Starks shook his head. He hadn't said one word about the Highlander's impetuous and dangerous charge across the pasture or how close he had come to getting himself killed. He hadn't offered criticism of any kind.

"You may go, then. And thank you both for your service. Paxon, tomorrow you will report back to Sebec in the morning and Oost in the afternoon to continue your instruction. Starks, please write down everything you've told me for the records on magic retrieval. Now go eat something and then get some rest."

And that was the end of matters for several weeks. During that time, Paxon began training with magic, as well as weapons, abandoning the heavy wooden sword in favor of his own blade. It was Oost Mondara who determined he was ready, and Oost who turned him back over to Sebec for his lessons on using magic. Paxon was surprised when he discovered it was to be Sebec, mostly because the Druid seemed so young—not much older than his student, after all. But it made sense that the Druid who had provided him with his lessons on the theory of magic's uses during their days of long talks and discussions should be the same one who provided his practical experience.

And he liked Sebec. Working with him was easy, and communication was uncomplicated and direct. With Oost, even now, there was a clear delineation between teacher and student, and Paxon never even thought about trying to cross that line. But Sebec was more a friend than a superior or mentor, and their relationship felt more like one of equals, though Paxon never doubted for a moment that the Druid was the more experienced and skilled.

This became clear on their first day of training together. Although there was no actual combat involved in learning how to use the magic contained in the Sword of Leah, it was Sebec who, from the beginning, understood the various ways in which it might be employed.

"You have to start thinking of it as a weapon that has multiple functions. You've seen it act to defend you, an instinctive reaction of the magic of the talisman when the holder is threatened. But there are likely other forms of protection it can offer, as well, if you know how to summon them. Perhaps it can ward you as a shield or covering, can thrust away, as well as shatter other magic. Maybe it can burn or strike a blow or become a thunderous wind or a heart-wrenching wail. Or be small or large, soft or loud. But everything it can do depends on your heart and determination. Your belief is as important as your physical strength. You need to believe in yourself and in your weapon both. Doubt is the enemy. Hesitation is potentially fatal."

Sebec began working with him on expanding his attack skills. The Sword of Leah's magic generated a powerful form of fire, very like what diapson crystals were designed to accomplish when used as a power source for the deadly flash rips. Technology had finally caught up with nature, Sebec opined. Once upon a time, technology had dominated and magic had been kept hidden away by those few who had use of it. That had changed with the Great Wars when magic had resurfaced. Now it was all changing back again as the Federation pursued ways in which the old sciences could be brought back into the world to replace magic once more, most particularly through the development of weapons.

There had been a time, more than 150 years ago, when it seemed this undertaking might have stalled permanently. The demonkind had broken free of the Forbidding and destroyed Arishaig and thousands of its people with it. The Prime Minister of the Federation had been killed along with almost half of the Coalition Council, and the government was in disarray. If ever there was a moment when the population's collective attention might have been turned to other efforts, this had been it. But instead Arishaig had been rebuilt, a stronger fortress than ever; the Coalition Council and its officers had been replaced by an even more militant body; and the once-stalled efforts at creating weapons and warships had intensified.

The belief among the Southlanders, Sebec said, had never changed. A strong military, dominant weapons, and aggressive tactics were what would keep them safe. History suggested this mind-set might never change, even after all the catastrophes and defeats endured, even after all the hard lessons administered. The Southland had its own particular worldview, and as the largest and most heavily populated of the Four Lands, the heartland of the Old World and its storied survivors, it viewed itself as dominant and entitled. It was this attitude as much as anything else that had led it astray repeatedly over the centuries, but that nevertheless continued to prove pervasive among its people.

Discussions on topics such as these filled gaps in the actual training efforts that Paxon underwent over the next few weeks. Sebec used the time between attempts at focusing the magic as opportunities to discuss related matters, providing Paxon with a broader perspective of the world. The Highlander did not discourage or disdain this instruction; rather, he looked forward to and appreciated it. Sebec, in spite of being so close in age, was far more knowledgeable about history and current events, and he had traveled extensively on behalf of the Druids during the time he had been at Paranor and so knew the whole of the Four Lands. Paxon was grateful for the chance to share in what the other had learned.

But it was mastering the skills needed to unlock his sword's potential that provided him with his most exciting and compelling moments. Because he could not wield the power of the Sword of Leah personally, Sebec was restricted to offering explanations on the nuances of a variation over and over. He was always patient and encouraging, every time, until Paxon would finally begin to comprehend what was needed and see his efforts rewarded. It was a slow, sometimes torturous process, but he wouldn't have traded it for anything.

So his training progressed, and the three weeks passed swiftly.

He was still in the middle of his education at the beginning of the fourth week when he was summoned once again before the Ard Rhys.

Climbing the stairs to the upper levels of the Keep and the offices of the Ard Rhys, he paused when he reached the closed door behind which she waited, taking a deep breath. He remembered the last time he had come at her summons, brought to her by Sebec to be sent on his first assignment as a protector away from Paranor.

Was this to be his second?

He knocked, heard her bid him enter, and opened the door. Aphenglow Elessedil was bent over her writing desk once more, fussing with several stacks of paper, her ink-stained fingers clutching a quill pen. He bowed in greeting, and she waved him toward a chair to one side. "Sit down," she ordered. "Pour yourself a glass of ale."

He found a pitcher and two glasses on a small table beside his chair and did as she had instructed. Sipping the ale, he glanced at the other glass, a possible indicator that someone else was expected.

Five minutes later, the knock came again. "Come," the Ard Rhys called out, and the door opened to admit Starks. The Druid was dressed in his black robes, and his sleepy expression suggested the summons might have caught him napping. With Starks, it was hard to tell. He smiled and nodded at Paxon.

"I have something new for the two of you to look into," Aphenglow announced, rising from her desk to face them. She motioned Starks into a second chair, and he sat down at once. "This one involves traveling into the deep Southland below Arishaig to a small farming community called Eusta. Five killings have taken place in a little over a month, all of them by what the community elders are describing as a wild animal. But this animal has been seen and walks upright on two legs. It also seems able to disappear into thin air. It may be a shape-shifter or a changeling or something else entirely, but it is not a normal creature. What we know from reading the scrye waters is that it has the use of magic."

"Why have we waited so long to respond to this?" Starks asked her.

"Deep Southland, Starks," she pointed out. "They hate us worse than they hate whatever's killing them. If the killings hadn't come so close together, they might have continued to ignore us." She shook her head. "Such fools. We offered help when we took the first reading, weeks ago. They turned us down. Now they've changed their minds."

"So the magic might come from this thing changing appearances?" Paxon asked. "Or do you think it comes from something else?"

Aphenglow smiled. "I don't think anything. It's up to

you and Starks to find out the truth. But see that whatever it is, it gets dealt with. Don't leave it alive. Bad enough that we are shunned when we could help; imagine the reaction if we can't help once we've been asked. The protocol is the same as before. Starks commands, Paxon protects. Don't get it mixed up." She sighed heavily. "Be careful with this one; I don't like things that hide behind false faces. Watch your backs."

"This doesn't have anything to do with Arcannen, does it?" Paxon said.

The Ard Rhys cocked an eyebrow. "You can tell me that when you return. Leave in the morning. Travel safe."

It was a long night for Paxon, who had trouble falling asleep. The idea of another assignment so soon was troubling. He didn't think he had done all that well the time before, and he had wanted to complete his training before having to go out again. But Starks told him they had no one else to act as protector for the Druids save other Druids, and he believed the Ard Rhys thought additional practical experience would be good for him.

He also pointed out that there had been a sharp increase in the number of readings of magic throughout the Four Lands in the past half a year.

"It all began about the time the scrye orb disappeared," he told Paxon before they parted that afternoon. "The orb was a companion magic to the scrye waters—different, yet serving the same purpose. Aphenglow found it in the wake of the events surrounding the breakdown of the Forbidding more than a century ago. It happened after she returned to re-form the Fourth Druid Order and build upon its work. The orb allows its holder to view magic of any sort if it manifests itself. It can let the holder know the nature and location of that magic."

"It disappeared?" Paxon repeated. "How did that happen?"

Starks gave him a look. "Not by accident, I can tell you, but the details are fuzzy. One day it was there, the next it was gone. Stolen, of course. But by whom? And who has it now?"

"But it's a magic," Paxon pointed out. "Wouldn't the scrye waters reveal it at some point? Surely it's been used."

"Yes, well, there's a problem with that. The one doesn't reveal the other. One magic negates another—a rare but sometimes unavoidable event—so we can't pinpoint where it is. We are still waiting for something or someone to let us know what happened."

He didn't have anything more to add to what he had told Paxon, and the Highlander realized how hard it would be to track something like that once it was gone. But he found himself wondering if whoever stole the orb might not be the same person who had given them away to Arcannen at Grimpen Ward. It would be odd if it weren't. There couldn't be two spies within the order, could there?

They set out the following morning aboard the fast clipper and with the same two members of the Troll guard as before. Starks was soon back in his favorite position in front of the pilot box, buried in another book, reading as if there were nothing better to do. Paxon moved to the bow, thought about doing his exercises, then abandoned the idea in favor of a nap. Sleep seemed more important.

They reached Eusta the same day, but very late at night. There was a small airfield occupied by a couple of worn-looking skiffs and one two-masted transport moored up alongside a maintenance shack, and no one around. They spent the night aboard their vessel, then rose at dawn, washed and ate breakfast, and walked into the village.

Eusta was small and worn down by age and weather. Most of the buildings were wood-sided and thatch-roofed, patched and crumbling. A handful of men stood outside a grain storage bin, talking in low voices, and Starks approached them, Paxon at his heels.

"Well met," he said. "My name is Starks. My companion is Paxon. We're here about the killings."

Because he was wearing his Druid robes, there wasn't much doubt about either who he was or why he was there. But it forced the men who were gathered to engage in conversation with him.

"Two more just last night," one answered. The man was big and strong, with huge forearms and hands. "Ellice and Truesen Carbenae, on their farm, a mile south of the village. Thing's not satisfied with taking just one anymore. Now it wants two."

Last night, Paxon thought. *While we slept.*

"Anyone see it happen?" Starks asked. "Anyone get a look at this creature?"

"Just those that are dead," growled a second man, his ferret features sharp and narrow, his eyes challenging. "They didn't have much to say about it."

Starks ignored him, eyes on the first man. "Can you take me there?"

"What's the point?" snapped Ferret-face. "You think you can catch a ghost? You think you're up to it, Druid? This thing is smart and dangerous. It will end up eating you for its next meal."

Starks turned. "If you are so concerned about me, why don't you come along? You can help."

The man smirked. He glanced at his fellows knowingly, then back at the Druid. "I don't help Druids."

"You've probably never had one ask you in the right way." Starks crooked his fingers and twisted them in the way Paxon had seen him do before in Grimpen Ward, and the man went rigid, unable to move. His face turned red with his futile efforts at freeing himself, his mouth opening and closing pointlessly. "There you are," Starks finished. "All ready to go. I'll even let you lead." He turned away. "Can we get under way?" he asked the first man. "What's your name?"

"Joffre Struen." Joffre glanced at his companion. "You really going to take him with us?"

Starks shrugged. "What do you think?"

"I think you've made your point."

The Druid nodded. He turned and gestured again, and Ferret-face dropped to the ground in a heap. "Don't let me see you again," Starks said, bending down to him, and then he walked away.

The journey to the farm took a little more than half an hour on horseback. Joffre Struen provided them with horses from the town stables, of which he was owner and manager, and led them south down a dirt road that quickly petered out into broad swaths of pastureland. The day was sunny and bright, the sky clear of clouds and deep blue. The landscape was rolling and grassy, with small patches of forest and plowed fields. It was good soil for growing, Paxon saw, and the crops were just starting to poke through the furrowed earth.

"Does this creature eat its victims?" Starks asked Struen at one point. "What does it do to them?"

"Tears out their throats and mutilates the bodies. Sometimes it dismembers them. Just rips them up."

"It doesn't eat them?"

The other man shook his head. "Not so far. It kills mostly at night, after dark. Probably catches them unawares. You can decide for yourself."

They arrived shortly afterward at a small farmhouse with a barn and a fenced-in pasture. Cattle grazed inside the fence, and chickens roamed the yard.

"Were any of the animals harmed?" Starks asked.

Struen shook his head.

"No damage to anything?"

Another shake of the head.

"Same with all the others who were killed?"

"Always the same. Hard to know what to think."

Paxon knew what he thought. This was something that killed for reasons other than protection and food. It killed because it was compelled to kill or because it liked to kill or maybe even both.

They reached the farmhouse and dismounted, tying the reins of their horses to a post and looking around warily. "Inside," Struen said.

They walked up the wooden steps to the veranda, opened the door, and went inside. The bodies were gone, but there were bloodstains everywhere. There were smears on the floor and walls, and on the furniture—most of which had been smashed. There were even blood spatters on the ceiling. It looked like the bodies had been thrown around in a rage. Paxon stared, trying to make sense of what he was seeing.

"Who found them?" Starks asked.

The stable owner shrugged. "I did. I came by to help with shoeing one of the field horses. I found the door open and them inside. I buried them out back. I couldn't stand to leave them like that."

Paxon was wandering about the room, picking out the debris that was recognizable, noting everything. "It looks like they were in the middle of eating dinner," he said.

Starks was back examining the door. "Was this door unlocked when you got here?"

Joffre Struen nodded. "Closed, but unlocked. But the windows are all broken out. I'm guessing that whoever got in and killed them probably came through that way."

"Were the others killed in their own homes, too?"

Struen shook his head. "Two were. The others were in various places around their homes. Out in the barn for one. In a pasture, for another. One was killed at the miller's, right by the grinding wheel—a young man who was visiting the daughter. The miller was away, down at the tavern. The young man was just leaving when the thing took him. The daughter heard the screams and hid in the cellar."

Starks and Paxon exchanged a look. "How many plates do you count?" the former asked.

"Three. Someone was visiting."

"Someone these people knew and let come inside."

"Otherwise, the door would be locked."

"If what killed them had to break in, it would have come through the door, locked or not. It had to be incredibly strong to do the sort of damage we're looking at."

"So the killer was a guest, a friend."

"Or at least a familiar acquaintance." Starks left the door and walked back into the room. "But I'm finding no traces of magic. All this was done with brute force. Let's walk outside, Paxon. Struen, can you give us a few minutes to look around?"

They left the big man standing amid the debris and walked out into the yard. Starks moved in leisurely fashion toward the barn, looking about the grounds as he did so. Once, he stopped to examine some wagon tracks, kneeling in the dirt to bend close and smell the earth. Another time, he poked with his toe at something that was lying on the ground, but didn't pick it up.

Inside the barn, they found the usual tack and harness for fieldwork, bags of feed and a bin of hay, and hand plows and scythes. This was a rudimentary farming operation, probably involving only the husband and wife.

Back outside again, Starks stopped and stood looking

off into the distance. "Three place settings, an unlocked door, and a dinner cut short maybe halfway through." He turned to Paxon. "Wagon tracks from yesterday and no wagon in the barn. Someone was here just before they were killed. But who?"

Paxon had no answers to offer. Together, they walked back up to the house. Struen had come out to stand on the veranda. "A little close in there," he said, shrugging. "Is there anything more you want to know before we go back?"

"Were the people killed connected to each other in any special way?" Starks asked him.

The stable owner shook his head. "Just that they were part of the community, most of them born here."

Starks nodded. "Let's go back. Can you help us find a room for the night?"

"Got you one already. At my place, above the stables. I use it now and then for visitors. There's no inn or rooms at the taverns. Hardly anyone outside the community passes through that isn't kin to one of the families. Besides, I was the one who sent for you. The others, they still think Druids are more the enemy than this thing that's killing them."

Starks swung up into the saddle of his mount. "We aren't the enemy, and we will prove it before we leave." He waited as Paxon remounted and swung in next to him. "Don't talk about this with anyone just yet. Let us do some more looking around first."

"You have an idea about this? Can you put a stop to it?"

Starks smiled, his calm demeanor reassuring. "Yes," he said.

II

THEY SLEPT THAT NIGHT ON MATTRESSES FILLED with straw in an unheated upper-level room in the stables that had likely once been part of the hayloft. They were given blankets, which was a good thing since it was chilly at night in Eusta, even as far south as it was, and the wind blew constantly. The cold didn't bother Paxon nearly so much as the wind's constant moan—a sound that sent shivers up his spine and suggested the presence of creatures he would rather not encounter.

When he rose the next morning, Starks was already up along with the sun, wrapped in his black robes and standing at the doors of the loft looking down on the shabby business district below. A few men and women were out on the street—there was only one—making their various ways from door to door, going about their personal business. There was nothing about their behavior to indicate that something was out there waiting to kill them off.

Paxon walked over to stand beside Starks. For a few moments, he didn't say anything, merely stood with him observing the town. "Did you mean what you said to Struen yesterday?" he asked finally. "Do we really have some idea of what's going on or who is responsible?"

Starks nodded. "We do. Or at least I do."

"Do you intend to share this information with me?"

"Of course."

Paxon waited a beat. "When, exactly?"

Starks looked at him. "Don't be so impatient."

"I'm just wondering if we are to spend today like yesterday, asking questions about the villagers and its outliers, rather than using magic. Can't you just track this thing we're hunting with your Druid skills?"

"Unless it uses magic, I have no way to track it. Its magic, Paxon, is of a different form. It's not a talisman, not a substantive thing separate from the user. It is a part of the user. Why, I don't yet know. Whatever it is, it has infected someone so completely that they change from human to animal in seconds. I don't think they can control it. I think it just happens, and maybe they aren't even aware of it."

"Is that possible?" Paxon felt doubtful. "How could you not be aware of something like that?"

"Mostly, you are in denial because it is too horrible to accept. You just don't let yourself think about it."

"So these killings aren't planned?"

"In the middle of a dinner at someone's home? As a young man prepares to leave his girl? Why bother to consume half a dinner and then attack? Why not wait until the young man is farther off?"

"But you have some sort of idea of how to go about finding the creature?"

"At the farm yesterday, there were wagon tracks, but no wagon." Starks was looking directly at him now. "I was able to sniff out traces of ground wheat. I found particles of milled grain."

"The miller's place."

Starks nodded. "A starting point, at least. We'll go there after we've gotten something to eat."

The breakfast options were not an improvement over the sleeping accommodations. There were no eating establishments in the town, so they were forced to eat what Joffre Struen was able to supply them, which consisted of a thick slice of dense wheat bread and a glass of warm ale with which to wash it down. It was less than satisfying, but it was probably the best that the stableman could manage, so neither Starks nor Paxon even thought about complaining.

When they were finished eating, they borrowed the horses once again, got directions to the mill, and set out. This time they rode east, traveling first on the main road and then turning off onto a rutted trail a quarter mile farther up. The trail ran parallel to a river that meandered its way into foothills that continued on toward distant mountains. There were no other people on the road, and only twice did they see any buildings—once, a shed nearly hidden from sight within a grove of fir, and later on a cabin that showed little upkeep and no indication of life.

Paxon kept searching the landscape they passed through, thinking to spy out a meaningful sign. But all he saw were glimpses of swift birds and squirrels in the trees and stationary cows in the pastures.

At the end of the road, the mill sat flush against the river, its great waterwheel turning slowly with the current, the grindstone groaning like a great beast from inside the building that housed it. They rode to within a dozen yards of the mill before spying the cottage behind it. They dismounted there, leaving their horses and walking up to the mill.

Within the near darkness, a shadow moved and the miller emerged.

"Well met, sirs," he said cheerfully, coming up to them and shaking their hands. "I thought you might be coming out this way eventually. I'm Crombie Joh."

He was a big, burly man with a shock of black hair, his shoulders massive, his hands callused and hard. He had lively eyes that shifted back and forth between his visitors, but never left their faces. His grin was open and welcoming.

Starks gave his name and Paxon's. "Is it true your daughter was here when it happened?"

The man sighed. "Iantha. Yes. The boy was more than a casual friend, I think. She doesn't like to talk about it. He had come while I was away. He was just leaving, and she had gone back inside. She heard the screams, ran to the door, and saw him pinned to the ground with something ripping at him. She knew right away what it was. She'd heard about the others. So she ran back inside and hid in the cellar until it was done."

"There was nothing she could do," Starks offered. Paxon wasn't sure if it was a statement or a question or even how it was intended.

"Nothing. Nothing anyone can do about a thing like that. Have you any ideas about this?"

"One or two."

"The townspeople don't trust the Druids. Don't like them, in fact. If it weren't for Joffre Struen, you wouldn't be here at all. I think it's a good thing you are."

"Were you out at the Carbenae place the other day?" Starks asked him, smiling.

The miller nodded. "Took them a load of feed. Midafternoon or maybe a little later when I got there. Didn't stay long. Left to get back in time for dinner. I was worried about Iantha, too. Don't like leaving her alone anymore since . . ." He trailed off with a shrug.

From the shadows behind him, a girl suddenly emerged. She was younger than Paxon by a few years, slender and pretty, her hair a soft dark brown, her eyes quick like her father's. She came forward a few steps and stopped, as if waiting for permission to approach.

"Iantha, come here," her father urged, holding out his hand.

She crossed the room, her eyes fixed on them, tentative in a way Paxon found endearing, but also troubling. She reached them and stopped.

"These are Druids, Iantha," her father told her. "Would you please tell them briefly what you saw that day? Just what you can manage, girl."

In a halting voice, Iantha related the events immediately leading up to the departure of the young man and his subsequent killing. She could not describe the creature or offer much in the way of details about the killing. She had gone into hiding at once, terrified of what might happen to her.

Indeed, she looked appropriately terrified even now, talking about it. She looked at the ground while she told her tale and kept her hands clasped tightly in front of her.

When she was done, Starks asked if she could show them where everything took place. She nodded without speaking and led them outside the mill and up to the yard fronting the cottage. She pointed out where her young man had mounted his horse and started to ride away. She showed them where she was standing on the cottage porch before she turned to go back inside. She walked them over to where the killing had occurred, although she would not go close to the stained, rutted earth.

Starks went over and knelt next to the killing ground, searching it carefully. The miller joined him, offering bits and pieces of information.

Iantha moved over beside Paxon and stood looking at him. "You seem nice," she said after a minute.

Paxon met her intense gaze. "I should be saying that about you, Iantha."

"Will you be my friend?"

He hesitated, confused by this. "Of course. But you must have lots of friends."

"My father doesn't want me to have friends."

He glanced over at the miller, who was suddenly looking right at him. "Why would that be?"

"He is afraid for me." Her voice was small, almost a whisper. "He thinks—"

"Iantha!" her father called out sharply. "Let the man be. He has work he needs to do."

Iantha moved away, head lowered. Paxon forced himself to smile at the miller. "She was just asking me about the Druids," he said.

The miller turned away, his attention on Starks once more. The Druid had risen and was looking around. Paxon glanced once more at Iantha, then walked over to join him.

"We should move along," he said to Starks—a completely inappropriate remark to a superior from a subordinate, but the miller wouldn't know this, and he wanted to get Starks alone.

The Druid nodded. "We might want to speak with you again later," he told the miller, extending his hand. "Thank you for your help. And for yours, as well, Iantha," he added.

They left the miller and his daughter standing in the yard of their cottage, walked back down to where they had left their horses, and mounted them. Starks took a last look around, saying as he did so, "Did you learn something you want to share?"

As they rode back down the trail, Paxon told him of his brief conversation with the girl. "She seems frightened. I don't know what's troubling her, but something is."

"We might infer that it has something to do with her father's story about visiting the Carbenacs to deliver grain and then leaving just before they were killed. Yet there was a third place setting at the table. It doesn't feel like we are being told everything, does it?"

"I would like to get Iantha alone for a few minutes,"

Paxon said a moment later. "She might say more when her father isn't around."

Starks nodded, urging his horse ahead. "Let's see what we can do."

They spent the remainder of the day visiting the sites of the other killings and speaking with the few people who had actually seen the creature responsible. All described it as wolfish and walking upright. No one had gotten a close, clear look at its face. All of the sightings had been at night and in shadows. One man said he had witnessed the creature ambush a rider who had passed him on the road while he was walking the other way. He said that when the creature was done with its victim, it had loped back into the trees, changing into something less animal and more human even as it did so.

They went back into the village to continue their search for further information, but everything had pretty much dried up. Even Joffre Struen, though trying to be helpful, could not think of anything to add that would help their efforts.

"What do you think causes the beast to change?" Paxon asked Starks as they sat in one of the two taverns the town had to offer, drinking from tankards of ale and mulling things over. "You said you believed it was spontaneous. But wouldn't something have to happen to trigger a reaction that severe?"

"You would think so," Starks agreed. His black robes were rumpled and sweat-stained, and his face was streaked with dust. "But I don't know what it is yet."

Paxon knew he was as grimy as the Druid, and he wanted to take a bath before eating anything—assuming they could find food somewhere. But mostly he wanted to know more about the girl, Iantha.

"Do you think we could go back there tonight?" he asked after a few minutes of silence.

"The miller's?" Starks shrugged. "I suppose. It will be dark, though. Are you hoping to catch the creature in mid-change?"

Paxon shook his head no. "I just want to talk to the girl again. I'm worried about her."

"She does seem a bit frail. She said he is afraid for her? Why would that be?"

"That's one of my questions." Paxon leaned back in his chair. "Do you think you can decoy him away for a few minutes when we go back?"

They talked about how to do so, already decided that waiting around until tomorrow was a waste of time and that going tonight made better sense. There was no guarantee the creature killing the villagers would delay doing so again, so the quicker they got to the bottom of this, the better.

"I still don't understand the nature of the magic involved," Paxon said a bit later. "If it isn't a talisman, how are we supposed to recover it? Killing the creature won't give it to us, will it?"

Starks shrugged. "I don't know. The Ard Rhys made it plain enough that the killings were to be stopped, no matter what. I have accepted those marching orders and put aside any consideration of recovering magic until afterward. There are all kinds of magic, Paxon. This is a new one, although I would guess that somewhere in the Druid Histories there is a record of one similar. Magic doesn't live in a vacuum; it always has a traceable source."

They finished their ale and then thought to ask the tavern owner if they could get dinner. He said that the answer was usually no but his wife was making a roast and for a reasonable price they might share it. Both Starks and Paxon were quick to agree, even though the price asked was considerably more than a meal would normally cost.

So they remained at the tavern through dinner, and then set out for the miller's place. They rode through the twilight toward the purple-and-gray foothills, turned off on the trail that paralleled the river, and arrived just before nightfall at the mill. The air was cool and windless, and the night birds were still. In the darkness before them, bats flew in sudden bursts from the trees and eaves of the house.

Just before they started to dismount, Paxon turned to Starks. "Do you think there is a possibility Crombie Joh might be this creature?"

Starks gave him a careful look. "I think anyone and everyone might be this creature. Remember that."

They walked up to the veranda, and Joh appeared in the doorway before they reached it. "Kind of late for a visit, isn't it?" he asked.

"We're trying to make the best use of our time," Starks said vaguely, greeting him with a handshake. "A few more things came to mind. I thought we could walk down to the mill to talk about them. Paxon can stay here with your daughter, just to be sure she's kept safe and sound while you're gone."

The miller frowned. "She could go with us. She should, I think."

"It might be best if she stays behind. What I have to tell you is not fit for young ears. It will remind her of the very things you've already said she needs to forget."

"Did I say that? Well, I suppose I did." He looked discomfited. "All right. If this doesn't take too long."

"I'll wait here on the porch," Paxon announced, already moving over to seat himself. "Unless you think she needs me to come in."

"No, no, you're fine where you are." The big man hesitated, then started walking. "Just for a few minutes, though."

Paxon sat alone in the darkness, conscious of the

weight of his sword where it pressed against his back, a comforting presence. His eyes were sufficiently adjusted to the darkness by now that he could see almost everything clearly in the mix of light from the quarter moon and stars. He could hear the steady rippling of the river as it flowed past the cottage some thirty feet away, its movement casting a silvery sheen in the moonlight.

Not a minute had passed before Iantha came through the door and sat down beside him.

"You came back," she said. Her eyes were huge in the darkness, her fine dark hair like a veil where it spilled over her face.

"I was worried about you. I didn't like what you had to say about your father. Why wouldn't he want you to have friends?"

"He's just trying to protect me. But I suppose it could be something else."

He waited, but she didn't say anything more. "Are you afraid of him?"

She stared at him. "What an odd question. No, I'm not afraid of him. He's my father. I'm just worried about him."

"Why?"

She shrugged. "He takes too many chances. He's brave, and he's strong, so he thinks nothing can hurt him."

"Like the creature that's doing these killings?"

She hesitated. "Maybe. Maybe something else."

She looked over at him and then without warning kissed him on the mouth, her hands gripping his arms to hold him to her. When she released him, there was a smile on her lips. "Did you like it?"

He smiled back. "Of course. But why kiss me?"

"Because. I told you already. You are nice. I like you."

"You don't even know me."

"You don't kiss people because you know them. You kiss them because you want to."

He wasn't sure that was so for most people, but maybe it was for her. They sat together in silence for a few moments, and then he said, "Why do you think your friend was killed by the creature?"

She shook her head. "I don't know. Maybe he did something to make it angry. Maybe he did something he shouldn't have."

"What about the other people? Did they all do something to make it angry?"

"I wouldn't know. I'm only guessing." She looked at him again. "Do you think it killed them for no reason?"

"I don't know why it kills. Maybe it was random. Maybe it just kills because it likes killing."

"That would make it difficult to find, wouldn't it?" she asked. "How would you ever find it? Unless you happened to be right there when it tried to kill someone, you never could."

"Oh, we'll find it," he replied.

Starks and her father were coming back from the mill, their dark forms emerging from the darkness. "Do you want me to come back tomorrow?" he asked her suddenly.

She leaned into him. "Yes. Father will be gone for several hours in the early afternoon, making deliveries. We could talk more then." She hesitated. "I have things I need to tell you."

She stood suddenly, pulling him up with her. "I like you, Paxon. I like you a lot."

Then she turned and ran back inside the cabin and did not come out again.

12

At noon of the following day, Paxon rode out alone to the old mill, taking his time as he went. The day was gray and cloudy, the smell of rain in the air, the dampness palpable on the chilly wind that blew down out of the north. Paxon was thinking about what waited, his mind on unanswered questions, some of which he would ask, some he might not. The answers he anticipated receiving did not put him in a good mood. His suspicions were aroused, had been so since last night, and his expectation of what he would find out today depressed him. But he was protector for the Druids, and so he would do what he knew he must to put an end to the creature.

He had talked it over with Starks after they had returned from Crombie Joh's mill yesterday, deeply concerned for the girl Iantha, worried that she was in considerable danger. It seemed obvious to him by now that the miller was the creature they were hunting, and his daughter knew it and was looking for a way to get away from him. Starks wondered why she hadn't been attacked before now, though he guessed maybe her father could distinguish between her and anyone else when he was the creature. But he agreed after hearing the details of her conversation with Paxon that there was cause for concern for her welfare and that something needed to be done.

"If I can be alone with her for an hour—with no danger of her father interfering—I think I can find out the truth," Paxon had insisted. "I think Iantha will tell me the truth."

Starks wasn't so sure, but he had agreed to let Paxon try. "You'll have to go alone," he had said. "She likely won't talk to you if I'm there. But you be careful, Paxon. We still don't know what's happening here. I know you like this girl, but she may be more under her father's control than you realize. She may even betray you to him."

But Paxon did not think this was so, believing instead that this was a chance to help someone who desperately needed it. With his sword to protect him, he felt more than capable of carrying out his effort to uncover the truth.

As he neared the mill, he slowed his mount, careful to keep watch and to listen for the miller's wagon. He believed the man had already gone to make his deliveries, but he couldn't take anything for granted. If he was seen, he would have to turn back. He couldn't let Joh discover he had been to visit Iantha secretly. Not without first knowing if his suspicions were correct.

But when he passed by the old mill and approached the cottage, he found Iantha waiting for him, already seated on the steps of the porch. She rushed up to him at once and took his hands in hers. "Tie up your horse in the trees across the way," she told him, a note of urgency in her voice. "Father is already gone, but if he should come back early, he won't know you're here."

Paxon did as she asked, then walked back over to the porch to sit with her. She went into the house and returned again with glasses of cold ale and a plate of fresh bread. "I'm so glad you came back, Paxon," she said, sitting close to him. "I feel so much better when you're here." She glanced at him shyly. "You must think me very forward."

"I think you are scared," he replied, his eyes on her face. "I came back because I wanted to see you, but also because I am worried about you. Do you have something to say about that?"

She seemed almost ready to speak, but then there was a hesitation in her response and a tightening of her shoulders. She shook her head. "Can we talk about something else first? Tell me about Paranor!"

He did, anxious to put her at ease, to give her a chance to collect herself so she could tell him what she knew. It would not be easy, talking about her father, revealing him as the creature that was killing the villagers. In spite of what he was, he expected she loved him and had been protecting him for some time now. She would know something was wrong, living with him as she was, and she would be torn between her love for him and her need to tell someone what he was.

They spoke together quietly for the better part of an hour, Paxon giving descriptions of the Druid's Keep, providing entertaining stories about various Druids, even giving her a brief explanation detailing his own training for the order. She was fascinated by everything—her eyes wide, her enthusiasm unbounded, and her questions unending. How did this happen? What did you do then? Were you ever frightened by what might become of you? On and on. But he could feel her loosening up, and it would not be long now before she was ready to talk to him about her father.

Still, he was aware of time slipping away; neither of them could be certain how much of it they had left. Patience was one thing, but unreasonable delay was another. Paxon needed to persuade her to talk to him before doing so became too dangerous.

So, finally, he took her hands in his and gently

squeezed them. "We have to talk about your father now. I need you to tell me the truth about him. You said you were frightened. What is it that frightens you?"

She dipped her head again, a protective gesture, and for a long time she didn't speak. She let him hold her hands and once or twice she squeezed them back, but her face remained hidden in the veil of her long brown hair.

"This is very hard," she said finally.

He nodded, waiting on her. She leaned forward suddenly and kissed him again. In spite of the circumstances, he found himself kissing her back.

"I like you so much," she said, breaking the kiss. "You are kind and patient with me. I'm going to hate it when you are gone. I will miss you."

"Just tell me," he encouraged her.

She shook her head. There were tears in her eyes. "I don't know how!"

"Does your father have something to do with all the killings that have happened in Eusta?" he tried, thinking a nudge might help.

She clenched her fists. "We shouldn't talk about this, Paxon. You should forget I said anything. In fact, you should leave now. My father will be back soon, and I don't want him to find you here. I'm sorry."

Paxon hesitated only a moment, and then he took hold of her by her upper arms and held her firmly in front of him. "You brought me out here to tell me something. I came because I believed you. This isn't going to go away, and neither am I. The killings have to stop, and if your father has something to do with them, Starks and I are going to find out."

Her eyes were suddenly wild. "You don't know what you are talking about! You don't know what you are saying!"

He nodded, holding her gaze. "Then tell me. Tell me

why your father isn't involved. Tell me where I am wrong. But I'm not leaving until you tell me something!"

She sagged in his grip, her head drooping. "I didn't want this to happen!" she wailed. "I only wanted you to like me. To be a friend! To talk to me! I just said whatever came into my head so you would come back. Can't you leave it at that? Can't you?"

"No, I don't think he can," a voice said from behind Paxon. He turned to look, and there was Crombie Joh, standing in the shadows less than ten feet away, hands on hips, face grim. "I told you that, Iantha. I told you he would keep after you until he found out everything."

"Everything?" Paxon echoed, taking his hands off Iantha and bracing himself as he faced her father.

The big man shrugged. A light rain had begun to fall, and his features were indistinct in the mix of gray light and shadows. He had the look of something more wraith than human. Yet his voice was the same, and his build hadn't changed.

"I knew you would come out here as soon as she told you I was leaving to make deliveries. Why did you do that? She likes you; she doesn't want to see you get hurt. And now you almost certainly will." An audible sigh escaped his lips. "Where is your companion?"

"On his way to join me," Paxon said quickly.

Joh frowned. "Oh, I doubt that. He would be with you now, if he was coming. He wouldn't be hanging back, biding his time. He let you come because you both thought Iantha would tell you what you wanted to hear about me. That I was the killer. That I was the changeling. That she had been covering up for me all along. Isn't that right? Isn't that what you were expecting her to tell you?"

"I thought she might want to help you."

Crombie Joh's laugh was mirthless. "That's very funny, Highlander. Very amusing."

Paxon got to his feet and drew out the Sword of Leah. He came down off the porch steps and advanced on the miller. "Why do you find it so funny? You don't believe she might want to help you?"

"Why, no, not at all. Exactly the opposite, in fact. I believe she wants to help me very much."

He was changing now, right in front of Paxon, his human form fading, something predatory and dangerous taking his place. The big body lengthened and stretched, the clothes shredding as bones and cartilage and muscles found new shapes and took on strange definitions. A wolf's head replaced Joh's own, jaws lengthening into a maw that was filled with gleaming teeth. Hands and feet became paws with great hooked claws. Dark, bristling tufts of hair sprouted all across the exposed parts of the strong body, up arms and down legs, covering head and shoulders until what Paxon beheld was all animal and nothing human.

Then, some inexplicable instinct—the Highlander never knew exactly where it came from or what triggered it—warned him to turn. It was so strong he flinched from its impact as he spun around, his sword held protectively in front of him.

Iantha was gone. In her place was another of the creatures.

"Shades!" Paxon whispered, not quite believing what he was seeing, not ready to accept what it meant.

There were two of them.

Both father and daughter were changelings.

This realization took place in a split second, and then Iantha was on him. There was no hesitation, no suggestion of any regret. She was no longer human; she was a predatory creature consumed by a bloodlust that swept away any other consideration. She meant to kill him on the spot, and she would have done so if his sword had not saved him. But the magic responded instantly to the threat, throwing up a burst of power that blocked the claws and teeth that slashed and bit at Paxon and would have crippled him. The force of the attack was blunted, but it threw the Highlander backward to the ground while at the same time causing Iantha to howl in rage and go tumbling away.

Paxon was aware of only bits and pieces of what followed next. As he struggled to rise, he caught a glimpse of Crombie Joh coming for him from the other direction, a bigger, stronger threat bearing down with growls and snarls, jaws split wide. Then a second explosion erupted, intercepting him, this one all white fire and blinding light that seemed to come out of nowhere. For an instant the gray light and heavy shadows vanished, the rain evaporated, and the world disappeared.

And there was Starks, emerging from the brightness even as it faded back into the day's gloom and damp, striding toward him, arms extended, smoke tendrils curling from his fingertips. The miller rose, shifted his attack to the Druid, and barreled toward his intended victim with terrible intent and unstoppable fury.

Paxon tried to find his way back to his feet, but his entire body felt as if a great weight had rendered it useless. His limbs had become soft clay, and his thoughts were scrambled and scattered. He was surprised to find blood all over the front of his tunic and down one arm, and he was suddenly aware of pain washing through him. In spite of his sword's magic and all his training from Oost, Iantha's attack had broken through his defenses.

Shaken by the realization and momentarily rendered too weak to arise, he watched helplessly as Crombie Joh launched himself at Starks, a huge and implacable threat. But Starks was equal to it, sidestepping the creature with practiced ease and sending a second explosion of fire into the side of its head. The miller screamed as the blow threw him off balance and sent him sprawling in the damp earth. His massive form crumbled, shaking all over, bristling hair singed and smoking. Starks followed him down, another blast of Druid Fire hitting the other's wolfish head. And then another.

All at once Crombie Joh was on fire, the flames consuming his now writhing body, fur and flesh alike blackened and smoking. The miller screamed and tried to rise. But his great strength was no match for the damage that had been done to him, and finally he fell back and lay still.

Starks wheeled on Paxon, gesturing. "Go after her!"

Paxon scrambled up, catching a glimpse of Iantha fleeing into the trees, her lupine form bounding through the shadows. He broke into a run, recovered enough now to give pursuit, his sword gripped tightly in his hand. A part of him was reluctant to hunt her like this, but he knew he had to. Even racing after her through the woods, through the layered shadows and clouded gloom, he recalled the young girl eager for his company. A lie, he told himself. But maybe not entirely.

He had planned it all with Starks ahead of time. The miller was the creature. They were convinced of it. The daughter was his accomplice, willing or no. She had told Paxon to come to her when her father was away, but Starks didn't think events would necessarily turn out as she had promised. So while Paxon would be allowed to go alone, Starks would follow and be there just in case the Highlander was being lured into a trap.

Which, in fact, was what had happened. What they hadn't counted on, what they hadn't considered, was that Iantha was another of the creatures, and that father and daughter had been killing the townspeople of Eusta together. Paxon could still hardly believe it. The shock of finding her changed and trying to rip him apart remained a sharp-edged memory in his head, tearing at him.

So now she must be stopped. She must be killed.

I do not want to do this.

I do not want to hurt her.

Conflicting thoughts warred within him. The race to catch her had taken him deep into the woods by now. Starks and the old mill were well behind him and out of sight. He was on his own. *Be careful,* he warned himself. *Remember what she is. Remember what she tried to do.* He could no longer see her up ahead, although he could hear her crashing through the brush and see the damage her passing had done.

And see the blood spots, too. She was injured.

Suddenly he was aware that he could no longer hear her. The world around him had gone silent save for the patter of the rain against the leaves and the sound of his breathing. He slowed and then stopped, listening. She was waiting for him. Perhaps in ambush, intending to catch him off guard, coming in reckless pursuit, giving her a chance to finish what she had started.

He moved ahead cautiously, searching the shadows, paying attention to every sound. Nothing. The trail of crushed grasses and blood spatters continued, so he knew he was going in the right direction. The trail had moved away from the deep woods and was now heading for the river. The trees were opening ahead of him to reveal the silver-tipped waters, and the danger of an ambush was fading. He picked up his pace. He could sense that she was near.

He found her at the river's edge, collapsed in a heap. She had reverted to human form, her clothes in tatters and blood everywhere. His sword had done more damage than he realized when it had deflected her attack. She was watching him come toward her, but making no move to do anything about it. Her hands were empty; she had no weapons.

He knelt beside her, and she gave him a weak smile. "I'm sorry, Paxon. I didn't want to hurt you."

"You should have told me," he said. "Maybe I could have helped you."

She shook her head. "There is no help for things like me. Father has been searching for a cure for years. Neither of us wanted this life. This curse. We change without warning. We do it together and separately both. We can't stop it."

She was dying, he realized. He fought down a sudden wave of anguish. "I know this. I know you wouldn't hurt me if you could help it."

Her voice was surprisingly strong. "It was the gemstone. Father found it two years ago buried beneath the house—beautiful and mysterious and glowing, like nothing he had imagined possible. He believed it to be a treasure of great worth. He thought we could sell it and become rich. He brought it inside the house and showed it to me. While he stood there, holding it in his hands, he was compelled to kiss it. It poisoned him. He didn't know it at the time, but he found out soon enough. The urge to kill consumed him after that. He tried to fight it, but it was too strong. He needed the relief the killing gave him. In those early days, he made his kills far away from Eusta, traveling to other villages. But after a while he couldn't manage to wait until he was far away and began killing our neighbors."

She coughed, and there was blood on her lips. "For a long time, I knew nothing of what had happened to him. The killings were still taking place far away, and he never spoke of them. And the change never came to me, even though I had kissed the gemstone, too. My father thought I might not have the curse. But eight months ago, it showed itself. I changed for the first time.

It happened while Father was away, and the urge to kill overcame me and I acted on it. I didn't know what to do; I was terrified. When finally I admitted it to my father, he told me the truth. He and I were the same."

She was crying softly. "He tried to protect me. But he couldn't even protect himself. We were the same, and we killed together, father and daughter. We shared in the bloodlettings. Neither of us could stop; neither of us could help the other."

She closed her eyes. "It hurts," she whispered, and he knew she was speaking of the pain her memories caused her.

He took her hands in his and held them. It was raining again, the droplets running down her anguished face. "Just rest a moment."

"Father is dead, isn't he?"

"I think he is."

"This will end it, then. Once I'm gone." Her eyes opened. "Find the gemstone, Paxon. Don't touch it. Just take it and destroy it. Promise me."

He nodded. "I will."

Her blood was soaking into the ground all around her, and her skin was growing whiter. "I could have loved you. I did love you. You were so nice. I just wanted you to be my friend. I didn't want to hurt you, even when I knew I would, I tried not to, Paxon."

Her eyes fixed in an unseeing stare, and she quit breathing.

"I know you did," he whispered, and released her hands.

He carried her body back to the mill and found Starks just getting ready to come after him. Together, they buried father and daughter in the deep woods, and then they began searching the cottage for the gemstone Iantha had warned about. It took them a long time to find it. Joh had hidden it well, perhaps because he was afraid of its power and wanted to protect against anyone else stumbling on it. They had to conduct their search cautiously because they didn't want to touch it accidentally in the process of finding it. They located it finally at the back of a cabinet in the miller's bedroom beneath a false drawer bottom. It was a wicked-looking thing, an irregularly shaped black orb with dozens of facets, their mirrored surfaces flecked with gold shards that glimmered and sparked like bits of dancing fire.

"A passive magic," Starks said, studying it carefully without touching it, using Druid magic to probe and reveal. "That's why it didn't register on the scrye. It only comes awake when the stone is touched. Otherwise, it lies dormant."

"Where did it come from?" Paxon said. "Who would have made such a thing? Or is it just an aberrant magic?"

Starks shook his head. "I doubt that we will ever know. What matters is what we do with it now."

He pulled the cabinet drawer all the way out and dumped the gemstone onto the cottage floor. He used the toe of his boot to roll it into a leather pouch, which he then stuffed into a worn feed bag he found in the mill. He rolled up the feed bag and its deadly contents into a tight ball and bound it with twine.

"That should keep it safe until we get it back to Paranor."

"What do we tell the townspeople?" Paxon asked.

Starks shook his head. "Not the truth. They wouldn't accept it. They wouldn't want to live with it. They would spend the rest of their lives wondering who else might be infected."

Paxon understood. "Well, we'll have to think of something to tell them that explains both the creature and the disappearance of Iantha and her father."

They talked about it at length as they rode back to the

village. Finally, Starks said they would offer a version of the truth. They would say they found out the miller and his daughter were the creature's next victims and tried to save them, but failed. Both died, but the creature was distracted long enough for the Druids to kill it. The creature was a changeling that assumed the shape of a wolf, as the witnesses had described. But it was dead now, and there was no further danger to anyone.

So they rode back into Eusta and returned the horses to Joffre Struen, giving him the details of the agreed-upon explanation and leaving it to him to tell the rest of the townspeople. Starks made it a point to remind him they were always available to come help should the need arise, and to tell the others not to be afraid or suspicious of the Druids. They were friends, and they would help if they could.

"About two out of five will believe that," Starks commented as they walked back to the spot where they had left the airship. "But that number's up from what it was before, and at the end of the day the problem is the same. We have to win the doubters, the disbelievers, and the antagonistic over one at a time."

They found the airship with no problem and boarded for home. Starks went back to his station in front of the pilot box and to his reading. After moving aimlessly about the decking for a time, Paxon settled down by the bowsprit to mull over what had happened. He kept thinking he should have realized the truth sooner; he could not shake the feeling he must have missed something he should have seen. Mostly, he thought of Iantha's young face and her eagerness to be liked—nothing you wouldn't find in any ordinary young girl. She hadn't been much older than Chrysallin, and it haunted him that a young girl's life could be cut short so easily and without any fault on her part. He realized anew how lucky he was to have gotten his sister free of Arcannen before something evil had happened to her.

He wished he could have done the same for Iantha.

He found himself wondering what the Ard Rhys would do with the deadly stone that had cost the girl and her father their lives. He hoped she would smash it into a thousand fragments and throw them into the sea.

Below him, the countryside passed away in a rolling carpet of plains and forests and fields with rivers angling through it all. The rain, which had started much earlier and continued to fall throughout the day, abated finally, but the gloom and a misty haze remained. Long before it became dark, they were enveloped in low-slung banks of clouds. Far away, distant from where they flew, lights began to appear in the towns and villages, fireflies against the closing darkness.

They spent that night in the Tirfing aboard ship. Paxon was unable to sleep, and he took the watch, sitting forward by the bowsprit once more, looking out over a countryside moonlit and calm beneath a clear sky, still troubled.

He was there only a short time when Starks came over to join him.

"Not happy with things, are you?" the Druid asked.

Paxon shook his head. "I should feel better about this than I do."

"You were sent to protect me, and you did. You were sent to help me find and destroy the creature that was killing the people of Eusta, and you did. You were sent to bring back whatever magic was at work, and you have." Starks nodded to himself. "That's as much as you can expect, Paxon. You might wish it made you feel better, but that isn't always how it is afterward. You have to accept that."

"I know. But I can't forget how she looked when she

was dying. She was a victim of what that gemstone had done to her. She wasn't a bad person. She was a victim. She shouldn't have had that happen to her."

"No one should. But life isn't fair, and the right thing doesn't always happen. You know that."

Paxon didn't respond. He did know. But he didn't like it, and he wasn't happy about how it left him hollowed out and dissatisfied.

"It just doesn't feel like we did as much as we could."

Starks gave him a nod. "This is how it is. Sometimes, it isn't so satisfying. Sometimes, people die. We do what we can, Paxon. You have to be at peace with that. If you think you need more, you shouldn't be doing this." He paused. "Maybe you should give that some thought."

He rose. "But I think you are doing exactly what you should be doing. You did well back there. You showed courage and intelligence. You have my approval even if you don't have your own. I'm going to bed. You should do the same."

He disappeared below, leaving Paxon to consider how much of what he had just heard he believed.

They reached Paranor by midafternoon of the following day. Starks told Paxon to go clean up while he gave his report and the sack containing the dangerous gemstone to the Ard Rhys. She would want to see him later, but he might as well look and smell a little better before that happened.

So Paxon washed and dressed in fresh clothes, then walked down to the dining hall to find something to eat. He was midway through an especially wonderful potato leek soup when Starks reappeared.

"She would like to see you right away," he said. He did not look happy.

Paxon didn't miss it. "What's wrong?"

"It would be better if she explained. Go to her working chambers. She's waiting for you there."

Paxon left the table and his half-eaten meal and went down the hallways and up the stairs of the Keep until he reached the door that opened to her chambers. He paused, a premonition already telling him that this was bad.

When he knocked, she called out at once. "Come in, Paxon."

He did, and found her at her desk, immersed once more in paperwork. The trussed-up feed bag containing the gemstone sat to one side. His eyes went to it immediately, and she gave him a tired smile. "You want to know what I will do with it?"

"Yes," he admitted.

"It will be sealed away in a special compartment in the catacombs beneath the Keep. We have others of this sort down there, as well." She paused. "We would destroy it, if we could, but such magic released from the confines of the stone would spread to other places and take other forms. We could end up with more than one dark magic, and it might even prove more dangerous than it is now."

"So you can't destroy it?"

She shook her head no. "Only contain it. But that's usually enough. Sit down."

He sat, waiting for her to say something more.

"As you know, we sent someone to keep watch over your sister and mother, just in case Arcannen returned. Sebec made the arrangements himself. He sent one of our own, a young Druid with only a year's experience in using magic, but life skills that made him a good choice. He was to shadow your sister and mother, and he was to make sure nothing happened to them."

She paused. "Yesterday, he was found dead on the streets of the city. It was made to appear as if he was the victim of a theft, but those who found him and reported back to us say it was something more. Whatever else it was, it wasn't a robbery. There were signs of magic in play. He was deliberately killed."

"My sister?" he asked quickly.

She gave him a steady look. "She's disappeared."

13

CHRYSALLIN LEAH WOKE TO A ROOM FILLED WITH shadows and emptiness, the only light seeping in through narrow cracks in a tightly shuttered window, the only sounds those she made when she stirred far enough to discover she was chained to the bed she was lying on. Her head was filled with cotton and her mouth was dry, but there was no cure on hand for either condition. She tested her limbs against the chains and found the former drained of strength and the latter secure. She was not going to change either condition right away no matter what she tried.

She lay back reluctantly, stretching her long legs and torso and waiting for her lethargy to fade, wondering where she was.

Or how she had gotten there, for that matter.

The events leading up to her present situation were far from clear. She remembered going to the Brew Tide to help Jayet. That had been later in the afternoon, when the tavern was just starting to fill up. The crowd had been boisterous and impatient. Everyone wanted to get served at once, and no one was prepared to wait. She was flying around the room, caught up in the excitement and laughter of the drinkers, smiling and joking with them, and loving every minute. Later that night, she and Jayet would go down to the river for a private swim. The cool water would wash away the sweat and the smoke and the tavern smells, and the day would come to a pleasant, relaxing close.

But the swim had never happened. What had? She had been serving the customers, carrying trays with tankards of ale and bowls of soup and plates of bread, and then . . .

She had gone outside. Just for a moment, to get a breath of fresh air, to escape the din.

And that was the last thing she could remember.

Now she was a prisoner in a dark room, snatched away from her friends and home without explanation, brought here for no apparent reason, chained to a bed in this dark room.

Except that right away she thought of Arcannen and the last time this had happened. Even if it had happened in a slightly different way, it still felt the same and she could not help thinking that once again this was the sorcerer's doing. She pondered the idea for long minutes. If it was Arcannen, was this still about the gambling debt she hadn't settled? Or was this an attempt to get at her brother? Was the sorcerer using her to get revenge on Paxon for what had happened at Dark House? She still wasn't sure what it was all about the first time. Had the sorcerer been after her for making a bet she couldn't pay and wanting to teach her a lesson, or was he after Paxon for reasons that were never made clear?

Whatever the case, she was beginning to grow steadily more certain that it was the sorcerer who had snatched her away.

She glanced down at herself in dismay, aware suddenly of a chill she hadn't noticed before. Sure enough, beneath the thin sheet that covered her, she was naked. Every last stitch of clothing had been removed. She gritted her teeth. Very likely she was back in Dark House, and whatever Arcannen's intentions, it would be a lot more difficult for Paxon to come to her rescue this time.

Chrysallin might have been only fifteen, but she was tough-minded and confident, more a young woman than a girl. She had grown up wild and reckless, and there wasn't much she hadn't tried. Constantly in trouble for one thing or another, she had learned much of what she knew the hard way. She had taught herself how to stand up to anyone, how to behave when she was threatened, and how to accept punishment when it was unavoidable. So she was not about to start panicking now. She was less than pleased that her clothes had been removed, but it was not cause for losing control.

Not yet, at least.

She took a deep breath and released it with a shudder. Someone was fumbling with the door handle. A key was being fitted into a lock and turning. She heard the lock release and watched the door open.

Sure enough, Arcannen stood in the opening, wrapped in his black robes and backlit by the hall light. He studied her momentarily in a casual, indifferent way and then came into the room, closing the door behind him. A quick touch to smokeless lamps on either side of the door chased the darkness away sufficiently that he and his prisoner could see each other.

"You seem to be doing fine," he observed. There was a touch of humor in his voice. "For someone chained naked to a bed."

"My brother will come for you," she said quietly, keeping her gaze locked on his.

"I certainly hope so. That's been my intention all along."

"So you were never really interested in collecting that gambling debt? That was just an excuse for luring my brother to Wayford?"

He crossed the room and sat down next to her on the edge of the bed, then reached out and ran his hand over her leg and up her thigh to her breast. "Oh, I wouldn't say that. Having you here promises to be lots of fun."

She felt a chill sweep through her, but managed to keep from showing what she was feeling. "You made that threat before. This is probably the best someone like you can do. A girl chained to the bed is the only way you'll ever get close to any woman."

He pursed his lips, a sneer forming. "Or in your case, any girl. But don't worry. I won't do anything to you. I won't make you work in the pleasure stalls or scrub the floors or service my guards. That's not for you. I want you in perfect shape for when your brother comes to trade for you."

She stared at him, the pieces suddenly coming together. "You want his sword. That's what you were after before, but you didn't get it. So you are still trying, aren't you? Me for the sword—that's the bargain you're hoping to make."

The hawkish features tightened. "The bargain I *will* make, Chrysallin. Your brother will give anything to get you back in one piece. Only this time I won't be caught off guard by his promises. And you won't be taken away quite so easily. This time things will be a little different."

She gave him a look, her resolve tightening. "Can you hurry it up? Or can you at least give me some clothes and take off these chains? How much trouble do you think a fifteen-year-old girl can be?"

"I'm not sure I want to find out. Chained to this bed and stripped of clothes, I don't think you can be much trouble at all. Dressed and let loose, perhaps a whole lot."

She searched her mind for an argument. "I have to eat and bathe and use the chamber pot or things will get really unpleasant. What if I give you my word I won't try to escape? What if I promise to wait until Paxon has a chance to come get me?"

Arcannen gave her a long, searching look and shrugged. "Not that I think you would keep your word for one minute, but you have a point about personal hygiene. Maybe we can reach a compromise."

He agreed to give her back her clothes and release all the chains but one clamped about her ankle, which would allow her to move about without leaving the room. Food and drink and water with which to bathe would be supplied. Guards would stand watch, but only come in to bring what she needed to eat and wash. She would give her word to stay put until he heard something from her brother.

She agreed readily—although he was right in supposing she didn't for one minute intend to keep her word about not trying to escape. He knew it, and she knew it. That wasn't how this game was played. If he wasn't putting her into the pleasure stalls or otherwise misusing her, he must consider her well-being important enough not to risk causing her harm.

"Of course, if you misbehave after enjoying my generosity of spirit, I will have to change the way I do things. Your living conditions could take a change for the worse rather quickly."

"What is it about that old sword?" she asked, ignoring him as he waited for her response to his threat. "Why is it so important to you?"

He shook his head. "Didn't your brother tell you? He didn't, I see. So why should I? Ask him when you see him. Ask him why he thinks I have gone to all this trouble to get hold of it. There's a mystery for you to solve, Chrysallin-of-the-many-questions. Why didn't I just steal it from you in the first place and have done with it? You don't have the faintest idea, do you?"

"No," she admitted.

He grinned wickedly. "If you change your mind about working here, just let the guards know. One of them will be in shortly to bring you clean clothes and release you from your chains. Behave yourself when he does."

Then he patted her arm, rose from the bed, and went out the door, locking it behind him.

He did not go far. Just down the hall and around the corner. Mischa was waiting in the shadows of an alcove leading to an outside balcony, eyes glittering with anticipation. "Is it done?"

He nodded. "I will tell the guard to bring her clothes and release her chains. All but the one that secures her ankle. Not that it will hold her for long. She will be out of it inside an hour. That girl is smart and determined. Are you sure this will work?"

"She is a better subject with those qualities than if she were slow-witted. She will be molded as you intend. She will become what you wish. A week's time, no more. Do you leave for Arishaig?"

"Tonight. Make sure you intercept her. Take her where you wish, but take her quickly." He paused. "And Mischa. Don't underestimate her."

The smile Mischa gave him was chilling. "She is no match for me, Arcannen. And you should know that I never underestimate anyone. So don't forget the terms of our agreement. I would be sad if you did, but you would be even sadder."

He stared at her a moment. "Threats now, is it? Just be certain you keep your end of the bargain."

Then he turned from her and continued on his way.

Arcannen had barely finished closing the door before Chrysallin was thinking of ways to escape. A single ankle chain and a lock on the door: Free herself of those and she was on her way home. The sorcerer was so smug, so convinced of his superiority over a fifteen-year-old girl that he believed her cowed. Or at least, he was convinced she would be unable to outwit him. Well, he was in for a surprise. She had no intention of waiting around for Paxon to come get her. She would be out of here and off to find him long before coming for her was necessary.

She lay back, thinking of Arcannen's face when he found her gone, imagining his rage. It made her want to laugh. It was too bad she couldn't be there to see it. But she brushed these images aside, reminding herself she wasn't free yet and that there were still obstacles to be overcome before she could take time to enjoy fantasies of Arcannen's unhappiness.

It wasn't long before the door opened again and a guard appeared with her clothes. He dumped them at the foot of her bed, released the locks and chains that bound her wrists—leaving the ankle chain in place—and departed without a word. She sat up and spent several minutes massaging her wrists, then slipped out from under the sheets and started to dress. Right away, she faced a problem. With a chain and cuff still fastened about her ankle, she couldn't put on her pants. Instead, she had to settle for slipping into her tunic and tying the sheet about her waist to use as a makeshift skirt.

Then she sat back down on the bed and felt carefully along the waistband of her pants until she found the tiny metal pick. Long and straight except where it curved at one end, it was a tool she always carried with her. Picking locks of one sort or another had become something of a specialty, although in this case it was more important than usual. Arcannen had left the lights on, so boosting her ankle and chain onto the bed provided her with enough light to pick the lock. It took her less than five minutes to free herself. Discarding the sheet, she pulled on her pants and boots, tucked the pick back into her waistband, and walked over to the door.

She stood there listening for a time, then carefully tried the handle.

Locked.

She looked around the room. What she needed was a weapon, but there wasn't anything at hand that would serve the purpose. She thought momentarily about the chain that had secured her ankle, but it was linked to a ring in the floor—and besides, it was too heavy for her to wield effectively. What she needed was some sort of club.

She looked around. There was not a stick of furniture in the room save for the bed, and the frame was metal.

Her jaw tightened.

She was not giving up.

Walking back to the door, she put her ear against the frame and listened through the crack. Nothing. She waited a moment, and then she knocked and called out, "Hey, can you come here a minute? I need help!"

There was no response. She waited a few minutes and then tried again. Still no response. Good enough.

Retrieving the pick from her waistband, she began working it around in the keyhole. It was harder going this time, the lock larger and less easily maneuvered. But in the end it gave a familiar *snick* and released.

Pocketing the lock pick, she gently twisted the handle and felt the latch give. Standing where she was, with the door partially cracked, she listened for sounds of someone waiting outside. When she heard nothing, she opened the door farther and took a cautious peek outside, looking first one way and then the other down a long hall. She was not anywhere she had been before. She was not anywhere she recognized. If she was back in Dark House, as she assumed, she had been taken to a different part of the building than where she had been kept before. This area was shadowy and empty feeling, as if no one was anywhere about.

Still, she took her time before she stepped from the room into the hallway and began edging her way carefully along the wall, stopping often to listen for the sounds of movement or voices. But everything was still. She had chosen to turn left, but she had no idea what way she should be going. She needed some sort of indicator to give her a sense of direction so she could figure out how to get free of the building.

When she reached the end of the hallway, she was facing a wall. No stairway led either up or down. She turned around in frustration, her fears heightening, and retraced her steps, working her way toward the other end of the corridor, forcing herself to keep her pace slow and steady. This time, she found that the hallway bent to the left, and in the dimness cast by the passage lights she could just catch sight of stairs leading down.

She was just starting ahead again—freedom in sight—when a door opened in front of her and an old woman emerged. The woman was bent and worn looking, dressed in a skirt and blouse that were stained and old, a scarf tying back her long gray hair, and high-top boots on her feet. She was hauling a bucket and mop, and she carried a collection of rags under one withered arm.

A cleaning woman, Chrys thought, freezing in place. Too late to go back or try to hide. She waited for the old woman to turn the other way, to not notice she was there.

Instead, the old woman turned directly toward her and froze. For long moments, the two just stared at each other.

Then Chrysallin raised a finger to her lips in a universally recognizable plea for silence. The old woman watched her, then nodded in agreement. Chrys moved in front, heading for the stairway. As she angled past, the old woman beckoned her to step close.

Leaning in, the other whispered, "There are guards at the bottom of the stairs. If you want out, there is a better way."

Chrys hesitated, then nodded. "Can you show me?" she whispered back.

The old woman nodded and wordlessly led her back the way she had come to a door she had already passed, opening it onto a hidden set of narrow steps. Motioning for her to follow, she led Chrys down three flights of stairs into a cellar crammed with boxes and smelling of damp and mildew. What light there was came from slits cut into the stone of the foundation walls, almost at ceiling height, and covered over with a heavy, diffuse glass.

The old woman led her across the cellar floor, winding through the stacks of boxes, avoiding places where water had pooled and cracks in the floor had opened. Once or twice, Chrysallin thought she saw movement in the shadows—quick and furtive. Rats. She stayed close to the old woman, her guide through this gloomy country she did not know. It took them a long time to reach the far end, and then they were at an old ironbound wooden door recessed deep in the stone of the wall. The old woman stopped there, released a series of locks and latches, and pulled the door open to the outside.

Chrys peered past the woman's stooped shoulders to a twilight in which stars were just beginning to come out in a darkening sky. In front of her, steps led upward to a street lined with houses and streetlamps. She could hear the distant sounds of voices and the movement of carriages and horses.

She could smell the fresh air of the city. She could taste her freedom.

She turned to the old woman who was watching her through rheumy eyes, hands clutched to her breast like a supplicant. "Go on, now," she hissed. "Run!"

Chrysallin almost bolted, but then she hesitated. "Will you tell me your name?"

The old woman smiled. "It's Mischa."

14

Expectations danced through Chrysallin's mind as she fled Dark House and Arcannen for places unknown but infinitely safer. She ran through the twilight and darkness toward freedom, thinking at first only to put distance between herself and her captors but then realizing a plan was necessary. Afoot, she could never hope to escape. She needed an airship in which to fly to her brother at Paranor. She needed to find the airfield she had found with Jayet the last time she was here.

It was not as difficult as she had imagined it would be. She remembered the route easily enough, and she found the landmarks that would guide her on her way. She tracked them successfully, one after the other, taking care to remain clear of crowds and unfriendly places, doing what she could to make herself invisible to those she passed. At first, her running drew unwanted attention, and so she slowed to a fast walk in places where there were crowds. But soon she was far enough outside the heart of the city that only a handful of other people appeared, and she broke into a run once more.

She was in sight of the airfield when the men came out of the shadows between buildings on both sides, and she was trapped. They swarmed over her, bearing her to the ground, pinning her arms and legs. She was tall and strong for a fifteen-year-old girl, and she was not easily taken. But in the end, she was taken nevertheless.

What happened after that was horrifying. She lost consciousness at one point while fighting to break free—a blow to the head delivered by one of her attackers that dropped her into a blackness in which she seemed to drift for a very long time. When she came awake, she was lying on a table in a darkened room, her arms and legs pinned in place by cuffs about her wrists that were pulled tight by ropes attached to rings set into the legs of the table. A sheet covered her, and her clothes were gone. Again. She was fuzzy-headed and oddly disoriented. She could barely make herself care about what was happening to her, although she was aware of her situation. She wondered who had her now. It had to be Arcannen and his minions, didn't it?

She tried to see through the darkness beyond where she lay, sensing there was someone present, hidden back in the gloom. But she couldn't make anything out. So she lay passively, having no other choice, waiting to see what would happen next.

She didn't have to wait long.

Almost as soon as she resolved to be patient, a door opened and men in hoods and robes entered the room. Smokeless torches were ignited on poles set at both ends of the table on which she lay, providing illumination that reached no farther than her immediate surroundings. The men—four in all—placed themselves at the corners of the table. None of them spoke. They just stood silently, looking down at her.

"Begin," said a muffled voice from the darkness.

They did. They went to work on her with callused hands, wooden clubs, metal implements, and vicious promises. They started with her feet and worked their way up her naked body. They left no part untouched. They were thorough and systematic in their efforts, and from the beginning it was clear they possessed neither sympathy nor compassion for her suffering. They hurt her every time they touched her. They hurt her in so many ways she lost count. She could not see what they were doing, and her inability to anticipate only added to her pain. She screamed and cried and begged them to stop, but nothing helped. It was as if they didn't hear her. It was certain that they didn't care. These were men who had done this before. They were men who enjoyed their work.

She passed out over and over, only to awaken in white-hot agony anew. The torture went on and on. The men paused several times to rest themselves, to drink from an aleskin, to throw water in her face, to wake her with slaps and harsh words, to rest arms grown weary with tightening and twisting and pressing and jamming. But mostly they kept at it. Time lost meaning for Chrysallin Leah. She pleaded for someone to tell her what was wanted. She begged to be told if this was punishment or an effort at persuasion. She gritted her teeth and tightened her muscles. She twisted and squirmed and hunched her body against what was being done to her.

She prayed after what must have been hours of suffering that she be allowed to die. Even death would be preferable to this.

When they finally stopped, backing away to admire their work perhaps, a tall figure stepped into view. Arcannen? But this was a woman, one she had never seen, her features arrogant and commanding, her posture rigid and upright. She was Elven, her hair gray, her face lined with age. She studied her captive for perhaps half a minute, made a few strange gestures, talked softly to herself as she did so, then turned and walked away.

Chrysallin was left alone then. The woman and the men departed, and the room was shrouded in darkness.

They had thrown the sheet over her once more, and she could feel the blood seep into the cloth and glue it to her skin. Her pain was a red-hot scream that flooded through her. She saw into the darkness through a screen of red, and there was a coppery taste in her mouth. She was certain the bones of toes and fingers were broken, but couldn't see them and was afraid to move them in any way that would let her know for sure. With this much pain, every brush against the tabletop was agony.

What was worse was the sense of defilement and emotional carnage. She was fifteen years old, and she had been subjected to things she had never imagined she would be forced to endure. Tears flowed down her cheeks at the thought of them. She was shaking with rage and pain and a terrible sense of loss.

Paxon would make them pay, she told herself. Paxon would do to them what they had done to her!

But how long would it be until Paxon reached her? How long before he could come to her rescue? All her plans of escape had vanished in the wake of the day's punishment. She no longer believed she could get free without Paxon's help; there was no other way. She had put herself in this situation the way she put herself in so many unfortunate situations—by overestimating her cleverness and skill, by reckless belief in her own ability to avoid anything. She had attempted to do what she had been told not to do, and now she was paying the price.

She thought for long minutes about the Elven woman who had watched it all. What did she have to do with Arcannen and her kidnapping? What did she have to do with any of this? She wanted something, but she seemed in no hurry to tell Chrysallin what it was. Today's torture had been an object lesson in the nature of control. She was letting Chrys know that she didn't care when she got what she wanted. What mattered was that

Chrysallin understood her captor could have anything she wanted from her, anytime she desired it. What she wanted the Highland girl to know was that she was in complete control.

That Chrysallin's life was in her hands.

They came for her again sometime later. She could not tell if it was day or night, but she thought it was a new day because she had slept and her pain had lessened marginally. They entered the room as before, the four men lighting the smokeless lamps at the head and foot of her table, and they ripped off the sheet without concern for the wounds that were torn open and the skin that was shredded. The woman slipped in while Chrysallin's screams were dying into whimpers, and the girl didn't even know she was there until she spoke.

"Begin," she said.

They did. All over again. It was a virtual repeat of the previous day, the pain beginning in her toes and working its way up her legs to her torso, and from there to her arms and head. It was a long, relentless assault on her body and mind, and there were times when she was awake that she thought she would go mad. On this second day, she blacked out repeatedly, which forced them to find more creative ways to bring her awake again so they could continue. A few new adaptations were applied, most involving underarms and ears. Burns were added to the repertoire of tortures, some applied with iron rods, some with coals. New damage was inflicted. Chrysallin could smell her own flesh burning. She could smell the stench.

At the end of this day, when the tall woman with the long gray hair and the Elven features came over to study her again, Chrysallin stared back, memorizing every feature, burning the hated features into her memory, wanting to be certain she would know her should she ever get out of this. She hated the woman with every fiber of her being, even more so than she hated the men that were carrying out her instructions. Chrysallin hated her enough that if she could have gotten free, she would have tried to kill her on the spot.

When the woman was gone, taking her creatures with her, Chrysallin was drained of energy and damp with sweat and blood. Her body throbbed and twitched with pain, and there was no relief to be found. Every shift of her limbs, however small, produced fresh agony. Attempts at waiting it out only caused her to be more aware of it. In the darkness, she could not see the damage that had been done, but she could tell it was considerable. She believed she would never look the same when this was over. She would be marked for life, both without and within. She would be rendered a shadow of who and what she had once been.

But she did not cry this night. She refused to cry. She would not let herself. Instead, she channeled her suffering into rage—a white-hot anger that made her want to scream and tear at things. She fed this rage with promises of what she would do to the gray-haired Elven woman once she was free. She gave it direction by thinking how she would inflict on her captor the same pain she was suffering. It was wishful thinking, but it gave her an outlet for her despair and for her need to respond and not feel entirely helpless. It gave her another life outside of the one she was enduring. It gave her a focus and a mission. She wasn't sure she could survive another day of what was being done to her, but she knew she was going to try if for no other reason than to deprive them of the satisfaction of watching her break apart. And, of course, the possibility of somehow gaining revenge.

She dreamed that night, and in her dreams she was in a desert crawling on her hands and knees across burning sands and jagged rocks, her body torn and bloodied and her strength almost exhausted. For as far as the eye could see, there was nothing but emptiness. No trees or water, no buildings, no people. Except that there was someone walking beside her as she crawled. When she managed to look up, she found it was her nemesis, the gray-haired Elven woman, keeping pace with her, glancing down now and then and smiling with satisfaction, showing no other emotion, saying nothing as they proceeded. The sun beat down, the heat rose off the carpet of the sand, and the woman never offered any of the water she drank from a skin she had slung across her shoulder.

The dream went on a long time—or at least it felt that way—past any semblance of reality, a steady progression of sameness meant to demonstrate what was already all too clear. Chrysallin's fate was out of her hands. Nothing was going to change. The suffering was going to continue.

And when she woke, brought out of her sleep by the reappearance of her captors for another round of torture, the dream became reality.

In the Federation capital city of Arishaig, Arcannen was visiting a variety of friends, associates, allies, and wielders of political power to whom he dispensed favors—or from whom he sought them. He had been connected to almost all of them for years, building relationships that allowed him to pursue his special efforts at acquiring and employing magic in spite of the strict laws against doing so—mostly because he made certain that those who looked the other way or openly supported him benefited from what he did. Among those who received him were Ministers of Defense, Treasury, and Transportation, several ordinary Ministers lacking specific offices but who came from populous cities, a pair of high-ranking commanders in the Federation army, and a handful of lesser sorcerers with whom he shared a common interest in liberating the use of talismans and artifacts that unlocked various forms of magic.

It was a tedious business, but he wanted to leave no one feeling snubbed. He was an important figure in the Southland world of banned magic, and all sought his friendship and support. They were to some degree frightened or at least wary of him, but he regarded that as a form of respect and did his best to encourage it. Unpredictability and the certainty of retribution should he be crossed were the strongest characteristics of his reputation, and he made good use of them. A while back, one of the lesser magic wielders living in Arishaig had let it be known that he would no longer consider himself an active part of Arcannen's network, but would go his own way. He was allowed to do so—in pieces, which made their way to the other magic wielders and a few key Ministers.

But while Arcannen did not shy from using violence or blackmail, mostly he accomplished what was needed through diplomacy and clever planning, always allowing others to share in his good fortune.

All of which was the point of this visit, but in particular regarding his plans for the Leah siblings, Paxon and Chrysallin. To do what was needed, he required the support of the prickly and sometimes recalcitrant Minister of Security, Fashton Caeil. Unfortunately, the Minister was the one man he could neither bribe nor intimidate, for Caeil was as powerful and ruthless as he was. He had been cultivating the man's support for years, slowly building an alliance that demonstrated his good intentions toward the Minister while at the same time drawing on the other's resources and powers to claim things that would otherwise have been denied him. Because without Fashton Caeil's assistance, Arcannen's involvement in acquiring magic from those who possessed it within the borders of the Southland would have been a dangerous undertaking indeed.

While Fashton had no use for the Druids and their rules, he also had no problem with using magic where it would benefit his climb to power. Like all of the members of the Coalition Council, it seemed, he desired the position of Prime Minister. But his plans far exceeded his grasp, Arcannen had determined early on, and so he was prepared to bend the rules for the sorcerer so long as it helped him on his climb up the political ladder. It was a bargain that had rewarded them both.

It was one that would continue to reward them if he could manage to keep Caeil from doing something foolish.

He mounted the steps to the Assembly, newly built and beautifully rendered amid the other buildings of the reconstruction. Arishaig was a new city. It had been destroyed by the demonkind during their breakout from the Forbidding more than a hundred years ago, and then subsequently restored. Larger and more opulent, reimagined in innovative ways by its builders, it was an amazing sight to those visiting from the lesser, older cities, and a wonder to those now living there. Wide avenues, parks and similar open spaces, a consistency of architecture, and an integration of businesses and residences helped soften the unfortunate sense of imprisonment created by the massive walls and gates that ringed the populace in steel and stone and which were touted by their builders as unbreachable.

Aside from the presumptuous nature of this claim, Arcannen found it all garish and showy. He liked things that looked used and a little out of plumb. He liked places that were weathered and worn and had withstood the test of time. Arishaig was fine for those who liked their beauty on the surface and cared nothing for the substance underneath.

This city would be destroyed again. Of that, he was certain.

Within the halls of the Assembly, he made his way to the offices of the Minister of Security, passing through several checkpoints and past numerous guards. Fashton Caeil bragged about his popularity with his people. Yet if that was so, why did he require so many guards? Someday, Arcannen promised himself, he would ask that question.

In any case, the guards let him pass with nothing more than a perfunctory greeting. He was well known here, and he was expected. So the searches and questions that others had to endure were not required of him.

The Minister's personal assistant, a man named Crepice who had been with Caeil since the beginning of his rise to power, greeted Arcannen with a smile that somehow managed to lack expression and led him to the inner chambers where his employer was waiting.

"Well met, Arcannen," Fashton Caeil greeted him cheerfully, immediately drawing the sorcerer's suspicion. Caeil was almost never cheerful. "Come, sit. A glass of ale?"

A big, corpulent man with thinning hair and close-set, piggish features, he had the look of someone who didn't quite understand the world and its people. But underestimating his intelligence would be a mistake; Fashton Caeil was very smart and very clever. Not much got past this man, and while he might look self-indulgent and vague, he was anything but.

Arcannen moved over to the chair offered and accepted the glass of ale. "You seem quite . . . satisfied this morning," he said in response. "Rather like the cat that caught the mouse."

"Well, yes. I've had quite a good week." Caeil sat across from him, settling his bulk into the chair gingerly. "Fresh possibilities for advancement have unexpectedly surfaced. I am looking at a rather exciting prospect. Our current First Minister seeks to step down. Age and time have fueled a loss of his interest in the battles of the political arena. My name has been mentioned as his successor. By more than a few, I should add."

Arcannen inclined his lean frame toward the other in acknowledgment of the announcement's importance. "It would be a well-deserved advancement."

"Yet I am cautious of such judgments. Much of what happens to us in life is due to chance and circumstances beyond our control. Being in the right place at the right time. Discovering that others have impacted us more than we know and for reasons that are not entirely clear. But hard work matters, too. There is an old saying: The harder I work, the luckier I get."

"If so, then you should be quite lucky indeed."

Caeil shrugged. "Tell me what news you have of our latest venture. How does it go? Are the pieces falling into place?"

The sorcerer nodded. "It goes well enough. But there have been changes to it. I was forced to rethink my plans a few weeks back when I discovered that the brother possesses an artifact of great magic, one that I must find a way to control. I thought to do so through the sister, but he managed to unlock the artifact's magic and rescue her. Pure chance. To counter this, I have retaken her and placed her in Mischa's tender hands. I think she will provide the impetus we need."

The minister studied him a moment and then shook his head doubtfully. "I mistrust this approach. It relies on mind control and deception of thought. Not the most reliable of tools."

"It requires a practiced hand, yes. It requires skill and

patience and careful application. But it works. I have seen the results."

"You put too much faith in Mischa. She is a witch, after all. Who can tell what such a person might do?"

Indeed, Arcannen thought darkly, ignoring the implication that he was of the same ilk. "She raised me, Caeil. She taught me everything I know of mind control. She is my solid and dependable ally."

"Yours, perhaps. Not necessarily mine." He made a dismissive wave of his hand. "This plan you have concocted is a fragile vessel."

"The plan will work as intended. The Druid order will become ours to manipulate, and you will be credited as the man who made it happen. Then your advancement beyond the position of First Minister to Prime Minister will be all but assured."

"And yours as caretaker of magic? It is a pleasant daydream. But I wonder if it is anything more."

"Think about it. Think of how it works. We deceive ourselves far more easily than others deceive us. Our false perceptions betray us. Our fears and doubts worm their way into our subconscious and cause us to believe what isn't necessarily true but becomes true through our own fixation on the possibilities. How do you think I managed to get the girl to believe she was able to bet in a game of chance where she had no coin? How do you think I managed to steal her away as easily as I did? She was no fool. She was young, tough-minded, and smart. But that only made her more vulnerable to the self-deception I instigated."

"Yes, but this new approach? What you are attempting now? I see that you might achieve your goals in the short term, but will they last beyond the day? Or the week's end? You condition her for a task that is innately repulsive and abhorrent to her. Will she not at some point realize what has been done to her?"

"Of course. It is unavoidable. She will doubt, she will equivocate, and she will mistrust her own perceptions. She will be enveloped in her inability to sort out truth and falsehood. But only one act is required of her. She will have her chance and the means to act on it. She will do what she has long since decided she must because she will believe unfailingly in its rightness."

Arcannen shrugged. "And if she fails for some reason, we have lost nothing. But if she succeeds, think of what we will have gained."

The big man drank his ale glass dry and set it aside. "But will the new Ard Rhys be as receptive as you think? What is to prevent his change of mind where we are concerned? What is to keep him loyal to us? How do we assure ourselves against a rebellion that will leave us where we are now?"

"Trust me," Arcannen hissed, smiling.

Caeil made a rude noise. "I trust no one. I wouldn't be where I am if I trusted people. No offense."

"None taken. But remember, you have nothing to lose in all this. You are protected against any possibility of discovery. You are safely out of its path. I am the one who must trust you. If I succeed, I must depend on you to fulfill your promise and give me what I want."

"Oh, there's no problem with that. Have I ever failed to act on your special requests? That prototypical flier you command? Those weapons no one possesses but the Federation High Command? Access to important figures in the government that would otherwise have been denied you? All freely bestowed. That and more, should you ask it, can be yours. They mean nothing to me. But advancement to Prime Minister and control of the Druid order—now, that is something of real worth. Give me access to power of that sort, Arcannen, and there is nothing I would deny you."

He stood, walked to the window, and looked out.

"But things have changed. We no longer stand in the same place we did yesterday. This new possibility of advancement to First Minister requires that we alter our relationship." He turned back. "After today, we can no longer meet here. We must find neutral ground where we will not be seen together by anyone. We must make clandestine arrangements. A future First Minister and past Minister of Security cannot be seen in the company of a sorcerer with your unfortunate reputation. You understand, I am sure."

Arcannen understood perfectly. This self-aggrandizing fool was already marginalizing him. He seethed inwardly as he gave Caeil a reassuring nod. "Whatever pleases you."

Fashton Caeil came forward, extending his hand in a gesture of false friendship. Arcannen accepted it, held it firmly, and smiled. As he did so, he looked the other man in the eye and held his gaze. "But we are still friends?"

The Minister's face took on an uncertain look. "Of course we are still friends."

Arcannen shifted his gaze and released his grip on the other's hand. He had read Caeil's eyes, and he knew he was lying. He meant to sever the relationship as soon as it was feasible to do so. Perhaps he even was thinking of doing so in a permanent manner.

"I must be going. I will contact you again soon with further news of our efforts. Congratulations once again on your impending appointment."

You had better hope I let you live to enjoy it.

15

FOR CHRYSALLIN LEAH, LOCKED IN THE DARKNESS of her torture chamber, the madness continued unabated.

She lost track of the number of times she was visited by the gray-haired Elven woman and her henchmen. She lost count of the number of ways they found to hurt her. After a while, everything started to blend together, and it seemed that the torture never stopped for more than a few minutes, and the pain never stopped at all. There were no longer times of relief, not even small ones; the whole of her existence was a single endless wash of agony and humiliation. In the darkness, she felt increasingly alone, abandoned, forgotten. In the hands of her captors, subjected to their terrible ministrations, she began to feel her mind slipping.

In the brief moments when the pain lessened—a marginal reduction, at best—she found herself wondering what had happened to her brother. She began to imagine all sorts of terrible things. He had not come for her, and therefore she knew something had prevented him from doing so. Perhaps he was a prisoner, too, undergoing the same horrible experience she was. Perhaps he was injured and could no longer find the strength to act. Perhaps he was even dead.

She grew steadily more depressed as her hope diminished and her certainty that her fate was determined grew. She began to wish it would end, that everything would be over, that she would be allowed to die.

All the while, her tormentors never spoke to her. She waited for them to tell her what they wanted, but it never happened. She listened for the smallest sound, the briefest whisper, anything that suggested a reason for her captivity. Once there was a hint of laughter, and she felt relief even in that, though it was at her expense. She waited for more, prayed for more, but nothing came.

They fed her a liquid that was not water and not anything else she recognized. It relieved her parched throat, and while at first she was reluctant to drink it, in the end she was grateful for anything that would quench her thirst and did not care what it might be doing to her. They gave her no food. They gave her no chance to move about. She lost all sense of time and space, all ability to think of anything but her agony and its endless reoccurrence.

Then, at some point when she had given up waiting, with no warning and for no discernible reason, the Elven woman appeared, bent close to her, and whispered, "Tell me what you know."

Chrysallin, her throat and mouth so dry and blood-filled she could not answer back, croaked in a desperate attempt to answer. But immediately a strip of cloth was tied about her mouth to prevent her from speaking. She tried to respond anyway, shrieking and crying into the gag, fighting to make the words take shape. Her efforts failed, and the Elven woman did not speak to her again.

In those few moments when she was left alone and awaiting the next onslaught of pain, she tried to make sense of what was happening. By doing so, she hoped she might find a way to free herself from the uncertainty that was eating at her. If she failed to do so, she knew she was going to continue on the road to madness. She could not survive what was being done to her without being able to imagine a rationale for its cause. Mostly, she thought it was about her brother. Mostly, she believed Arcannen was responsible. But she never knew for sure, and her belief was a slippery, elusive thing that she could never quite hold on to.

She was on the verge of losing her grip entirely when the door to her prison opened and a shadowy figure slipped into the room and came over to stand next to her. Although no sounds issued from the newcomer's mouth, Chrysallin knew right away that this was not one of her tormentors, but someone new. Hands touched her gently, moving to her wrists and ankles, releasing her bonds. Arms came around her shoulders and gently helped her into a sitting position.

"I would have come sooner," Mischa whispered, holding the girl close. "I tried. But they watch you so closely."

Chrysallin tried to speak, but the words stuck in her throat. She nodded instead, hugging the old woman back.

"There, there," the other cooed, stroking her back, patting her softly. "Let's get you out of here. Can you stand?"

Chrysallin shook her head. "Can't . . . don't look at me, please."

Mischa made a titching sound. "They've gone too far. This is beyond reason. Here, I've brought you some clothes. Let's get you dressed. You'll be fine now. I'm here to help."

Chrysallin was crying, tears streaming down her cheeks as she slipped into the clothes Mischa had brought, trying not to look at herself and at the same time to shield her battered, bloodied body from the old woman, ashamed of what had been done to her. She was so grateful she could barely manage to keep from breaking down completely, the emotions she had kept bottled up during her imprisonment now threatening to undo her.

"Shhh, shhh. It's all right. I'm taking you out of here to somewhere safe. Just dress yourself. Hang on to me, if you need to."

Chrys was shaking as she pulled on the clothes, the pain of her open wounds and damaged body causing her to gasp aloud. She eased herself carefully into the confines of the cloth, biting her lip against the rawness of the pain. It took her several long minutes, but Mischa never asked her to hurry.

"Lean on me," Mischa told her. "Just stay with me."

They moved toward the door, Chrysallin hobbling on feet and legs too damaged for anything more, supported by the surprisingly strong old woman. She managed to keep from crying out when her movements caused sharp stabs of agony, although she could not contain small gasps and groans.

"You know what they want, don't you?" the old woman whispered as they slipped through the doorway and started down the empty hall beyond.

Chrysallin shook her head no. Her eyes scanned the shadows ahead, searching for the gray-haired Elven woman.

"They didn't tell you?"

Another shake of her head.

"You don't know anything? All that time they tortured you, and they didn't tell you anything?"

Chrysallin was crying again, unable to respond.

"Then I will tell you!" Mischa hissed, "as soon as we are safely away. I will tell you what these monsters want!"

She guided Chrysallin ahead, moving at a steady pace, not rushing her, helping her to stand, speaking to her in low, hushed tones, reassuring her that everything was going to be all right. The girl listened, clinging to the words as she would to a lifeline thrown in a violent dark sea, desperate to believe that this was the chance she had prayed for, a way out of her misery, a way back to her home and family. She forced herself to ignore her pain and her fear, concentrating on putting one foot in front of the other, telling herself that each step brought her that much closer to freedom.

They went out of the building and onto a street, but this was not a place Chrysallin recognized. The avenue was narrow and dark, the surrounding buildings crowded close, shadows cast everywhere, the sun shut away. It was barely daylight, the air gray and damp. The stones on which she walked were wet with a recent rainfall, and she had to be careful not to slip and fall.

They went only a short distance before Mischa turned her into the doorway of another building, and they went inside. From there they followed a hallway to a set of stairs that took them up one floor, then down another hall a short distance to where Mischa lived. Once inside her rooms, the old woman helped Chrys into a comfortable chair and brought her hot tea to drink. Mischa's home was a living space, kitchen, and two back rooms the girl assumed were bedrooms. She couldn't see beyond that. She sipped at the tea and waited for her rescuer to seat herself on the couch across from her.

"You listen to me, girl. You listen close. There's things happening that might be not so much to your liking even beyond what's been done to you. There's schemes and trickery afoot, and that Elven woman is right in the middle of it. Now you and your brother have been brought into the mix, as well, and you might find it to your advantage to do something to change that soon."

"How?" Chrys managed, her voice a croak, rough and blunted.

"By getting far away from here. By finding your

brother and telling him what I am about to tell you. By being smarter and quicker than the witch woman and the sorcerer."

"What . . . do you . . . know?"

The old woman leaned toward her, dark eyes intense, lips compressed into a thin line. Her bony hands clasped together as she rested her elbows on her knees. Her hawk eyes fixed on the girl.

"Arcannen is ambitious," she said. "He is not satisfied with being just what he is now. He has much bigger plans for his future. They begin with destroying the Druids and taking their magic for himself, and he has found a way to do this. Before the month is out, a Druid will assassinate the Prime Minister of the Federation. When that happens, the Southland cities will rise up and crush the Druids once and for all. Then Arcannen will step into the void their departure has left."

Chrysallin shook her head in confusion. "What . . . has this . . . to do with me?"

"You are the bait, girl. You are the spark to light the fuse. Arcannen will do this time what he set out to do before—trade you for that sword your brother carries. When the killing takes place, it will be with that sword, and the Druid who carries it out will be as much a pawn as you are. He will have done to him what's been done to you. Do you understand me?"

"Tortured?"

"Now you have it. Tortured enough that the will is bent but not quite broken, the Druid's spirit collapsed and made malleable enough that he will do whatever it takes to get free of the pain. Wouldn't you have done the same, if I hadn't come to rescue you?"

The Highland girl nodded. Indeed, she would have done anything.

"But you can stop this from happening. Listen close

now. That woman that commands the torture? Do you know her?"

Chrysallin shook her head no.

"She hides the truth about herself. She pretends to be one thing when she is another. I have seen her reveal herself. When she is not here, she is in Paranor. She is a Druid!"

Chrys was staring at her. "How do . . . you know this?"

The old woman smiled. "I've cleaned Dark House for fifty years, and never a word of complaint, never a day taken that was not given to me. I am as much a part of that place as the furniture and less recognizable. They see right through me. They do not even realize I am there. They think me a crone with no mind and no purpose but to serve them."

She paused, winking. "That's how I found out about you. That's how I learned they caught you and brought you back again after the first time. They talked when I was in hearing, and never knew I was there. Arcannen and his witch woman—they were both of them so much smarter than an old cleaning lady. They let everything slip out, saying how it would work, what it would do for them, when it would happen. I listened at the door to the room where you were held for other bits and pieces, knew what you were going through, but couldn't get to you. Until now."

Chrysallin could barely take it all in. It felt like another terrible dream, this whole tale of intrigue and deception. Her brother and herself made pawns, the Sword of Leah used for murder, the Druids infiltrated and subverted by the sorcerer's magic, an assassination planned—could any of this be real?

"The Elven woman . . . is a Druid?" she repeated, her mouth gone dry again, her words scratchy and harsh.

Mischa nodded slowly, then rose and came over to

the girl, bending down so that her lips were right next to Chrysallin's ear. "But not just any Druid. Oh, no. She is disguised in clever clothes, that one."

She stepped back and locked eyes with the girl. "The gray-haired lady, Chrysallin Leah, is the Ard Rhys!"

At Paranor, in Aphenglow Elessedil's personal chambers, Paxon Leah sat facing her, his face horror-stricken. "How could this have happened?" he demanded.

Some days earlier the Druid assigned to keep watch over his mother and sister had been killed, and Chrysallin had disappeared. All this while he was off with Starks in the Southland village of Eusta, trying to track down the changeling that had been preying on the people living there. It was so impossible to believe that he was still trying to get his mind around the idea.

"Arcannen?" he asked.

She shook her head in a gesture of uncertainty. "It would seem likely, but we don't know for certain. No one saw what happened to her. No one saw any sign of Arcannen. Chrysallin simply vanished. Someone took her, and now we have to find out where she is. We are looking."

"It has to be Arcannen. He's still trying to get at me through Chrys." He rose quickly, his weariness forgotten. "I have to go find her."

"Sit down, Paxon," she said quietly.

Even though her voice was soft, there was iron in it—an unmistakable authority that he responded to instantly. Slowly, he lowered himself back into his seat. "You can't expect me to do nothing," he said to her.

"No, but I can expect you not to do something foolish. Before you go looking for your sister, you have to think it through. You have to know what you are up against. If Arcannen took her, he did so for the reason you already set out—to get at you. So he will be expecting you to come looking for her. He will be waiting for you. He will have a plan to take you prisoner, as well. Or at least a plan to persuade you to give him your sword. It won't be like it was before. You won't get your sister back so easily. You realize that, don't you?"

He nodded sullenly. "I realize it. But at the end of the day I still have to go. I have to find him and deal with him. I have to save Chrys."

"Then do so with a plan, not with little more than emotions and hope. Starks must have taught you that much in the time you've been with him."

Paxon exhaled wearily. "He did. More than you know. You're right. I have to give this some thought. He won't have Chrys with him even if I find him. He will have her hidden away somewhere. He will use her as barter for the sword, but he won't give me a chance to get her back without first giving up the sword."

She stood up. "I want you to take Starks with you. He will provide balance to your impetuous urges. He will be a voice of reason and protect against foolish decisions. Listen to him. Do what he tells you. He has a lot of experience, and he tends to be calm even when things come closest to being out of control. Will you accept his help?"

"Of course. But he might not want to do this. It isn't his problem."

"I've already spoken with him about it. He has agreed to go with you and offer what help he can." She paused. "He likes you, Paxon. He respects your determination and courage."

"I would be grateful to have Starks come with me," Paxon said at once.

"Then take today to talk about it with him. Think it through. Consider your options. Leave tomorrow, after you have done so. Remember that you won't be helping your sister if you act out of haste. You can only help her

if you are better prepared and smarter than whoever
has her."

He stood then and faced her. "Don't worry. I'll remember. But whatever it takes, I will get her back."

Then he went out the door to find Starks.

Mischa sat down again, eyes still fixed on Chrysallin.
"Drink your tea, get some liquid in your body. Then
you should sleep. You'll be safe enough here."

"They'll be . . . looking for me," Chrysallin said.

"Arcannen's away. His minions will look once they
find you gone, but that won't happen right away. Even
when it does, they won't know where to start. They
won't know how you got free or where you might have
gone once you did. They'll look, but mostly they'll wait
for his return."

"But I . . . should go before . . . that happens. While . . .
I still have . . . a chance to do so."

"Not in your condition. You aren't strong enough.
Drink, now," she repeated. "All of it. You leave after
you've rested a bit, gotten stronger, clearheaded enough
to know what you're about. I can't go with you. If they
find me gone, they'll know. I have to stay here, keep
working, and not let them know I was the one who
helped you. No choice in this, girl. I'm at risk now, too."

Chrysallin nodded quickly. "I know."

All the while, the pain that had racked her body for
the time of her captivity continued to throb and pulse, a
constant reminder of her weakened and debilitated condition. She tried to pretend it was getting better, but she
could tell it wasn't. Even without knowing how bad it
was, she could be certain it wasn't good. How many
bones had been broken? How many ligaments torn?
How many organs irreparably damaged by the torture
she had suffered? She wanted to get a look at herself in

a mirror, but she didn't see one anywhere and didn't want to ask the old woman to give her one.

She could only imagine how she looked. She was grateful to Mischa for not saying anything about it, for letting the matter be.

She set down her tea. "Is there . . . somewhere I can rest? Just for a little while?"

Mischa led her to one of the two bedrooms in the back of her home. It contained a single bed, a nightstand, and a chest of drawers. She guided Chrysallin to the bed and sat her down. "Sleep here. As long as you want. I'll be close by. I don't go back to work until tomorrow. By then, you can be on your way."

"Where should I go?" Her voice was getting stronger now, clearer.

"Go to your brother. Go to Paranor to find him, if you must. But be aware of the danger you face if you do. *She* will be there. Home is Leah, but Leah is not safe, either. Arcannen will just come for you again. Best if you get to your brother. Just remember the Ard Rhys is not what she seems. Stay away from her."

"But it's Paranor. How can I avoid her?"

Mischa shook her head. "I don't know. I just know you don't want to fall into her hands again. Into Arcannen's hands. If you do . . ."

She trailed off, looked away, and stood up. "Wait here."

She left the room, was gone for a few minutes, and then returned. She sat next to Chrysallin on the bed. "Here," she said. She handed the girl a long, slim object. It was wrapped in a soft cloth, but was hard underneath.

It felt like a knife.

Chrysallin looked at the old woman. "If you are threatened by Arcannen—in any form—use this," the old woman said. "It's what you think it is. But very special. Use it without hesitating, without thinking. There will be no time for either. Can you do that?"

Chrysallin nodded slowly, thinking of the pain and anguish, remembering what had been done to her. "Yes."

Mischa stood. "I'll leave it with you. It belongs to you now. Keep it safe." She started away. "Keep it for when you are threatened. Especially by the Elven witch. Remember what she has done to you. Remember she will try to do it again."

She stopped at the door and turned back, her face haggard, her eyes intense. "I will keep watch while you sleep. As long as I am able. At least until I have to return to Dark House to work on the morrow. But I will be back for you. Rest well, girl."

Then she went out the door and closed it softly behind her.

It was nearing nightfall when Grehling made his way toward Dark House from the airfield with his delivery. A small box had come in during the afternoon, shipped from Arishaig for Arcannen. Normally, he would have brought it over at once. But Arcannen was not in Wayford now in any case, and he saw no need to rush. He waited until his shift at the airfield was finished—his father had given him the night off—before making the delivery.

He had no idea what was in the box and didn't care to know. All that mattered was getting it where it was supposed to be and ending his involvement. His attitude toward the sorcerer had not improved since the incident with Paxon Leah and his sister, and he doubted that would change anytime soon.

He was closing in on his destination when he saw the old woman Mischa coming out of an alleyway beside the building where she lived. Right away he froze in place until she paused to look behind her, and then he stepped quickly into the deep shadows of a doorway. It was already hard to see, the light leached from the sky by night's arrival and by rolling clouds that had blanketed the city since sunrise. Pressed back against the walls of the alcove, he watched the old woman creep into view like a predator in search of food and start down the street toward Dark House.

Immediately he decided to wait awhile before continuing on. He didn't like Mischa. He couldn't have said what it was exactly, only that his fear and dislike of her was a tangible thing and he suspected she was evil in a way that matched Arcannen. She and the sorcerer were two of a kind, twin dark stars in a firmament of scheming and machinations. He had only spoken to her a couple of times, and a couple was more than enough for him to form an opinion. It wasn't that she threatened him or tried to harm him. It was his conviction that she could do either—and it wouldn't cause her to lose much sleep if she did.

Even the way she moved was unnerving. Like a spider. He was small and skinny, so there wasn't much of him to spy, but he was frozen in place nevertheless. People often didn't see him because he was not particularly noticeable. He used that to his advantage here, willing her not to look in his direction but to keep moving ahead.

She did so, disappearing around a corner and moving out of sight.

He glanced back at the building. A single light burned in a window on the second floor. The rest of the building was dark.

That was probably where she had her rooms.

He wondered why she seemed so furtive around her own home, as if not wanting anyone to see where she was coming from. She lived there, after all; everyone knew it. So why all the stealth and suspicion? Why all the casting about, as if afraid she would be seen?

He wondered suddenly what her place was like inside. He wondered what she kept in there.

Grehling gave her almost half an hour before resuming his delivery. Then he hurried on, dropped the package at the front door with the guards, and went his way, the matter set aside, but not forgotten.

16

Chrysallin Leah's sleep was dark and deep and filled with nightmares. In succession they flooded her troubled mind, stealing away the momentary peace she had experienced after being rescued by Mischa, returning her to a sense of impending doom.

The first began in a meadow where she walked through sunlight toward a river, accompanied by her brother. Paxon was cheerful and his laughter was bright, and she felt his strong presence as a reassurance of her safety and freedom. She felt buoyant and at ease as she traversed a carpet of meadow wildflowers and smelled their sweet scent wafting on a soft breeze.

But soon she sensed a lessening of the wildflower presence as the swatches of color and the smells on the air diminished and then faded completely. She was in a pasture now, its carpet all dried and browned, the green of the fresher meadow grasses having disappeared. The skies had lost the sun's brightness, and clouds had moved in to curtain the blue. She slowed, hesitating, and as she did so she felt something grapple at her ankles and wrap about her legs. She looked down and found herself entwined by saw grass and weeds, whipcord tough and working hard to bind her in place and hold her fast.

She struggled to break free, but the weeds and grasses were too strong, and finally she could not move at all. In desperation, she turned to find her brother, but he had disappeared. She cast about desperately, calling out his name, trying to discover what had happened to him. She could not believe he had left her like this, without a word of warning.

When she looked again to where she had last seen him, the gray-haired Elven woman who had bound and tortured her in Dark House was standing in his place, smiling. Her lips moved, shaping words that Chrysallin understood, even though they made no sound.

Tell me what you know.

Chrys screamed in terror, grasping for the knife she knew was tucked within her belt and finding it missing. She wrenched furiously at the grasses, but they only clung all the tighter to her. She clawed at strands and stalks, trying to pry them away from her, but they refused to budge.

Then tiny bugs emerged from the earth beneath her feet and began to climb her legs, working their way under her clothing and into her boots. She could hear the gnashing of their tiny teeth, and then they were biting her, tearing at her flesh. She felt her skin break and her blood begin to flow. She collapsed in despair, shrieking.

The bugs were suddenly all over her.

Abruptly, the meadow with its bugs and withered grasses and the gray-haired Elven woman disappeared into blackness, and she was alone again. She felt herself rising, and when the light returned, she was standing on a mountainside, high up in the clouds, wind whipping snow and particles of ice against her skin. She wore no coat, hat, or gloves. The cold was bitter and relentless as it tore at her clothing and lashed her skin. She stared about, looking for where she was supposed to go, thinking there must be a trail leading down. Yet she could barely see beyond her outstretched hand where it braced her against the cliff face.

Eventually, she took a few tentative steps along the narrow path on which she stood. But the path led neither up nor down, and she could not see if that changed beyond where she crept along its slender length. She kept going nevertheless, knowing she must get off this mountain. If she stayed where she was, she was going to freeze to death. She would die if she did not find shelter.

Then an opening in the cliff wall appeared and she ducked hurriedly inside. She was in a huge cave, one that stretched away in all directions before her. The walls gave off a pale greenish light, a glow that chased back the darkness. Time slipped away as she proceeded deeper into the cavern, losing sight of where she had entered, finding that the walls ahead did not seem to get any closer as she went.

She was thinking of turning back again when the gray-haired Elven woman appeared, emerging from the shadows right in front of her. She drew up short, cringing involuntarily at the other's approach. She took a step back, intending to flee. But the other stopped, hands at her side, smiling in a way that suggested to Chrysallin that flight was pointless.

Lips formed familiar, soundless words: *Tell me what you know.*

Then the shadows layering the walls lifted and became vague figures that took shape and approached like wraiths through the cavern gloom. Chrysallin backed away, but everywhere she turned, the shadows were closing in on her. She forced down the scream rising in her throat, fought back against her fear as it threatened to suffocate her. The shadows were close to her now, and there was nowhere for her to go, no avenue of escape open, no chance of finding help.

When they reached her, she had her hands up to her

face and her eyes squeezed shut, and she could feel their touch on her body like the icy fingers of creatures long dead and frozen.

Help me, she begged the darkness. *Please, help me.*

The shadows draped her, and her breathing was cut off.

Seconds later she was standing on the cliffs above an ocean, looking out over a vast blue expanse of empty water. The cliff on which she stood was a thousand feet high, and its precipice was rocky and barren save for small tufts of sea grasses. Below, the face of the cliff disappeared into the water, a smooth sheer surface from which to tumble. She found the urge to do so almost irresistible. Strangely inviting. She could throw herself over, fall unimpeded to the ocean's depths, and escape the nightmares that plagued her. She was aware of them, even in her dreams, knowing they would come again and again, never-ending visual impressions of what threatened her. It was almost more than she could stand, and relief could only be found if she were to give herself up to a watery tomb.

The sense of hopelessness she felt at what was happening to her was overwhelming. It was relentless and purposeful, and there was nothing she could do about it but jump and be done with her life. Why not give in to the urge? Why not save herself from further pain and fear? Was her life so precious that she would endure it even in the face of such misery?

Again, the gray-haired Elven woman materialized out of nowhere, standing close, looking at her, smiling.

Suddenly she found a well of strength she didn't know she possessed—a strength given life by the hatred she felt on looking at this monster. Her rage was fueled by thoughts of what she would like to do to this creature, of how good it would feel to make her suffer for what she had done. White-hot and unchecked, her anger burned through her, providing fresh purpose and determination.

With a cry, she launched herself at the other, hands outstretched, intent on tearing the other's face off, of obliterating her smiling presence.

But when she reached her, the Elven woman wasn't there, had become a wraith that faded away, and Chrysallin passed through her empty image and toppled over the cliff's edge and began to fall. All at once, she knew she had made a mistake. She didn't want this to happen. She didn't want to die. She had been tricked.

Too late. She was plunging toward the flat, hard surface of the ocean, and she knew that when she struck she would be killed on impact. There was no hope; her fate was determined. But the fall went on and on, and it would not end. She screamed now, and curled herself into a ball as the wind rushed past and the sound of the waters below lapping against the cliff face reached her ears. *Soon now*, she kept thinking. *Any second*.

But still she fell and did not stop.

She woke in the bedroom in which she had fallen asleep, still in Mischa's home. But now she was lashed in place again, spread-eagle across the bedding, her arms and legs held fast. The men who had tortured her were back again, gathered close, watching. Their eyes glittered in the light of smokeless lamps that cast their shadows on the walls behind them, larger than life. They held metal implements that would cut and rend. They were stripped to the waist, their muscled arms gleaming. None of them spoke a word as they stood there watching her, waiting.

Then, from the darkness, the familiar voice said softly, "Begin."

Chrysallin twisted and thrashed in response, trying to break free, to escape what was coming, and as she did so she caught sight of Mischa's severed head resting on a platter on the nightstand next to the bed, eyes open and staring.

Then the pain began anew.

Aphenglow Elessedil was working through the contents of an address she was planning to present to the Coalition Council of the Southland Federation—one of the rare personal appearances she would make in the coming months—when Sebec appeared in the doorway of her offices in response to her summons. He entered quietly and she could tell at once from the look on his face that he knew something was wrong.

She set aside her speech and turned to him. "Have you inventoried the storage chambers lately?"

He didn't speak right away. Instead, he closed the door behind him and came all the way in. His young face was strained, and there was a hesitancy to him that suggested whatever it was he had to tell her was not something he could relate easily.

"We've had another theft," she said finally.

Which would make four altogether, including the disappearance of the scrye orb. She thought she had put a stop to it. She had placed wards on the doors to the storage chambers where the magic artifacts and instruments were kept cataloged and sealed away. She had used magic that only she and Sebec could unlock, the latter given access from the first because she trusted him in his role as personal secretary in a way she had seldom trusted anyone in her 150 years of life, and because someone besides herself had to have access to the chamber in case anything happened to her. She had determined long ago that once the Druids had found and recovered lost magic, it must be kept safe from misuse and irresponsible hands.

But someone had breached her protective efforts three

times in recent months, stealing magic for reasons that were not entirely clear. It was a given by now that it must be one of them—a Druid acting alone or on behalf of an enemy of the order, a rogue who had penetrated her usually thorough assessment of an applicant's suitability. It had been a bitter discovery on learning of the first theft, and it hadn't become any easier to accept with the ones that followed.

Now this.

"Another?" he repeated. "What is it that's missing this time?"

She took a steadying breath. "The Stiehl."

The blade the assassin Pe Ell had used to kill Quickening, the daughter of the King of the Silver River, centuries ago in Eldwist, the lair of the Stone King. Its blade was so sharp, it could cut through rock. It had vanished and reappeared time and again over the years until finally it had been recovered and sealed away for good.

The Stiehl had been accorded special treatment, the wards that protected it complex and layered. No one should have been able to get to it.

"You're certain, Mistress?" he asked.

She nodded. "I had decided to do a survey of the artifacts, comparing the actual items to our listings in the catalog, when I noticed the wards that protected them were broken. At first, I couldn't believe it. I thought I must be mistaken. I even searched the entire set of chambers, every nook and closet, every shelf and container. It took me all afternoon. But it wasn't there. It was gone."

She watched Sebec's brow furrow in dismay. He understood the seriousness of what she was telling him. It was one thing to have the scrye orb stolen—a magic that, while important, was not particularly dangerous. But the Stiehl was another matter. Here was a killing weapon against which there were few protections. All sorts of bad things could happen if this blade fell into the wrong hands.

Only the loss of one other artifact would be more devastating. But the crimson Elfstones, or draining-Stones—which had been recovered by Redden Elessedil from within the Forbidding decades ago and given over to the order by his brother, Railing—were not housed in the chambers that contained the other artifacts. She kept them in her own chambers, in large part because after all these years she was still toying with the possibility of returning them to the Elves.

"Do you have any idea at all who took it?" he asked, referring again to the Stiehl.

"None at all. Like the other thefts, it was carried out when no one was around. The wards were negated and bypassed, and the weapon found by someone who clearly knew where it was being kept. I had a careful look about when I realized what had happened, thinking I might find some hint of who had been there. But whoever did this knew what they were doing." She paused. "Did you inventory everything after the last theft? Are we sure the Stiehl was still locked away at that point?"

"I inventoried everything after every theft. So, yes, it was still where it was supposed to be."

"When was that? Maybe two weeks ago?"

"About that."

"Hardly any time at all. Our thief believes we are helpless to stop him, so he continues to steal."

Sebec shrugged. "It seems we *are* helpless."

A dark possibility crossed Aphenglow Elessedil's mind—one so repulsive she almost dismissed it out of hand. But then she considered what was at stake and made a decision. She rose to face him. "These artifacts being stolen are increasingly more important. I must be concerned now for the safety of the crimson Elfstones. They've been safe enough in my quarters, but I think I should move them to the artifact chamber. I will do so this afternoon. Will you assist me in setting the wards?"

"Of course," Sebec said. "Though perhaps you should leave the Elfstones where they are since they've been safe enough so far."

"No, I think it would be better to move them. I will create new wards for the entire chamber. No one will be allowed inside but you and me until further notice. I will ferret out this thief or I will catch him in the act. The stealing stops now!"

"Yes, Mistress," the other acknowledged.

"Send Starks and Paxon to me. I want to speak with them before they leave."

Sebec nodded, backing toward the door. She was furious, and she knew he had seldom seen her like this. But an Ard Rhys had a breaking point, just like everyone else. She had reached hers, and she was not likely to calm down again until the thefts were resolved.

When he was gone, she took a deep breath, reconsidered at length the dark possibility that had occurred to her earlier. The more she looked at it, the more likely it became and the unhappier she grew.

But there was no help for it. It was what it was, nightshade by any other name still deadly poisonous. When she was finished thinking on it, she exhaled sharply to relieve the tension that had built up within and set about making herself a pot of tea.

It was midday of the following day when Arcannen arrived back in Wayford, his personal airship—courtesy of Fashton Caeil—with its distinctive raven emblem emblazoned on the mainsail setting down in its assigned space. Disembarking, he crossed the airfield, leaving his crew and personal attendants behind, choosing to go alone to his meeting with Mischa. Having finished his business with Fashton Caeil for the moment, his attention was refocused on Chrysallin Leah. By now, she should be sufficiently subverted that she would carry out his plans for the Druids. Mischa was resourceful and relentless when it came to mind alterations, and she would be no less so here where she knew how much was at stake.

Nevertheless he was anxious about this plan, even if it was his own. So much depended on everything falling into place at just the right time and in the right way. A failure on any front would scuttle the entire effort, and the most obvious risk lay with how the girl would respond to what was being done to her.

He intended to extract a further guarantee from Mischa this very day that her magic was doing what she had promised.

Tall, spare, and shadowed within his cloak and cowl, he cut an imposing figure as he passed the field manager's boy where he worked on repairs to a parse tube set up on blocks close by the business office. The manager himself was present, sitting inside the building, visible through the viewing window, head bent to whatever task currently occupied him. He waited for either of them to glance up at him, but when neither did he dismissed them automatically from further consideration. The boy was occasionally useful, his father less so. Neither had an important place in his life. Even so, he supposed he was more comfortable passing them by unnoticed.

But then he stopped abruptly and turned toward the boy, a new thought occurring to him. He considered it momentarily, then he walked over. Now the boy was looking up at him, an uncertain look on his face.

"Do me a favor," the sorcerer said to him. "You remember the Highlander I asked you to direct to Dark House a few weeks ago?"

The boy nodded.

"If you see him again, if he flies into Wayford, alone or with others, I want you to come at once to Dark House and let me know. Can you do that?"

The boy nodded once more, but didn't say a word.

"You're certain you can do this? You understand what I am asking. I don't want the Highlander to know what you are about."

"I understand," the boy said.

"There will be something in it for you, if you do as I say."

The boy nodded, but didn't respond. A bit slow, Arcannen thought to himself, but reliable. Though he wondered suddenly how Paxon Leah, on his earlier visit, had managed to find a way into Dark House without alerting his guards. Had the boy told him?

He dismissed the idea; the boy would never risk the consequences.

He left the airfield behind and walked down the streets of the city, eschewing carriages and horses, feeling the need to stretch his legs and wanting to be alone. Passersby gave way to him, most moving all the way over to the other side of the street. He knew they were frightened of him, and it pleased him to see them demonstrate it openly. It was always better to be feared than respected. Respected men could be approached; they could be talked to and reasoned with. But feared men were simply to be avoided; reason and small talk were out of the question.

He walked not to Dark House, but a short distance farther on to where Mischa's home was located on the second floor of a seemingly empty building. He took a few moments standing on the walkway of a side street where he could make certain no one was watching him, then crossed to the other side and moved quickly down the alleyway. The lock on the outer door of the building was familiar to him, and he released it easily. Once inside, he passed into the hallway beyond and went up the stairs at its end and down a second hall to Mischa's front door.

There he paused, listening to the quiet before knocking softly—one loud, three soft—the agreed-upon signal. Time passed, then the locks released, the door swung open, and Mischa stood there looking out at him.

He was surprised at her appearance. She never looked particularly well, because she was old and withered and worn. Still, she almost always seemed composed and steady, even in the most stressful of times. Not today. Today she looked haggard beyond anything he had ever seen, her features contorted, her mouth twisted in a grimace, her eyes ablaze with intensity and raw emotion.

He jumped to an immediate conclusion. "You've killed her," he said.

The grimace turned into something even more horrible. "Likely she'll kill me first. Come inside."

The crone turned away and walked into the living area without a glance back. Arcannen followed, closing the door behind him. "She's all right, then?"

She wheeled back, and the sharp eyes fixed on him. "That depends on your point of view. She's where I want her to be, but she is strong, that one, fighting me every step of the way, and I can't be sure at this point if I've persuaded her or merely captured her attention for a time."

"That sounds ominous."

"Mostly, it's aggravating. She has a strong mind—much stronger than anyone else's I've worked on. She has a core to her that defies explanation. There's something there. What is her history? What is there about her that might explain this?"

Arcannen shrugged. "You know the family. Kings and Queens of all Leah once, now simple folk. The brother wields the sword, compels the magic by virtue of his bloodline. Maybe she could, too. Maybe that's her strength."

"Strength, yes. But are you assuring me she has no magic?"

"None that I know of. But most of what I know was recently learned. Only since I became aware of the sword. It seems the girl talked about it regularly at the tavern, though apparently no one there paid much attention. Even the tavern owner, who was the one who told me about it, insisted it was just another legend, another wild tale. Where was the proof that this weapon was anything special? It was nonsense. But I knew better. That was when I first began considering the possibility that I could acquire the weapon by holding her for ransom, and then you could turn the boy to our cause by altering his mind as you are altering the girl's. Of course, that's all changed now."

Mischa shook her head. "Well, there's something more to her than what's on the surface. I don't like it. She should have succumbed by now. But she's still hanging on, clinging to something I can't identify. We may have her convinced of what is happening and who is to blame, but it would be a good idea if we set her to her task as quickly as possible. The longer she lives outside my influence, the more likely she will come back to herself when we don't expect it."

"Perhaps you need more time with her?"

She gave him a look. "If I do much more to her, I will break her entirely. Then she will be useless. What we need is to keep her close another day and then speed her to your chosen destination and put an end to this business."

"Another day? I think we can manage that. But are you sure that is enough to do the job?"

"I'm not sure of anything, sorcerer. I'm working with smoke and mirrors. I'm groping in the dark. But I have the skills and the experience, so don't you worry yourself. I'll make her our cat's-paw. I'll turn her to our uses and set her abroad to be the weapon you intend."

"Let me see her."

The witch hesitated. "Very well. But only for a minute and only through the doorway. You cannot enter the room; it would disturb the magic's workings. The skein is delicate and complex. Only I can enter until its work is done."

Arcannen nodded his agreement, and she led him down the hallway to the back rooms, stopping at the last door on her left. The door was closed, but flashes of light shone from beneath it, illuminating patches of flooring.

She looked back at him. "Say nothing when I open the door. Do not move from where you stand."

Again, he nodded, irritated by now. Did she think he knew nothing of the magic she worked?

But he held his tongue, intent on making his own determination about how matters were proceeding. Mischa grasped the latch and carefully lifted so that the door swung open wide and everything within was clearly revealed.

The entire room was crisscrossed with bands of wicked green light, all of it pulsing softly. The bands ran everywhere and in no discernible order. Chrysallin Leah lay on a bed near the back of the room, her body covered in a thin sheet. The lines wrapped all about her, and it seemed as if many passed through her body. She twisted and squirmed in their grasp, her movements feeble and ineffective. She moaned softly, and sporadically she emitted small gasps.

Arcannen nodded to himself. She was deep in the nightmares Mischa had conjured for her, caught up in visions that would shape her thinking. She believed herself to be in the hands of the gray-haired Elven woman and her henchmen, being tortured and disfigured in an effort to divulge something of which she was unaware and they would not reveal. Her fear and rage were being directed toward her tormentors, deliberately and exclusively, and particularly toward the Elven woman.

He had seen enough. He nodded to Mischa, who closed the door softly and secured the latch. "She comes to us more and more, Arcannen," the old woman said. "Her thoughts and actions become less and less her own and more and more ours. She will do what she is being trained for when the time comes. You could see it for yourself."

"But she resists?"

"More than I would like. But not enough to change the eventual outcome. Another day, perhaps two, and she will be unable to function using free will. She will become our puppet, and she will do what she is being conditioned to do. Trust me."

He trusted no one, but he nodded anyway. "Let us hope so," he said. He turned away. "Come get me at Dark House when she is ready. I will take charge of her then and speed her on her way."

He went through the house and down the hallway to the stairs without looking back.

17

In spite of what Arcannen might have thought about the boy, Grehling was anything but slow. When the sorcerer departed the airfield and walked past him on the way into the city, the boy once again deliberately kept his head down and his eyes lowered so as to pretend to be absorbed in his work. But that didn't mean he wasn't thinking about the conversation that had just taken place. Why was the sorcerer so interested in the Highlander's return? Knowing what had transpired during his first visit, it seemed unlikely Paxon Leah would consider coming back again. Yet Arcannen seemed to think it was possible.

And where was the other going now? Back to Dark House? Alone and on foot and without his guards? That was odd. He had seen Arcannen come and go from the airfield countless times over the years, almost always traveling by horse or carriage and with his collection of bodyguards close at hand.

But not this time. Grehling wondered why.

He waited until Arcannen was safely past and out of sight before lifting his head to look in the direction the other had gone, wondering again what he was up to. Because leaving as he had, alone and on foot, suggested he was up to something that he wanted to keep private.

He glanced over at the sorcerer's airship, where the crew was dropping light sheaths and pulling down radian draws, securing the vessel in place. The guards Arcannen kept for protection milled about, looking bored and disinterested. Curiosity nudged the boy's thinking, prodding at him like the poke of a finger against his arm. What was going on?

Almost immediately he found himself thinking back to the previous day and his sighting of the witch Mischa creeping about as she left for Dark House from her rooms in that all-but-empty building she occupied. He couldn't have said why he connected the two—besides knowing that the witch was in Arcannen's service and he had seen the two with heads bent close on more than one visit to the pleasure house—but he sensed he might be guessing right.

With the airfield safely under his father's watch and no work that demanded his immediate attention, there was nothing to keep him from finding out if he was right. So he abandoned his task of repairing the skiff engine, told his father he was walking into town to look for spare parts, and set out. It was an obvious indulgence, a way of satisfying his curiosity and maybe seeing something he shouldn't—an attraction for any fourteen-year-old boy—but he gave in to it readily with a boy's excitement at embarking on an adventure. He didn't do so with foolish disregard for the danger he was risking, because he understood that well enough, but he didn't shy away from brushing up against it, either.

Down through the city he went, and he had only gone a short distance when he caught up to the sorcerer. Hard to mistake that tall, black-cloaked form, and he began following at a safe distance, staying out of the center of the roadway and up against the buildings. Arcannen didn't slow, didn't turn aside, and didn't glance around. Apparently, he was unconcerned about the people around him, and after a while Grehling began to think he had been mistaken.

But as they neared Dark House, Arcannen paused at the corner of a side street, the one that Grehling knew led to Mischa's building, and took a long, slow look around. The boy was already pressed back in the shadows by then, out of view of the sorcerer, little more than a part of a building wall. He stayed there for a long time, not bothering to try to peek out until he was certain Arcannen had moved on.

A quick glimpse confirmed that he was right about where the sorcerer was heading, and he began following him once again, more cautiously now, aware of the other's heightened watchfulness. But Arcannen must have been satisfied he was alone; he had already moved down the side street and was out of sight. Grehling hurried after him and by the time he caught up to him again, close enough to see what he was doing, Arcannen had moved all the way down the alley to the exterior door of Mischa's building, released the locks and latches, and was disappearing inside.

Standing on the side street across from the alleyway, Grehling considered his options. He had satisfied himself that his hunch about Arcannen was accurate, but he still didn't know anything about the reason for the visit. He couldn't shake the feeling that it had something to do with Paxon Leah, even if the Highlander wasn't here. Of course, he hadn't been here the last time Arcannen had told the boy to keep an eye out for him, had he?

But Paxon's sister had, a prisoner in Dark House.

It was too far-fetched to believe she was a prisoner again, but Arcannen might have found another way to lure the Highlander to Wayford. Whatever the case, it was worth waiting around a bit to see what might happen next. All he had to do was be careful not to be seen.

So he moved down the street a short way and ducked into a second alley in which boxes had been stacked near a refuse bin. From there, he could see the entrance to the alley Arcannen had taken without being seen from across the street in turn. He hunkered down, put his rear end on the ground and his back against the building wall, and waited.

Grehling was slender, almost bony, not very tall or muscular—sort of your average fourteen-year-old. If he had to get away quickly, he could run very fast. He was good at following without being seen, at getting into places that were locked up, and at thinking things through in a thorough and logical way. He was something of a wizard himself when it came to airships, able to take them apart and put them back together almost mindlessly. He could fly them, too. He was a better pilot than his father; his father had said so. But if it came to a fight, he was in trouble.

He was afraid of both Mischa and Arcannen, and he did not want to be found by either of them. So he made sure the alleyway in which he was hiding opened at both ends—which the one leading to Mischa's door did not—so that he had an escape route if he needed one. He would have loved to go up to the door of Mischa's building, pick the lock, and have a look at what was inside, but he knew such an intrusion was far too risky to attempt. For now, at least, he would have to make do with watching and waiting.

The minutes slipped away, and Arcannen did not reappear. The boy grew impatient, but stayed where he was. He occupied his time with thinking about Paxon and his sword. Grehling really admired that sword, and he wished he could have it for his own. But he imagined it was a family heirloom, passed down from father to son, and Paxon would never part with it. He wondered if he could find a sword like that for himself. Was such a thing possible? He couldn't imagine there were too many weapons of that sort lying around waiting to be found.

He was still daydreaming when a flicker of motion from across the street caught his eye, and Arcannen reappeared. Grehling, sitting quietly behind the refuse heap, watched as the sorcerer reached the opening of the alleyway and turned toward Dark House. The boy could see his face clearly, but could not read anything into his expression. He waited until the other was out of sight before rising and moving to where he could see the black-cloaked form disappearing from view.

He wondered what he should do. But there really wasn't anything more he could do at that point, and he had almost made up his mind to return to the airfield when he heard a door slam from across the way and backed quickly out of view once more. Seconds later Mischa appeared, pausing at the head of the alley to look about, just as Arcannen had done moments earlier, before turning the opposite way the sorcerer had gone and shuffling quickly up the street. Grehling edged out from his hiding place so he could see where she went, watching as she continued on up the street until she was out of view.

The boy hesitated. Here was his chance to have a look inside the building. It was risky, but maybe the risk was worth it. Who knew what he might find? What if the sword was in there? Paxon's black blade? What if Arcannen had stolen it and was keeping it hidden there?

He crossed the street quickly, dashed up the alley, and stopped when he reached the door. The only lock was on the latch plate, and he could tell at a glance it would not keep him out. He used the pick set he had been carrying with him since he was ten, and he had the door open in seconds. If the witch had used magic to secure the entry, he would have been in trouble. But there didn't seem to be any present. Not that he could know for certain, of course. Still, when he tried to enter, there was no problem. Good enough. If they found out later someone had broken their wards, he wouldn't be there anyway.

Inside, he looked about. The entire ground floor seemed abandoned. He followed the hallway to the back of the building and the stairs that led to the second floor. He remembered the location of the window where he had seen the light the previous night when he had caught the witch slipping out. He would look there first.

It occurred to him suddenly that if she was only going out for a few minutes and intended to come right back, she might not think it necessary to use magic to secure the premises. He thought he might be wise to hurry his investigation. The only way down from the second floor was by using the stairway or going out a window. Whatever happened, he didn't want to be caught up here when Mischa came back.

He went up the stairs to the second floor and turned down the hallway to where the witch's rooms were located. He stood before the door and put his ear against it, listening. No sounds were audible. He tried the handle. Locked. Again, he produced the picks, working the locks cautiously until he heard each release.

Pushing down on the handle once again, he opened the door and stepped inside. He was standing in a space with a couch and two chairs, a small dining table, and a stove. A hallway farther back led to several closed doors. He glanced around, assuring himself there was nothing lurking in the room's deep shadows before he started down the hall. He stopped at a pair of closed doors, one on either side of the corridor. From beneath the door on the left, flashes of wicked greenish light were visible.

Now he was afraid. Really afraid. There was magic at

use inside that room; he was certain of it. But he had no idea what sort of magic; he could not know what he would find if he opened the door to see. He was carrying no weapons, and he wasn't big enough to stop much of anything that might come after him. He wondered suddenly if he had overstepped himself by coming in here in the first place. Maybe he should have let well enough alone until Paxon reappeared—if he was coming at all—and tell him what was happening and let him decide what needed doing.

But then he got angry with himself. He was not a coward, and he was acting like one. He could risk a quick look, couldn't he? He had gotten this far. He was fast enough that he could slam the door shut again and flee down the hall and out of the building before anything in that room could get to him. Flashes of green light didn't mean anything. Since when could that hurt you?

Since the Federation had found a way to reshape rough-cut sets of diapson crystals to create flash rips, he answered himself.

But what would something like diapson crystals be doing here? This was a witch's lair, and magic was what would be waiting inside.

He took a deep breath, tightening his resolve. He would crack the door, he told himself. Just a bit. He would peek inside and see if anything threatened. If it did, he would run out of there immediately.

He could do this.

Even so, he almost didn't. He almost listened to his worst fears and turned around and left. He almost gave it up then and there because he couldn't think of any real justification for taking the sort of risk that opening that door would likely yield.

But then, almost on impulse, angry and impatient

with himself, he pushed down on the handle and cracked open the door.

What he saw was confusing and scary. Bands of light crisscrossed the room, running everywhere in irregular patterns before converging on a bed near the back of the room where they wrapped about someone who was lying there. He could tell it was a person, even in the indistinct greenish glow. A thin covering outlined a body that jerked and shuddered and writhed in response to whatever the light was doing to it.

It was a surreal moment, and Grehling almost closed the door and fled. This was beyond anything he understood, and he needed to tell someone about it right away. But who would he tell? Who was going to come back here and go up against the witch? And likely face Arcannen, as well?

So he hesitated, trying to make out the prisoner's face in the dim light. He was unsuccessful until a twisting of limbs and body brought her face into view, and he found himself looking at Chrysallin Leah. He stared in disbelief. So Arcannen had recaptured her and brought her back to Wayford, after all. But what was being done to her? What were these bands of light intended to accomplish?

Whatever it was, it wasn't good. It was clear the witch's magic was attacking her. He had to forget about getting help and get her out of there himself. There was no one else. A fourteen-year-old boy trying to get help with the story he would have to tell would only be laughed at. He would be ignored. Even the soldiers at the Federation army garrison would brush him off. Besides, he couldn't let her continue to suffer like this. She was in obvious pain, in some sort of agony caused by the bands of light. She needed his help at once.

But what was he supposed to do?

He stood there, undecided. Time was running out.

The witch would be returning. He had to act quickly. But anything he wanted to do began with entering the room. If he did that, would he be trapped in Mischa's web, as well? Would he become bound up like Chrysallin?

There was only one way to find out.

He stuck his arm into the room. When nothing happened, he stepped inside the door all the way.

Immediately he was assailed by images of Chrysallin in strange places, a gray-haired Elven woman nearby, and various dangers threatening. The images filled his mind, buckling his knees with their darkness and intensity. He took another step, and the force of the images pressed down harder on him. They scrambled his thoughts, and on the bed Chrysallin Leah thrashed violently.

He closed his eyes to concentrate on steadying himself and took another two steps into the room. When he opened them again, the lines were fragmenting and losing focus, beginning in some places to curl up like burned threads and in others to fall away completely. There was a strange buzzing sound as the pulsing of the greenish light intensified.

Keep going, he told himself.

He continued on, moving with slow, steady steps toward the bed and the girl, trying to block out the images and to concentrate on what he knew he must do. The bands of light were collapsing altogether now, blinking into darkness, falling away. They offered no resistance as he passed through them, shredding and fading at his touch. Though the images continued, they were losing force, flickering in and out of his consciousness. His passage through the room was obviously disrupting the magic, and it gave him heart and persuaded him to continue.

By the time he had reached the bed, the bands of light

had disappeared almost completely. He knelt by the girl and shook her gently.

"Wake up," he urged. "Chrysallin? Can you hear me? Wake up!"

And she did, her eyes opening to find his face, horror-filled and despairing. "Who are you?"

"Grehling Cara. I'm a friend of your brother's."

Then her look changed to one of hope, and she sat up quickly and threw her arms around him.

"Thank you, thank you," she whispered in his ear, holding on to him tightly. "Thank you for coming!"

"We have to go," he said. "Quickly. Can you walk?"

He helped her stand, but she was clearly in a great deal of pain in spite of the fact that she seemed to have suffered no obvious injuries. He checked her over surreptitiously, conscious of her near nakedness and embarrassed to be looking, but he could find no wounds.

"You have to walk. I can't carry you. But I can help support you."

She was dressed in a night shift, and there was no sign of her clothes anywhere. He would have liked to find her boots, at least, but there was no time for a search. With one arm about her waist, he walked her toward the bedroom door.

Midway there, she stopped, looking back, glancing around. "Mischa," she said.

"Back any minute." He started her moving again. "We don't want her to catch us here."

"But her head? What happened to her head?"

He had no idea what she was talking about, and he didn't want to take time to find out. So he just kept moving her toward the front door, helping her stay upright, one arm wrapped firmly about her slender waist. She was muttering to herself about things he couldn't understand, every so often mentioning the Elven woman and Arcannen and her brother. It was enough to con-

vince him that whatever was going on, it had to do with
bringing Paxon back to Wayford. It also convinced him
that the sorcerer and the witch were deadly serious
about making this happen or they wouldn't have gone
to all the trouble to kidnap the girl a second time and
then layer her with bands of magic intended to . . .

He paused in his thinking. To do what?

In point of fact, what were those bands? He really
didn't know. But he would find out, once he got somewhere safe and could talk to Chrysallin about it.

"Keep moving," he said. "You're all right now. You're
doing fine."

She murmured something unintelligible, but gripped
him more tightly with the arm she had slung across his
shoulders. She was tall, taller than he was, and it was
awkward trying to steer her. She was keeping upright,
but it was taking everything she had to do so.

"Don't look at me," she said at one point, and he
thought she must be embarrassed by her lack of clothes
and wished he could find a robe or shawl with which to
cover her.

But there was no time for that or anything else. He
had to get out of the witch's rooms and her building and
safely away. Time was something he didn't have to
waste.

He reached the door and flung it open and abruptly
found himself face-to-face with the witch. There was no
time to think, no chance to do anything but react. He
slammed his fist into Mischa's snarling face, catching
her flush between her eyes. He was small and not much
of a fighter, but desperation and fear lent him unexpected strength and the blow packed real force. Her
head snapped back, her eyes rolled up, and down she
went.

Leaning Chrysallin against the wall, he bent over the
witch, made sure she was unconscious, then pulled off

her boots and put them on the girl. In less than a minute, he had his arm around Chrysallin once more, steering her down the hall to the stairs, down the stairs to the first floor, then down the passageway there and out the door to the alleyway.

Whatever he was going to do now, he thought worriedly, he had better do it fast.

18

Emerging from Mischa's building into the alleyway with Chrysallin clinging to him, Grehling was surprised to find that dusk was setting in. He'd paid no attention to the time of day while tracking Arcannen and then freeing the girl, and he was vaguely disturbed to find he no longer had much daylight left. He supposed this was an automatic reaction to a change he hadn't anticipated, but he also knew it was a response to not wanting to be caught out in his present circumstances after dark.

He slowed at the alley entrance and peered both ways down the street beyond. A solitary cart was ambling along from his right, pulled by a donkey and driven by an old man. No one was in view to his left, in the direction of Dark House. It was as much as he could have hoped for; one old man did not suggest problems. But he was still dizzy from punching Mischa in the face and having to half carry Chrysallin out of the house, and feeling less than able to deal with much of anything more.

Especially Mischa.

If she caught up to him now . . .

He wondered suddenly if she knew who he was. He didn't think so, but he couldn't afford to take the chance. That meant he couldn't haul Chrysallin back to the airfield and try to hide her there. If the witch had recognized him, she would bring Arcannen right to his front door. He had to get Chrysallin out of the city altogether if he wanted to be sure she was safe. He had to return her to her brother.

But first he had to get them both off the streets of the city and out of sight.

The cart with the old man and the donkey rolled past, and he turned to Chrysallin. "Can you walk yet?"

She shook her head. "I don't know. I don't think so."

At least, she seemed a bit more lucid. She was no longer muttering to herself and sounding as if she were drunk, even if she still looked it. He eased her out of the alley and turned her down the street. She was doing better with supporting herself, not entirely able to let go of him and still staggering slightly, but making an effort at walking alone. Fortunately, this was a part of the city where a boy walking with an intoxicated girl wouldn't attract much attention.

But it was a long way to the airfield, if he intended to go there, and now he was thinking maybe he should, in spite of the danger. If Mischa had recognized him, she would come after him. But whether she did or not, Chrysallin Leah was not safe in Wayford and had to be taken somewhere else. To do that, he would need an airship to fly her there.

Which meant going to the airfield.

But afoot it would take forever.

He was sweating heavily now, and the fear that had been temporarily submerged by his earlier excitement was resurfacing. What had he done? He still couldn't believe it. He was risking his life for a girl he didn't even know for reasons he couldn't quite define. He knew it was the right thing to do, but it was so foolish it bordered on insanity. He had heard the stories of what Arcannen did to his enemies. He knew what was likely to happen to him if he were caught out at this point.

And Mischa's reputation was no less terrifying, and her response unlikely to be much different than Arcannen's.

"We have to walk faster," he muttered.

But Chrysallin was moving as fast as she could, and even after long minutes they had only gotten a few blocks away and were still on the main road. He was beginning to panic now, in danger of losing what little confidence he had left. He had to find a new plan, change what he was doing to something that made sense, and get off the street!

Then he remembered Leofur Rai.

She lived not two blocks away, just off this roadway, tucked back down a narrow pass-through. He didn't see much of her anymore, but she might be willing to help him. Of the alternatives he could manage to conjure, this was the best one.

Chrysallin had begun muttering to herself again, slipping in and out of lucidity, head drooping, body starting to sag. She wasn't strong enough for this yet, and it further convinced him that getting her to a place where she could rest was essential. He moved her forward, speaking to her softly as he did, urging her to keep going, to be strong, to remember she was free and would soon reach her brother.

They were just words and maybe even wishful thinking, but they kept her going. He could tell she heard him and was responding, but her focus was limited and her strength barely equal to what was required of her.

Nevertheless, he got her to the side street and into the pass-through, and in moments they were standing at Leofur's door. He tried to imagine for a moment what his reception would be like, but failed to manage an image that could do it justice. So in the end, he simply knocked, stepped back from the entry, and waited, doing his best to keep Chrysallin steady as she swayed

drunkenly, trying to put together in his head the words
he would need to persuade Leofur to help.

When the door finally opened, there she was, exactly
as he remembered her. Brilliant green eyes, honey-
colored hair artificially streaked with silver, perfect features, not very big, sort of on the short side, but
immediately unforgettable. He'd fallen in love with her
the moment his father hired her to care for him—she
only fifteen, he still a child and not yet even aware of
what real love was, but spellbound even so. His mother
was dead by then, and his father didn't want him to
grow up without a woman's hand. So Leofur had been
brought in to care for him in those years before his father remarried, and even at eight years of age he was
smitten from day one.

A hopeless infatuation, of course, but it was one he
still remembered as if it had happened yesterday. When
she left, he had thought he might follow her. But by then
he was realizing how hopeless it all was, and so he had
chosen not only to quit thinking about her but also to
not see her again.

That had been three years ago, and this was the first
time he had been able to make himself come looking for
her. She gave him a flat, expressionless look, her smooth
face hiding the surprise that flashed momentarily in her
eyes.

"Can we come in?" he asked, trying his best not to
give away his own feelings on seeing her again. "Please?"

She stood where she was, her gaze shifting between
the girl and him. "How bad is this?" she asked finally.

"About as bad as it could be," he admitted. "We need
to get off the streets right away."

Without another word, she stepped aside, holding the
door open to allow them to enter and then quickly closing it behind them.

"Sit her down at the kitchen table," she told him, hurrying ahead to move several stacks of clothes she had been sorting. She glanced back at him as she did so. "I wondered if I would ever see you again."

He nodded, his face gone flaming red. "I just couldn't," he said.

At the end of things, he had told her he loved her. Just before she left them to go back to her own life. He thought maybe she might take him with her. But instead she sat him down and told him she couldn't do that. He would have to stay with his father until he was old enough to be out on his own. What she was telling him, of course, was that she didn't love him in the way he loved her. It was a terrible moment; he had felt destroyed.

"Who is this you have with you?" she asked.

"This is Chrysallin. She's from the Highlands. Arcannen took her prisoner and locked her away in Dark House. He's working with that old crone, Mischa."

He went on to tell her everything—all about the first kidnapping that was meant to lure Paxon Leah to Wayford, the rescue and escape that followed, the second kidnapping and how he had learned about it by chance, and his own rescue of Chrysallin that had brought him here.

"I couldn't leave her. I couldn't let what was happening to her continue."

"Which was some sort of magic?" Leofur turned to the girl. "What were they doing to you?"

Chrysallin looked startled. "I asked! I begged them to tell me! But they wouldn't answer. Not the Elven woman. Not any of them. They just kept hurting me! They cut me and broke my bones and pulled the skin from my body. They used metal tools to make the pain worse, and all I could think about was how they were taking me apart, destroying me. The way they were making me look . . ."

Leofur shifted her eyes to Grehling questioningly. *What?* She mouthed the word soundlessly.

He shook his head. *I don't know.*

"Where are you hurt?" Leofur asked the girl.

"Everywhere! Can't you see?" She was instantly hysterical, wild-eyed. "Look at me! No one can see me like this."

Leofur moved over to sit next to her, taking her hands in her own. "But there's nothing wrong with you, Chrysallin. Everything is fine."

The Highland girl gasped in disbelief. "How can you say that? Look at my hands, my fingers. Look at my body!"

And she ripped open her nightshirt to reveal a perfectly flawless breast and shoulders.

Leofur gently pulled her garments back together and took Chrysallin in her arms and held her as she sobbed uncontrollably. "I think it would help if you would lie down. But first let's give you something to help you sleep."

She prepared some tea—or something that looked like tea—made of leaves she poured from a small pouch. Chrysallin drank the pungent liquid obediently, now and then glancing to make certain Grehling was still there. When she was finished, she allowed herself to be led over to the couch and placed on it. Leofur brought out a blanket and wrapped her in it, and in moments she was asleep.

Leofur motioned Grehling to join her at the kitchen table. "Well, something's certainly been done to her. She thinks she's been tortured, but there's not a mark on her. How did this happen?"

"Mischa used magic." Grehling fidgeted, nervous still in her presence. "Bands of greenish light. They were all over the room when I found her, hundreds of them, wrapped around her like ropes. She was twisting and thrashing, and she was clearly in pain."

"She has to be made to understand there's nothing wrong, that it's all in her mind. But it can wait until after she sleeps." Grehling started to reach for the bag that contained the leaves used to make the tea given Chrysallin, and quickly Leofur held up her hands. "Not that, Grehling," she said sharply. "There's more in that tea than what you need just now. Here."

She rose, went to the cupboard, and brought out a different mix, then set about reheating the kettle. "I'm sorry I waited until this happened to come see you," he said. "I shouldn't have stayed away."

She grinned, her cheeks dimpling. "No, you shouldn't have. But that's all right. I've been waiting for you. I thought you were just still trying to grow up and hadn't quite gotten there yet."

"Still haven't gotten there," he said with a shrug. "But I couldn't wait any longer. I didn't know where else to go."

"That's all right. You're welcome here." She paused, her smile fading a bit. "I thought you stayed away from me for other reasons."

He shrugged. "I've heard some rumors."

"Some of those rumors might be true."

"I didn't pay attention." He had, of course. But he would never admit it because he didn't want what he heard to be true. Not of Leofur. "Anyway," he added, "it doesn't matter. I've done plenty of things that aren't so good, too."

She stared at him a moment, a vaguely amused expression on her face, and then she nodded. "What do you want me to do for this girl? Hide her? This is Arcannen we're talking about. I'm in as much trouble as you. I'm looking at real danger here."

"I know. I shouldn't have come."

"I'm not saying that. I'm saying you have to decide what you want from me so I can tell you if I am prepared to offer it. I need to know what's at risk if I agree to help you further. Do you want her kept here? Or do you want me to see about helping you get her out of the city? He's going to be searching for her when he finds her gone, isn't he?"

Grehling nodded. "He and Mischa might already be searching."

"Do they know about your connection with her?"

"I don't know. Mischa saw me leaving with her, but we've never met face-to-face, so she might not know who I am."

"But you can't take chances."

He shook his head. "I thought I might try to get Chrysallin to the airfield and into my flit and fly her back to Leah. But the walk to the airfield is too long; she's too weak to make it."

"And too much under the influence of the magic, whatever it's doing." Leofur poured tea into cups for both of them. "Anyway, even if you somehow manage it, by the time you get there Arcannen or his men will already be watching. You know his reputation as well as I do."

Something in the way she said it stopped him. "You don't have anything to do with him, do you?"

She cocked her head, the vaguely amused expression returning. "No, I don't have anything to do with him."

"I didn't think so." But now he wished he hadn't asked. "What do you think I should do?"

"You shouldn't go back to the airfield or your house. You shouldn't go anywhere near either one." She thought about it a moment. "I could slip you out of the city in a wagon or cart, even though it might take a day or two to arrange things. But you might have to do it anyway, just because it would be the safest choice."

He shook his head. "No. We're miles from another city of any size. Or an airfield where I could find a ship. Anyway, I don't have any money."

She laughed. "You are sad, aren't you? A rescuer with no means to effect a rescue." She reached out and took his hands in hers. "I'm glad you came to me, Grehling. It's good to see you again. I've missed you."

"I've missed you, too," he admitted. "It's never been the same without you. Father remarried, and she's nice enough, but we're not close. I work at the airfield, but I'm pretty much on my own most of the time. I miss talking to you. Father tries, but . . ."

"Your father was never much of a talker," she said. "But he was kind to me."

She looked like she might say something more, but then she stood up abruptly and looked out the window into the darkening twilight. Nightfall was settling in, the shadows enveloping the surrounding buildings, the light gone out of the sky.

"Let's think about this," she said. "Why don't we sleep on it? Night's almost here, and you must be very tired after what you've been through. Your friend's already asleep. Why don't you join her? You can have a place beside her on the floor. I have some blankets and a sleeping pad you can use."

Though anxious to be off, to be moving away from the danger, Grehling saw the wisdom in her advice and gave a nod. He would be able to think more clearly and act more quickly after he slept. He watched her as she walked over to a closet, brought out the promised pad and blankets, and laid them out neatly on the floor next to the couch where Chrysallin was sleeping.

"We'll talk about this in the morning," she said. She came over, took his hands once more, pulled him to his feet, and kissed him on the forehead. "There, just like when you were a little boy."

She smiled and turned him toward the sleeping pad. "Lie down, now. Go to sleep."

He did as he was told, slipping off his boots and shirt and crawling beneath the blanket as she extinguished the lights. He lay there in the dark, listening to her move away—down the hall and into her bedroom. He listened to her movements afterward, picturing her.

He understood in that moment why he had never really managed to forget how he felt about her.

He wasn't sure how long he was asleep before he heard Chrysallin thrashing, but he was awake instantly as he jerked upright from beneath the blankets and hurriedly knelt beside the couch, trying to calm her.

"It's okay," he said, his voice a rough, sleep-fogged whisper. "You're safe! Nothing can hurt you here."

But she was having none of it, her eyes open and staring, her limbs gesturing wildly, her words jumbled and lacking any recognizable meaning. She kept saying something about the Elven woman, about her brother, and about a black knife. She raved about her pain and suffering, begging and begging her tormentors to stop, to let her go. He held her and whispered reassurances, soothed her with hushing and with the touch of his hand as he stroked her long hair. He did everything he knew how to do to calm her, but it was only after a long time that she went still again.

When he lay her back on the couch and adjusted her blanket, it seemed as if she had gone back to sleep.

But when he lay down again himself, he heard her call softly, "Grehling?"

"I'm here."

"I had a dream. Another dream. A nightmare. It was bad." She paused. "I don't know what's real anymore."

He waited, and then said, "I'm real. Your being here with me is real. Being safe is real."

"Maybe. But everything I thought was real before wasn't. Now I can't be sure of anything."

He heard her shift positions so she was lying on her side, looking down at him. "I still hurt everywhere. I can still feel the pain from what they did to me. I can still remember them doing it." She took a long shuddering breath. "But there doesn't seem to be any physical damage. I touch my fingers and hands and arms—which I thought were all torn apart and broken—but they're just the same as always."

"Everything about you is fine. You don't have any damage anyone can see. You look just the same. When it gets light you can see for yourself. All those things you said happened to you—they didn't. Something was done to make you believe they happened, but they didn't."

She was silent for a long time. "I imagined it all?"

"You were made to imagine it, I think."

"Maybe not all of it."

He hesitated. "No, I think maybe everything."

"Not the Elven woman. Not her. She was real. She was there every time I opened my eyes. Mischa was real. You said so yourself. They were both real, but maybe Mischa is dead now. I saw her head on a table."

Grehling squeezed his eyes shut and then opened them. "I don't think she's dead. And neither do you. Think carefully. You saw her when we escaped. I struck her with my fist. You saw that happen."

"Did I? I'm not sure. I don't know if I remember that. I think it was the Elven woman. She was the one you struck."

The boy sighed and yawned, reluctant to have this discussion now. "I have to sleep. So do you. We can talk about it in the morning. But I'll be right here if you need me."

"Promise?" she asked softly.

"Promise."

"Thanks."

"You're welcome."

Silence. His breathing deepened and his eyes closed. He was almost asleep again when he heard her say, "When I see her again, I'm going to kill her."

He didn't have to ask who she meant.

19

WHEN MISCHA SHAMBLED INTO HIS OFFICE AT Dark House late that evening, a huge bruise on her forehead and both eyes blackened, Arcannen knew at once what had happened.

"The girl got away," the witch spat, confirming it.

It was with some effort that he managed to keep his composure. "How did she manage that?" he asked.

She slumped into a chair, her head in her hands. "She had help. A boy. I don't know where he came from, but he must have broken into the building, found her, and taken her out."

"He was able to free her from the magic?"

"Apparently. It wasn't that hard. If you were determined enough, you could walk into the room, break the web apart, and free her." She looked up, her face twisted in pain. "You will remember I told you to be careful not to go into the room when we looked in on her. That was the reason. The strands have a powerful effect on the intended subject, but are otherwise weak."

"This just happened?"

"A short time ago. I went out for ingredients for the potions that form the bands. When I returned, they were coming out the door. The boy hit me before I could stop him." She pointed needlessly to her forehead. "When I woke again, they were both gone."

He hesitated, thinking it through, resisting the urge

to leap up and do something. Haste now would be a mistake. The damage, however bad, was already done. He glanced out the window to his right. Darkness had settled in, the light gone out of the world for another day. Another complication.

"How far along do you think the process was? Is she sufficiently subverted by now that she will do what you have set her to do, even though she has been freed?"

Mischa gave him a dark look. "The magic needs time; there isn't an exact way to measure how much. You know that. It varies with each subject's strength of will. She has already endured a stronger dosage than most, and still I was not satisfied that she was completely won over. Yes, she is deep under. But another day would have been better."

"Well, we don't have another day now, do we?" He only barely managed to conceal his disdain for her incompetence. "So what is your best guess?"

The witch was silent for several long moments. "A better chance that she will than she won't, I suppose. But if I could get her back—"

"Yes, you would be happier," he interrupted. "And we would both like to get our hands on this boy. Did you recognize him?"

She shook her head. "I may have seen him somewhere. I can't be sure. But I'll remember his face. Sooner or later, I'll find him."

Very helpful, I'm sure, Arcannen thought. "He must have had some connection to her," he mused aloud. "Otherwise, why would he bother to help her? For that matter, how did he even know where to find her, whatever the connection? It wasn't like her stay with you was public knowledge. You must have done something to give it away."

"I did nothing to give anything away!" she spat at him. "Everything was done as we agreed. No one was allowed to see anything. She was not allowed to know anything. For her, it was all a dream. Nothing was real, but it all felt real. For anyone watching, there was no way to know who she was or why she was there." She sat back. "Are you going to do anything about this?"

He shrugged. "She will either go to ground or try to get out of the city. I will send men to watch the airfield. I will send others to search the streets. But I have to assume we won't catch her again. If whoever helped her takes her to her brother, things might still turn out the way we want them to."

He paused, remembering suddenly. "Did she take the knife with her when she left?"

The witch reached into her robes and pulled out the Stiehl. "I doubt she even thought of taking it, as deeply under the magic's spell as she must have been." She placed it on the table between them. "The boy probably knew nothing of it. It was still sitting on the nightstand where I left it."

He was furious now. Use of the knife was essential to his plan. A weapon against which there was no defense, it would have assured that matters were concluded as he had intended from day one. Now he would have to rely on opportunity and luck.

"That's too bad," he said through gritted teeth. He got to his feet then, irritated beyond measure. "I have work to do. Maybe we can find her after all. You never know."

She staggered up with him, still clearly not recovered from being struck. Well, she was old, after all, witch or no. "I'll not leave this to chance or luck, Arcannen. You have your men watch for her, and if they find her let me know. In the meantime, I intend to track her down myself. That boy thinks himself so clever, but he doesn't know he's already marked himself just by breaking into my rooms. I can track him using magic, and I will. It might take a day or so, but I will find him."

She straightened. "When I do, you can have the girl back again after another day of treatment, but the boy is mine. I will use him a bit, experiment on him, and then make him disappear for good."

She turned and shuffled out of the room, bent and shapeless and somehow more loathsome for seeming so pathetic. But she was immensely dangerous, and he never forgot it when he was in her presence. The evil she exuded was palpable, and he would not have liked to be that boy once she went hunting.

The Stiehl lay on the table in front of him where Mischa had placed it. He looked down at it thoughtfully, then reached out and picked it up. There was still a chance it might find a use in his plans. If not in one way, then perhaps in another.

He slipped it into his black robes and went out to summon his men.

Mischa left Dark House and went out into the surrounding streets, seething. She hated having to go to Arcannen like that, hat in hand, admitting her failure to hold the girl prisoner as she had been charged to do. She loathed having to confess like a penitent schoolgirl. But mostly she burned with rage at having had this brought about by a mere boy. As she said to the sorcerer, there was definitely something familiar about him. She had seen him somewhere, although she could not remember where just at the moment.

But she would, she promised herself. At some point, she would.

She shuffled her way back to her rooms, passing through the darkness like one of night's shadows, ignoring the few other denizens of the time and place who passed her by. Most knew her on sight, even faceless and obscured. All avoided her. Arcannen was right: She had the look of a harmless old lady, but she was anything but. Mischa was a creature capable of great evil.

She was thinking even now how she would dissect the boy while he was still alive, listening to him plead, smiling at his misery. Oh, he would be made to regret what he had done to her, of that there could be no doubt.

But finding him came first.

How best to do that?

When she reached her building, she paused at the entry and examined the lock. Picked by someone who knew what he was doing. So the boy was a little thief with talent. She touched the lock and the door frame. His essence was all around her, caught on the materials he had touched. She smelled the air. It was there, too.

She went inside, aware of the pounding in her head, but unwilling to let it subside while it fed her hunger for vengeance. The walk upstairs was slow and painful, her head throbbing, regret and impatience eating at her. If she had only come back from her errand a little sooner. Just a little. But she knew to put that aside. In the end, she would have what she wanted.

At the door leading into her room, she paused. Once again, she read the signs of the boy clearly. Enough to track him. Enough to hunt him down. If she had the proper creature to do the hunting.

She went inside and closed the door behind her. Not yet midnight. Still plenty of time. She walked to the center of the room amid the frayed remnants of her carefully constructed web of magic, now in tatters, all of it destroyed, all of it invisible to the ordinary eye. She could even sense the boy here. Yes, there was enough to work with. But the magic would be strongest in the bedroom where the girl had been wrapped in it and the remnants of it still remained to mingle with the boy's scent.

Stretching her thin arms wide, she summoned new magic, using words and gestures, elements and memories, her skills brought to the fore by years of practice and a sizable measure of self-confidence. When she had this mix collected and roiling within the room's empty confines, she left momentarily to bring back potions and a brazier. She lit the brazier, set a small kettle on the flame, and threw in the potions. A fresh glow of pale green surfaced and a terrible stench from the kettle assailed her nostrils. But to her the smell was sweet and welcome, and she breathed it in.

Once the air was filled with her smoky brew, she spoke the words of power and made the necessary gestures to enhance them—to invest them with her own emotions and dark imaginings—giving life and breath to inanimate substance. It was a rigorous, grueling effort, but anger and pain gave her strength.

Slowly, the thing she was making took form.

Initially, it was little more than an amorphous cloud, but as the magic grew stronger and more cohesive it took on human shape. Enough so that it developed arms and legs to go with its elongated body. It hung there in midair, a twisting embryo, a replicant of a nightmarish vision coming to life in the gloom and smoke and shadows. No sounds accompanied its birthing save those of the witch's muttered incantations and labored breathing, and the faint hiss of venom expelled by the creature's expansion.

When everything else was done and the making all but complete, she infused her creation with weight and strength, and it sank from midair to stand upon the floor, taking final form and becoming what she had intended all along. It stood before her, misshapen in the way she had intended—a long, lean torso; short, powerful legs; multi-jointed arms meant to sweep up and gather in; skin like serrated leather; hands and feet ending in huge claws—and it acknowledged her with a voiceless inclination of its blunt face. It had a tiny slit for a mouth, a huge snout for smelling scent, and narrow yellow eyes that could see equally well in darkness or light.

She let it stand before her as the air cleared of the magic's detritus and the room was restored to its earlier condition, studying its features, admiring her handiwork. It stood quietly, showing no signs of impatience, looking about incuriously, breathing slowly and evenly. The long, lean body was muscular in a way that promised quickness and strength in equal measure. There was intelligence in its gaze, too, and the suggestion of a capacity for extreme violence. She would need both if it was to serve her properly.

A hunter, she thought, *pure and simple.*

She walked to the window, parted the curtains she had drawn earlier, and peered out. The night was still young. Plenty of time to find wayward children. Not many people would be abroad at this hour, and most would likely be sleeping. She thought the boy and the girl might have found shelter by now. Exhausted and frightened, they would be hoping to spend the night undisturbed. The girl might have escaped, but she would not be able to travel far in her present condition. The magic would have eroded her strength and left her barely able to walk. She would not be far from where Mischa stood now; it was almost certain that the boy had not yet been able to get her out of the city.

No, they would still be here. Somewhere. Here, where her creature could track them down and reveal them.

She walked back to stand before it, gathering up a handful of scent and shredded magic as she went, a clutch of essence from both the boy and the girl. She cupped it in both hands and held it out to the beast. It bent forward to inhale the scent, its snout wrinkling to reveal the teeth hidden within its mouth.

"Hunt them!" she hissed.

Aboard their Druid airship, Paxon Leah and Starks approached the city of Wayford, its lights a glimmering carpet in the otherwise deep midnight darkness. They had gotten a late start, and their arrival was well after the time they had intended. But delaying another day was unacceptable to the boy, and Starks—his usual nonchalant attitude evident once again—had simply shrugged and agreed they should set out immediately.

It was the Ard Rhys who had delayed them, calling them to her quarters just as they were about to depart—a summons delivered by Sebec with such urgency that it was clear any refusal would be a mistake. Paxon was hopeful the delay would be only momentary, but it soon became clear that it was not to be. She brought them inside and sat them down, standing tall and strong before them in spite of her age and normally gentle demeanor.

"Someone has taken the Stiehl," she announced. "The theft was discovered yesterday, but the knife could have been taken anytime since your last inventory. What this means is that the most dangerous weapon we possess is now in the hands of someone who probably has plans for using it."

Paxon had never heard of the Stiehl, but it was easy to conclude from the darkness of her voice as she announced its theft that it was an important artifact.

"We have no idea who took it?" Starks asked.

"Not yet, but I have taken steps to find out. We have someone in our midst who is both a thief and a traitor to the order. This most recent theft makes four in the past year. The Stiehl is the most dangerous—the other three, including the scrye orb, considerably less so. You were summoned so that I could warn you to be careful. It is not altogether impossible that any of these weapons, but especially the Stiehl, might be used against you. This theft has Arcannen's mark on it, and you are embarking on a journey to find him. Don't be careless when you confront him."

Starks nodded and rose. "We are not the careless sorts," he said. "Is there more?"

"Only this. If you should find the knife, be certain that you bring it back."

When they left her chambers, Starks explained to Paxon about the history of the blade—how it was recovered by Walker Boh on his quest to the land of the Stone King and then brought to Paranor when the Keep, closed since the death of Allanon, was reopened. It was an ancient weapon forged of rare metals and infused with dark magic so that it could cut through anything, no matter how strong. It had been kept safe for most of the past thousand years, locked away in the Keep. To have it taken and returned to the larger world where it could be used for any number of terrible purposes was unsettling.

"I want to talk to Sebec," Starks announced. "He will be the one making inquiries. I want to know what he has found. I want to hear from him directly."

Together, they tracked down and confronted the young Druid, who gave them what information he had and asked Starks if he knew anything about anyone entering the artifact chambers. The conversation lasted longer than Paxon believed was necessary, but he kept his thoughts to himself and paid attention to what was being said. As it was, they learned nothing useful, and their plans for leaving were delayed by more than half a day.

But now they were approaching their destination, and Paxon's thoughts of the missing blade and the efforts mounted by the Ard Rhys to find it were forgotten in his focus on the search for Chrysallin. A fresh tension began to build, fueled by a mix of fear and expectation. She had been taken from her home almost a week ago. By now, anything could have happened to her. He was terrified that she might already be damaged in some unchangeable way. Arcannen didn't seem above exacting revenge simply because his earlier efforts had been thwarted. And while Paxon believed he had more in mind than simple vengeance, he couldn't quite make himself rule out the possibility. Whatever the case, there was ample reason for him to hurry his efforts and to find his sister with all possible haste.

Starks had said nothing much of what he thought they should do, which was frustrating. He was the leader of this expedition, and Paxon would have liked to have known hours ago how they were going to go about it. But Starks had concentrated his efforts on flying, and Paxon had been reluctant to bring up the matter himself. He knew Starks had a penchant for not speaking of future events until they were close to being upon them.

But now, climbing down from the pilot box and standing together on the darkened airfield by the manager's office, he turned to Paxon and it seemed he would say something about their plans. Instead, he said, "Where is the field manager?"

Paxon glanced around and pointed. "There's someone over there."

The airfield manager was shambling toward them, coming from somewhere out among the moored aircraft. When he reached them, he tipped a battered cap and said, "Well met. Do you require service?"

Starks nodded back. "Our ship needs to be watched over. Can you do that for us?"

"For tonight?"

"Perhaps tomorrow, too." He glanced at Paxon. "It's late for a visit," he said, lowering his voice. "Sleep might be a better choice."

Paxon shook his head doubtfully. He didn't like the idea of waiting. "Is Arcannen about?" he asked the manager. "Is he in Wayford?"

"Flew in this afternoon," the man answered.

"Traveling alone?"

"If you don't count his crew and his guards."

"No one else?"

The man shrugged. "My son would know; he sees things better than I do. But he's not here. Matter of fact, he left right after Arcannen flew in and didn't come back." He scratched his beard. "Been wondering about that. He's late for the night shift. Usually I can depend on that boy."

"That would be Grehling?"

"That's him. Able and smart, though he's got an independent streak a mile wide." He shook his head. "You never know."

Instantly, Paxon had a dark premonition. He faced Starks squarely. "I don't want to wait on this. I want my sister back."

Starks studied him a moment, and then he nodded. "All right. Let's go get her."

20

It was well after midnight when Starks and Paxon began their walk toward Dark House. The former led the way, wrapped in his familiar black robes, hooded now and shadowy against the worn cobblestones, and Paxon kept close behind. The Highlander felt the weight of the Sword of Leah pressing against his back with every step he took, a reminder of what most probably lay ahead. He did not think for a minute that any rescue of Chrysallin would come without a struggle. This time would not be like the last. Arcannen would be fully prepared, aware of the power of the Sword and looking to catch him off guard one way or another.

Out of the corner of his eye, he watched the movement of shadows from within alleyways and along walls. Bits and pieces of darkness, layering and separating, changing shapes by the instant. They might be human or animal, tree limbs or bushes, or they might be nothing at all. He kept his focus on the roadway ahead, not trusting his vision, using his other senses to warn him of possible danger. The deeper into the city they went, the less easy it became to see what waited. A skein of fog was settling in, forming in a mix of cold air and city warmth, clogging the streets and alleyways as it slowly expanded, snaking this way and that in search of fresh space, flooding yards and open spaces, banking up against stone walls. It thickened steadily, tightening until they were enveloped.

Starks slowed, studying the whiteness that obscured the way forward, clearly unhappy. He glanced over at Paxon, nodded to one side, and led him off the street and onto the walkway.

There, he stopped and lifted his face to the sky.

"Something is out there," he whispered.

They were only blocks from Dark House now, so Paxon assumed the Druid believed that whatever he was sensing had something to do with Arcannen. He waited patiently as Starks stood silent and unmoving, eyes closed.

Then, abruptly, the Druid started forward again, and Paxon went with him. The Highlander found himself wondering about Grehling. Was it possible the boy had done something foolish and run afoul of Arcannen? He had been willing to risk himself earlier by telling Paxon how to break into Dark House. He had some experience dealing with both the sorcerer and his lair, so he might have been willing to take a further risk.

But he couldn't know of Chrysallin's kidnapping, could he?

Although, hadn't he known of it before? Just by being present on the airfield when she was brought in? Was it too much to think he might have seen something this time, too?

In any case, he was worried for the boy, and he promised himself he would make sure Grehling wasn't in any danger before he left Wayford.

Thoughts of Chrysallin's fate haunted him. He couldn't stop imagining all the things Arcannen might have done to her. Might even now be doing to her. He tried to tell himself that the sorcerer was after him, not her, but even that didn't quite dispel the horrific images his mind seemed determined to conjure up. Guilt plagued him. Chrysallin should never have been involved in all this in the first place. She had nothing to do with any of it, a pawn the sorcerer had played to checkmate Paxon, bait to bring him to the hook. He hated that he was the cause of the situation she was in. He berated himself for leaving her unprotected. He should have turned down the offer to go to Paranor to train. He should have stayed with her and been ready when Arcannen resurfaced, and then he could have put an end to him.

But he knew that was foolish. What chance would he have had? He'd never killed anyone. He'd never before used magic. He had barely managed to wield the power of his sword the first time he'd gone to bring Chrysallin back. Only with the training he had received at Paranor in the use of arms and magic would he be able to survive a second encounter with the sorcerer.

And even then, he would be at extreme risk.

A cat darted across the roadway, a blur in the haze, a phantom. Paxon started in spite of himself, though Starks seemed unaffected. The fog was everywhere now, swirling gently in the night air, shifting to open and shut windows all around them, revealing momentarily parts of buildings and streets before closing about once more.

The minutes slipped away. Paxon lost track of where they were. In the fog, it was impossible to find anything to tell him. But Starks kept moving ahead, seemingly aware of where they were and where they were going, steadfast in his passage. Streetlamps burned out of the haze now and again, never bright enough to reveal much, but indicators at least that they were still keeping to the roadway and had not wandered off into the endless dark untethered from reality.

"There," Starks said finally, pointing ahead.

Paxon stopped next to him. For a moment, he couldn't

see anything different. Then the fog shifted slightly, just enough that he could make out the front entrance to Dark House and a scattering of lights burning in the windows.

The Druid turned to him. "We'll try going straight in. I will go first. You will watch my back. There will likely be someone on the door. I will deal with whoever that is. Keep your sword at the ready, but don't use it unless we are attacked. We might get lucky enough to reach Arcannen before he is warned."

He paused, waiting. Paxon nodded. "We have to find her," he said. "Whatever else happens, we have to save her."

Starks gave him a crooked grin. "We will."

They crossed the street, went up the short set of steps that led to the front door, and stopped. Starks moved Paxon out of the line of sight offered by the peephole, but stood fully revealed himself. He pulled back his hood, adjusted his robes, and knocked.

The window on the peephole opened. "Name?"

"I'd rather not give it," Starks replied with a rueful grin. "I'm just a man looking for a glass of ale and some personal comfort. Can you provide some of each, perhaps?"

The slide closed and the locks released. The door opened. Starks remained where he was, smiling at whoever was standing on the other side, not rushing in or showing any urgency.

"Lovely evening," he said.

Then he stepped through the door. There was a muffled reply, a gasp, and finally a more distant grunt of surprise. Paxon peered around the door frame to find Starks holding a burly doorman pinned flat against the wall, his mouth working like a fish out of water, but with no sound emerging. Farther down the hall, a second man lay slumped against one wall, unmoving. "Close the door," the Druid said.

Paxon did so. Starks moved close to the doorman, and their eyes locked. "Listen carefully," the Druid said to his captive. "I will ask some questions. You will answer them. If you disappoint me, I will break your neck." He paused, studying the man. "Is any of this not clear? Nod if you've understood it all."

The man, now turning an interesting shade of purple, nodded vigorously.

"First question. Is Arcannen in Dark House?"

The man nodded.

"Is he on this floor?" A negative shake. "Upstairs, in his office?"

Affirmative nod.

"Are there guards with him?"

Another negative shake.

"Has he gone to bed?"

The man hesitated, managed to shrug. Then, an uncertain nod.

Starks reached out with his free hand, pinched the man's neck hard near the shoulder, and the man collapsed in a heap.

"There will be more guards. We need to avoid being seen. There are back stairs down the hall and off to the left. Come."

They moved down the corridor without encountering anyone else. Once again, Paxon was struck by the lack of guards and protections. Just as he had the first time, he sensed the possibility of a trap. But Starks seemed unconcerned, and so they reached the side passage and the stairway without incident.

Again, Starks paused, his voice a whisper. "Arcannen's personal quarters are on the third floor. We will look for him there. If we find him, we will subdue him, then look for your sister."

"I know where she was last time," Paxon offered.

Starks nodded. "She won't be there this time. The sorcerer knows you are coming. He will have moved her. But we might find someone who knows where he is keeping her."

The Highlander nodded.

Together, they began to climb the stairs.

Arcannen sat at his desk, studying charts on supplies of potions and elixirs, on ingredients used in the construct of magic and conjuring forms he favored. It was busywork, admittedly, but he was not sleepy and he had done all he could about Chrysallin Leah for the moment. After Mischa had left, he had summoned a dozen of his guards and sent some to search the streets and some to watch the airfield. Chrysallin would show up at one place or the other. They would find her.

If Mischa didn't find her first, of course, using her usual golems and familiars to track her down. He didn't favor such things himself, preferring more reliable magic, but the witch had learned her skills differently than he so he had to accept her as she was. Besides, if her efforts yielded results he might even be inclined to forgive her for letting the girl escape in the first place. He might begin viewing her once again as indispensable to his plans.

He might, but not likely.

It always came down to the same thing. You could only rely on yourself. It didn't matter about skills or experience or promises or good intentions or anything else when it came to placing your faith in another person—even someone you were close to, someone who had raised and nurtured and mentored you. You were always the first, best choice for making sure matters turned out the way you wanted. It wasn't always possible for you to handle everything personally, but it was always possible for you to choose which things you would.

In this case, he had made a poor choice leaving Chrysallin Leah in the witch's hands rather than keeping her close to him in Dark House.

Water under the bridge now. He would have to hope that either she was recovered so she could be treated further, or she would manage to find her way to Paranor and the Druids.

He leaned back in his chair, the lists and charts momentarily forgotten. He supposed his worldview was different from that of most, but he believed it the only realistic one. Strength was the measure of success, both physically and intellectually. Showing weakness led to failure, and any deviation from your goals only demonstrated your lack of commitment. The world did not give you anything for free; it did not provide help to those who did not look for opportunities and take advantage of them. Moral codes merely held you back; they placed unnecessary restrictions on your options and locked you in place. A willingness to ignore convention and rules was necessary if you were to achieve anything.

He knew how others viewed him. But how others viewed him was not his concern. None of those people would do anything for him. What they wished was to see him driven into the ground, a beaten man. They were jealous of his power and his achievements, and they hated him for his ability to do what they were afraid to do.

They called him wicked and evil; they labeled him a monster. It made them feel better to act as if he were a poison they must avoid at all costs. But strength did not come from belittling others and hiding away behind pretense and subterfuge. It did not come by doing what others thought admirable and consistent with their beliefs. It came from bold, determined action, from a willingness to ignore everything but the goal desired. It came from resilience and commitment.

His connection to and use of magic allowed for most of this. He could overcome almost anything simply by calling on what he had mastered over the years in the black arts. He had developed an affinity for using magic, an emotional and psychological bond that infused him with deep satisfaction when he summoned it, and while it might be argued that his attachment bordered on addiction, he felt the trade-off well worth it. Others might shy away, but they would never have what he did, would never attain what he had.

Thus, in this present situation, he was attempting something that no one had ever succeeded in doing, not just through careful planning and an understanding of how best to exploit weakness that others would not even recognize, but through fluid adaptation to changes and reversals such as the one involving the girl. He was attempting to bring down the Druid order.

Ambitious, yes. Impossible, no. It could be done, and he was in the process of doing it. If nothing further occurred to disrupt his already somewhat entangled plans, he would accomplish it within the month. And once he had done so, the benefits would be enormous. With the active support of his spy inside the order and the services he intended to exact from the recalcitrant and unreliable Fashton Caeil, he would become, overnight, the most powerful magic user in the Four Lands. He would be nicely positioned to see either the total destruction of the order or its rebuilding under his leadership.

He had barely completed that thought when one of the men he had sent out earlier appeared in the doorway, out of breath and red-faced.

"What's wrong?" he asked quickly.

"That Highlander is back. With one of the Druids. I

just saw them land at the airfield. They're on their way here. I ran all the way, just ahead of them, to tell you."

Arcannen nodded, staying calm. "Go back downstairs and get something to eat. Stay there."

When the man was gone, Arcannen considered his options. He wanted the Highlander and his sword, but the presence of a Druid complicated things sufficiently that he didn't think engaging them at this point would be a good idea. Since he no longer had the sister, he had nothing with which to bargain. He could pretend he did, but it would be better to wait until he had the girl back in hand.

He picked up the charts and shoved them into a deep drawer, closed and locked it, and put the key in his pocket. If he hurried, he could get out of Dark House before they arrived. This is where they would come, searching for him, but if he wasn't here they would be at a loss as to what to do. There were plenty of places he could go to ground until they lost interest or word reached him that Chrysallin was recovered.

Of course, there was always the danger they would stumble on a wandering Chrysallin Leah, but even that might work to his advantage. The boy would want to keep his sister safe. He would know he could not do that in Leah. So he would take her to Paranor and the Druids. Things would proceed from there as he had planned.

Meanwhile, he could put his time to better use. There were other pieces to his plan that needed setting in place.

He finished putting everything away, walked to the door, and peered out into the hallway. No one was visible. They couldn't have gotten there this fast anyway, he chided himself. Why was he worrying about it? He went out into the passageway, started for the main stairs, and paused. Just in case, maybe he should avoid the main entrance.

He turned about and went the other way.

When he reached the back stairs, he started down.

Several blocks away, Chrysallin Leah was dreaming. She had fallen asleep again finally, exhausted from her struggle to remain awake, but had succumbed at last to the horror that waited. The gray-haired Elven woman was back, pursuing her through woods that were deep and dark and monster-haunted. She was everywhere Chrysallin looked, and it made no difference where the girl went or what she tried to do to escape. Her tormentor was always there, close at hand.

Other things hunted her, as well, their bodies shapeless and their faces blank and empty of expression. They crept through the shadows and out of dark holes. They dropped down from trees and walked out of walls of mist. They did not speak, but their intentions were clear. Even absent a show of teeth and claws, she knew they meant to hurt her. And she was already in so much pain, her body torn and ripped, her insides bruised and bleeding. No part of her had been left untouched when the Elven woman and her voiceless henchmen had tortured her earlier, and she remembered every last thing they had done to her.

So she darted here and there, turned this way and that, dodged the creatures that came at her, each time just barely avoiding them. But their pursuit was relentless, and she could not get clear. The chase went on and on, and her frantic, useless efforts drove her half mad . . .

Wake up!

Hands were on her, shaking her, holding her fast. She tried to cry out, but fingers sealed her mouth and would not let her.

"Chrysallin!" a voice hissed. Her eyes flew open, and Grehling's face was right next to hers. "We have to go!"

She was hopelessly confused, still wrapped within the remnants of her dream. Where was she? The boy—she knew him, could almost speak his name—who was he? She tried to sit up, but her body screamed with pain, and she lay down again at once.

"Chrysallin, look at me!" he snapped, taking hold of her shoulders. "The witch is after us! Mischa! She's sent something to find us. It's right outside the door!"

She went cold all over at the mention of Mischa, and recognition came flooding back in a series of images and memories. Ignoring the pain, she struggled up, his strong hands helping her to her feet. A faint wash of light penetrated the curtains covering the front window, and she caught a glimpse of something big and black moving past, just outside the building wall.

The creatures in the dreams! They've found me!

Panic surged through her, and she backed away hurriedly, looking around for an escape. She saw Leofur Rai then, standing not six feet away, facing the door, a sleek metallic weapon cradled in her arms, pointed forward. Chrysallin had never seen anything like it. It was encased in black metal with a stock and barrel, and she could see Leofur's finger resting on a trigger near the joinder of the two.

The young woman glanced over and gestured with her head. "Get out of here, both of you! Go down the trapdoor in the floor behind you. Go now!"

Grehling was hustling her backward, away from whatever was waiting just outside the front door. She heard a scratching sound and saw the door handle lever downward and catch on the lock.

"Quickly!" Leofur hissed. "There's no—"

In the next instant the door burst inward, torn from its hinges as a huge black shape appeared in the opening. Leofur's weapon discharged a fireball that shot across the space separating her from the intruder and exploded into it with such force that it was thrown backward through the doorway and into the street.

By then Grehling was shoving Chrysallin through the trapdoor and down the ladder to the passageway below, practically leaping after her. A moment later Leofur reappeared, clambering down to join them, pulling and bolting the trapdoor behind her.

She pulled out a smokeless torch from a niche in the wall and lit it. "This way," she said without preamble, starting down the passageway, smoke curling from the barrel of the strange weapon.

"Did you kill it?" Chrysallin heard Grehling ask breathlessly as he rushed her along through the near darkness.

"Didn't do much of anything to it. Confused it, maybe." She didn't look around, didn't slow. "Keep going."

The corridor ahead branched, and she turned left. The passageway twisted and turned with sets of stairs and ladders leading upward all along the way.

"What is that thing you used on it?" the boy persisted. "I've never seen one before."

"There aren't many," Leofur shot back over her shoulder. Her eyes were dark with anger and frustration. "They're still experimental, a part of the Federation's weapons development program. Handheld flash rips."

"How did you get one?"

She glanced back at him. "Contacts in my business. A bargain, a trade. What difference does it make? It wasn't enough to stop that thing back there, was it? What have you gotten me into, Grehling?"

Not him, Chrysallin thought, *not him. What have I gotten us into? I'm the one responsible.*

Behind them, they heard a prolonged ripping of metal and wood. The trapdoor was open.

I'm sorry, I'm sorry! She screamed it in silence, screamed it to no one and everyone. *So sorry!*

She was coming apart again, the momentary sense of balance she had achieved when the creature had broken down the door and she had begun her flight thrown off kilter. The nightmares were back, the face of the gray-haired Elven woman right in front of her eyes, the pain and anguish surging through her in waves. She could feel herself moving, but was losing all sense of what she was about.

"Up here!" Leofur hissed at them as they reached a set of wooden steps cut into the earth.

They scrambled up to another trapdoor, which the young woman threw open, leading them through in a rush. When they were free of the tunnels, she dropped the door back into place once more and sealed it with locking bolts. They were standing in a warehouse, the space cavernous and dark. Crates were stacked against the walls and piled up in the center of the room. Windows set high up near the eaves let in what little light the room allowed.

With Leofur still leading the way, they rushed across the space, skirting the stacks of boxes and crates, to where a small door opened near the rear of the building and led back out onto the streets. They emerged panting for breath, their strength sapped, but their fear of what tracked them providing fresh resolve.

Leofur wheeled on the other two, the weapon held ready, the barrel still smoking. "We have to go to the airfield, Grehling. I don't care what's waiting there. That thing found us once; it will find us again." She thrust the flash rip at him. "If this won't stop it, I don't know what will. We have to get out of the city!"

Grehling nodded. "All right. We'll find a way. Chrysallin! You have to stay on your feet. You can't fall! Can you do it?"

There was nothing she could say. She didn't think she could make it to the next corner, let alone to the airfield. Her mind wandered momentarily, and she wondered where she was and where Paxon was and why she was hurting so badly. She wondered if the terrifying Elven woman was anywhere close. Or Mischa.

Mischa!

Suddenly she was looking right at her, standing not ten feet away.

Chrysallin screamed.

21

PAXON AND STARKS HAD JUST FINISHED THE CLIMB to the second floor of Dark House and were rounding the corner to begin their ascent to the third when Arcannen appeared above them coming down. They saw one another at the same time and all three immediately stopped where they were.

"I want my sister, Arcannen!" Paxon shouted up to him.

The sorcerer seemed nonplussed. Then he smiled. "We all want the same thing, boy," he called down. "All three of us. I don't have her. I don't know where she is. Like you, I'm looking for her."

"You're not trying to tell us you didn't take her, are you?" Starks demanded.

Arcannen shook his head. "I took her. I brought her here. I intended to bargain her back to the boy in exchange for his sword and his services. I admit that. But she escaped me. I don't know how she did it, but she did."

"You want us to believe she's not here?" Paxon snapped angrily.

"I don't much care what you believe. I have no purpose in lying. You'll search Dark House in any event, but you won't find her. Not if you look until next year's turn to summer. She's gone, and that's the truth, like it or not."

Starks gave him a look. "I might better be willing to believe you if I could have a quick look into your mind. A touch or two would be enough, and I can know for certain if you are speaking the truth. Do you object to waiting where you are until I can come up and do this?"

"Now, there is a request almost no one else in the Four Lands would dare to make of me, Druid. Actually, I do object. Strenuously. I don't like others laying hands on me if they aren't meant to offer pleasure. Take my word or leave it. That's all you are entitled to."

Starks shook his head slowly. "You've stolen the girl away twice now. You have violated her rights and broken the laws of numerous lands. I think you have forsaken any entitlements. You are probably entitled to common justice, but nothing more."

Arcannen's face darkened. "You will never be my judge. Not you or any of your kind. And not that callow boy you bring with you on this fool's errand. Back down those stairs immediately or be prepared to be judged yourself."

Paxon started past Starks, drawing out the Sword of Leah. "I've had enough of you—"

But Starks grabbed him and threw both of them down on the stairs, just as a rush of fire burned through the air not a foot above their heads, trailing heat and smoke and exploding into the wall on the landing below. For a moment, they lay where they were, the air about them obscured by smoke and ash, and then Starks was on his feet, pulling the Highlander up with him.

"Kindly don't do that again!" he snapped.

They rushed up the stairs to the third floor, but Arcannen was already gone. They cast about hurriedly for some indication of where he had gone, then Starks sprinted for the other end of the hallway and the front stairs. He reached them just in time to see Arcannen's black robes flying out behind him as he leapt over the railing on the landing below all the way to the first floor and sprinted down the hall beneath them.

They gave chase, every bit as fleet of foot as their quarry, but cautious of what they might be running into. They flew down the stairs and then charged along the corridor the sorcerer had taken, barely avoiding a surprised guard coming the other way, bowling him over without stopping. They went through a doorway into an empty and darkened kitchen, catching sight of a door closing at the other end of the room.

"He's got a bolt-hole somewhere!" Starks shouted as they ran. "He's trying to reach it!"

He would find it, lock the way in, and go out the other end, Paxon realized. Anything to slow them down. Anything to lose them. But they couldn't allow it. No matter if what he had told them was true or not, they had to catch him before he had a chance to get to Chrysallin.

Ahead a door slammed and locks snapped into place. They rounded a corner and came face-to-face with a small, ironbound oak door.

"Step back," Starks said.

With both arms raised, he summoned a roiling ball of blue fire, broke it in half with his bare hands, and sent each part slamming into one of the hinges. The hinges melted in seconds, and the door sagged open. Starks wrenched it aside, and they charged into the room beyond. It was small and empty, a space for cleaning supplies. A window hung open at the far end, leading to the outside world. Starks hurried over, took a cautious look, and started to climb through, Paxon on his heels.

"Watch out!" the Druid shouted suddenly, throwing himself backward.

An explosion of fire erupted from without, filling the opening, engulfing Starks as he tumbled back into the room in a smoking heap. For an instant he was afire, and then a sharp gesture with one hand extinguished the flames and he was left singed and gasping for breath. Paxon rushed to help him to his feet, but the other pushed him away.

"That's what happens when you get careless," he said.

He tried it again, more cautiously this time, and there was no response. By the time the two were outside Dark House, standing in a side street, Arcannen was gone.

"Rat stink!" the Druid said softly. "He can't have gotten far. But which way did he go?"

They were searching the darkness when they heard the scream—shrill, terrified, and close at hand.

"Chrys!" Paxon exclaimed at once. "That's Chrysallin!"

At the same moment Starks pointed. "There he goes! Arcannen! Through those buildings!"

Paxon caught a glimpse of Arcannen as he fled down an alleyway a block over in the other direction from the scream.

Starks seized his arms. "Go after your sister. I'll chase Arcannen. But watch yourself, Paxon. Remember your training!"

Then he was rushing away, racing to catch up to the sorcerer. Paxon shouted after him, warning him to be careful. He hesitated, almost persuaded that he should go with him.

But then he heard his sister scream again, and he turned the other way and began to run.

Chrysallin Leah tore away from Grehling's hands and moved back against the wall of the building in horror, pressing her hands against her mouth to keep from screaming. All she could think about was Mischa's head sitting on a bedside table, eyes vacant and staring. Even knowing she was alive, even remembering how Grehling had punched her, she couldn't seem to forget. Yet here she was, come out of nowhere and not with any good intentions in mind. Not with any promise of offering her a chance to escape the gray-haired Elven woman. She could tell that much just from the expression on the other's face, even if she ignored everything else she knew.

For just an instant everyone was frozen in place. Then Leofur swung the barrel of her weapon about, pointing it at Mischa. But the old woman held her ground defiantly.

"Still the same foolish girl you always were, I see," she hissed.

Then she made a quick gesture, and almost immediately Leofur's eyes went blank, her face slackened, and her expression turned empty. She lowered the flash rip absently. Chrysallin was cringing in terror, images flashing before her eyes of a return to her prison and a reappearance of the Elven woman, of terrible things being done to her, of endless pain and suffering.

Suddenly Grehling was standing in front of her, facing Mischa. "Get away from her," he shouted angrily.

"I've been looking for you, boy," the old woman hissed at him. "I've something special in mind for you."

Something inside Chrysallin snapped. "Don't touch him!" she screamed at the old woman.

The girl rushed past the boy, finding strength she didn't know she had, and threw herself on the old woman, bearing her to the ground. Thrashing and screaming, they rolled about, locked together. Grehling stood transfixed, took a hesitant step toward them, then raced over to Leofur and shook her hard. "Wake up, Leofur! Wake up!"

And she did, her eyes snapping open in shock. She stared about, clearly confused.

"Help me!" the boy shouted at her, pointing to Chrysallin and Mischa, fighting on the ground.

Together, they rushed to pull the two apart, not stopping to think about what might happen afterward. The instant they separated the two, Mischa began screaming as if demented, trying to scramble to her feet, dark words pouring out of her twisted mouth. Leofur kicked her down again and stepped on her throat, pinning her in place. Grehling pulled Chrysallin to her feet, dragging her away from the other two.

"Leave her!" Grehling screamed at Leofur. "We have to get out of here!"

But Leofur had other plans. One fist cocked, she hit the old woman with such a powerful blow that Mischa went limp instantly.

In the next instant the door through which they had escaped from the tunnels burst open, and the black thing that had been tracking them surged through. All three cried out in shock, but it was Leofur who brought up the flash rip and fired into the creature once more, this time knocking it down the walkway into the shadows.

"Run!" she screamed.

They did so, although Chrysallin's efforts at running were hopeless, and the best they could manage was a fast walk with Grehling supporting her once more. Behind them, Mischa was already stirring and the creature was struggling back into view.

There was no hope for them, Chrysallin realized. No hope at all. They couldn't run fast enough, they had nowhere to hide, and the weapon Leofur carried—while helpful—would not keep the creature down. She fought to control the fear and despair that swept over her, listening as Grehling asked Leofur, "How many more times can you use that thing?"

"It carried six charges," she replied. "Two are gone. Got any ideas?"

"Not the airfield. It's too far!"

"City Watch? There's a station somewhere close."

"I know it. We'll go there. Straight ahead!"

They picked up their pace, down the empty city streets and through the darkness, fear nipping at their heels.

Behind them, Mischa hobbled into view, her face bruised and bloodied, already in pursuit. But as she did so, she was casting anxious glances over her shoulder.

A terrifying struggle was taking place just behind her.

Paxon Leah was at its center. Having separated from Starks, he had raced in the direction of his sister's scream and arrived just in time to see Chrys and two others—one of whom looked like Grehling—disappear around a corner. An old woman had just scrambled to her feet and was limping after them, but she glanced back and saw him rushing toward her. Slowing momentarily, she gestured at something behind her, called out a few quick words, then continued on.

In the next instant a huge black creature came out of the shadows and lunged toward him.

He reacted instantly, bringing up his sword, calling on its magic, shielding himself as the beast smashed into the shield it formed to protect him. The creature struck with such force that Paxon was knocked backward several steps. But the blow had no effect on the creature, which righted itself and came at him again, this time trying to sidestep the sword and get around whatever magic it was using. Paxon feinted and parried, stepped quickly one way and then another, outmaneuvering his attacker through footwork and anticipation, trying to reach it with his sword. But the creature was canny enough to avoid his efforts, dodging and weaving with each sweep of the blade, studying Paxon's defenses as it did so, looking for a weakness.

After several tries, it found one. It dropped flat and with one long arm swept Paxon's feet out from under him. He dropped backward, just managing to keep his protection intact as the creature swarmed on top of him, first blocking its efforts and then, with a surge of energy, throwing it backward and away.

Dropping the shield, he rolled to his knees and stood as the black thing launched a fresh assault. But this time, he centered the magic in the sword itself, turning the sharp edge into the creature as it tore at him. The blade had a razor's edge, and abetted by the magic, it sliced off both clawed hands as the attacker closed in.

Paxon stepped away, stunned by what he had done. The creature looked at its severed wrists, but it made no sound. Its face was impossible to read. No blood came from the wounds. It stood there, seemingly bewildered. Then, slowly, impossibly, the wounds began to close, and the blunt, ragged ends to re-form. New hands appeared, growing out of the wounds left where the old hands had been cut off, and they were shaped exactly the same.

The creature waited until it was completely whole again, then slowly approached Paxon once more. For the first time, Paxon was uncertain. He wished Starks were with him. The Druid would know what to do about something like this—something that clearly involved the use of magic. But Starks was gone, and he was alone. He would have to figure this out himself because if he didn't . . .

There wasn't time to finish the thought because the creature was on him once more, this time trying to knock the sword from his hands. Quicker than thought the clawed hands got past his shield and tore at his wrists. He only barely managed to hang on, using the sword to hack at the creature's head. The blade slipped sideways, partially blocked by a sudden arm swing against the flat side, but the edge bit deep into the creature's shoulder and lodged there.

Frantically, Paxon fought to free it. The creature was ripping at him, and only the thinnest of shields was keeping it from tearing him apart. He felt himself beginning to panic as they surged back and forth, and he knew if he gave in to it he was finished. He screamed at the creature as a way of focusing the magic, as a means of strengthening his determination. He put everything he had into the effort, fighting harder to yank the blade loose.

But the Sword of Leah was wedged tightly in place in the creature's body, and no amount of effort would free it.

It was his training that saved him. Oost Mondara had taught him to always take the path of least resistance, to remember that when one thing failed to work it simply meant you should do the opposite. Don't ever force a result; take a different approach. So instead of continuing the struggle to break free of his adversary, Paxon Leah channeled the blade's magic not into escape, but into attack, forcing the blade in deeper. The creature jerked and heaved its body immediately in response, a clear indication that it was in trouble. It stopped trying to get at Paxon and turned its attention to the blade instead, trying to wrench it free.

Paxon pressed his attack, going right at the creature, forcing it back, riding it to the ground. The creature writhed and struggled, and the sword blade bit deeper into its body, sinking in almost to the hilt. How the creature could still be alive was troubling, but Paxon was determined to end it here.

Then the creature gave a mighty heave of its body, and the blade wrenched loose at last.

Paxon straightened and went after the creature in a rush. Down came the Sword of Leah in a series of quick, fluid strikes that relied as much on Paxon's training as on the weapon's magic. The creature absorbed blow after blow, struggling to rise, but unable to fight its way clear of the blade. Paxon did not let up, attacking with renewed purpose as pieces of the creature separated from its body. It was thrashing wildly now, still without making a sound or shedding a drop of blood, its distress evident from its desperate efforts to break free.

Finally, the Highlander managed to damage both the creature's arms sufficiently that it could no longer defend itself, and with one mighty swing he took off its head. At once, it went limp, its head rolling slowly away on the rough surface of the street.

Wounded and bleeding, Paxon stood there waiting for it to re-form. But this time there was no recovery. The pieces of its body lay scattered and still in the lamplight and shadows, and the only sound in the aftermath was Paxon's labored breathing.

Not all that far away, Chrysallin Leah had fallen to her knees and was struggling to rise. "I can't go on!" she gasped.

Grehling pulled on her shoulders and arms, trying to get her back up. "You have to! She's coming!"

Chrysallin was terrified. It was clear to the boy that her strength was gone, her body drained of whatever energy she had possessed earlier. Even her fear, as intense as it was, was not enough.

"Move back over there, into the shadows," Leofur ordered the pair, gesturing toward an open alleyway where an arched covering of interlocking stone blocks offered a small amount of concealment. "Hurry! We'll make a stand there. I'll deal with Mischa myself."

She still had her weapon, and it still carried four charges, so there was some reason to think they could slow or disable the witch when she appeared, especially if they caught her off guard. Grehling helped Chrysallin struggle back to her feet, and together they limped over to the covered alley and moved back into the shadows. Leofur was last in, and she stayed by the entrance and peered back down the street they had just come up, searching for their pursuer. The silver streaks in her blond hair glimmered in the faint light cast by the streetlamp across the way as she cradled the flash rip.

"Do you want to sit down?" Grehling whispered to Chrysallin.

She shook her head no. "I better stay on my feet."

"I could go for help. Alone. I could find someone at a City Watch station, I think."

Chrysallin grabbed his arm and held on. "Don't leave me, Grehling. Please. Stay with me."

She was begging, the urgency in her voice unmistakable. She couldn't help herself. Being left alone again would be the end of her. She would rather die than fall into the witch's hands a second time.

The boy understood. He put his hand on top of hers and squeezed gently. "I'll stay," he promised.

"She's coming," Leofur hissed at them from the alley entrance. She crouched lower and brought up the barrel of her weapon.

Then abruptly Leofur stiffened, muttering something unintelligible, lifting up slightly from behind her cover to peer out into the streets, then turning sharply in their direction.

"She's gone!" she hissed at them in a mix of anger and disbelief. "She was right there and she just vanished into—"

She never finished. An explosion threw her backward into the darkness next to them, the flash rip flying out of her hands, stone and brick shattering as part of the archway wall collapsed. Leofur went down and was still, blood on her face and arms, her eyes closed.

Mischa appeared in the opening, bent and withered and terrible. Her crone's face was twisted with a mix of hatred and satisfaction, and her mouth was working hungrily—chewing, chewing. Smoke rose from the tips of her fingers, and her eyes glowed blood red.

"There you are!" she exclaimed as if surprised and excited. "Hiding back in a corner like rats! Oh, but that is what you are, isn't it? Little rats, caught in a trap! How sad! How unfortunate for you! And now you've lost your fierce protector and her weapon. Whatever will you do?"

Gone was any pretense of being Chrysallin's friend. She was in full-blown witch mode, and Grehling knew what was in store for him. "Someone will see what you are doing!" he snapped at her, placing himself in front of Chrysallin while wishing he could be anywhere but.

"Goodness! They will? Should I run and hide then, like you? Will I be safe from these people?" She cackled. "Or should I just ignore them like they mean nothing to me? Which they do!"

She moved a few steps closer. "I have had enough of you, boy! I think maybe I will put an end to you before I take little Chrysallin back for more tender loving care. You almost wrecked everything, but my work is not easily undone." Her gaze shifted. "Is it, Chrysallin? You remember, don't you? Everything the gray-haired Elven woman did to you? Every torment and travesty committed on your young body? Every pain you suffered? You remember. And you know what you will do when you find her again, don't you? Would you like to find her now? This very moment?"

She made a smooth series of loops and whispered softly, and the Elven woman appeared, standing off to one side, smiling. Chrysallin shrank from her, buried her face in her hands, and began to shake all over.

"Yes, you remember," Mischa teased, clearly enjoying the girl's response, excited by it. "Listen to her! Can you hear? She whispers something to you! Listen. Listen closely!"

A deep silence followed, unbroken save for the sound of Chrysallin Leah whimpering. Then the Elven woman, still standing there, watching everything, leaned forward and spoke.

Tell me what you know.

The words must have been intended to produce a particular response from the girl, but certainly they couldn't have been intended to produce the one they got. Chrysallin went stiff with shock, and her hands dropped from her eyes to knot across her chest, and her face twisted with sudden rage. She no longer looked like a young girl. She no longer looked anything like herself. She looked like a demon. She screamed—quick, piercing, and furious. She screamed in a way that Grehling had never heard anyone scream before. The sound of it dropped him to his knees; he clapped his hands over his ears to protect them. She screamed with every fiber of her being, and the sound of it assumed both shape and substance.

At first it was everywhere, a force unleashed and gone wild. But then it redirected itself as Chrysallin turned to the Elven woman. The scream slammed into her and she shattered into fragments born on a sudden wind, tiny shards scattering everywhere.

By now, Mischa was backing away, her crooked form bent low, her face horror-stricken. She brought up her hands to defend herself, weaving spells, creating protections. But the scream took on new power as it reached her, lifting her off the street as if she were weightless and slamming her into the wall of the building behind her. It held her pinned there as it penetrated her flesh and bones and turned them liquid. She became a smear that splattered and flattened and then ran down the wall in red rivulets like too much paint.

And just like that she was gone.

Grehling wasn't sure what would happen next—not to him or to Leofur, not when it appeared that Chrysallin might be completely out of control—so he crawled to where she stood screaming and grabbed her ankle. The scream increased, wavered slightly as she looked down and saw him, and abruptly ceased.

"Grehling!" she whispered, dropping to her knees, her face aghast, tears streaming from her eyes. "What happened?"

The boy gave her a look, pulled himself up beside her, and grasped her hands. "I was hoping you could tell me."

22

Arcannen wove his way through Wayford's city streets, at first aimlessly and then increasingly with a destination in mind. His initial reaction was to lead the Druid and the boy a merry chase before setting out for the airfield and the ship that would convey him to safety. To that end, he chose a circuitous path that took him down alleys, into courtyards, across parks and grassy dividers, and eventually through buildings so tightly packed together that it was impossible for anyone to know which doors he had entered or exited.

Yet the pursuit continued. It got close enough at one point that he saw the Druid's black robes from a window as the latter entered the building in which he was hiding. All of his tricks and subterfuges were failing him, and it became increasingly clear that he was going to have to attempt something more drastic than simple flight.

A confrontation was a last resort. The Druid might easily be his equal in a battle of magic, especially one as clearly experienced as this one seemed to be. Risking everything by going one against one was not his preferred method of engagement, in any case. Subterfuge and deception were highly preferable. Flight and avoidance were survival tools he understood and embraced when dealing with those whose skills he did not want to underestimate.

Besides, there were ramifications to killing a Druid that he did not particularly wish to test. There were consequences for acts of that sort that had a tendency to seriously disrupt your life.

Still, he was running out of options. If he made a break from his flight pattern now, the Druid would know for certain he was trying to reach the airfield and might well find a way to get there before him. What he needed was a scheme for trapping the Druid somewhere long enough to allow for a clear escape path and time to use it.

So as he ran, his mind was racing, too, thinking of a way to put a stop to his pursuit. But everything he considered was uncertain at best and foolhardy at worst. He had to anticipate that the Druid not only had the same skills and experience also that he did but that he could anticipate him, as well. So whatever solution he came up with, it had to be clever enough that the Druid would fail to recognize it until it was too late.

It also had to be something he could set up and trigger quickly, because the chase was tightening.

He rushed out of the back of his latest building bolt-hole, turned up the street, and saw the grain warehouse. Sudden inspiration infused him, and he knew how he might stop the Druid once and for all. He kept running, thinking his plan through, then slowed just enough as he reached the entry to the building to be sure the Druid—exiting the building behind—caught sight of him.

Then he broke the lock and hurried inside.

A quick look around revealed grain-filled wooden bins sitting on platforms under loading chutes. Ramps ran the length of the room on both sides, and vented windows opened out from high on the walls to let in light and air. He checked to be certain there were release doors on the bins near the floor, then began weaving invisible threads that he attached to the latches.

Gathering up the loose ends of the threads, he moved to the very back of the room and concealed himself in the shadows of the last bin on the left. When the Druid entered the room, he would pull the threads, releasing several tons of grain onto the warehouse floor. The Druid would be buried in seconds, dead or damaged badly enough that he could not immediately follow.

If things worked the way he anticipated, it would end up looking like an accident, a fluke release of the contents perhaps caused by the Druid. He would be gone from the scene and in no way implicated.

He waited patiently, eyes on the door.

But nothing happened.

When he started to think something had gone wrong, he heard a small noise behind him and turned to find the Druid looking at him.

"You should know better than to expect an old trick like that to work," the other observed.

The sorcerer rose, dropping the ends to the invisible threads to the floor. No point in holding on to those. He gave the Druid a nod. "I suppose you want me to come with you?"

"Indeed. We need to clear up what's become of Chrysallin. A visit to the Ard Rhys might help sort it out. You might even learn something about boundaries and appropriate behavior."

Arcannen shrugged. "I have nothing to hide."

As he walked past the Druid, his hand strayed almost of its own volition to the pocket inside his robes where the Stiehl was hidden—surreptitious movement hidden from the other's watchful eyes. He would have to be quick. He closed his fingers about the weapon and waited until they had reached the back door to the warehouse. Then, without any haste or sudden movements, he slowed his approach. The Stiehl was out and ready for use when he turned back, its flat black blade a swift, wicked shadow. He struck at the Druid, and even though a protective wall of magic was already in place, the Stiehl went right through it and into the other's exposed body.

The Druid grunted sharply and took a quick step back. But Arcannen followed him, striking again and again until the Druid was down on the floor, his blood everywhere. Not until he was no longer moving and his eyes were open and staring did Arcannen cease his efforts.

The sorcerer gave him a final look, then turned and hurried out the warehouse door.

By the time Paxon Leah reached his sister and her companions they were out of the covered alleyway and gathered on the still-dark street, huddled against a nearby building wall. The girl with the silver-streaked hair was bloodied and unconscious and Chrysallin was practically catatonic. Only Grehling was in any shape to talk to him, and the boy tried to explain what had happened while Paxon held his sister in his arms and waited for her to regain some recognizable level of awareness.

"She's been acting oddly ever since I took her out of Mischa's quarters," Grehling finished. "She keeps saying she's been tortured, that she's in pain and all torn up and broken. But look at her. There's hardly a mark on her. And she keeps talking about a gray-haired Elven woman being responsible."

"This is Arcannen's doing?" Paxon pressed him.

"Mischa works for him, so whatever she did to your sister, it was at the sorcerer's bidding. I've seen them both going in and out of the building where Chrysallin was being held. That's what led me to her." He paused. "What's the reason for all this?"

Paxon didn't know. He had assumed Arcannen took Chrys in order to force him to give up the Sword of Leah. But if he had tortured her to the point where she believed she had received injuries she hadn't, the reason must be more complex. Whatever had been done to his sister, it clearly involved subverting her mind.

"Chrys," he whispered, bending close, "can you hear me? It's Paxon. I'm here. You're safe now."

Her eyes were open and staring off into the distance. If she heard him, she wasn't giving any indication of it. Her face had a stricken look, and her hands were balled into fists.

He looked up again. "What happened just now?" he asked the boy. "I saw the old woman coming after you. Was that the witch?"

Grehling had moved over next to Leofur and was cleaning off the blood on her face and arms with a piece of cloth torn from his shirt. "Chrysallin couldn't go any farther; she was ready to collapse. So we hid in that alley. Leofur had this weapon—a kind of portable flash rip. She'd already used it twice on this creature that was tracking us. A beast of some kind. Did you see it anywhere while you were looking for us?"

"I saw it, and you don't have to worry about it anymore. Go on. Tell me the rest."

"Leofur was going to use this weapon on the witch. But somehow the witch tricked her and everything exploded in her face and she went down. Then Mischa came after Chrysallin and me. She taunted Chrys about the torture and the gray-haired Elven woman. And then the Elven woman was there—she just appeared. She said something—I couldn't hear what—and Chrysallin seemed to lose all control of herself. She started scream-ing. It wasn't like anything I've ever heard. It was terrible! The Elven woman just blew apart. Then Mischa was pinned against the wall and crushed. There was nothing left!"

Paxon looked down at his sister. How could she have caused any of this to happen? What was going on? He hugged Chrys tightly, as much to reassure himself as to try to get through to her, but there was no response. She just knelt there, leaning up against him, looking at nothing.

The young woman Grehling called Leofur was stirring now, coming awake, moaning softly and holding her head as she sat up. She glanced around, saw Paxon with Chrysallin, nodded to him, and said, "You're Paxon."

"You're Leofur," he responded. "Are you all right?"

She looked down at herself, running her hands over her arms and body and nodded. "What happened to Mischa?"

"We don't know exactly," Grehling answered. "Are you sure you're all right?"

"I'm fine. What do you mean, you don't know?"

"Chrysallin did something to her. She screamed at her, and Mischa exploded against the building wall in the alleyway. There's nothing left."

Leofur gave him a doubtful look. "Help me stand up."

The boy did as she asked, and when she was on her feet she started back toward the alley, staggering a bit as she went.

"Are you trying to make sure?" Grehling called after her, getting up to follow.

"I need to get my flash rip back," she threw over her shoulder. "Want to help me find it?"

He went after her at once, and she stopped to let him catch up. When they were out of sight, Paxon bent close to his sister and began whispering.

"Listen to me, Chrys. I don't know what's going on here. You have to wake up and tell me. You don't need to worry about Mischa. She's dead. You're with me now. You're safe. No harm can come to you. I won't let it. I'll take you to Paranor and keep you there where no one can get to you. We have Healers who are very good at helping people who have been treated the way you have. They can make you better. Can you understand me?"

No response.

He hugged her tighter, stroking her hair. "I love you, Chrys. I'm so sorry this has happened. I would do anything to take it back. I hate myself for not doing a better job of looking after you. But don't leave me. Come back from wherever you are. Everything will be all right if you do."

Grehling and Leofur reemerged from the alley ruins and came toward him. Leofur was carrying a strange weapon, one he had never seen before. She had called it a flash rip, but as far as he knew no one had ever seen a flash rip this small. It made him wonder what other sorts of weapons you could find in the Federation that maybe even the Druids didn't know about.

"How is she?" Leofur asked, kneeling next to him. She seemed better now, her voice strong, her gaze steady as she looked at him.

He shook his head. "I can't get a response. She won't speak to me."

The young woman gave him a reassuring smile. "Give her time. She's been through a lot, but she's a very determined girl. She's stronger than you think."

"Can you do something for me?" he asked her abruptly. "Can you accompany Grehling to the airfield and find out if Arcannen has flown out of the city? Or at least if his private airship is still there? I need to know where he is. And ask if anyone has seen a Druid about.

I came here with a Druid to find Chrys. His name is Starks, and he was chasing Arcannen when I saw him last. Would you see if anyone knows anything about what's happened to him? If you find him, tell him where I am."

"I can do it by myself," Grehling announced at once. "Leofur is hurt. She can stay with you."

"I don't doubt for a minute you can do it on your own," Paxon said quickly. "There doesn't seem to be much you can't do. But it wouldn't hurt to have someone with a portable flash rip to watch your back."

"He's right," Leofur agreed. "I'm coming with you."

"If you catch sight of Arcannen, don't go near him," Paxon added. "Don't try to stop him, don't even let him see you. Just come right back here and tell me."

They nodded in response and started off together, and quickly they were out of sight. Paxon picked up Chrysallin and carried her over to a doorway where they were partially hidden from anyone coming down the street. Not that it was likely anyone would; it was still an hour or two until sunrise. But it didn't hurt to be careful. Not when he didn't know where Arcannen had gone.

He found himself regretting that he had let Starks go off on his own. Paxon was supposed to be the Druid's protector. That was what he had been trained to do, and in this case he had abandoned his duty to go after his sister. He didn't like it that Starks had been gone so long. He should have returned by now, Arcannen in tow or not.

He knew it was silly to worry. Starks was more than able to take care of himself. He was better trained and more experienced than Paxon, and during the times they had spent together it had been more a case of the Druid protecting Paxon than the other way around.

Time passed slowly as he sat in the doorway shadows

cradling Chrysallin in his arms. She never changed expression, but eventually she fell asleep, her head falling onto his chest, her body sagging down against his. He kept still afterward, hoping that sleep would do what his words and comforting had not. When she awoke, perhaps she would be herself again, the nightmare behind her and the absence of any recognition of what was going on around her a thing of the past.

Dawn arrived in a dull brightening of the eastern sky, chasing back the reluctant shadows inch by inch. A handful of people came out of doors and down the streets, some passing by without seeing them, others slowing for a quick look. No one spoke to them. No one asked if they needed help.

Then Grehling reappeared, coming out of nowhere to kneel down beside them, his young face intense.

"Anything?" Paxon whispered, not wanting to wake his sister, who was still asleep.

The boy nodded. "A little. Arcannen arrived at the airfield not long before we got there. My father saw him. He was alone. He crossed the field to his vessel, woke his crew, and they released the mooring lines and took off. He didn't say anything to my father about where he was going."

"Starks?"

"Leofur's gone hunting for him. He didn't show up at the airfield. I waited until just a little while ago to make sure. She'll let us know when she finds him."

"She doesn't even know where to look," Paxon muttered absently, more worried now than ever.

"She doesn't have to know," Grehling said quickly. "Other people will, and she knows everyone. She will ask around, and someone will tell her where he is."

The boy settled back against the wall across from him, watching Chrysallin. Neither said anything for a long time. The morning began to brighten and the shadows to fade. More people filled the street beyond their alcove, moving in groups, beginning their day's work. Tucked away in their shelter, they occupied an island of calm among the steady movement and sounds only yards away. But their uneasiness was palpable.

"She looks better now that she's sleeping," Grehling offered finally. "I think she will be all right when she wakes."

Paxon wasn't so sure, but he knew the boy was just trying to be helpful. So he nodded in agreement. "You were very brave to rescue her," he said.

Grehling shrugged. "I didn't know what I was getting into. I just thought something felt wrong. Then, when I saw her, I knew it was Arcannen's work, trying to get at you again. He wants your sword, doesn't he?"

Paxon nodded. "How did you know?"

"Everybody wants something like that. Especially someone like him. A sorcerer's tool, he probably thinks. He spends all his time collecting such things. Mostly, he steals them. But whatever it takes to get hold of them, he will do. He told me that once. He said that's how you got by in this world—that if you wanted something, you found a way to get it, no matter what."

"But you don't agree?"

Grehling managed to look insulted. "Of course not. Do you?"

"No."

"I didn't think so."

They were quiet again after that, still waiting on Leofur. Chrysallin awoke and began staring into space once more. Both Paxon and Grehling tried talking to her, asking her questions, offering her further assurances that she was safe and that no one would hurt her again. But still she did not respond.

It was approaching midmorning when Leofur finally reappeared. She returned from a different direction than the one she had taken earlier with Grehling, catching them both by surprise. She approached at a brisk walk, her eyes fixed on them, her posture ramrod-straight.

She stopped in front of Paxon and took a deep breath. "I have news of your friend. It's very bad."

He knew at once what it was. He knew it as much from her tone of voice and the look on her face as from the words themselves. When she spoke them aloud, he already knew what she was going to say. He held up his hand in a belated gesture to forestall hearing them. But it was too late. She was speaking, and the words were cutting at him like knives.

23

Arcannen's nerves showed no sign of giving way in the face of what he had done until he had reached his airship, woken the crew, and lifted off. Then all at once his hands were shaking and he was damp with sweat. He had killed a Druid. He had committed the one act he had warned himself against, the one act he had known would bring him the worst kind of trouble. Now the Druids would hunt him until he was found and killed. He could argue all he wanted about why that wouldn't happen—the passage of time would take the edge off the urgency of finding him, changes in the order would result in an agenda where punishing him was a lesser concern, whatever. But the truth was inescapable: Sooner or later, he was going to have to answer for what he had done.

He cursed the Druid for being so persistent, for continuing to hunt him long after any reasonable person would have given up. He cursed himself for believing his ambush would be enough to stop the other. He should have kept running, should have made better choices, should never have given the man the chance to come after him in the first place.

But it was all water under the bridge now, wasn't it? It was all beyond a place where he could do anything about it. He was stuck with things the way they were. Regrets and hindsight and disgust were all shackles that threatened to slow him down and ultimately to undo him. What he needed to remember was that if he kept a clear head and acted quickly enough, he might still find a way to get clear of this mess. After all, it wasn't the first time he had put himself in danger. It wasn't the first time he had made a mistake that threatened to cost him everything.

But it was the first time he felt really, truly threatened.

Still, a solution to his problems was already nudging him, whispering in his ear—a plan that would free him from the immediate threat of Druid retaliation. It had come to him—as so many things did—when he least expected it. He was fleeing the scene of the killing, not yet seen by any of Wayford's citizens, still not exposed nor his deed revealed. It gave him the opportunity and time to escape from the city, and it was while he was coming up to the airfield and making for his airship that the idea had begun to take shape.

If he could find a way to shift attention away from himself, he would have a chance to disappear until matters settled down. If he could give the Druid order a distraction to occupy its time, a matter that was more pressing than finding him—a threat so immediate and troubling that its members wouldn't hesitate to focus all their efforts on dealing with it—he could salvage this debacle.

And by *debacle* he meant his disrupted plans for gaining control of the Druid order through Paxon and Chrysallin Leah.

The plan as originally conceived had long since fallen apart. The goal, however, remained the same: Find a way to take control of the order, then subvert it sufficiently to turn it to his own uses. In the beginning, after he had inadvertently discovered that Paxon Leah had in his possession a talisman believed lost, one quite possibly infused with extraordinary magic, his goal had been simple—he would claim it for himself. His first impulse was simply to steal it. But then he had remembered he lacked a means to unlock its magic, that only a member of the Leah household could do so. Therefore, he had taken Chrysallin Leah as a way to make her brother do his bidding.

But that effort had failed when Paxon Leah discovered the power of the sword and by doing so found a way to rescue his sister. For a time, it seemed he would have to forget the whole idea of using the boy; he was in the Druid camp after that, living at Paranor and not likely to return for a second encounter without bringing help.

Then he had come up with the idea of taking the girl a second time and using her in a different way. She was better suited to what he had wanted to accomplish in the first place, and maybe the boy could be brought around, as well. Using Mischa to subvert her thinking, he would make her his pawn—one who could be conditioned to perform without hesitation a single act when the opportunity was given her.

She would kill the Ard Rhys.

Such a thing had seemed impossible at first glance. But Mischa was talented, and she had turned more than one unwilling subject into an obedient servant. Give Chrysallin Leah enough reason, fill her with enough hatred, subject her to enough emotional and psychological suffering, and she would react instinctively against one she perceived to be an implacable enemy. The torture would not have to actually happen; it would not be necessary to physically damage her. It need only be perceived as real by the victim to accomplish what mattered—to leave her so obsessed with gaining freedom from and revenge upon her perceived torturer that she would use deadly force against her at the first opportunity.

All that, Mischa now claimed, she had accomplished. Chrysallin Leah was terrified of the gray-haired Elven woman who had stood by and directed her endless suffering—a woman who wasn't even there, but who was as real to the girl as the pain she had experienced. A woman who looked exactly like Aphenglow Elessedil. The first time Chrysallin Leah came face-to-face with the Ard Rhys, she would try to kill her. She wouldn't be able to help herself. She would use whatever weapon she could find, whatever tool lay close at hand, to put an end to the Druid leader.

To help her with this, Arcannen had arranged for Mischa to leave the Stiehl where Chrysallin could find it. But when she had escaped, she hadn't even bothered to take the blade with her. He had worried from the beginning that Chrysallin Leah might not react as Mischa believed she would—that she might simply break down and be unable to function, reverting to a helpless victim. But the witch said the girl was very strong and very determined, and once she was free of her imprisonment she would be driven by the memories of what she thought had been done to her and would act quickly and directly. She would not see herself as helpless. She would see herself as needing to prevent any chance of ever again becoming her enemy's prisoner. She would be driven to seek revenge for acts that were embedded in her memory like spikes.

All that was needed was a way to put the Ard Rhys and the girl together in the same room. And that would have been arranged if the girl hadn't somehow found a way to escape through Mischa's carelessness. It might still happen, of course. If her brother found her before the witch did—which was entirely possible—he would take her with him to Paranor to keep her safe. He would want the Ard Rhys to have a look at her. He would not understand the danger of what he was doing. Not until it was too late.

It was an ambitious and admittedly uncertain plan, but it was worth trying so he had carried it out. Now, of course, the outcome was highly improbable given the extent of the disruption that had occurred. Mischa could believe whatever she wanted, but he was a realist and he knew that the chances of Chrysallin Leah doing what she had been conditioned to do had fallen off dramatically.

Though he was willing to wait and see before writing off its chances altogether.

And with the Druid dead and a full-scale hunt to find and punish him inevitable, his plans for gaining control over the Druid order were evolving anew. The opportunity was still there. His path to the Druid archives and their collection of talismans and magic was still open to him. All he needed to do was to widen it a little, to smooth things over sufficiently that access was assured.

He thought he knew now how to make that happen. Not as he had planned in the beginning, but as he now determined was necessary.

A fresh plan, a fresh start.

It would begin in the Federation city of Arishaig.

In another part of the skies, some hours later, Paxon Leah was winging west toward Paranor. He was aboard the Druid airship he had flown to Wayford, bearing his still-catatonic sister and the body of his friend and companion Starks back to the Fourth Druid Order. He had intended to fly back alone, thinking to sail the airship single-handed.

But flying an airship the size of a Druid clipper was risky in any case, and more so here, where he was distracted by what had happened to him and by his sister's need for constant attention. It was Leofur Rai who pointed this out and Grehling who was quick to back her up. He should not be flying solo; she and the boy would accompany him, offering assistance where it was needed, either in sailing the airship or in providing care and companionship for Chrysallin. Once she was safely returned to Paranor, they would find a way home again. In the end, he saw the wisdom in what they were suggesting and reluctantly agreed.

It was his reluctance to permit *anyone* to be around him just now that had caused him to resist the offer in the first place. He was still in shock over what had happened to Starks, and he did not think himself fit company. The loss of his friend was something from which he did not think he would ever recover. The guilt he was feeling was enormous. In part, he blamed himself for not going with the Druid in pursuit of Arcannen. In part, it was his sense of having failed again—a pattern of lapses that seemed to mark his entire brief career as a Druid protector. Only this time it had cost a life.

He brooded about it on the flight north, whether standing at the controls or sitting with his sister. The other two did not try to engage him in conversation, clearly aware that if he wanted someone to talk to he would let them know. Neither made any attempt to distract him from his dark mood. They were simply there to help him where they could, doing what was needed to keep him on track to complete his return to Paranor and to those who might better be able to address what had happened.

They flew through the remainder of the day and into the night, lighting the ship's guidance lamps, tracking their way across the darkened terrain under a cloudless sky brightened by an almost full moon and millions of stars. They encountered no other vessel or any form of disruptive weather, and it was still several hours before dawn when they reached their destination.

Trolls from the Druid Guard met them on the landing platform that connected to the north tower and swiftly bore Starks away. Because of the hour, Paxon was sent to his quarters while Chrysallin was taken to the healing center and Grehling and Leofur to rooms on the visitor level. There would be plenty of time to give reports after they had rested. The Ard Rhys would be informed. For now, sleep was what was needed. Matters were handled in the usual efficient manner, and all four were dispatched to their beds.

Paxon slept until noon. His sleep was deep and dreamless, and when he woke Sebec was waiting to receive him, lingering just outside his room.

"Come with me," he said. "The Ard Rhys is anxious to see you. At present, she is speaking with the boy and has just finished interviewing the young woman. Leofur, isn't it? I'll take you to sit with her until it is your turn to report to the Mistress."

He paused as they walked toward the dining hall. "I am very sorry about Starks. I know you will miss him greatly."

Paxon said nothing. There was nothing to say.

Then he stopped suddenly. "I should see about Chrysallin."

Sebec slowed, but shook his head. "Please wait on that, Paxon. The Healers are working with her just now, trying to find a way to bring her out of her catatonia. She is deeply under the influence of her self-induced withdrawal, and so far nothing anyone has said or done has been strong enough to bring her back. It might be best not to interrupt their efforts."

Although he didn't like the idea of not going immediately to see Chrys, he understood Sebec's reasoning and let the matter slide. But he made the young Druid promise to inform him the moment the Healers were done working with his sister—even if it was for just a short time—so that he could go to her. She might not know him yet, but he still thought his presence might be enough to help her recover.

Minutes later, he found himself sitting with Leofur Rai in the dining hall. Sebec had returned to the Ard Rhys, and the two of them were off in a corner by themselves.

"Did you sleep?" he asked her, knowing she would wait for him to speak first.

She nodded, her silver-streaked hair rippling in the sunlight. "Better than I thought I would after what happened."

"Your wounds are better?"

"Fine. Healing."

He looked down for a minute. "I can't thank you enough for what you did. Taking Chrys into your home, sheltering her when you knew how dangerous it was, making a stand against that black thing, facing down the witch—I can't imagine how hard that must have been."

"Sure you can," she said. "You did pretty much the same. You ended up saving us from Mischa's creature, and Chrysallin saved us from the witch. We came through it because we each made a stand when it mattered."

"Still, I owe you for that."

She shook her head. "You don't owe me a thing. No one does."

The way she said it puzzled him. "So you knew Grehling when he was much younger?"

"I helped his father raise him for a little more than four years. Do you want to eat something? I'm pretty hungry."

He found he was hungry, too, and they went into the kitchen to see if there was any food to be had and emerged with full plates. They ate in silence, and when they were finished Paxon said, "What sort of weapon did you use on Mischa's creature? I've never seen anything like it."

Her nose wrinkled in something that suggested distaste. "A handheld flash rip. They're new. A fresh invention from the Federation that relies on a set of specially faceted diapson crystals for its power. Word is, they're working on other things, too. Weapons development is high on their list of priorities. They intend to rebuild their army."

From what it once was before the demons broke free of the Forbidding and destroyed the old city of Arishaig and most of its army. He hesitated. "How did you come by one?"

She shrugged. "Payment for a favor. A foolish, impulsive gesture on the part of the original owner, in my opinion. But he's not likely to complain. Tell me about your sword."

She was clearly uncomfortable talking about the flash rip, but he didn't want to say too much about his talisman, either. "An ancient weapon. It's been in the family for many generations. It was infused with magic by the Druid Allanon for one of my more famous relatives, Rone Leah."

"And Arcannen knew about this sword? And that was why he took Chrysallin—he was trying to get to you?"

"Grehling's been talking to you about this?"

"Some of it. Some I figured out on my own. Am I right?"

"He's kidnapped Chrys twice. The time before he was trying to make a trade for the sword. This time, I don't know what he was doing. Except that he knew I would come after her, so maybe it was the same thing again—a trade for my sister. But he tortured her, didn't he? Or the witch did. I don't understand the purpose of that."

"Maybe there wasn't any purpose. Maybe it was just to teach her a lesson. Arcannen has done it before. He tortures his girls at Dark House when they disobey."

Paxon shook his head. "But he knew I would find out."

"Maybe he just didn't care." She ran her fingers through her streaked hair. "And he didn't do it himself. Chrysallin told Grehling that her torturer was a gray-haired Elven woman who stood by and watched the whole thing. She kept asking Chrysallin to tell her something—I don't know what. Chrysallin apparently didn't know, either. When Grehling brought her to me, she was barely coherent. It's hard to know what happened to her."

Paxon leaned back. "The Healers will help her. Once she's better, maybe she'll be able to tell us more. Whatever the case, I intend to go after Arcannen myself."

Leofur pursed her lips thoughtfully. "I've been thinking about something. Did you know the Ard Rhys spoke to me about all this earlier, while you were still sleeping? She asked me to tell her everything I could about what happened."

"Sebec told me."

She paused. "Well, maybe this doesn't mean anything, but I couldn't help noticing that the Ard Rhys could be the woman Chrysallin described."

Paxon almost laughed aloud. The idea of the Ard Rhys being responsible for Chrysallin's torture was ridiculous. But then he caught himself, wondering suddenly if there might be a connection he wasn't quite seeing.

"Tell me what Chrys said about this Elven woman," he demanded.

*   *   *

By the time Arcannen landed his cruiser in Arishaig's main port, he was already firmly settled on his plans. He had used the entire trip to mull them over, and he was satisfied that he had thought them through carefully and should proceed to execute them. *Execute*—a good word for what was needed. The ramifications of what he would do here would be extensive, but they would diminish considerably the chances that the Druids would be coming in search of him anytime soon. He just needed to hide himself for a sufficient length of time for events to proceed to a logical conclusion. How that would all play out, he wasn't sure. It didn't matter. His goals, his needs, and his plans would not be changed by what happened after today.

He disembarked the airship with orders to be ready to lift off at a moment's notice and for no one else to leave, even for a moment. He was wearing the black robe he kept in the onboard locker for situations of the sort he was confronted with today. He spent much of his time disguised as someone else, and the black robe—which was, in fact, one belonging to the Fourth Druid Order—would provide him with the look he required for today's work.

It was the first of two pieces to the disguise he would assume.

The second was the change he had made to his facial features. Temporary, not permanent, and good for at least several hours, so that whomever he encountered or who happened to get a look at him would be able to describe him accurately to those who would come looking for him later.

He summoned one of the carriages that were always waiting at the edge of the field by the manager's office and ordered the driver to take him to the Assembly and the chambers of the Coalition Council. He rode inside the closed passenger's compartment with the curtains drawn and did not bother looking out. He was wrapped in his black robes and had his hood pulled up over his head, leaving only his face and hands visible. He was already deep in character, assuming the behavioral traits of the man he was impersonating. For the next two hours, or however long it took, he would become that man, and those who saw him would have no reason to doubt what they were seeing.

He experienced a brief moment of regret that things had failed to turn out the way he had wanted, but that was the nature of attempting to manipulate others. You had to be fluid in your thinking and in your decision making. Matters had a tendency to go awry no matter how well laid your plans. Arcannen knew this. Never so much so as in this case, but what was required to right the situation was the same as always. He must adapt and he must do so quickly.

And no one was better at it than he was.

When he arrived at the imposing edifice that was now called the Assembly, he paid the driver with Federation credits and ascended the steps leading to the building's primary entrance. He knew his way and did not have to ask for directions. His robes and the emblem they bore identified him well enough that he was barely slowed at the checkpoints. A few of the guards gave him a look of recognition, and one even saluted him. Good enough. His disguise had not been uncovered. When his business was over, his identity would be confirmed. Eventually, the truth might surface, but by then his plans for the Druid order would have come to fruition as intended.

He wound his way through the Assembly hallways, keeping to himself, doing nothing to suggest that he desired conversation with anyone. In short order, he was standing at the entrance to the offices of the Minister of Security. Here, he was stopped briefly, his identity apparently not so well known. Eventually Crepice emerged to confront him.

"Isaturin," the aide greeted him, bowing slightly. "We welcome you to this ministry."

He bowed in return. "I am appreciative of your hospitality. I hope to speak with Minister Caeil. Is he available for a brief conversation?"

Crepice hesitated, his eyes shifting away momentarily and then back again—assessing the situation. Arcannen recognized the look. He was deciding what he should tell Isaturin—a man who was clearly antagonistic toward this office and its avowed purpose.

"Come into the waiting room and let me find out if he can see you." Crepice had decided favorably. "I am sure something can be arranged."

He guided Arcannen from the outer office to the reception area beyond and motioned for him to take a seat in one of the chairs set against the far wall. Then he disappeared through the familiar double doors that led to Fashton Caeil's chambers. Arcannen sat down and waited, thinking through how he would handle what must happen next. Crepice would be right outside the chamber doors, so he would have to be careful.

He had only a few minutes to wait before the doors opened anew and out walked Caeil, his corpulent frame garbed in scarlet robes, his face flushed, his arms outstretched in greeting.

"What a surprise!" he enthused, grasping both of Arcannen's hands in his own. "This visit is long overdue and much welcomed!" He paused, as if remembering something. "Although I have heard it said in certain quarters that your feelings for this office are not of the warmest sort."

Arcannen nodded and managed a regretful look. "Times change. Attitudes evolve. I think a meeting between us is long overdue. I am hopeful that a reconciliation between the Federation and Paranor might begin at this very meeting."

"Wouldn't that be wonderful?" Caeil released his hands and stepped back. "Come in, then. Let's sit down and discover what sort of agreement we can achieve."

Leaving Crepice to close the doors behind them, they entered Caeil's chambers and sat, Caeil behind his desk, Arcannen in front of it. The minister bent forward to lessen the distance between them and smiled. "So, Ambassador Isaturin, what is it I can do for the Fourth Druid Order and its esteemed Ard Rhys?"

Arcannen motioned for him to lean even farther forward, and then he bent closer himself—a gesture that suggested that secrets and confidences were about to be shared.

"Well, Minister," the sorcerer replied, the Stiehl already in his hand and held just out of view below the desktop, "you can die."

In a quick, practiced movement, he snatched the front of Fashton Caeil's robes with his free hand, yanked him across the desk, and buried the Stiehl at the base of his throat, severing his vocal cords and spinal column. Caeil went limp, his mouth opening and closing, and Arcannen pinned him to the desk while he worked the edge of the black knife blade back and forth, separating the other's head from his shoulders.

It was over in seconds. The minister's heavy body slumped to the floor, but his head—eyes wide in shock, mouth hanging open—remained atop the desk.

Arcannen took a moment to study his work, then carefully set the knife on the floor to one side, where it would be found, and stepped back. There was a little blood on the sleeves of his robe, but he was able to wipe most of it off on the dead man's body. If he kept his arms folded against him when he left, nothing of the smears would be seen. He gave Fashton Caeil a last look. The Minister might still be alive if he hadn't given himself away on their last visit. But suggesting that meeting in public was no longer an option was a clear indication of the direction in which things were going. Caeil's usefulness as a resource was at an end. He would serve better by drawing the Federation's attention to the Druids, and the Druids' attention away from Arcannen as a result.

He took a moment to compose himself, making certain he was back in character as the Druid Isaturin, and then he walked to the door and opened it. Crepice was sitting at his desk, but he got up immediately as Arcannen appeared. The sorcerer waited until the man was close enough, then reached out quickly, grasped his neck, yanked him close, and twisted his head sharply to one side. Crepice went limp instantly.

Arcannen caught the body in his arms and dragged it behind the desk, leaving it there, out of sight.

Then, still in character as Isaturin, he walked through the doors leading out, closed them behind him, nodded to the guards standing watch and disappeared down the hall.

24

Aphenglow Elessedil was talking with Grehling in her chambers, urging him to tell her what had happened to Chrysallin Leah.

"So when you found her in Mischa's quarters, she was strapped to a bed in a room that was crisscrossed by glowing lines. But you could walk through these lines and they shredded and disappeared? They didn't hurt you? You didn't feel anything?"

The boy thought about it. "They didn't hurt me, but they did something to me. They made me see images of Chrysallin and a gray-haired Elven woman. Chrys was in trouble; she was in pain. And—"

He stopped suddenly, staring at her. "And what?" she encouraged him. She needed to understand what had happened. "Go on, Grehling. Tell me everything."

"The gray-haired Elven woman looked like you." He hesitated. "In fact, it *was* you."

"You're certain about this?"

He nodded. "But then the images went away when I broke enough of the threads. So I got her free and took her out of there. She was in a lot of pain. She kept saying she had been tortured and no one could bear to look at her ever again. She seemed to think that she had broken bones and that there was blood all over her; it was hard to make sense of it all. I couldn't see anything wrong with her. She looked fine to me. But I didn't ask her about it. She was too upset. I just wanted to get her away. We bumped into Mischa right outside the door, coming back from wherever she'd gone, but I hit her hard enough to knock her out. We ran then, and I took Chrysallin to Leofur's house."

He went on from there, describing how Leofur had taken them in and they had slept until the black creature broke down the door and then Leofur saved them by using her weapon and taking them down into the tunnels. But the creature had followed them, Mischa had appeared, and again they had fled until they were caught by the witch and trapped in an alleyway.

"But then something really strange happened," he continued, his voice suddenly becoming more intense. "Mischa started taunting Chrysallin. She kept reminding her about the gray-haired woman—the one who looked like you. She asked her if she wanted more torture. Then the gray-haired woman appeared and said something, and Chrysallin went crazy. She started screaming—and I've never heard anything like it! It was terrible. I tried covering my ears to shut out the sound, but nothing helped. Then the gray-haired woman exploded. The witch started backing away, but she was thrown against the wall and smashed apart. And all from the screaming! But Chrysallin didn't seem to know what had happened afterward. She even asked me if I did!"

Aphenglow didn't say anything in response for a long time, turning away to walk to the window and look out over the walls and towers of the Keep. "Chrysallin didn't do anything with her hands, didn't speak any words? She just screamed?"

"That's what I saw," Grehling affirmed.

You don't suppose, Aphenglow thought, an idea occurring to her that was so unexpected she was momentarily startled.

She turned back to the boy. "Why don't you go have something to eat in the dining hall? Paxon and Leofur might be there. I'll have Sebec take you."

The boy started to leave, then turned back. "Do you know what's wrong with Chrysallin?" he asked her.

She smiled. "I might."

"Can you help her?"

"I intend to try."

She watched him depart, closing the door behind him, and then she turned back to the window once more. She would have to see the girl at some point, although she would need to be careful about how she handled it. If Chrysallin thought her responsible for her current condition—if she believed Aphen was the one who had overseen her torture—she would not be very receptive to a visit.

Normally, this wouldn't be of much concern to an Ard Rhys. The defenses of her magic would be more than enough to protect her from any harm the girl might try to cause her in retaliation. But this tale of screaming that was strong enough to cause a human being to simply disintegrate was disturbing. It could be it was an aberration resulting from a form of wild magic—one either due to a birth defect or attained through exposure or physical contact—or it could be what had occurred to Aphenglow immediately on hearing of it. It could be an indication that Chrysallin Leah had been born with a heretofore-submerged command over the Ohmsford family's generations-long magic they called the wishsong.

After all, she was the great-grandchild of Mirai Leah and Railing Ohmsford, the product of a mixed bloodline with a very long history of magic use. Paxon Leah possessed the same blood and carried the same history in his genetic mix, but he had shown no trace of having use of the wishsong. It was entirely possible that the sister had it and he did not. There was a history of that within the family—of the magic sometimes skipping entire generations before resurfacing. It was also true that the ability to summon the wishsong did not always appear right away. Sometimes, it took years to reveal its presence.

But it was a magic embedded in the use of the bearer's voice, the sound capable of achieving almost anything for a practiced user. If not controlled or if released spontaneously, the result would very likely be the one Chrysallin Leah had experienced. Terrified, threatened, and enraged, she would have struck out blindly, giving voice to the mix of feelings roiling inside of her. She would not necessarily have even been aware of what she was doing, and the result would have shocked and confused her.

It all fit. Yet Aphenglow could not be certain unless she revealed to the girl what had happened and then convinced her she needed to find a way to deal with what it meant.

But how best to do that?

She would start by telling Paxon what she suspected. He would have to come to terms with the fact that his sister might have the use of a magic that had not surfaced in the Leah/Ohmsford bloodline for several generations—an incredibly powerful magic that she would need to learn to control. He would probably have to help her do that. It would require that Chrysallin be given time and opportunity to fully recover from the damage she had suffered at the hands of Arcannen and Mischa. It would demand patience and understanding and guidance.

She didn't know if the young man was up to it. She thought he might be, given the level of maturity and determination he had demonstrated in his efforts to master the skills taught to him by Oost Mondara and the lessons imparted by Sebec, but she couldn't be sure.

No one could.

She stepped away from the window and started for the chamber door. She had another matter to occupy her attention just now. She had put it off for days, but she could do so no longer. She must go down to the artifact chamber and discover if anything had disturbed the wards she and Sebec had placed over the vault that housed the crimson Elfstones. The Stones themselves were safe enough; she had taken no chances with that.

All that mattered was whether or not another theft had been attempted.

Paxon was still deep in conversation with Leofur about his sister when Sebec reappeared. "They've finished with her for now. She's sleeping, but you can sit with her. Would you like to do that for a few minutes?"

He didn't have to ask whom the young Druid was talking about and he didn't hesitate to break off with Leofur. "Can we continue this later?" he asked, already getting to his feet.

She gave him a nod, and he was off. With Sebec leading, he departed the dining room, went down the hall to a set of stairs, climbed one level, went down another hallway, and at the very end entered a large ward sectioned off into a collection of rooms with walls and closed doors and open compartments separated only by curtains. The Healers, whether they were Druids or not—Paxon couldn't tell for certain—were all dressed in white, men and women alike. There were eight or nine in evidence, all bustling about, going this way and that, some singly and some in small groups. A few glances were directed his way, but no one spoke to him.

He had not spent much time in the healing center during his stay at Paranor and did not know his way around. But Sebec, who was obviously familiar with everything, led him forward to one of the enclosed rooms, knocked softly on the door, turned the latch, and peeked inside.

He turned back to Paxon. "I'll let you stay with her alone. But not for very long. The Healers will be back shortly. I'll come for you when they are ready. I'll knock first. Don't open it unless I do."

Paxon went inside and heard the door close behind him. Chrysallin was not, in fact, sleeping, but sitting on a chair staring off into space. She was dressed in a white gown and slippers. She had been washed and her hair had been combed. He walked closer, noting once again that there were no marks on her, no evidence at all of any sort of torture. Whatever had been done to her, it was all in her mind. But she believed the terrible things she spoke of had actually happened, and that was all that mattered.

He knelt beside her and took her hands in his own.

"Chrysallin, can you hear me? It's Paxon. It's your brother. Please, look at me. Let me know if you can hear me." No response. He kept talking. "Chrys, we're going to help you. You've been hurt, but there is no damage to your body. The torture you experienced wasn't real. It all took place in your mind; you were meant to believe it was happening when it wasn't. But we are in Paranor now. There are Healers here who can help you. They are working to find a way to make you better. Everything will be all right."

Then he talked to her about their childhood. He told her stories she would remember of when they had played together as small children. He reminded her of adventures they had gone on in their backyard. He tried kidding her about the time he had chopped off her long hair and made her cry. He talked about the trips they would take together on the airships, freighting cargo from Leah to other cities in the Four Lands. He told her how good she would be at crewing and piloting, how much she had learned, and where they would go and what they would do once she was well.

He asked her to come back for their mother, who loved her and missed her. He told her he wanted to take her home.

He talked to her until he was talked out, and then he held her to him and sang softly, stroking her hair and rocking her. A long time passed. He kept thinking the Healers would come back, but they didn't. Maybe Sebec had told them to wait a bit, to let Paxon have time with her. Perhaps the Healers believed he might have better luck than they had in bringing her out of her withdrawal.

Then he stopped everything and just held her in the quiet of the room, trying not to cry, holding back the tears that threatened to come with every dark thought about how she might never get better. Eventually, he put her back in her bed and tucked her in, sitting next to her for another long period of time, watching over her. But she just lay there, her eyes open and staring.

He was finally getting ready to leave when a soft knock sounded at the door. Sebec, he thought. Releasing his sister, he rose and walked over. When he opened the door, the Ard Rhys was standing in the opening.

"Sebec said . . ." she started to whisper, and then she trailed off as she saw the expression of shock on his face as he turned quickly to look over his shoulder. Her gaze shifted past him, and she locked eyes with Chrysallin, who was suddenly sitting up in bed.

Paxon saw the shock and surprise mirrored on his sister's face an instant before she began to scream. He reacted instinctively, throwing himself in front of the Ard Rhys to protect her, propelling her backward through the door and into the hallway beyond. But he was too slow. Chrysallin's scream struck him like a hammer blow, slamming into him with such force that it knocked the breath from his lungs and his feet out from under him. Locked together with Aphenglow Elessedil, he was thrown into the wall beyond. They went down in a tangled heap, and Paxon lost consciousness.

When he came awake, Sebec and the Druid Healers were there, pulling him off Aphenglow. The treatment room door had been closed again, and he couldn't see what was going on with Chrys. But the screaming had stopped, so he knew the attack was over. The Ard Rhys lay next to him, still unconscious, the Healers bent over her. They would both likely be dead now, he thought, if the impact of the attack hadn't carried them back out the door, beyond where his sister could see them.

Or had she somehow realized who he was and instinctively held back? Or perhaps the Ard Rhys had managed to summon magic in time to protect them both. Would such magic come to her as his did to him when he held the sword—an instantaneous response that required no act or even thought to summon it?

Sebec knelt beside him. "What happened?"

He breathed in deeply and exhaled. "I'm not sure. She came to the door and knocked. I thought it was you or the Healers, so I opened the door. Chrysallin woke and saw the Ard Rhys and reacted at once, screaming . . ." He closed his eyes at the memory. "The force of it threw both of us out of the room and into the hallway. That was the last thing I remember. I blacked out."

Sebec looked confused. "Why did your sister scream at the Ard Rhys? They've never even met."

The scribe didn't know about the possible resemblance between the gray-haired Elven woman of his sister's torture experience and the Ard Rhys that Grehling had described to Leofur, so Paxon told him. "Perhaps she just attacked as a response to what she thought she was seeing; I'm sure she was terrified she was about to be hauled back for more," he finished.

"Well, whatever she thought, she hurt my mistress; I don't know how badly just yet. The Healers will have to spend more time with her before we know. You shouldn't have opened the door without being sure it was me, Paxon."

The Highlander cringed at the rebuke, thinking he hadn't done anything wrong. Sebec had said not to open the door until he knocked, and Paxon had waited until he heard a knock. What was the Ard Rhys thinking, coming to Chrysallin's room in the first place?

But he said nothing, letting the matter be, anxious to get back into Chrysallin's room to see how she was. He asked Sebec if he might do this, but the young Druid told him he would have to wait, that the Healers had sedated his sister and would be working on her again as soon as she woke.

So instead, the Highlander went back down to the dining hall to look for Grehling and Leofur. He didn't find them there, but he was told they were walking in the gardens just outside. When he left the building to have a look around he found them almost immediately, and while the three of them strolled through the flower beds and hedgerows he revealed what had happened.

"She came right to Chrysallin's room?" Grehling asked when he had finished. "That's strange."

Paxon looked at him. "What do you mean?"

"This morning I told her I thought the gray-haired Elven woman looked just like her. She asked all about it, wanted to know everything. She knew exactly how Chrys felt about her."

Paxon started to reply, but then stopped himself. He needed to think this through before he said anything more. Something about this whole business troubled him, but he couldn't be sure yet what it was.

So he changed the subject, talking instead about his plans for Chrysallin should the Druids be unable to help her. If that happened, he told them, he would take her to the renowned Gnome Healers of Storlock in the Eastland. If anyone could help his sister, they could.

Then he asked of their plans for returning to Wayford. After a hesitant exchange of glances, Grehling said they were just waiting for someone to offer them a way back. Unless Paxon needed them to stay, of course, which they would be happy to do. The Highlander told them they had both done more than enough, and he would look into helping them find a way home.

Then abruptly he decided, almost before he realized what he was doing, that he had a much better idea.

In point of fact, he was feeling useless sitting around Paranor doing nothing while Arcannen was still out there somewhere. He knew if he asked he would not be allowed to go looking for the sorcerer. But the loss of Starks burned like a hot iron inside him, and he was not going to let his killing go unpunished. He knew the Druids would be content to wait until the right opportunity presented itself, but that was not enough to satisfy him. This was personal; he continued to view Starks's death as his fault. He could not shake the feeling that he had failed his friend, letting him down when he was needed most. All the arguments as to why this wasn't so didn't make a whit's worth of difference. His own truth was what mattered, and he felt strongly that he had to do something about it.

Then again, the matter of Arcannen notwithstanding, he felt a compelling urge to do something more to help Chrysallin. Dark worries about the deep withdrawal she had embraced rode his shoulders like vultures. She seemed safe enough under the care of the

Druid Healers, yet he could not make himself sit around waiting for a recovery that he knew might not happen. He believed he could serve his sister better by returning to Wayford, and Grehling and Leofur had provided him with the excuse and opportunity he needed to act.

It was late in the afternoon when he found Sebec again, and even then it was only by chance. He was scouring the halls looking for the Druid scribe, hoping he would be allowed to visit Chrys, when the other appeared right in front of him.

"How are you?" he asked Paxon, then immediately shook his head, as if dismissing the answer. "A stupid question for me to be asking. I need to apologize for what I said earlier. I was frightened for my mistress and I took it out on you. Please forgive me."

Paxon shrugged. "There's nothing to forgive. I should have asked who was out there before I opened the door. How is the Ard Rhys?"

"She seems better. She suffered no broken bones, only cuts and bruises. She's sleeping now." He shook his head. "But she's frail at best and not so strong as once. These sorts of injuries are worrisome."

"I was wondering. Could I see my sister now?"

"You can look in on her, but she's still sleeping. They want her to rest for as long as possible. They think she suffered quite a shock seeing the Ard Rhys appear unexpectedly like that." He paused. "Maybe I shouldn't tell you this, but they gave her a very strong dose of a sleeping potion. They are hoping she sleeps for several more days. They think she might have a better chance of recovery if she does."

A better chance of recovery. The words felt cold and taunting. It reaffirmed his certainty about what he had decided to do.

"I want to take Grehling and Leofur back to Wayford," he said abruptly. "They've been here long enough. They need to go home."

Sebec pursed his lips. "I can have Troll guards take them. You don't need to go."

"I know I don't. But I want something to do, something to take my mind off Chrysallin. If she's to sleep another day or two, this gives me time. I promised them I would see them safely back."

Sebec studied him carefully. "You don't intend to go looking for Arcannen, do you?"

"Not unless he's in Wayford. But after killing Starks, I don't think we can expect him to come back there anytime soon."

Sebec clearly didn't know what to think, so he gave the Highlander a noncommittal nod. "Do what you need to do, Paxon. I'll tell the Ard Rhys when she wakes."

Paxon left him there, took time to look in on Chrys and sit with her a short while, watching her sleep, and then found Grehling and Leofur and abruptly announced that he was taking them to Wayford. Neither said anything right away, both leaving wordlessly to gather up their few possessions. Soon they met him back at the airfield by the skiff he had chosen for the journey.

But Leofur, on returning—carrying her flash rip cradled in her arms—said, "Why are you the one doing this? You, personally? Why not someone else? Shouldn't you be staying here with your sister?"

"I said I would help you find a way back." Even to himself, he sounded defensive. "Besides, Chrys was given a sleeping potion. They don't want her awake again for a few days. I might as well do something useful."

She stepped close. "I don't know you all that well personally, but I know enough about men in general to know when they aren't telling me the truth. Suppose you tell me why I have that feeling about you."

Grehling had moved closer, too. "What's wrong?" he asked, looking from one to the other.

Paxon weighed his choices, and then he made his decision. "I want to have a look inside Mischa's quarters. Maybe there is something that can help Chrys get better. A potion, an elixir, something written down about what was done and how to undo it. I don't know. I just want to look around."

She gave him a long, steady look. "Then you ought to just say as much. Let's get going."

They flew through the remainder of the day and all through the night, switching off regularly on the controls in the pilot box, each one taking turns at steering the airship. They were all experienced fliers, even Leofur, and they knew how to navigate by the stars and a steady scanning of the moonlit terrain, staying not far off the ground as they proceeded south across the Dragon's Teeth and down the length of the Runne River to Rainbow Lake and then on toward Leah and the deep Southland.

Paxon managed to sleep a few hours during their flight, but spent most of his time awake, much of it musing on the direction his life had taken. Only months earlier, his world had revolved around the airfreight business and his mother and sister. Now the business was gone, he was miles from his mother and his Highland home, and his sister was even further away in another sense and in danger of never coming back. He had made a life among the Druids of Paranor, but he wasn't one of them and they might blame him—as he blamed himself—for the death of one of their order.

He was adrift in a world he didn't fully understand and wasn't even sure he believed in, struggling to keep his feet and maintain his determination, trying his best to balance the vicissitudes of a much-changed life. Everything he had done was buttressed as much on faith as on knowledge, and that wasn't about to change with this current endeavor. His world was a confusing and treacherously shifting ground, and he did not see that he had any better way to deal with it than simply to keep marching on.

It was nearing morning when they arrived in Wayford, the sun a golden haze on the eastern horizon, the sky clear and promising as the night fled west. They landed at the airfield amid receding shadows and splashes of sunrise light, setting down close to the manager's office so they could arrange to moor the airship. Grehling jumped down and went on ahead to speak to his father, whom he had already spotted inside the office, while Paxon and Leofur tied off the mooring lines, drew down the light sheaths, and coiled the radian draws.

The Highlander and the young woman were just finishing up when the boy hurried back over, clearly excited as he scrambled up the rope ladder and jumped over the railing and onto the decking beside them. "Father just told me," he whispered, as if caution were advised. "Arcannen flew in late last night."

Paxon straightened at once. "What time?"

"An hour or so after midnight. He moored his ship, left his crew aboard, and went alone into the city. He hasn't come back. He told Father he might be gone as long as tonight and not to tell anyone he was here."

"But your father told you anyway?" Paxon asked, one eyebrow arched.

Grehling gave him a sheepish grin. "He tells me everything."

Paxon was already buckling on his sword. "I'm going after him."

"I'm coming with you!" Grehling declared.

Paxon held out both hands to stop him where he was. "No, you're not. You're staying here."

"But you might need help! You can't face the sorcerer by yourself."

Paxon only just kept himself from saying, *So I should face him with a fourteen-year-old boy?* "It's too dangerous. I won't let you risk your life for me. You stay right here and keep watch for his return."

"But I want to—"

"No, Grehling." Leofur cut him short before he could finish. "Paxon is right. You have to stay behind this time. It *is* too dangerous."

"Thank you." Paxon gave her an appreciative nod.

"Which is why I'll be going instead," she finished, hefting the flash rip in the cradle of her arms to emphasize why. She faced down Paxon defiantly. "Don't say anything stupid. You need someone to watch your back. I can do that for you."

He saw the determination in her eyes and nodded. "Let's get going."

25

Side by side, Paxon and Leofur walked from the airfield down the roadway leading into the city of Wayford. The road was mostly empty, the lamps in the residences either still off or just being lit. There were a few people abroad—those who began their workday early—but they passed without doing more than nodding or waving. Ahead, the larger buildings of the city were vague shadows in the gloom of the fading night.

"Why are you doing this?" Paxon asked her finally, unable to let the matter rest any longer. "You barely know me. You have no reason to risk yourself like this. Not after what you've already done."

"I didn't know there was a limit on how much help you could offer people," she replied, deadpan.

"I just mean it's unexpected."

"It would be odd if you were *expecting* me to come with you, wouldn't it? Like you say, we don't know each other that well."

"But why are you coming?"

She looked away a moment and then back again. "Several reasons. I think what you are doing is important. Not so much where Arcannen is concerned; more for helping Chrysallin. What was done to her is terrible. I've experienced something like that. I want to see her get better. This seems to me to be one way she could."

She shrugged. "I thought I might help you with that part, but try to talk you out of the other."

They reached the outermost buildings of the business district of the city and she pointed him down a different street than the one he was intending on taking. "No point in doing the expected. Better if we go the back way."

"You've had something done to you like what was done to Chrys?" he asked.

She nodded. "Yes. But I don't want to talk about it."

"You just want to talk to me about leaving Arcannen alone. Even knowing how I feel about what happened to Starks?"

She looked over again. "I like you, Paxon. Even knowing as little about you as I do, I like what I do know. You care about your sister and you would do anything to help her. You are willing to sacrifice yourself for your friends. You aren't afraid of things that would scare the pants off most people."

He laughed. "Don't worry. I'm plenty scared."

"Maybe. But it hasn't stopped you from doing the right thing."

"But going after Arcannen isn't the right thing."

"Going after medicine or information that will help Chrysallin is the better right thing. That's what you need to realize."

She turned him down a side street, and by now he was completely lost. "All right," he said. "I'll think about it. I will. But I'm not making any promises."

"Just weigh the two. Take their measure. Think about what needs doing the most."

They walked in silence for a time, turning down one small street, alleyway, and pass-through after another, the shadows deepening around them in spite of the sunrise.

I like you, too, he said to himself.

All at once they were in front of an entry that led into a small residence sandwiched between larger buildings. The door to the house had been smashed in, and all that remained were pieces of wood and iron hinges.

He looked at her in confusion. "My house," she said, heading through the open entry. "Mischa's creature found your sister here and tried to get at her. This is where we escaped into the tunnels."

They walked inside, and she looked around distractedly. "Some small damage, but nothing that can't be put right. Everything valuable is tucked safely away. Like the charges I need for the flash rip. Wait here."

She disappeared in back. He stood looking around. It was odd that she had been gone for days and no one appeared to have looted the place. In almost every scenario he could imagine, that would have happened. He wondered again about who she really was.

When she rejoined him, she was dressed in different clothing—shirt, pants, boots, and gloves, all in black. She was checking the flash rip's diapson crystal chamber as she came up to him. "All charged up," she announced, snapping the cover closed. "If we run into the sorcerer or any other sort of trouble, I don't want to find myself one load short."

"You still don't have to come," he told her.

She smiled, tossing back her silver-streaked hair from her face. "Yes, I do. I want to."

They left the building and went back out into the street, turning in the opposite direction from the one in which they had come. Leofur was doing the leading again, and Paxon—because he was lost anyway—had to be content with letting her. Some of what he was viewing appeared familiar, but it was difficult to be certain.

Dozens of people were in the streets by now, the sun fully up and their day begun. Carts and wagons rolled through, horses trotted by, and the silence had given way to the sounds of people and their activities.

"Where now?" he asked her finally, trying to be heard over the din.

She grabbed his arm and pulled him close to her, lifting her head to his ear. "Mischa's quarters. All right?"

He nodded, and she released him. "Good choice," she might have said, but he wasn't sure.

Before long they were standing at the head of an alleyway running between two buildings. Paxon believed they were close to where he had done battle with the black creature a few days earlier.

Leofur gestured to the building on the right. "Mischa's rooms are on the second floor," she whispered. "We have to be really careful from here on. I'll lead until we get inside, then you take over."

He already had his black sword free of its sheath and grasped firmly in his right hand. "Go ahead."

They entered through a wooden gate overgrown with vines and greenery that made it barely visible beneath a shadowy overhang. The alley was empty, and the windows of Mischa's building were dark. There was no sign of life. The sounds of the city that had surrounded them earlier had become faint and distant. When they reached the door leading off the alley, Leofur paused to test the locks. But they were not secure, so she opened the door without trouble and led them inside.

She paused there a moment so they could listen to the silence. Then she led Paxon down a hallway to a set of stairs and up to the second floor. Again, she paused. Satisfied, she took him to rooms about halfway down to the other end of the hall, opened the door cautiously, and led him inside.

The rooms appeared empty. Paxon, sword held guardedly in front of him, moved from room to room to make sure. When he reached the bedroom in which Chrysallin had been tortured and saw the bed on which she had been tied down and the detritus from the broken threads of magic lying in lines of ash and cinders across the floor, he had to back out again right away.

"I'll search in here," Leofur offered. "You take the rest of the rooms."

So they hunted through the witch's chambers for the better part of two hours, carefully searching for hidden panels and stashes, for books and papers on which conjuring and magic might be written. They tested floorboards for looseness, searched walls for hollow places, and turned the furniture upside down. In the end, Paxon even went into the adjoining rooms, which were all vacant and mostly empty of furniture, and searched them, as well.

They found nothing.

"This can't be right," Paxon said as they stared at each other in frustration. "There has to be something. She would keep her important supplies and writings for her magic close."

"Grehling said he rescued Chrys when Mischa went out to retrieve some potions and ran into her just outside while she was coming back with them. So her store of supplies should be here." He looked around. "But she's hidden it well. We've searched everywhere."

"She would, wouldn't she? She was a witch, and she would have been careful to protect herself." She paused. "If it were me, I would use magic to conceal everything."

He nodded slowly. "Of course. It's here, but we just can't see it."

Leofur nodded. "A Druid could show us. We should have brought one along."

Paxon thought instantly of Starks, who would have come without hesitating. He compressed his lips and shrugged. "There's someone else who likely knows."

She nodded slowly. "I knew we'd get to that. You won't let go of it, will you?"

"Not when it's the only way."

"We don't even know where he is."

"Dark House."

She nodded reluctantly. "Probably. But why would Arcannen help you?"

"He wouldn't. Not willingly."

Her face tightened and despair reflected in her eyes. "Don't do this, Paxon. Wait for some help."

"If I wait for help, he'll get away. He'll be gone, and I might not find him again. I might not have any chance of finding whatever Mischa's got hidden in here."

"You're thinking of Starks. This is about avenging his death."

He stepped close. "I promise you it isn't. I'm doing this for Chrys. That's the truth. Believe me, please."

She shook her head. "I suppose I do believe you. Although I don't know why." She sighed heavily, and then took hold of his arms and turned him toward the doorway. "I want to believe you, so I will. Don't disappoint me. Let's go find him."

At Paranor, Aphenglow Elessedil had come awake. She ached from head to foot from Chrysallin's attack, but her thinking was clear and sharp. She lay in her bed for long minutes, gathering her thoughts. In a chair nearby, one of the Druid Healers dozed, head lowered, hands clasped in his lap. The curtains were drawn and the room was dark, so she could not tell what time it was, although she could see slivers of light through tiny gaps in the fabric.

She was thinking of what had happened to her when she had come face-to-face with Chrysallin, but mostly she was thinking about what she now knew of the theft of the artifacts from the Druid vault. She was carrying this burden alone for the moment, unwilling to speak with anyone else about it. She had known who the thief was for a short while now, but had let the matter be because she wasn't certain how to handle it. Unusual for her—but then the truth about who had committed the thefts was unusual, as well.

Worse, it exposed a failing in her with which she had not managed to come to terms. It made her realize how very long she had been Ard Rhys. She found herself thinking of Arling, now gone for more than a century and a half—the sister she loved so much and had tried so hard to protect. In the end, she had failed her sister because Arling had sacrificed herself to save the Four Lands, and Aphen had let her. With Arling gone, her mother and her beloved uncle Ellich long since dead, and even steady, dependable Seersha passed away, she had been left alone. She had other family, but they were not close. She had separated herself from Arborlon and made her home at Paranor. The Druids were her family now, and she had given her entire life to caring for them.

Perhaps that was why it hurt so much to know that one of them had betrayed her.

She sat up finally, unwilling to remain abed any longer, and when she did so the Druid dozing in the chair woke up. "Mistress!" he exclaimed in horror, and he leapt up to prevent her from rising.

"No, no," she insisted, warding him off with arms extended. "I'm well enough to get up and walk around. Please let me do so."

He did, but only after he had helped steady her and made certain she wouldn't fall. "I should examine you, Mistress."

"Why don't you wait on that and go find Sebec for me, instead," she said gently. "Ask him to come here. When we are finished, you can conduct whatever examination is needed."

He left reluctantly, and she took the opportunity to wash her face in the basin by her bedside and run a comb through her long gray hair. She watched herself in the mirror as she did this, thinking she really had lived too long. The Druid Sleep was a gift but it didn't make her happy. It didn't bring back the time she had lost. It didn't bring back the people who were gone. It didn't even provide a sense of contentment.

There was a knock on the door and Sebec entered on her invitation. The young Druid looked haggard, his face drawn, his eyes mirroring his concern, but he smiled at once when he saw her back on her feet. "Mistress! Thank goodness!"

He came over to her and knelt at her feet, taking her hands in his own and kissing them. "I'm so sorry for what happened. It was my fault. I didn't know the doctors hadn't sedated her yet. They said they were going to. I almost killed you!"

She grasped his hands and brought him to his feet. "Hardly. I was just a bit stunned from the blow. She has real magic in her voice—a dangerous power for one so young—but I don't think she knows anything about it. Is she sleeping now?"

"The Healers gave her a strong potion. They want her to rest for several days before they begin treating her again. The shock was significant, they say."

"I imagine so. Where is Paxon?"

Sebec hesitated. "He flew the boy and the young woman back to Wayford."

She gave him a measured look. "And you let him do this?"

"I don't think I could have stopped him."

"You know what he intends, don't you? He intends to go looking for Arcannen."

"He said he just wanted something to do."

Aphenglow released his hands and walked over to

pour herself a glass of water from the pitcher on the dresser. "I want you to get him back here. I want a contingent of Druid Guards to fly to Wayford, find him, and escort him home. Send Oost Mondara. Right now, Sebec."

She said it with enough emphasis that her disapproval was clearly evident, and he almost ran out the door to do her bidding. She watched him go, disappointed all over again. Some things you couldn't do anything about, she supposed. Some things had to be left to run their course.

She walked to the window and pulled open the curtains. Daylight streamed in. From the position of the sun, it appeared to be midmorning. A new day had arrived.

She walked to her wardrobe, pulled out fresh clothing, shed her nightgown, and began to dress.

She did not see Sebec again until midafternoon. She imagined he had decided to keep his distance until he was certain her anger had abated, occupying himself with other duties. She was confident he would do as she had told him and dispatch Oost and the Druid Guards immediately, so she saw no reason to follow up on that. But she couldn't stop thinking about Paxon, still so young and headstrong. She worried that he would find Arcannen before help could reach him.

She was afraid that the rescue attempt would come too late.

But she had done what she could, and there were other matters she must deal with.

She'd spent the morning with the Druid Healers being poked and prodded, listening to advice—don't try to do too much right away, get lots of sleep, drink liquids, if you feel weak sit down and wait for it to pass. All of it was well meant but unnecessary. She was sore, but getting better by the minute, ready to resume her duties as the Ard Rhys of the order.

So after she had eaten lunch—her first meal since waking—she returned to her office to examine documents that had now been awaiting her attention for days. Much of it was busywork, the sort of paper shuffling she deliberately put aside and ignored for as long as possible. But with her limited strength and mobility, this seemed an excellent time to catch up.

She was still in the midst of her efforts when Sebec knocked on her door and entered. She could tell at once from his expression that something was seriously wrong. But she forced herself to sit back and wait for him to get up enough nerve to tell her.

"Mistress, we have visitors," he announced. "A Federation warship has arrived. It carries a full complement of Federation soldiers and the Prime Minister himself. He wishes to speak with you at once."

She gave him a measured look. "What does he want to speak to me about?"

"He wouldn't say. He said it was strictly between the two of you. He is waiting just outside the north gates."

She took a moment to digest this news. The current Prime Minister of the Federation was a welcome change from Drust Chazhul and Edinja Orle and a few others she had been forced to deal with over the years. By all accounts, he was a decent and honorable man whose service to his people and conduct toward the other Races of the Four Lands had proven exemplary. Hard-nosed and fiercely loyal, he was nevertheless neither venal nor treacherous. She believed she could trust him.

She rose. "Arrange for a contingent of the Druid Guard to accompany me. No one is to act precipitously. No one is to do anything unless I am attacked. Am I clear about this, Sebec?"

The young Druid nodded hastily and backed out of

the room. She gathered up her black robes and followed him into the hallway beyond and along its length to the stairs leading down. Once outside the building, she crossed the open courtyard to the north gates, squinting against the bright sunlight. By then, the contingent of Druid Guards she had requested had caught up to her, flanking her protectively, a silent presence. She ordered the gates opened and walked outside the Keep into a broad splash of sunshine.

The Federation warship was moored right in front of her, its huge dark hull casting its black shadow over her as she walked forward, leaving the Druid Guards behind. A small gathering of Federation officials and soldiers stood off to one side of the warship.

The Prime Minister separated himself from the others and came toward her. He was a spare, elderly man, white-haired and bearded, his blue eyes still sharp and knowing.

"Well met, Mistress Elessedil," he greeted her. "Thank you for agreeing to meet me like this. It is important that everything be done out in the open. An appearance of trust is crucial in this situation."

She wondered what he was talking about, but let him steer her aside, well away from the others, choosing a spot where they were out of hearing. "What's happened?" she asked, facing him squarely.

He met her gaze and held it. "Yesterday morning, a Druid entered the chambers of Fashton Caeil, our Minister of Security, and murdered both him and his assistant. The Druid who did this was seen and recognized by Federation soldiers stationed at the entry to the Minister's chambers. He was positively identified. It was Isaturin."

Aphenglow pursed her lips. "So have you come to Paranor to ask me to turn him over to you?"

The Prime Minister shook his head. "Not exactly.

The identification is suspect. I have reason to believe it is false even though the soldiers were quite clear about seeing him and hearing his name spoken. Or perhaps it is exactly because of both. It seems odd to me that a killer would allow these things to happen if he had any intention at all of hiding his identity. Then there's this."

He reached into his robes and pulled out a long black knife. "It is the murder weapon. It was found lying on the floor next to the body of Minister Caeil. Do you recognize it?"

She nodded. "It is called the Stiehl. It is a Druid artifact that was stolen from our archives some weeks ago. May I see it?"

The Prime Minister handed it to her. "That blade is very sharp."

"That blade," she said, giving the weapon a careful examination to be certain of what she was holding, "will cut through anything. There is no defense against it except for certain forms of magic." She looked up at him. "It was left behind by the killer?"

The other nodded. "And so it proves a further cause for my suspicion. Who would be foolish or careless enough to leave behind clear evidence that they were in some way affiliated with the Druid order? Was it simply forgotten in the heat of things? Was it dropped by accident? All of these seem unlikely to me."

"The Stiehl was last seen in the hands of a sorcerer called Arcannen several days ago in Wayford. It was used to kill one of my Druids—a man who had gone to find him and bring him back for punishment."

The Prime Minister's smile was chilly. "I thought as much. Arcannen's name has surfaced repeatedly during our investigation of this killing. He was listed on Minister Caeil's register as visiting him at least six times in the last four months. He was clearly a man known to the Minister who came and went regularly." He paused.

"Rumor has it that he has significant use of magic, including the ability to change his appearance."

Aphenglow nodded. "I expect that is true. So you don't think Isaturin is responsible for any of this?"

"I would be surprised if he was. Fashton Caeil was an ambitious man with plans for improving his situation in the Coalition Council. I have heard he coveted my own position. It seems likely that he overstepped himself with this sorcerer and paid the price for doing so."

He paused. "My only confusion comes from not understanding why the killer believed I would be convinced it was Isaturin. Given what we know, his efforts seem amateurish."

"I agree. Whatever else he might be, Arcannen is no fool. There is something else at work here." She considered. "I wonder if his intent in all this was not to fool us, but simply to delay us in our efforts to come after him. He knows we hunt him for his killing of our Druid brother. Perhaps this additional killing was meant to cause enough confusion to give him an opportunity to escape. And to make certain at the same time that the exact details of what was going on between the two never came to light."

"Perhaps he hoped I would act precipitously and simply assume the worst about you," the Prime Minister added ruefully. "It would not be the first time such a thing happened in the history of Druids and the Federation. And, in point of fact, it is happening to some extent now, as well. Others are already making judgments about these killings, which is why I came to you myself so we could have this talk. Can you be certain Isaturin was here yesterday when the killing was done?"

"I can find out immediately," she answered.

She called back to her guards and asked for Sebec to be sent to her. When the young scribe appeared, she asked him about Isaturin. "I want to know if he was here all day yesterday and the day before. I want to know if he left the Keep to go anywhere at all in that time. Will you check the logs and speak with the airfield watch?"

Sebec set off at a run. She turned back to the Prime Minister. "So the rumor of a Druid murderer is already being given credence?"

"He was seen and identified." The Prime Minister shrugged. "On the surface, it seems unquestionable that he is guilty. But you and I know better than to rely on what appears on the surface."

She nodded. "I am grateful to you for coming to settle this matter yourself."

"I fear we do less than we should to cooperate. Our inbred suspicions and long history of conflict drive us apart more often than not. This seemed a good opportunity to try to change this rather unfortunate habit."

She offered the blade back to him, a gesture she felt appropriate, but he quickly held up his hands, indicating he did not want it. "It belongs here, locked safely away. Do you think you might have better luck doing that this time?"

She didn't miss the irony in his voice. "When we lock it up this time, it will not be taken from us again," she replied.

"I am pleased to hear that."

So they stood together in silence for what seemed to Aphen an endless amount of time, waiting on Sebec. When he finally returned, he was flushed and out of breath. Before saying anything, he looked questioningly at the Ard Rhys.

"Just give your report, Sebec," she told him.

"Isaturin returned from Arishaig five days ago. He has not left here since. The logs and the guards all confirm it."

She sent him away and turned back to the Prime Minister.

"Well, Mistress, we have our answer," he said. "I am satisfied. But let me ask a favor of you. Would the Druid order be willing to undertake a hunt for the real killer? Would you be willing to assume responsibility for finding him?"

She nodded slowly. "I had already decided on this. If I can bring him back in one piece, he will be brought before you and made to answer directly for his actions."

The Prime Minister held out his hands. "I offer peace to you, Mistress. Now and in the future."

"I offer friendship, Prime Minister," she replied. She took his hands in her own and squeezed gently. "Safe journey home."

She watched him return to his companions and board the warship. She continued to watch as the vessel released its moorings and lifted away. She kept watching until it was out of sight.

A crisis averted, a promise of peace offered, and an affirmation of friendship given in return—all in a matter of minutes, she thought. *What other surprises does this day have in store?*

26

THE CITY STREETS WERE TEEMING WITH PEOPLE
and clogged with carriages and animals by the time
Paxon and Leofur exited Mischa's building and began
walking toward Dark House. To all appearances, they
were just another couple passing through the city, but
that was only because Leofur had slung her flash rip
over one shoulder and closed it away beneath her cloak.
While one or two pairs of eyes might have strayed to the
black sword strapped across Paxon's back, it didn't
draw nearly the attention the flash rip would.

In any event, no one stopped them. Midday was
approaching, and the smell of foods cooking and the
laughter and voices of men and women enjoying their
noon meal rose on all sides. The Highlander was acutely
aware of how hungry he was; he hadn't eaten anything
since the previous night. He glanced at the girl and took
note of her pinched face.

Impulsively, he pulled her over to a cart serving hot
beef sandwiches and bought two. Standing in front of a
makeshift counter with tankards of ale added to the
purchase, they gulped their food and drink like starving
wolves. Once finished, they exchanged a look at each
other's grease-and-ale-smeared faces and laughed in
spite of themselves. Offering thanks to the vendor, who
barely acknowledged them, they set out anew.

It took them only a short while to reach their destination. Paxon slowed when it came in sight, hanging back against the wall of a building across the street and down a bit from Dark House, gathering his thoughts. They weren't so much about what he was going to do as how he was going to do it. It would probably be better to wait until nightfall and then go in. The traffic would have abated and the darkness would help conceal them. But waiting wasn't an option. There was no guarantee that Arcannen was even there; waiting until it got dark didn't improve the odds.

Still, going in now meant doing so in broad daylight with eyes everywhere. Even attempts at sneaking through the back, where Paxon had gone before with help from Grehling, would leave them dangerously exposed. The other choice, of course, was to walk up to the front door and use the flash rip to force their way inside and try to catch the sorcerer by surprise. If there were guards and if he was anywhere but on the first floor, they would likely fail in their efforts.

He turned to Leofur finally, perplexed. "I don't know how to go about this. We need to get inside, but we have to do it without causing a disturbance that will alert Arcannen. We have to be able to get to him before he has a chance to flee again."

Leofur nodded. "One of the reasons I came with you," she said, "was to show you how that can be done."

He stared at her. "You can get us inside Dark House?"

She nodded. "Right through the front door. Want to give it a try?"

"But how can you do this?"

"I just can. Do you want me to try or not?"

He hesitated, unsure of what he was letting himself in for. But to persist in asking her how she could manage it seemed wrong, too. If she was saying she could do this, she probably could. And he didn't have a better idea to offer up, as he had already admitted.

"It's in your hands," he said.

They left their place by the wall and walked into the thick of the crowds passing by and crossed the roadway. When they reached the far side, Leofur went straight for Dark House, stopping when she reached the bottom of the steps leading up to the front door.

"You wait here," she told him. "No arguments, no questions," she added quickly.

He was surprised, but he did as she asked nevertheless. If she could get them inside, he wasn't about to interfere. He watched her climb the short flight to the door and knock once. When the door opened, she spoke with someone briefly, and the door closed again. Without looking at him, she made a gesture behind her back for him to remain where he was. He did so, still wondering what was going on.

When the door opened once more, a different guard was standing there, burly and scarred, filling the doorway with his bulk. He spoke to Leofur softly, nodded a few times, and finally glanced down the steps at Paxon. After a moment, he nodded to her and stepped back to let her pass. She glanced down at Paxon this time and beckoned him to come with her.

They walked through the front door together, the burly man in the lead, passing any number of guards as they traversed the length of the hall ahead to a set of stairs and started up. Paxon had no idea at all what to expect. Leofur hadn't said anything about what was going on, and he couldn't see any way of asking now. He had to trust her; he had to believe she was doing the right thing. Even if it was becoming increasingly hard to do so.

On the second floor, the burly man took them into a small room with a desk and a guard sitting at it and directed them to chairs set to one side. When they had seated themselves, he left without a word.

The guard at the desk was bent over a chart of some sort, his attention focused on whatever was written on it. Paxon glanced at Leofur, who nodded back. He mouthed the word *Arcannen,* and she looked at the ceiling. He took that to mean the sorcerer was still here, upstairs somewhere. But he still wondered how they had gotten into Dark House so easily. If Arcannen was really here, surely he would have given warning against allowing anyone to come in like this.

After a few moments, Leofur got up and walked over to the guard at the desk. She bent close and when he looked up she put a cloth concealed in her hand over his nose and mouth; he collapsed immediately. She wiped her hand off on his shirt, threw the cloth away, and turned to Paxon.

"He's upstairs in his office, getting ready to flee the city. We have to hurry."

They went out the door and found the hallway beyond empty. "What did you just do to that guard?" he asked her.

She glanced over and grinned. "Just a little trick I learned growing up."

"What sort of trick?" They were out in the hallway now, heading for the stairs leading up.

"Something that puts you to sleep for a while. Why do you care?"

He shook his head. "I just want to know what's happening here. I feel like I don't know anything. How did you get us through the front door?"

"Easy," she answered. "I know these people."

"How do you know them?" He could not keep the tone of incredulity from his voice.

"I used to work here." She turned on him, a hint of anger reflected in her eyes as she ran her hand through her silver-streaked hair. "How much more do you need to know? Any more questions you need answers to?"

Only one, he thought, but he realized he already knew the answer. She was young and pretty—what kind of work did he think she was doing here? Maid service? Scullery labor? Scribe? He bit back the rest of what was on the tip of his tongue and simply tracked her up the stairs to his impending confrontation with Arcannen, angry and disappointed.

Arcannen had just finished gathering up the record books for his various businesses when the knock on the door sounded. "Come," he said, barely looking up as Fentrick entered and stood there as if he had no idea why he had come. "Is there a problem?"

"I just need to tell you something."

"All right. Tell me."

"Leofur is here."

He looked up at once. "What does she want?"

"To see you before you leave, she said."

"And you let her in?"

The burly guard shrugged. "You said that if she ever came around, I was to—"

"Yes, yes, I know. You were to let her in." Arcannen made a dismissive motion. "But now is not a particularly convenient time for her to be here. I should have told you as much, I suppose. But I keep hoping you can figure these things out by yourself." He heaved a deep sigh and accepted the inevitable. "Where is she?"

"Waiting in the guard room with her friend."

His response was much quicker this time. "What friend?"

"A young man. Tall, dressed in woodsman's clothes. Wears this black sword strapped across his back." Fentrick sensed immediately that he had made a mistake.

"She said it was all right! She said you wouldn't mind, that you knew who it was."

"Matter of fact, I do," he said quietly, straightening up, realizing what was about to happen. "One flight down, you say?"

"In the guard room. She did say the visit was something of a surprise, so I shouldn't tell you they were here. She made it sound like it would spoil something if I did. But I just wasn't sure . . ."

He trailed off. Arcannen sighed. Saying he wasn't sure about this or anything else, for that matter, was the understatement of the year. Fentrick was steady and mostly reliable, but he wasn't quick-witted or astute enough to realize when he was being used.

And what was Leofur doing with Paxon Leah? How had they even managed to meet? It was impossible! He experienced an abrupt sensation of things slipping away from him, as if he could no longer control even the smallest events in his life, as if all his efforts at building something were being torn down around his ears.

He glanced at the boxes of records. There was no time to salvage them now. He would have to abandon them. He would have to run. "I'm leaving," he said to the other man, coming out from behind his desk in something of a rush. "After I'm gone, make sure you gather up these records and boxes—"

He didn't finish. The door exploded inward, torn off its hinges, pieces of wood and metal flying everywhere.

Paxon and Leofur rushed through the opening, the former with his black sword drawn, the latter with her flash rip held ready to fire a second charge. Through a haze of smoke and ash, they could see Arcannen seize the guard who had admitted them into Dark House, using him as a shield as he backed around the desk.

Paxon raised his sword in readiness, easing forward. "Let him go," he ordered the sorcerer.

Arcannen ignored him, his eyes fixed on Leofur instead. "You could have just knocked," he hissed at her. "My door has always been open to you."

"Ever wonder why I never take you up on that?" she snapped. "Why don't you stop hiding behind other people?"

The sorcerer's eyes shifted to Paxon and back to the young woman. Paxon could see the anger and desperation reflected there. "I don't think I want to have this conversation just now," he said.

"Paxon thinks you should have a talk with the Druid order," she retorted. "Maybe you can explain to them why you killed one of their members."

"Please let me go!" Fentrick gasped sharply.

"I don't think they would like my explanation, Leofur." Arcannen was dragging the guard deeper into the room, toward the back wall. "Why are you doing this to me, anyway? What's in it for you?"

"Nothing you would ever be able to give me!"

Paxon was hearing this conversation, but not quite understanding what it was about. Or maybe he understood all too well. Whatever the case, he didn't care to listen to any more of it. He was standing within five feet of the sorcerer by now, close enough to act if Arcannen resisted. "Either you come out from behind your guard or I'm coming right through him!"

Arcannen was looking at him now, a direct, challenging gaze. "You are, are you?" The black eyes glittered. "But do you intend to go through those men behind you, as well?"

It was an old trick, but both Paxon and Leofur instinctively shifted their gazes, casting a quick look over their shoulders. It was enough. Arcannen shoved the hapless Fentrick into Paxon and brought both hands up just an instant before Leofur could level her flash rip. A flash of light caught her squarely in the chest and knocked her backward into the wall, where her head slammed into the wooden boards. She collapsed instantly, the flash rip falling to the floor beside her.

Paxon kept his feet, if only barely, shoving Fentrick out of the way and charging at Arcannen as the terrified guard righted himself and staggered out the door. The sorcerer crouched against the wall, hands held out in what appeared to be a defensive posture, but was not. A flaring of white fire burst from his fingers into Paxon, the fire hot and crackling.

The Sword of Leah scattered it in shards.

Arcannen tried again, this time with a flame that was even hotter and separated in three parts so that it came at Paxon from different directions. But the Highlander stood his ground and did not panic, wielding the sword as Oost had taught him, choosing his targets and blunting their force with responses that were as swift and accurate as the movement of his eyes from one to the next. The fiery strikes burst apart, pieces of flame flying all over the room, leaving scorch marks everywhere.

Arcannen roared in anger and shifted his stance once more, hands weaving, words pouring from his mouth in a rush of hissing and growls. Light flashed between them, and suddenly the sorcerer was holding a sword encased in fire. It had substance and a clearly defined shape, and the flames burned bright green.

Paxon took a step back, uncertain about this new wrinkle, waiting to see what would happen. Arcannen feinted casually, the strange weapon flaring each time he did so. "Did you think you were the only one who knew how to use a sword?"

He rushed at Paxon with a flurry of blows that the latter only barely managed to block as he sidestepped the worst of it and tried to get at Arcannen from the side. But the other was agile and his movements smooth, and it was instantly clear that he had real skill and experience with his weapon. He blocked Paxon's counter-attack easily, turning it aside with little effort. They separated and then met in a clash of blades, sparks and flames exploding from Arcannen's sword as it collided with Paxon's. Back and forth they surged, each one fighting to overpower the other, to cause him to slip, to lose his footing, to grow weary and fail.

Finally, Paxon thrust the other away from him, seeking space in which to maneuver. Arcannen laughed cheerfully as they began to circle each other. Then, abruptly, the sorcerer turned and fled the room. Paxon raced to catch him, but Arcannen was waiting just outside. As Paxon charged through the doorway, he only barely managed to block the other's sword as it swept past his head. Even so, the impact of the fiery sword against his own blade knocked him sideways into the wall. Arcannen was on him instantly, hammering at him, trying to break through his defenses. For an instant Paxon faltered, sensing he was overmatched. But his training and his determination saved him again. He blocked the sorcerer's blows and regained his momentum, first stopping the attack and then forcing the other man to give ground.

Again, Arcannen turned and fled, this time for the stairway. He was screaming for help, yelling for his men to come to his aid. A handful did, appearing at the head of the stairs, blocking Paxon's way as their leader rushed past them. But the Highlander never slowed. Giving the battle cry of his ancestors, the one all boys learned almost as soon as they were old enough to walk—*Leah! Leah!*—he went right through them.

He was down the stairs and on top of Arcannen before the other could reach the front door. Again they met in a clash of metal and fire, the sounds of the blows and their own heavy gasps from the effort filling the hallway. Paxon was wearing down, his strength ebbing, but he sensed that Arcannen was even more exhausted. At one point, in what the Highlander took to be an act of desperation, the sorcerer tried using magic to create a lumbering giant encased in armor. But Paxon slammed into the image fearlessly, and shattered it with a single blow.

Arcannen was retreating, step by step, now clearly interested only in escape. Smoke and ash filled the hall, clouding the air. Both men were bloodied and battered, their faces blackened and their eyes red with fatigue. Rage was present in their locked gazes, reflected in the glint of their eyes. Paxon was thinking of Starks, of how he had died. He was telling himself that the man he was battling had killed him and could not be allowed to go unpunished. He was telling himself that he was the one who must make that happen.

What Arcannen was thinking was unreadable. But his eyes said it was dark and dangerous.

They were alone now, the hallway empty save for them. The guards who remained upright had either fled or gone into hiding. No one was coming to Arcannen's aid. Paxon felt a sudden rush of adrenaline. The sorcerer's guards had abandoned him, his strength was fading, and his hopes for escape were disappearing.

He rushed Arcannen anew, sword lifted, yelling out once more—*Leah! Leah!*—intent on finishing this. Arcannen snarled something in reply and held his ground. When they collided, the impact staggered both. Weapons flashed and clanged, and the blows the men exchanged were fierce and unrelenting. They surged back and forth across the hallway, fighting from one wall to the other and back again. The minutes dragged on; the struggle continued.

Finally, as they backed away from each other yet again, muscles screaming with fatigue, mouths open and gulping for breath, Arcannen held out one hand in a warding motion. "You can't win this," he gasped.

The Highlander laughed, drawing in huge breaths. "I *am* winning it. Hadn't you noticed? Why don't you just give it up and come with me?"

"Back to Paranor? Back to your Druids? You know what would happen to me."

"You shouldn't have killed Starks!"

Now Arcannen laughed. "You think I didn't know that even before it happened? You think I wasn't trying to avoid it? But he tracked me and would not quit! I just reacted; it was instinctive."

"It doesn't change what happened. It doesn't mean you shouldn't answer for it."

Arcannen sighed. "You have an answer for everything, don't you? How simple the world must seem to you—all black and white." He paused, shaking his head in dismay. "How did you find out I was here in the first place? How did you even know I would come back so soon?"

Paxon shook his head. "I didn't. I came here to find something to help Chrysallin."

The sorcerer nodded. "Mischa's subversion. I'd forgotten about that. You took your sister to Paranor? What happened?"

"She attacked the Ard Rhys."

"That was what I intended. Only she was supposed to use the Stiehl, and she didn't have it with her."

"So it would have been the Ard Rhys who died, not Starks." He lowered his sword and leaned on it. "Well, because of what you and Mischa did, my sister is now catatonic. I came back to find something to undo the damage."

Arcannen nodded. "Take away the bad dreams. Make

her forget the gray-haired Elven woman and all the torture that never happened. Her belief that she was physically damaged when she wasn't." He took a deep breath and exhaled sharply. "I can give you that, Paxon."

Paxon straightened. "What? What did you say?"

"You heard me. I can make your sister well again. I have an antidote that will do so. Do you want it? Then, I'll make you a bargain. The antidote for my freedom."

Paxon was incensed. "I'm not going to do that!"

"I give you a potion that will make your sister well, and you let me go free. Why not?"

"I'm not letting you go!" the Highlander screamed in rage. "You're not getting away again."

The sorcerer shrugged. "If you want your sister back, you should think it over. That potion is the only thing that can help her, and I'm the only one who has it now that Mischa is dead." He smiled. "You did this to yourself, you know."

Paxon almost attacked him anew. But he kept thinking about why he had come back in the first place and of what Leofur had kept reminding him. He had not come back to find Arcannen, but to save Chrys.

"You're lying," he snapped. He lifted his black blade, held it ready. "You would say anything to save yourself!"

"I have the potion you need, Paxon Leah. *That* is not a lie; it is the truth. Do you want your sister back or will it make you feel better to see my head spiked on Paranor's walls? It's your choice. But you have to decide."

Paxon shook his head. "No. I can't let you go."

"Well, you don't exactly have me pinned to the ground yet, do you?" Arcannen lifted his flaming sword anew, readying himself. "Besides, there will be another day for you and me. Another time. Even if we don't settle it now, don't you think we will end up settling it eventually?"

Paxon did think so. It seemed inevitable.

He hesitated.

When he returned for Leofur, she was just coming out the front door of Dark House, as battered and smoke-blackened as he was, her hair all wild and spiky. Carrying her flash rip tucked under her cloak, she stepped clear of the building's walls with a quick look behind her and walked down the steps into the roadway to meet him.

For a moment, they just stood there. "Did you get him?" she asked.

He shook his head. "He got away." Then he grimaced. "Actually, I let him go."

She stared at him, her eyes surprised and wondering. "Why?"

He sighed. "Because he agreed to give me this in return."

He reached into his pocket and brought out the tiny bottle the sorcerer had found for him when they returned to Mischa's rooms. The witch had indeed hidden her potions and elixirs with magic, but Arcannen had known right where they were and how to reveal them.

"He said it would make Chrys forget all the bad things that happened to her, and that she would come back to herself." He hesitated. "You're going to tell me he was lying, aren't you?"

Leofur shrugged, then shook her head. "He probably wasn't. Even though he has dozens of other unpleasant characteristics, he tends to be truthful. He doesn't see any reason not to be. Besides, I don't think he wants to come up against you again right away, and you'd hunt him down if he lied."

"I'll hunt him down anyway."

She nodded. "You made the right choice."

"I hope so. I hope he didn't deceive me. But you know him better than I do."

"I know him better than anyone."

He felt a surge of renewed disappointment and unhappiness.

"Because you were his . . ." He couldn't finish. He couldn't make himself say it.

"Because I was his *what*?" she asked, frowning.

"His . . ." He stopped again. "His lover."

She almost laughed, a grin spreading over her features. "Is that what you think? Well, think again, Paxon Leah. I was as special as anyone could be to a man like him." She reached out and gripped his shoulder hard. "Because I'm his daughter."

27

She told this to no one in the years following her departure from her father and Dark House and the beginning of her life as caregiver for Grehling. Few who lived outside the walls of the building had ever seen her; fewer still knew who she was. During her early years, she was kept tucked away in rooms of her own and not allowed outside the building without an escort. She was fed, clothed, and educated in the manner of girls who were fortunate enough to enjoy a better social standing in the city, but she was denied their companionship. Dark House was her home, but it was also her prison.

She never knew her mother; she never even found out what happened to her. Her mother was simply never there, and no one would talk about her. She was raised by the women who worked for her father, raised in a home where strange men came and went by the hour, raised in dark and oppressive and carefully guarded surroundings that, by the end of things, she came to hate. She might have grown up there, but by the time she left to help look after and raise Grehling, she had come to realize the truth about her father.

"So that's how you got us into Dark House so easily," Paxon said. "They knew who you were because that's where you grew up."

They were walking back to the airfield, Paxon getting ready to leave for Paranor and the Druids.

"Some of them did. I feel badly about deceiving Fentrick. He used to play with me as a child. He and I were great friends at a time when I had no other friends. Now that's gone."

"You did it for me," the Highlander acknowledged. "I am very grateful."

"Don't think you're so special, Paxon," she said quickly. "I did it because it was the right thing to do. I knew when Grehling brought Chrysallin to my front door that if I let them inside, I was crossing a line. Everything would change, and the past—maybe all of it— would be wiped away. I made that choice. That's all."

"Was it your father who gave you the flash rip?" he asked.

"He thought I needed better protection living away from Dark House. He made me promise never to tell anyone I had it. That's all I really want to say about it just now. I would appreciate it if you didn't say anything to Grehling. He thinks a lot of me, and he might have a hard time understanding. I already told him I had nothing to do with Arcannen."

Paxon nodded. "I won't say anything to him or anyone else. There's no need. I'm just glad you're all right. I was worried when I saw you slammed into that wall. By your own father."

"My own father regards me as a failed experiment. I am an embarrassment to him. He wants me to be his daughter, and he can't understand why that is so difficult for me."

"But he attacked you!"

"In his eyes, I attacked him first. I allied myself with you, his enemy. I severed whatever ties remained between us. He had taken pains to do special favors for me in the past, even after I left, even though I never asked for them. I think after this, maybe that part of my life is over."

They were nearing the airfield now, the first of the masts and light sheaths of the moored vessels rising up ahead of them. "Don't misunderstand me," she added quickly. "I've wanted it to be over for a long time. There's really nothing between us now but our blood ties. I'm glad he's gone. And not likely to be back anytime soon."

Paxon gave her a rueful look. "You'll probably think the same thing about me once I've left, knowing what I was thinking about you."

She nodded. "I might. You don't seem to have a very high opinion of me."

"I made an assumption about what you were doing in Dark House that I shouldn't have made. I apologize. I don't know what I was thinking."

"I've never had a problem with what people think about me. You included."

"After what you did for me, how you helped me with your father, the way you stood by me when I was in danger? I will never forget that. And I don't want you to be angry with me. I like you a lot. I want us to stay friends."

She regarded him coolly. "It might be possible," she said. "Why don't we wait and see?"

At the airfield, Grehling came rushing out to meet them, throwing his arms around Leofur, who rolled her eyes and then hugged him back. The boy hugged Paxon, as well, and asked to hear the whole story of what had happened to them in Wayford. Paxon told him, Leofur adding bits and pieces here and there, but he was careful to stay away from the family connection between the young woman and the sorcerer.

"You did the right thing, taking the potion so you could help Chrys," Grehling announced. "You can always go after Arcannen later. You can find him again, if you really want to."

"I hope you're right," he said, ruffling the boy's hair.

"In fact, I'll go with you!" Grehling declared. "I can help you track him down and bring him back. I can be your pilot. Can't I, Leofur?"

She gave him a smile. "You can be anyone's pilot. No one knows more about airships than you do."

Paxon reached out to shake the boy's hand. "You and me, then. We'll talk about it another time."

Grehling ran off, and Paxon turned to Leofur. "I meant what I said. I won't ever forget what you did for me. I hope I see you again. I hope you will want to see me."

She stepped back, looked him over, and shrugged. "I've seen worse than you come through my life. Let's think about it. Go back to Chrys for now. Take care of her. Help her get better. Put all the bad things behind you for a while. Then let me know if you decide I'm not one of them."

So he flew out of Wayford aboard his skiff, setting a course for Paranor. He could have used at least a few hours of sleep before going, but he couldn't wait to return to Chrysallin and give her the potion. He tried unsuccessfully to convince himself that it would work, that Arcannen had not deceived him, that Leofur knew her father better than anyone probably did. One way or the other, he had to find out if there was any chance his sister could be cured. Putting it off only made matters worse.

He traveled through the remainder of the day and into nightfall, a solitary craft in the growing darkness, its masts and railings fore and aft lit by running lamps and guided by the stars. He passed back over the Rainbow Lake and up the channel of the Runne River to the Dragon's Teeth. It was nearing midnight by the time the lights of the Druid's Keep came into view and he felt the first twinges of serious doubt about what he was doing.

The possibilities he envisioned were almost too much for him to face.

What if Arcannen had given him poison, and he was meant to poison his own sister as retribution for the trouble he had caused the sorcerer?

What if the potion was something other than a remedy? What if it was intended to turn Chrys into something terrible?

What if it was useless, a mix of water and coloring? What if it made her worse?

But he tamped down his fears because in his heart he believed it would work and Chrys would be made well.

He set down the skiff on the landing platform, climbed out, and hurried into the Keep. A few of the Trolls serving as Druid Guards took note, but none of them spoke to him. Once inside, he went straight to the healing center. Almost everyone there was asleep, including the Healers, but Paxon ignored them all and went into the room where they had been keeping Chrys when he left.

She was still sleeping, but he managed to wake her; the sleep potion was beginning to wear off by now. He helped her sit up, whispering to her that he was back and could help her. But even so she made no response and went right back to staring into space without seeing anything. Nothing had changed. He spoke her name, hugged her, talked to her a bit, and waited for an indication that she was in any way better. She was not. There was no sign of recognition, no awareness.

He brought out the bottle with the potion in it and held it out where she would see it. "I want you to drink this. I want you to trust me." He hesitated, wondering if he should give her any sort of warning about other possibilities. In the end, he simply said, "I love you."

Then he put the bottle to her lips, tipped her head back slightly, and poured the liquid into her mouth. He watched her throat work as she swallowed. When she had taken it all, he held her by the shoulders and waited for a response.

Nothing.

He continued to wait, the minutes passing and the room's silence deepening. He peered into her eyes, looking for something to reveal itself. Finally, her eyes closed and she slumped into his arms. For a terrible instant, he thought he had killed her, that his worst fears had come true. But then he felt her throat and watched the rise and fall of her chest, and realized she was sleeping.

He took the chair she had vacated and sat watching her for a long time afterward, mulling over what he had done, telling himself he had not made a mistake, that the fact she was sleeping was a good sign. Time passed, and his thoughts drifted to the events of yesterday. He relived his battle with Arcannen, rueful and disappointed that he had failed to bring the sorcerer back to Paranor, that he had in some way failed Starks. He found Leofur's face continually resurfacing amid his other thoughts. He could see her expressions, hear her voice, and recall the way she moved.

He could not stop thinking about her.

At some point, he fell asleep.

He was still sleeping when cool fingers touched his cheek and a familiar voice called his name. He stirred awake, sleep-fogged and lethargic. Hands gripped his shoulders and fingers squeezed gently. *Leofur,* he thought.

But when he opened his eyes, he was staring at Chrysallin.

"Chrys," he whispered.

She nodded, tears in her eyes. "Where have you been?"

"I came as quickly as I could. I'm sorry it took so long."

"I was afraid, Paxon."

"I know."

She gave him a puzzled look. "But I can't remember why. I can't remember any of it."

He smiled. "It doesn't matter now. It's all over. You're where you belong."

And she hugged him to her.

He waited for the Druid Healers to arrive and then went straight to bed. He should have gone to the Ard Rhys, but he couldn't make himself do anything more. He was so exhausted he didn't think he could put words together to tell her what had happened. It didn't matter now, anyway. Chrys was well. The struggle to save her was over. Everything else could wait.

He slept then and did not come awake again until it was almost midday. It took him a long time even then to make himself climb out of bed, wash, dress, and go off to give his report to the Ard Rhys. He took a few minutes to stop at the healing center and let the Druid Healers treat the injuries he had incurred battling Arcannen and Mischa's creature before continuing on to find the Ard Rhys.

He was almost to her chambers when he passed Oost Mondara in the hallway.

"You are a whole lot of trouble, Paxon Leah," the Gnome declared abruptly, coming to a stop. "Why is it you aren't ever where you're supposed to be?"

Then he glowered at the speechless Highlander enigmatically before continuing on.

Aphenglow Elessedil was still in her office when he knocked. She rose to greet him and embraced him warmly. "We were very worried about you, Paxon. Sit down and tell me everything that happened."

He did so, omitting only the part about Leofur's relationship with Arcannen. It took him a while to go through it all, but the Ard Rhys sat quietly and did not interrupt. He took special pains to describe the difficulty he experienced in letting Arcannen escape after he had brought him to bay, choosing to help Chrys rather than capturing the sorcerer.

"I think you made the right choice. I spoke to her earlier today." She smiled at the look on his face. "The Healers told me she was fully recovered. But I had to see for myself. I had to know how she would react to me. It was all done carefully and with an eye toward her safety. She did not attack me. She didn't even know who I was."

"So Arcannen was telling the truth after all?"

"It seems so. She remembers almost nothing of what happened to her. Certainly nothing of her torture and her suffering. Not even much about Mischa—just a vague memory of an old woman."

"She doesn't remember any of it? Not the black creature or the gray-haired woman? Not the escape with Grehling?"

"She remembers the boy helping her. She just doesn't remember any of the things related to the nightmares and the pain. I didn't want to ask her too much all at once. There will be time for that later. There is one thing, though. And I wanted to ask you before pursuing it. She doesn't remember anything about using the wishsong."

"I wasn't there when it happened," he said, "but I guessed that was what it was from the description Grehling gave. Chrys had never used it before then; there was never anything to indicate she had inherited it. I don't think she knew."

Aphenglow nodded, her brow wrinkling, her face thoughtful. "There is a history of it surfacing in various members of the Ohmsford family after they have reached a certain age. It doesn't always manifest itself right away. In Chrysallin's case, I would guess the shock of what she experienced at the hands of Mischa and the threat of having to go through it again brought it out. Chrys just reacted to her fears by voicing them, and the magic came alive."

"But she doesn't remember it now?"

"Not a bit of it. My dilemma is what to do about that. She harbors a powerful magic. She's locked it away inside, but it could surface again at any point. What do we do? Do we let it be or do we find a way to reveal it to her and teach her to master its use?"

"If she doesn't remember now, maybe she won't remember at all. I don't think she should be reminded of anything that happened." His voice tightened. "I don't want her put through anything else right away, Mistress."

"Nor do I," she said. "I think we should let her be. But I wanted to hear you say it. For the time being, at least, while she is still healing, we should keep it to ourselves. Maybe she will remember at some point, and when she does we will have to be ready to tell her the truth. Now, tell me how you are."

He said he was fine, a bit battered and bruised, some scrapes and burns, but no broken bones. He had been to the healing center before coming to her and was treated for his injuries. Mostly, it was feeling good about Chrys that strengthened him.

"She'll remain with us for as long as she wishes— certainly until we know there are no aftereffects from what she went through." She paused. "One thing more. Are you well enough to undertake a short journey?"

The way she said it told him she was expecting him to say yes. It also told him this was important, and she wanted him to be a part of whatever was going to happen.

"I can travel," he answered.

"I have something I need to do, and it isn't going to be very pleasant. But as protector of the Druids—officially now, your trial period is over—I need you to bear witness. We leave in the morning."

She dismissed him then, leaving him to wonder at the nature and purpose of her mysterious outing.

28

HE MANAGED TO STAY AWAKE UNTIL SUNSET, trying to set his internal clock back on a regular schedule so he would sleep well that night. While still awake, he spent his time alone, thinking about what Aphenglow Elessedil had told him. He was no longer in training to be a Druid protector; he now was one. Hearing her pronouncement had generated a mix of emotions. He was excited to be a part of the Druid order, feeling that in spite of everything that had happened, he had found the home and the life he was looking for. He knew he wasn't as proficient or skilled as he should be, but he believed that he would become so in time. But it felt strange and vaguely disconcerting to be making such a drastic shift away from everything familiar and reliable. Gone was his Leah home and its familiar surroundings; gone his life as a shipper and flier of freight. Gone, too, for all intents and purposes, were his family and friends. Now he was a swordsman in service to the Druids. He would be asked to shoulder much greater responsibilities and challenges, and his family and friends would be found in Paranor.

He did not regret this change in his life; after all, he had sought it out willingly. He did not now wish it reversed. But having it actually come to pass, no longer only a possibility but a full-blown reality, was a bit unsettling. So he took time to consider its ramifications.

He turned it about and examined it. He pictured himself in his new role and tried to envision how he would behave given what he believed would be required of him.

He sat where he could watch the Druids pass by on their way to engage in and complete assignments. He caught sight of Sebec a number of times but the young Druid always appeared to be in a great hurry, and Paxon didn't want to interrupt his work even though he was anxious to share his good news. Of all the Druids he had met, Sebec was the one he liked best and felt closest to. He imagined it would be fun having him as a daily companion.

He ate an early dinner, sitting with Avelene and a couple of the other Druids he had come to know, talking about his elevation to Druid protector, exchanging jokes and laughter about the job's exaggerated demands on his skills and intellect. Afterward, he went to visit Chrysallin and spent more than an hour talking with her about everything that had happened to them, staying until she grew so tired she was falling asleep.

Then he went off to bed himself, exhausted and happy, and slept undisturbed until morning.

He was at breakfast the following day when Sebec came for him. "The Ard Rhys is ready for you," he announced.

Paxon followed the Druid along the corridors of the Keep toward the landing platform attached to the north tower where they would find the Ard Rhys waiting.

"Do you know what this is about?" he asked Sebec at one point.

The other shook his head. "But I'm to go with you."

This was unexpected. The Ard Rhys hadn't said anything about Sebec accompanying them. He wondered what other surprises awaited him.

The Ard Rhys greeted them when they reached the

landing platform, waiting for them beside her personal cruiser with Captain of her Druid Guard Dajoo Rees and two of his men. Apparently, there was no one else accompanying them; when they boarded, they were alone. The Ard Rhys did not offer an explanation for what they were doing or even speak to them again once they had released the mooring ropes and set out. Instead, she indicated a bench astern and had them sit there while she stood in the pilot box and set their course. The Trolls worked the lines and light sheaths, and no one said much of anything.

The day was bright and clear and beautiful, and Paxon soon forgot about her reticent behavior and air of mystery and spent his time looking out over the countryside and exchanging comments with Sebec. He was tracking their course as they went, familiar with the countryside they were passing over—coming down out of the forests surrounding Paranor to the Dragon's Teeth, from there proceeding through the Kennon Pass to the Borderlands, and then turning west to follow the Mermidon River as it ran on toward Arborlon and the Westland.

When they finally set down, they were well out into the grasslands of the Streleheim, far distant from much of anything.

As they disembarked onto the flats amid miles and miles of emptiness, Paxon felt for the first time that something wasn't right. The sense of uneasiness he experienced as he looked around was palpable, but he kept silent and waited to see what would happen.

"Where are we?" Sebec asked finally as they walked out onto the flats.

The Ard Rhys stopped and turned to face him. "Our destination. This is where we part company."

"What are we expected to do out here?" He looked confused.

"Not *we,* Sebec. Paxon isn't going with you. Nor I. You will go alone."

Sebec stared. "Go where? I don't understand."

"I think you do." Her voice was soft, but her eyes were hard as she faced him. "You crossed a forbidden line, Sebec. You have to accept the consequences. You know that."

Sebec's face changed, turning pale, all expression leaching away. "This isn't right. You've made a mistake."

"I wish that were so. I wish I had. But we both know the truth. You were the spy in our midst, the traitor who stole the artifacts of magic and gave them to Arcannen, the one who kept him informed of the details of all our undertakings. Why did you do it?"

"I didn't! I didn't do anything!" He was incensed, outraged. Arms in the air, hands clenched into fists, he was gesturing wildly. "You're wrong about this! It wasn't me! How could you think it was me?"

"Are you telling me it was someone else?"

"Yes, that's what I'm telling you!"

Paxon could not believe what he was hearing. A part of him wanted to jump in and defend Sebec—his friend, his teacher, his companion. But he held off, waiting to hear the rest of what the Ard Rhys had to say, thinking—hoping—she would somehow turn out to be wrong.

"How could I think it was you?" she repeated. "Well, I'll tell you. I never suspected it was you in the beginning, never once even considered it could be you. But when you took the Stiehl, I began to think more seriously about the possibility that it might be. I couldn't get past the fact that only you and I had clear access to everything in the artifact chamber. A skilled user of magic, trained properly, could negate those wards, no matter how cleverly laid down, so long as he or she knew how it had been done. You qualified. Even then, I thought it must be someone else, prayed that it was, that you weren't the one responsible. I had so much faith in you. I believed so strongly in your loyalty. Could I have been that badly mistaken?"

She shook her head. "So I decided to test you. I told you I had decided to place the crimson Elfstones in the chamber vault. I let you help me layer in the wards. Essentially, I gave you the keys to open them. When I examined those wards several days ago, they had been taken down and put back. Only you could have done that because only you would have known how to both remove and replace them in the exact same way. Which you had to do to protect yourself because when you opened the vault you discovered the Elfstones weren't there. Of course, they never were. I kept them tucked away in my chambers and installed an empty box for you to find."

She paused, assessing his expression. "But then you did something even more foolish. You sent me to speak to Paxon without warning me I would find him in his sister's room. And afterward, while I lay recovering from her attack on me, you agreed to let Paxon go alone to Wayford, knowing what he intended. It was all too much. Taken as a whole, it removed any doubt."

"I cannot believe you are accusing me!" Sebec shouted. "How can you do this to me?"

"How could you do it to me?" There was a dangerous look in her eyes. "I don't know when I first started to suspect you, Sebec. I can't be sure because all the while I kept telling myself I must be wrong. I *wanted* to be wrong."

"You *are* wrong!" he screamed at her.

"I am so very disappointed in you. I trusted you, and you betrayed me. You betrayed the Druid order. I think this is all Arcannen's doing, but I need for you to tell me I'm right."

She stepped close to him and seized his hands. "Am I right? Look at me! Am I?"

He started to say something, his face angry and harsh, but then his face changed as his eyes locked on hers and her hands tightened about his, almost as if he were a puppet whose strings had been cut. "Yes."

"Why did you do it?"

Sebec looked stricken, his defenses gone, his denials pointless. Paxon knew at once that the Ard Rhys had done something to him, perhaps used magic to render him compliant, but whatever the case he was defenseless in her grip. "You wouldn't understand."

She looked startled. "What wouldn't I understand? Tell me!"

He blinked rapidly. "Arcannen picked me up off the streets when I was thieving and lying to stay alive and gave me a home. He cared about me when no one else did! He raised me and trained me in the uses of magic. He told me I was meant to do something important, something great. I would have done anything for him."

"You were spying for him from the beginning?" she asked in disbelief.

"He was the one who sent me to you. I was to make you like me enough that you would trust me. I was good at doing that, even when I was on the streets. I could make people believe anything. Arcannen told me it was a gift I should put to use. He sent me to Paranor to become a Druid and get close to you. I did that. I became your favorite. I was your shadow, and everything you did I reported back to him."

"Shades, Sebec," Aphenglow whispered. "Don't you understand what he did to you? Don't you realize how you were used?"

The young Druid dropped to his knees and began to cry. "I'm so sorry. Please forgive me. Don't hurt me. Please, Mistress!"

She released his hands and stepped away. "You chose your path, and now you must travel it to its unfortunate end. I wish I could offer you a different alternative, but your actions ultimately led to the deaths of Starks and the young Druid on the streets of Leah. The extent of your betrayal gives me no choice." She turned away. "Come, Paxon. Time to be going."

The Highlander hesitated, still staring at Sebec in disbelief, and then he started to follow her.

"Paxon, wait!" Sebec cried out, struggling to his feet. "Don't leave me like this! Help me! Tell her how much I did for you! Tell her how good I was to you! Ask her to spare me! Are you just going to let this happen?"

The Highlander almost responded, wanting to do something to change things, knowing what was coming. But the Ard Rhys took his arm in a firm grip and turned him away. "Let him be."

Together, they walked back to the cruiser and climbed aboard. The Trolls, with Captain of the Druid Guard Dajoo Rees leading, went past them toward Sebec as they did so. Momentary wails of despair rose, cries of *"Spare me! Give me my life!"* And then silence.

When the Trolls returned to the airship and set about casting off the mooring lines and preparing to lift away, Paxon was sitting on the bench he had occupied with Sebec on the flight out, still staring fixedly at the deck planking. At the last possible moment, unable to help himself, he lifted his head and looked back.

Sebec's body lay sprawled on a blood-soaked patch of ground, separated from his head. As the airship slowly began to rise, his remains grew steadily smaller and finally shrank away to nothing.

After they had been airborne for a time and Paxon had begun to recover his composure, the Ard Rhys came back to sit beside him. "I wish there had been another choice," she said quietly.

The Highlander exhaled sharply, running his hands through his red hair. "I trusted him. I liked him. I don't understand."

She shook her head. "People are capable of terrible things. We think we know them, but we really don't. We let ourselves be deceived because we are always expecting the best out of those who seem willing to provide it."

"He was always so respectful when talking about you. 'My mistress.' He called you that constantly. He helped me with my training; he seemed to want to make things easier for me. But all along he was thinking of ways to help Arcannen. Even if it meant I got hurt. Or killed. Chrys, too. He knew what he was doing. He had to. How could he live with himself?"

"He would have explained everything away, given the chance to do so—telling himself and all of us it was necessary or unavoidable. He would have been able to provide reasons for all of it. A basket full of justifications. Sebec had so much potential; he could have done everything he said he wanted to do without giving in to Arcannen. But he didn't see it. He believed there was only one choice—to use us, to betray the Druid order, to embrace the roles of traitor and spy."

Paxon straightened and looked at her. "What do you think will happen when Arcannen finds out?"

She met his gaze and held it. "Does it matter?"

"I don't suppose so."

"What matters right now, Paxon, is how all this has affected you. I brought you out here for a specific reason. Not because I couldn't have told you about Sebec in Paranor and left you behind while I dealt with him, but because I thought it was important for you to see for yourself what is sometimes required of us. Of you, as a

Druid protector, every bit as much as the Druids themselves. Things of this sort have happened before; they will happen again. There will almost certainly be disappointments and deceptions in your life with us. There will be times when you hate yourself for what you have to do. There will be times when the choices will be as difficult as the one you made in Wayford when you let Arcannen go free in order to help your sister. You came to us to find a purpose in your life, a path that would lead you to something important and meaningful. But following that path can also break your heart."

She was talking about herself and Sebec. She was explaining to him how hard it could be to accept the way things sometimes worked out.

"I haven't changed my mind," he said. "I still want to be at Paranor. I still want to do what you've asked of me."

She smiled then, and the creases in her brow lessened marginally and the light in her eyes brightened.

"Then you shall have your chance."

If you loved *The High Druid's Blade*, be sure not to miss the next thrilling novel featuring Paxon, Arcannen, and a young musician struggling to contain the wishsong magic:

THE DARKLING CHILD

Here's a special preview.

I

Paxon Leah was sitting on a bench in the courtyard gardens of Paranor, paging through documents written more than five hundred years earlier that recorded the events in the life of the Elf King Eventine Elessedil, when Keratrix came for him. He could tell immediately from the scribe's solemn face that something was wrong.

"She's asking for you," the other said without preamble. His eyes seemed tired and haunted. "She says it's time."

Paxon stared. On a beautiful, sunny day like this one? On a day when everything felt right, and it seemed that the world was at peace and life could go on indefinitely? How could this be?

That was what he thought as he measured the scribe's words and let their meaning sink in. He didn't have to ask what Keratrix meant. He knew. He had known this was coming. She had told him so herself.

Aphenglow Elessedil, Ard Rhys of the Fourth Druid Order, was dying.

He rose at once, wordless and shaken, and followed Keratrix from the gardens into the tower that housed her private chambers. The Ard Rhys kept to herself these days, weakened by age and worn down by both the demands of her office and the passage of time. She was housed on the lower floors, no longer able to handle the stairs and the climb that going to her former chambers and to the upper reaches of the main tower required. She had not been in the cold room in over a year. She had not used the scrye waters once in all that time, relying instead on her chosen successor, Isaturin, to carry out her duties. She was in stasis, waiting for the inevitable. If the truth were told, Paxon believed, she was anxious for it to arrive.

And now, apparently, it had.

"Is she sure?" he asked Keratrix as they walked. When he looked at the young Druid, he was reminded of Sebec. Five years earlier, Sebec—then scribe of the Druid Order—had been his closest friend at Paranor, and the betrayal of that friendship was a wound that still burned in his memory.

Keratrix—slight and small, scarcely a presence as he wafted ahead of Paxon like a wraith in the shadowed hallways—barely turned. "She insists she is quite sure. I asked this, as well."

Of course he would. Keratrix was efficient and thorough; he would not leave something like this undone.

"I can't believe it," Paxon whispered, almost to himself, though he knew Keratrix must have heard.

And he could not. Five years he had spent as the personal paladin of the Ard Rhys, as the High Druid's Blade. She had brought him to Paranor at a time when he was drifting. She had offered him the position in large part because of his heritage as a bearer of the magical Sword of Leah. She had given him over to training and had kept watch from a distance as he struggled to find his place. When his sister Chrysallin had been taken by the sorcerer Arcannen, Aphenglow was the one who had helped him to get Chrys back and then found a home for her at Paranor—even though Chrysallin had been sent to kill her and had almost succeeded. And all the while, she had been beset by Sebec's betrayal and Arcannen's scheming to gain control of the order.

But perhaps even more important than that, she had taken Chrysallin into the order as a student in training, aware of the importance of the gift she possessed and the need to find a way to manage it. For like her brother, Chrysallin Leah bore a legacy of magic. Paxon's was the ability to unlock the power of the Sword of Leah. Chrysallin's was the presence of the wishsong, which she had inherited as a direct descendant of Railing Ohmsford. However, Chrys remained unaware of her powers. Arcannen had kidnapped her in an attempt to use her as a weapon against the Ard Rhys, but the subsequent trauma of the events that followed had wiped away any memory of those powers. Still, Aphenglow was convinced that her memory would eventually return.

So she had let Chrysallin remain at Paranor, keeping close watch over her and waiting for the moment when her magic would resurface and she could be given over to members of the order who would help her learn to master it—who would train her in its usage and teach her of the importance it held not only in her own life but in the lives of those around her.

So far, that moment had not arrived. To this day, Chrysallin remembered nothing, and no sign of the magic had reappeared. Now, as the Ard Rhys prepared for the end of her life, the task of watching over his sister would fall to Paxon. He was ready to accept this, he believed. More ready than he was for what waited just ahead.

As they neared the entry to Aphenglow Elessedil's room, the door opened and Isaturin appeared. Tall, gaunt, strong-featured, and steady in his gaze, he seemed lessened in all aspects as he approached Paxon. Undoubtedly, he was coming to terms with what the

Ard Rhys's passing would mean for him. He was her designated successor, the next Ard Rhys, and the new High Druid of what would continue as the Fourth Druid Order. He had known of his future for many years; she had made certain of it. But it was one thing to know what lay ahead of you and another altogether to have it standing there at your doorstep.

"She is waiting for you, Paxon," Isaturin said, slowing to meet him. "She doesn't have much time, and the journey ahead of us is a long one."

Paxon stared. "Journey? Do you mean her dying?"

Isaturin shook his head. "No, not that. She will explain. Hurry now. No lingering."

He moved away, leaving the Highlander looking after him in confusion.

Keratrix touched his arm. "Go in, Paxon. I'll wait out here."

Paxon went to the door, knocked softly, and heard her voice in response. Though he could not understand her words, he took a deep breath and entered anyway.

"Paxon," she greeted him.

That single word almost undid him. Everything she meant to him, everything she had done for him, all they had shared together seemed caught up in the moment. Memories flooded through him, some sad, some happy, all incredibly vivid—a jumble of connections realized in seconds. He stood where he was, weathering the onslaught, frozen in place.

Then he looked up from the spot on the floor to which his gaze had fastened and saw her. Whatever he had expected to find, it wasn't this. She was sitting up in her favorite chair, a blanket spread across her knees and her hands in her lap, clasped together. She looked old, but not sick; worn, but not broken. Her face radiated strength and certainty, and she had about her an aura of invincibility that caused him to blink in disbelief.

"You thought perhaps to find me abed and failing?" she asked. "You thought I might be breathing my last?"

He nodded, unable to speak.

"It doesn't work that way. High Druids go to their end with some measure of dignity and strength so they can face what awaits. Sit with me."

He took the chair across from her. "You don't look as if you are dying," he admitted. "You look very well, Mistress."

Her face was lined by her years and the stresses and struggles she had endured and survived. She was very thin, and her skin had the look of parchment wrapped about bones. He had seen pictures of her when she was young—portraits and sketches executed by Druids who possessed such skills as would allow them to capture her image accurately. It was said she had been beautiful—tall and strong, a warrior Elf and the descendant of Elven Kings and Queens. He could see traces of that in her even now—small indicators of what she had been years ago.

"Kind words, Paxon. But in spite of what you think you see, my passing is at hand. I must go to my rest in the way of all leaders of the order—and for that, I require your company. I wish you to make the journey with me to the Valley of Shale and the Hadeshorn, where I will be met and taken home. I would like to leave at once. Though I may look strong, I can feel myself failing. It is a scary thing to be strong one moment and know that in the next your life will be over. Will you accompany me?"

"Of course," he said at once. "Should I arrange transport?" He paused. "What happens once we get there?"

She gave him that old, familiar smile. "Best wait and see for yourself. I am not as certain of it as I would like to be. And don't give any further thought to arranging for an airship. Isaturin is taking care of that now. Just sit with me. Keep me company."

Paxon sat back. "Do the others in the Druid Order know this is happening?"

She shook her head. "Keratrix will tell them once I am gone. If he tells them now, there will be an unending line of mourners and well-wishers, and I don't think I can bear that. I want to depart this world quietly. When my sister Arling left me all those years ago—when she embraced the fate decreed for her and transformed into the Ellcrys—well, that was quite enough trauma and emotional turmoil for several lifetimes. My departure will be considerably less dramatic."

She gave a deep sigh and leaned back. "Ah, Arling, I wish I could come to you one last time." She closed her eyes, and tears streaked her cheeks. Then she wiped them away unself-consciously and smiled at Paxon. "I have never gotten over losing her. Not even after all these years."

Paxon shifted uneasily, not knowing what to say.

"I have revealed the situation with Chrysallin to Isaturin as the next head of the order," she said. "I have told him of my fears and of my plans for her should her memory of the wishsong resurface. He will act in my place as her mentor and teacher when it becomes necessary. But I rely mostly on you to keep watch over her, Paxon. You are closest to her and likely to notice first if any changes occur. She will be safe at Paranor from everything save herself. You must help her with that."

"I will," he promised.

She straightened, and for a moment he thought she intended to rise. But she remained seated and added, "At some point, Chrysallin will discover the truth. I am convinced of it. I don't know what effect it will have on her, but you need to be there to help her through it. So don't fool yourself into thinking this will never happen.

I worry that your decision not to tell her is more an avoidance than a kindness. You hope she will never remember what happened to her, what she had to do to save herself. But she will, Paxon. One day, she will. Don't fail in this. Tell her soon. Chrysallin's power is well documented in the records, and it is a powerful and sometimes unpredictable weapon."

He leaned forward. "I have been considering it. I am aware of the arguments for why I should tell her now. But I cannot get past the danger it poses if I am wrong."

She studied him a moment. "I know you would like this to simply go away, but I don't think you can depend on that. So telling her in advance might be best. Use your good judgment on how to go about it if you decide to do so. She will listen to you. She adores you. Five years ago, it would have been hard to reveal the truth to her. But now she is grown; she is a woman, and her strength and maturity are much greater than when she first came to us."

He found himself amazed that Aphenglow Elessedil would take the time and effort to try to help with his sister when there was so much else she might be doing. But she was still Ard Rhys of the Fourth Druid Order, and she would have her priorities firmly in hand even at the end of her life. She would not deviate from who she had been and what she had done for well over a hundred years. That was her nature, a direct result of the demands of her position. She would want to set her house in order.

"I owe you so much," he said, the words escaping him before he could think better of them. "You've given me this life, and I will never forget that."

"You earned what you have, Paxon," she said quietly. "No need to thank me for that."

He basked in her smile. "Can I bring you something to drink? Or eat? Before we set out?"

She shook her head. "We are not sitting here so that you can do something for me. We are here so that I can do something for you. Part of it is warning you of the risk to your sister. Another is warning you to beware of Arcannen. Do not think him gone for good—no more than Chrysallin's wishsong. He is a dangerous man with a long memory. He will be back for you and for Chrys. He will not tolerate leaving what you cost him unavenged. He will not be able to live with the humiliation and regret. When you least expect it, he will surface again, and he will seek to exact a price for what he has suffered."

"I am not afraid of him," Paxon declared at once.

"You should be. He nearly undid the Druid Order before you stopped him. He is capable of great evil. Watch out for him. Be careful of yourself and your sister."

She paused. "One last thing. Isaturin will need time to learn his place as Ard Rhys. No one can prepare for this until they hold the office. It was so for me; it will be so for him. Help him adjust. Give him your support. Keep him safe. You are fully grown into your paladin shoes, a young man with great skill and the good sense to know how to use it. Make use of it for him. Be his right hand and protector in these early months of his service to the order. Now take my arm."

She reached out, and he rose quickly to assist her. Her arm caught hold of his and she levered herself to her feet smoothly, suddenly seeming younger and stronger. She smiled at the look on his face.

"Now we can go," she said.